WELFARE WIFEYS

K'WAN

WELFARE WIFEYS

A Hood Rat Novel

St. Martin's Griffin ❦ New York

This is a work of fiction. All of the characters, organizations, and events por-
trayed in this novel are either products of the author's imagination or are used
fictitiously.

For my girls

WELFARE
WIFEYS

PROLOGUE

Blood In, Blood Out

IT HAD BEEN A LONG NIGHT. FROM THE TIME THEY HAD opened up shop, fiends had been coming back and forth scoring slices of ready-rock happiness, lining the pockets of the death dealers who slung it. Rock Head had been beyond thrilled when 2:00 A.M. finally rolled around and he was able to close up shop. All that was left to do was lock the remainder of the drugs away and bag up the money before he closed down for the morning. Getting money in Pittsburgh was hardly as glamorous as what he was used to in Harlem, but he had to make do with it, at least until he figured a way out of the mess he'd managed to get himself into.

Originally from Harlem, Rock Head was a mid-level nobody who was more of a thorn in the side of everyone who knew him. He made his money jacking and slinging, depending on however he was feeling that day, and blew his money frivolously on purple haze and chicks. Rock Head's appetite for the flesh of young girls was almost insatiable, and this was the beginning of the end of his problems. Rock Head had developed quite a name for himself based on his exploits with underaged girls and it all came back to bite him in the ass when he woke up handcuffed to a hospital bed.

Rock Head had been the victim of a robbery he'd orchestrated, that had gone horribly wrong, leaving several people dead and him shot. He'd initially thought the police were holding him in connection with the mass murder they'd found him in the middle of, but the rabbit hole ran much deeper. They had him on seven counts of statutory rape and seven counts of attempted murder. Rock Head was HIV positive and intentionally passing it to the young girls. Rock Head was able to offer up information on some cats he knew and barter himself a bail while he waited on his court date. Needless to say that he fled the moment he got out, but his new fugitive status with the police was the least of his concerns. In order to get his escape pass he had to lie on one of the illest killers in the five boroughs. He knew that for as long as the killer lived he would always have to sleep with one eye open.

Trying to take his mind off his past life, Rock Head busied himself at stuffing the trap money into his Louis Vuitton knapsack and eating the last of the sausage pizza that sat on the table amid the money and drug packages. He wasn't sure where the pizza had come from but he was glad to have it as it had been hours since he'd eaten. He had gotten to the last few bites when he felt his stomach starting to bubble. Leaving the money and the drugs on the table he bolted to the bathroom to relieve himself.

Rock Head had barely gotten his pants down when a river of shit came spilling from his insides. The smell was so rank that he had to cover his nose while he took his dump. As he sat there reading a magazine he felt a cool breeze against his thigh, which drew his attention to the bathroom window that was just above the bathtub. He cursed under his breath as he had constantly told his workers about leaving the window open because it was broken and therefore difficult to close again.

"Dumb muthafuckas," Rock Head cursed as he reached for the roll of toilet tissue that was sitting on the edge of the tub. He leaned over to wipe his ass when the shower curtain flew back and he realized that he wasn't alone.

"Why don't you hold that pose for me?" the man who had been hiding behind the curtain said in a low tone. His face was almost completely covered by the hoodie and sunglasses he was wearing, but Rock Head could see the sneer on his bowed lips. In the man's hand he held a long-barreled .357 that looked like it had seen better days.

"Chill, B, the money and the drugs are on the table," Rock Head said nervously.

The hooded man slapped him viciously across the face causing Rock Head's head to bounce off the wall. "Oh, I'm gonna take your bread, but that ain't what I came for." The man grinned devilishly at Rock Head, letting his shaded eyes run from Rock Head's sweat-covered face and linger on his exposed buttocks.

Rock Head's eyes went wide with shock. "Oh, hell nah, I ain't off no homo shit so you're just gonna have to blast me." Rock Head tried to spring to his feet, but the man slapped him again and sent him spilling to the floor.

"Don't nobody want a taste of your shitty ass so calm down," the hooded man told him.

"Then what do you want?" Rock Head asked, terrified to hear the answer.

The man smiled and showed two rows of diamond and gold teeth. "To make a point." He grabbed Rock Head by the back of his shirt and yanked him to his feet. "Walk with me, my nigga, while I tell you a little story." He shoved Rock Head out of the bathroom without allowing Rock Head to pull his pants up, making him waddle like a duck while he steered him toward the table and pushed him roughly into the seat. "The thing you niggaz don't understand these days is that when you fuck around in the streets, then you're married to the streets. She's your mother, your lover, and your whore. Your everything. When bitch ass niggaz disrespect that code and pull some ho shit, it's like pissing on the memory of every nigga whose movie ended on them same corners they were trying to get up off."

"Yo, my man—" Rock Head began, but the hooded man ignored him and continued talking.

"I loved the cold streets of Harlem more than I loved my own mother, and someone tore us apart. Can you imagine what it's like to be ripped from the bosom of your sweetheart without having a chance to make love to her one last time?" the killer asked no one in particular. He was starting to make Rock Head nervous and he wasn't sure how much longer he would be able to hold his bowels. "The hole it punched in my soul can probably never be mended, but I pressed on knowing that one day we would be reunited and all would once again be right with the universe." He looked down at Rock Head who was sweating and squirming in the chair. "You don't look so good, playboy. Judgment got you nervous?"

"Nah, my stomach is bubbling, man." Rock Head rocked back and forth with his arm wrapped around his gut.

"Don't tell me my gift didn't agree with your stomach? I thought rats could eat just about anything." The hooded man spun the pizza box playfully.

"Oh, my God, you poisoned me?" Rock Head started sticking his finger down his throat to gag himself. He vomited pizza and liquor onto his legs and brand-new Jordans.

The hooded man laughed. It was a familiar laugh, but Rock Head was so rattled that he couldn't place it. "Relax, I just doused it with baby laxative. Poisoning you would've been too merciful a death, and for what y'all done to me mercy is not an option. You stole something from me and now I intend to steal something from you."

"Look, dawg, I don't know what you're talking about. I don't even know you," Rock Head said nervously.

"I think you know me pretty good." The man removed the sunglasses so that Rock Head could see his lifeless eyes.

"Oh, God, it's you!" Rock Head panicked. He tried to leap from the table and bolt for the door, but the man tripped him and Rock Head went sprawling.

The man picked Rock Head up and shoved him back in the chair. "Now why you wanna go and hurt my feelings like you ain't glad to see me, especially with there being so much unfinished business between our respective peoples?"

Tears ran freely down Rock Head's face. "Listen, blood, I didn't have anything to do with that. I'm just a worker."

The hooded man paused as if he was weighing the truth of Rock Head's words. "Yeah, you ain't never been much more than a lap dog, but now you're gonna be a message." The hooded man pulled a long kitchen knife from the pocket of his hoodie and began to trace a line down Rock Head's face with it.

"Please, don't cut me," Rock Head whimpered.

"Nah, I ain't gonna cut you, Rock Head, but I am gonna get my point across, *literally.*" The hooded man suddenly flipped the knife and stabbed one of the packages spilling cocaine all over the table. "Go on and get you a taste, blood," the man urged him.

"Nah, I don't sniff," Rock Head said.

"You're either gonna sniff or you're gonna bleed, it don't really make me a difference," the man said while testing the sharpness of the knife with his fingertip. A trickle of blood ran down his middle finger while he watched it curiously. "I'm waiting."

With trembling hands Rock Head ripped off a piece of the pizza box and scooped a little coke onto it. He looked at his tormentor nervously before snorting it. He immediately went into a fit of sneezing and his eyes began to water. "Damn, you satisfied now?" Rock Head covered his nose.

The hooded man glared at Rock Head. "You must think I'm fucking with you." He grabbed Rock Head by the back of the neck and yanked him up from the chair. Rock Head struggled as the man forced his face down into the pile of cocaine. "Breathe, muthafucka," the hooded man ordered as Rock Head continued to squirm. "Since you can't seem to get it right on your own let me help you out." The hooded man positioned the knife between Rock Head's butt cheeks. Rock Head knew what was about to happen but it still didn't prepare him for the pain when the knife entered his rectum and stole his breath. "That's it, breathe *real* deep," the hooded man whispered into the dying man's ear, twisting the knife. Only when Rock Head had stopped screaming did the hooded man release his grip.

With a focused look on his face he took the shit-stained knife and cut Rock Head's tongue from his mouth and stuffed it in his pocket. "Blood in, blood out," the hooded man said to the corpse before tossing the smeared knife into the pizza box.

It would be almost twenty-four hours before Rock Head's body was discovered. The story of his gruesome execution would make front-page headlines in several newspapers. When one of the detectives was quoted as saying, "This was the work of an animal," he had no clue how close to the truth he had been.

PART 1

Drama for An Appetizer

Chapter 1

TRAFFIC WAS PRETTY LIGHT AT THAT TIME OF MORNING on the Saw Mill Parkway. The south-bound lanes were just starting to become congested with cars and people making the commute into the city proper to start the workday, but the north was wide open, which was a blessing considering the way Brasco was driving. The engine of the Honda Civic whined as he sped up the road, weaving in and out of traffic and occasionally checking his rearview for troopers. He didn't give a shit about a speeding ticket, but it would be hard to explain why he had a sawed-off shotgun stashed under a blanket in the backseat. After spending the last eighteen months on Rikers Island on a probation violation he had no desire to be caged again.

That summer had been a bad one for his little family. China had been killed in a botched robbery, Silk lost her life in a shoot-out with the police, and Tech had been executed by a rival faction, leaving only the junior members of the group to carry on the legacy, but their reign was a short one. Acting on a tip from a confidential informant the police had closed the net on their little gang. Brasco, Nefertiti, and Ashanti found themselves snatched off the block and thrown into jail on what turned out to be a trumped-up charge offered up by a snitch named Rock Head from 140th Street. Brasco knew that they were clean and would beat the case, but what he hadn't counted on was the warrant out on him. Needless to say it was considered a violation of his probation and an automatic ninety days. The extra five months came from a stabbing incident between him and a Crip who had been talking crazy. Brasco was eventually cleared of the crime, but it took time to prove his innocence.

Nefertiti didn't have any priors so they let him walk with a slap on the wrist, but little Ashanti had gotten the worst of it. He was a minor with no relatives who would claim him so he became a ward of the state, sentenced to a boys' home until he turned eighteen, which would've been in another three years had it not been for the letter Brasco's aunt had gotten in the mail.

Resting on the dashboard was the latest issue of *Don Diva*. On one side there was a mug shot of a cat named Gutter who had been the Adolph Hitler of gangbanging before being murdered by his enemies. The reverse side was a crisp picture of Don B. and his Big Dawg Entertainment crew, which now included one of Brasco and Nefertiti's closest comrades, The Animal. Animal looked like a little boy standing among the hardened soldiers of Don B.'s army, but he was arguably the most dangerous of them. Like all of them Animal had been a product of the streets and at the rate he was going destined to die in them, but fate had given him a pass. Brasco smiled proudly when he had received the issue in the mail and saw his friend posted up on the cover as a part of one of the biggest rap labels in the country, but it was the scribe inside the magazine that had him the most excited.

"How much farther is it?" Nefertiti asked while fumbling with the CD player. Plies's "Hundred Years" was replaced by Murs's "L.A."

Brasco slapped Nefertiti's hand like he was a child trying to touch a hot stove. "Nigga, have you lost your last mind?" Brasco snarled and switched back to the Plies CD. "Take Off" blared through the speakers, rattling the rearview mirror. "Nef, how you gonna change the CD when my cut is about to come on? You know I ride to this shit." Brasco began mouthing the words.

"Man, I don't know why you listen to this country muthafucka. Shit, he ain't even got a platinum album out," Nefertiti said.

"Because this nigga is talking to the cats like me. Plies might not have a number one album, but I'll bet you hear this shit bumping in every rock house in the hood. Nef, it ain't always about what you sell, but what you represent. Although I wouldn't expect a nigga like you to understand," Brasco said and went back to concentrating on the road.

"And what do you mean by that?" Nef turned to face him.

"I mean what I said. Me and you are two different kinda niggaz, homey."

Nefertiti turned the radio down and got Brasco's full attention. "Brasco, you acting like we ain't been jacking together since we was shorties. Don't my gun go off like yours?"

Brasco looked at him, wondering if he should keep it a hundred or sugarcoat it. He reasoned that he and Nefertiti went too far back to dance around the subject so he spoke from his heart. "Yeah, ya gun go off, but you ain't shooting to kill nobody. Nef, I ain't trying to say you won't lay your murder game down, but while I'm shooting to take a nigga outta the game, you're shooting to get him off ya back."

"So now I'm a pussy?" Nefertiti was beginning to get agitated.

"Never that, my nigga. Nef, I'll take you and Ashanti in my corner going to battle over a hundred of the illest cats you can find, next to Animal of course. We family, blood, but I know if given the choice you would let a nigga live to keep that kinda evil off ya soul, whereas I'm going for the kill. A live enemy equals a loose end that you'll always have to worry about. Nef, just because me and Ashanti are rotten doesn't mean that you have to be. God makes us all different and I respect you for being who you are."

"Whatever, man," Nefertiti said and occupied himself by staring out the window. For as long as he had been riding with the crew they had teased him about not being as bloodthirsty as the rest of the hounds. More often than not he would laugh it off, but he did have his moments where he could get caught up in his feelings about it. Nef was so caught up in his thoughts that he almost didn't notice that they had exited the parkway. Brasco did the speed limit as they drove through the sleepy town of goodness knew where. They had gone west for about a mile when Brasco turned off on a dirt road that led deep into a wooded area. After moving deep into the shoulder he threw the car in park and started flipping through the magazine.

"What the hell are we doing back here? I thought we were going to see Ashanti at the boys' home?" Nefertiti asked. He wasn't sure how comfortable he was with the way Brasco had stopped them in the middle of nowhere. His mind suddenly began to have flashes of how they did the kid in *Alpha Dog* and it filled him with dread.

"We are," Brasco said, never bothering to look up from the magazine.

Nefertiti was about to question him further when he heard shouting coming from somewhere on the other side of the woods. He looked over at Brasco, who was just smiling as the shouting grew closer. Nefertiti swung around nervously when he heard the bushes ruffling a few yards away. By this time his imagination had him so wound up that he almost shit his pants when Ashanti came bursting out of the shrubbery, with two angry-looking men hot on his heels.

Ashanti was dressed in a green sweat suit that looked like it was two sizes too small and a pair of strap-up sneakers. He wove this way and that in a complicated pattern like he was trying out at a football combine, occasionally bounding over logs and fallen branches. The dark-skinned man, who was wearing a blue shirt and khakis, tried to tackle Ashanti, but the lithe boy made a sharp cut and the man went skidding into the dirt. The second man, an older white gentleman with salt and pepper hair, managed to get out past Ashanti and stood between him and the car. He smiled arrogantly knowing that he had Ashanti trapped, but froze when the heard the telltale slide of a shotgun behind him.

Brasco stood wide-legged in the dirt with the shotgun braced against his shoulder, drawing a bead on the man's back. "Break yo self, white boy," Brasco snapped.

"Hey, take it easy, kid," the man said. When he attempted to turn around Brasco pressed the shotgun in his back.

"They don't pay you enough for what you're about to do," Brasco whispered in the man's ear. "Let's go, lil homey!" he shouted over to Ashanti.

Ashanti made sure that there was extra swagger in his walk when he moved past his former jailers. He stopped short of the man Brasco was holding at gunpoint and sized him up. All of the counselors at the boys' home were assholes, but this one had been especially cruel to little Ashanti. Without warning Ashanti drew his hand back and slapped the man so hard that the sound scared off a family of geese that had been swimming in a nearby pond. The man went to the ground in a heap holding his jaw that had already turned bright red and was beginning to swell.

"I told you one day I was gonna get ya ass back, pussy." Ashanti kicked him for good measure before jumping into the backseat of the car and making his escape.

"YOU SHOULD TURN THIS BITCH around so I can let one of them pussies hold something," Ashanti said, stroking the shotgun with a look of lust in his eyes. It had been quite some time since he held a gun, and the feeling was akin to a junkie relapsing.

"Shut up and give me that damn gun before you shoot one of us by accident." Brasco snatched the gun from him and handed it to Nefertiti.

"What the fuck just happened?" Nefertiti asked, looking from the gun to Ashanti nervously. He kept checking the mirrors to see if they were being followed.

"A jailbreak, what the fuck does it look like?" Ashanti laughed.

Nefertiti shook his head in frustration. "Only y'all two niggaz can cook up some shit like this and manage to rope me into it too. We're gonna fuck around and go to jail."

"Stop crying, Nef. Their system is so jammed up that they ain't even gonna bother to look for me once we cross the county line. If anything I just freed up a bed for the next poor bastard they toss in that bitch. Brasco, I can't tell you how happy I was when you sent word that you were busting me out, even if it did take your ass forever to make it happen. If I had to spend one more month in that joint I was gonna lose it."

"You know you wouldn't have been in there that long if we were still heavy in the streets. Dawg, a nigga was on twist when they laid me down. When I touched the streets again I had to build from the ground up," Brasco explained.

"I thought Nef was out there holding it down from the kites he was sending me. Son, sent up mad pictures of him with mad bitches and popping bottles with some lame ass niggaz from uptown," Ashanti said.

Brasco looked at Nefertiti and then at Ashanti. "Holding it down? Man, this nigga was working in the stockroom at B.J.'s while we were locked up."

"Chill, son, you know with all the heat on us I had to keep a low profile. Me working up there was just a front," Nefertiti boasted.

"Front my ass, Nef. The only reason your monkey ass ain't still working at B.J.'s is because they caught you stealing them frozen shrimp and fired you!" Brasco laughed.

Ashanti shook his head. "Shrimps, dawg?"

Nefertiti tried to act like he was mad but couldn't hold back the laugh any longer. "Shrimp, steak, and whatever else I could get my hands on. Every first, third, and fifteenth I'd be posted up right in front of the check-cashing spot getting my sling on. Them government checks were going from the state to the broads to my hands. I was killing 'em!"

"Nef, your ass is crazy," Ashanti said, wiping a tear from his eye. "Yo, Brasco, let me see the kite, son."

Brasco handed him the letter that had been tucked in the magazine. Ashanti was so shocked that he read it twice. "I can't believe it, dawg. Son, do you know what this means?"

Brasco nodded his head and grinned wickedly. "It means that all these bitch ass niggaz are about to fall in line."

Chapter 2

MALIKA STOOD UNDER THE WARM SPRAY FROM THE shower head as it beat down on her shoulders and back. She lathered up the loofah and began to wash her breasts one at a time. She took extra care around the areolas, relishing in the sinful sensation that traveled the length of her body. It had been quite a while since Malika had been with a man and even as her body craved one's touch, she refused to settle just to get a nut.

She grabbed the nearly empty bottle of Mane & Tale shampoo and began lathering her long auburn dreads. It took her almost a full ten minutes to make sure she had washed them thoroughly, and she knew they would take almost three times as long to dry. On more than one occasion she'd thought about cutting them but could never bring herself to do it. Malika was rinsing the last of the shampoo out of her hair when the water suddenly became ice cold. She staggered back, almost slipping in the shower. She quickly adjusted the knobs this way and that, but the water was still cold.

"You can't be serious!" Malika huffed. Housing had cut the hot water . . . again. From the pissy elevators to the abrupt hot water interruptions, Malika hated public housing. Growing up in the affluent neighborhood of Jamaica Estates all her life, she was totally underprepared for the bullshit that came with living in public housing. She'd thought she was spiting her parents when she'd left the nest, but had she known what was waiting for her behind door number two she would've listened to her mother.

MALIKA HAD BEEN THE PRIDE of their household. She had an older brother and sister; she was the baby of the family and the one who showed the most promise. Her father was a respected professor at NYU and her mother an RN at Jamaica Hospital. As a child she wanted for nothing, but her parents also made sure she was kept on a very tight leash. Her father was a devout Muslim, but her mother wasn't, so this often caused conflict in the house. When the issue of religion was raised her father reluctantly agreed to let the children choose their own path but he always made sure that the presence of Islam was felt in their house.

Like most young girls, Malika started feeling herself when she hit high school. She attended MLK in Manhattan as opposed to Stuyvesant like her parents had wanted. They thought it was because she hadn't been accepted, but unbeknownst to them Malika had intercepted the acceptance letter and destroyed it so they'd have to agree to let her go to King. From the first day Malika had taken the long train ride to Manhattan to attend her new school she was hooked on her newfound freedom.

Attending high school in itself was exciting to Malika, but to be so far out of her parents' reach only added to the thrill. It didn't take long for the boys to notice the pretty caramel shorty with the supermodel smile and silky locks and Malika soaked up the attention she got. While attending school in Queens she often came across the same faces from year to year, but at King all the flavors were different. It was like a great big stage and the once quiet and reserved Malika found herself auditioning for the leading role.

The summer before her junior year Malika was a victim of her first crush. He had been a Brooklyn cat named Suede who hustled in the projects near her neighborhood. Suede had money, cars, and the attention of every girl within a ten-block radius. Suede had chased young Malika for almost three months before she would even entertain a conversation with him. Their courtship went from the chase, to dating, to her being pregnant by the older man.

Malika's father went through the roof when he found out she was pregnant and had it not been for her mother he surely would've beaten the baby out of her. He was angry at his daughter for deviating from what they'd taught her about being careful, but he was also very hurt. He had watched his own mother struggle to raise him and his sisters, and couldn't bare the thought of having his own child throw her life away. Malika's father had given her an ultimatum: abort the child or get out of his house. So she left.

Suede got them a small apartment in the Bronx that they could call their own. It was only a studio, but it was theirs. Malika continued to go to school, but as the baby grew in her stomach it became more and more of a struggle, and Suede's moodiness didn't make it any easier. It seemed like the further along she got in her pregnancy the more distant he became, often not coming home for days at a time. Suede was totally out of order, but she put up with it rather than risking him leaving her. The more she put up with the more Suede attempted, even giving her an STD during her sixth month of pregnancy. When she confronted him about it he slapped her and accused her of giving it to him from her whoring, even though he was the only man she had ever been with.

Suede eventually got arrested and left Malika to take care of the bills and him while he was away. She continued to go to school and work a part-time job at Wendy's, but the stress of juggling both of them in her current condition eventually became too much, forcing her to give one up. School wasn't paying her bills so she let it go and toiled at Wendy's until she was thirty-two weeks into her pregnancy. She was scared, alone, and broke, but she held it together and gave birth to a beautiful baby boy that she named Solomon. From the first time she held him she knew that it was impossible to love anyone or anything the way she loved her new son. The first years were the roughest for them, with Malika having to go without eating some nights so that her son wouldn't. Just before Solomon's third birthday she got the news that Suede had been released from prison, but for some reason he hadn't bothered to tell her that he was getting out. She found out through a friend that he was staying with his mother in Manhattan, so one snowy day she bundled little Solomon up and took the long trip into Manhattan.

She wanted to surprise Suede, but she was the one who ended up surprised when she showed up on the doorstep only to find Suede living with another girl, who was also pregnant by him. Suede looked at Malika like she was the dirt on the bottom of his shoe and told his new girlfriend that she was just an obsessed little girl who was trying to pin another man's baby on him. Malika showed him obsessed when she opened his forearm up with a box cutter. That was the last time she saw Suede. Her first crush had damaged her heart beyond repair so Malika threw herself into raising her son and trying to get her life back together. From that moment on she vowed that the only man she would ever let into her heart again would be Solomon.

MALIKA HADN'T REALIZED THAT SHE was crying until she blinked and a tear rolled down her cheek. She laughed because her tears were warmer than the water. Ignoring the frigid cold Malika hurriedly washed away the rest of the shampoo and soap and jumped out of the shower so she could finish getting dressed. With towels wrapped around her body and hair she stepped out of the bathroom and tripped over a sneaker that had been carelessly left in the hallway.

"Damn it, Solomon," she cursed, snatching the sneaker up and making her way down the short hall to his bedroom. Before she reached the door she could hear the music coming from the room. It was a lewd song about money, clothes, and of course hos. She recognized the cut from a new mix tape that Big Dawg Entertainment had released called "Welcome to the Jungle," featuring Don B. and his newest artist The Animal. Malika pushed the door open and looked at her son in shock.

At the age of twelve Solomon was almost as tall as Malika, but weighed about ninety pounds soaking wet. He was dressed in a red Black Label T-shirt she'd bought him for Christmas and a pair of skinny jeans that she certainly hadn't bought. More of a shock than the feminine jeans was the red bandana hanging from his back pocket. He never heard Malika when she walked into the room, but he felt it when she suddenly smacked him upside the head.

"What the f—" Solomon started but caught himself. "Ma, why you hit me for?"

"You're lucky I didn't punch you in the damn face." She snatched the bandana. "What the hell is this?"

"Huh?" Solomon asked dumbly.

Malika grabbed him by the front of his T-shirt and hauled him in close. "Boy, don't play with me. What are you doing carrying this damn flag?"

Solomon looked at the flag as if he were seeing it for the first time. "That ain't no flag, Ma. Flags have stripes and stars. That's just an old sweat rag."

Malika gave him another pop with the hand holding the sweat rag. "Solomon, you know I ain't no square, so cut it out, okay? The people and things you choose to identify yourself with can have life-altering consequences, especially this little game right here." She waved the bandana in his face. "In certain neighborhoods this piece of cloth could cost you your life. I'll kill you myself before I let the streets have you. Do you understand?"

"Yes, Mommy," Solomon said timidly.

"And where did you get those tight-ass jeans, because I know I didn't buy them?" She frowned at the jeans.

"These joints are fly, Ma." Solomon spun around so she could get a good look at them. "I used the money Grandma sent me for my birthday to buy them. Do you like them?"

"No I don't like them. Boy, it looks like you're wearing spandex." Malika tugged at the jeans, but they had no give.

"Ma, you bugging. All the kids are wearing these," Solomon told her.

"Well, not my kid," she shot back. "Change them jeans before you give yourself a yeast infection." She snapped the bandana at him playfully and left the room. Fifteen minutes later they were both dressed and ready to face the world.

AS SOON AS MALIKA AND Solomon stepped into the hallway they smelled it. It was like the smell of burning paper, with an acidic bite. Malika sighed and made her way to Stairwell A and peered inside. Then she shoved the door to Stairwell B open and scared the daylights out of Shakes, who nearly dropped the crack pipe he was sucking on.

"Damn it, Shakes!" Malika snapped.

"Girl, you know better than to be sneaking up on an old man like that." Shakes gave her a rotten-toothed grin. He was dressed in a wrinkled business suit and dirty overcoat. At one time Shakes had been a master booster, but now he was just another addict trying to escape the reality of his life.

"And you know better than to be smoking that shit on my floor. I asked y'all not to do that." Malika folded her arms.

"Come on, baby girl, it's cold on them streets." Shakes pulled his jacket collar up as if the chill had suddenly made it inside the stairwell.

"Then smoke them rocks in your own damn house."

Shakes gave her a bewildered look. "And have my mama kill me? I don't think so, baby. So, other than busting the balls of honest crackheads like myself, what you been up to, Malika?"

"Trying to keep crack heads from trying to get high in my staircase," she joked. "Nah, I'm just out here trying to get in where I fit in."

"Malika, girls like you don't fit in, you carve your own niches. You ain't like the rest of these little girls."

"Shakes, how do you figure that and we all live in these same nasty ass projects?" she asked.

"Because you've got the good sense to see outside these project bricks," he replied. "Malika, I know you ain't no angel, but you ain't into all kinds of foolishness like the rest of these chicks. I watch the young girls floating around these projects from sunup to sunup keeping company with different men and cussing like they ain't got no sense."

"Shakes, one could question your sense for still smoking them rocks," Malika said.

Shakes looked at the pipe that he had only just realized that he was still holding and shrugged. "Old habits for an old fool. You know how it can be."

"Ma, elevator!" Solomon called. He was holding the elevator door open and tapping his foot impatiently.

"I'll catch you later, Shakes." Malika waved and got into the elevator.

The tiny steel car was hot, greasy, and rank, as it was most of the time. Malika and Solomon had to stand nearly pressed against the door to avoid stepping in the puddle of urine in the center of the elevator floor. After what seemed like an eternity the elevator reached the first floor and they rushed off, holding their noses. As usual the local knuckleheads were standing in front of the building, taking up space. It seemed like no matter what time of day or night Malika came in they were always there. Most of them were relatively harmless, but there were the few who were just trouble, which was the case with the young boy holding the door for Malika and Solomon.

"What's good, Malika?" Scar asked. His shifty dark eyes rolled over her body. He was a young block star from the projects who wore trouble like a second skin. Scar had gotten the name because of the scar that stretched from his left temple to the tip of his nose. As the story went, Scar had wrongfully cut a man in one prison and ended up bumping into him in a second prison where the favor was returned. Out of all the young men who hung out in front of Malika's building Scar was probably the worst, constantly causing trouble and filling the younger boys' heads with gang propaganda.

"Not much," she replied and kept walking.

"What's good, buzz'n?" Scar gave little Solomon dap and the boy's eyes lit up.

"Solomon," Malika corrected Scar.

"Huh?"

"Solomon. His name is Solomon," Malika repeated.

"My fault, Ma, I didn't mean nothing by it," Scar told her with a crooked grin.

"It's all good." Malika took Solomon by the hand and hurried toward the avenue. "I want you to stay away from that boy, do you hear me?" she told Solomon once they were out of earshot.

"Ma, Scar is cool. That's the big homey," Solomon said proudly.

"That snake is not *your* homey, and I'd better not catch you in that lobby with him and the rest of those junior delinquents. Do you hear me?"

"Okay, gosh," Solomon grumbled. He knew that his mother only rode him to protect him, but he hated when she treated him like some stupid kid who didn't know what was happening on the streets. In Solomon's mind he was technically the man of the house and therefore it was his job to make sure his family was good. Day in and day out, he watched his mother struggle just so that they could have a little and it tore him apart inside. He vowed that one day she would be able to just kick her feet up while he took care of things.

As they stood on the curb waiting for the light to change so that they could cross the street and catch the number seven bus, a gold Acura pulled to a clumsy stop at the curb. The door flew open releasing a cloud of weed smoke and profane lyrics that were blasting from the speakers. A girl slithered from the car dressed in a pair of tight-fitting jeans and spandex shirt. She had a bit of a gut, but her small waist and curvaceous hips drew attention away from it. The light breeze blew her rich black weave, making her look like Farrah Fawcett at a photo shoot. In her manicured hand she held the six-inch heels that had given her feet enough hell so that she wore her broke-down thong flip-flops in the chill. Between her MAC-coated lips she twirled a cherry lollipop back and forth while the driver gave her his parting words. She laughed and blew him a kiss, releasing him from her spell and allowing him to compose himself enough to drive away. Jada Butler was a bad chick and she dared anyone to tell her different.

"What's up, Jada? I'm surprised to see your ass out and about so early," Malika greeted her.

"Girl, I'm just coming in," Jada said proudly. "What's up, Sol? Boy, you're getting just as big and fine as you wanna be." Jada smiled at Solomon, showing off the fifteen grand in dental work she'd had done.

"Yeah, I know you see me, J, but you need to see *about* me," Solomon capped.

Jada laughed. "Listen to this one."

"You better watch that mouth of yours." Malika pointed her finger at her son.

"It's all good, Malika. You know it'll be years before his little ass even has an idea of what to do with all this." Jada slapped herself on the ass.

"I doubt if he'll be able to handle you even then. So where are you coming from this morning?"

Jada popped the lollipop from her mouth and waved it like a conductor's wand as she spoke. "Girl, ol' boy from the Knicks had a party in Atlantic City and a friend of a friend had the hookup, so you know I had to be in the building. When I tell you that it was some *things* in the building, it was some things in the building. I hit your phone to see if you wanted to roll, but when you didn't answer I ended up having to take that dusty bitch Renee with me, and you know the girl ain't got no home training."

"I was probably studying when you called; you know I don't take no calls during crunch time," Malika reminded her.

"You still taking them online classes?"

"Six months away from an Associate's in business management." Malika held up crossed fingers.

"Malika, you're better than me. After spending twelve years in school I couldn't see myself doing another day let alone two more years just to get some piece of paper that says I'm qualified to do something that I already know how to do anyway."

"That piece of paper is gonna be me and my little man's ticket outta these projects," Malika said seriously.

"There's easier ways to getting outta the projects than busting your brain with those books and paying the government back for the money you had to borrow to get the ball rolling in the first place. Chicks like you hustle backward, Malika. You're pretty and smart, so it wouldn't be nothing for you to find somebody willing to lighten that load of yours and take you up outta here, you just gotta know how to go about it."

"Jada, you're twice as pretty as me and you've been in these projects all your life," Malika pointed out.

"That's by choice, baby-boo. I've lived in plenty of places, but it ain't nothing like my projects. Look, my whole family is here so I ain't never got a problem with a babysitter, and the fact that I ain't gotta pay no light and gas frees up money for other shit."

Malika thought on it. "But don't you get tired of all the bullshit that comes with living here? Scar and his boys play the lobby twenty-four/seven and if I had a dollar for every time the hot water was cut off or the elevators were broken, I'd be a rich woman. I'm not knocking what you're saying, Jada, but I don't think I could spend the rest of my life living off the mercies of Public Assistance and this jacked up ass housing system."

"Now hold on, little Ms. Sunshine." Jada placed her hands on her hips and looked at Malika seriously. "I've worked different jobs since I was eleven years old. Even when I got pregnant with my son I had a gig downtown stuffing envelopes. I've given the state enough of my time and money, so it's only right that they return the favor. For as long as the state is knocking out the bulk of my rent I ain't gotta do much other than rest and dress," Jada said with a snap of her fingers.

"I feel you, Jada, but I'd still rather go get it than have it given to me."

"Which is why ya ass is broke and man-less now," Jada teased her. "But on the real, I ain't mad at you for the moves you're making, Malika. If I had as high a tolerance for bullshit as you do then I might not be out here living by my wits now."

"It ain't never too late, Jada."

"Yeah, but I think I'm gonna have fun with it for a while. Let me take my ass upstairs so I can lie down. I ain't been to sleep in almost forty-eight hours." Jada yawned.

"Do, you and I'll catch up later. You still gonna be able to style my hair tonight?" Malika twirled a hand full of her locks.

"Yeah, as long as you come by at a decent time. I heard my cousin is in town and I'm trying to catch up with her before she breezes again."

"I ain't seen Gucci in a minute, what's up with her? Does she still date that rapper?" Malika asked.

"Yeah, she's still all wife'd up to that psycho muthafucka. Cuzo sure picked a live one with him. I don't even try to understand their relationship, but I'm loving the benefits she gets from being a superstar's wifey. I'm trying to get her to hook me up with one of them cats, and it ain't necessarily gotta be a rapper. The way them niggaz from Big Dawg get money I could probably do pretty good for myself with one of their hype men." Jada laughed.

Malika shook her head. "J, I don't know how you balance your kids and this rock and roll lifestyle of yours."

Jada winked at her. "It's an art, baby. Maybe one day when you come up for air outta them books I can give you a lesson or two." Jada rubbed Solomon's cheek as she passed him. "Bye, cutie."

"Imma holla at you later, Ma." Solomon blushed.

"Boy, bring your thirsty ass on." Malika pulled him by the arm to the bus stop.

Chapter 3

JADA WALKED UP THE AVENUE, SUCKING HER LOLLIPOP and switching her ass hard enough to dislocate her hips. She turned the attention of just about everyone she passed, including the females. As she cut down the path en route to the stairs leading to her building she spotted two local stoop rats sitting on the bench, sharing a cigarette. The one rocking the head scarf and mean-mug was named Boots. She was a brown-skinned girl with a decent body, but a face that took a special kind of love or several shots to stare at for too long. Boots was washed up, but thought that she still had a shot at greatness. With five kids by almost as many men it was a stretch at best that anyone would take her for more than what she was, a jump-off. Jada couldn't stand Boots and the only reason she hadn't whipped her out yet was because she was one of her cousin Gucci's best friends. What someone of Gucci's caliber could see in a girl like Boots was beyond Jada's comprehension, but she let it be to keep the peace.

The second girl wasn't a hard-faced baby-making machine with a chip on her shoulder, but she was no less trifling. With big doe eyes and an inviting smile she had the face of an angel and the wit of a snake. Sahara was a pretty dark-skinned girl who had moved

WELFARE WIFEYS   29

to the projects from West Africa six or seven years prior. When she was ten years old she was sold into slavery by her uncle and had been shuffled from port to port all around Europe as the play thing of those who had the money to spend for her. When she was fifteen she managed to garner the attentions of an underworld figure from New York who dealt in international trafficking. Together they plotted the robbery and murder of Sahara's latest owner and fled to New York. Six months after arriving the man Sahara had fled with was found dead at the scene of what the police were calling a dope deal gone wrong. For a time Sahara floated from borough to borough doing what she could to survive, until she had managed to locate some cousins of hers who were living in the projects and opened their home to her. It didn't take long for Sahara to get a taste of the darker side of New York life and become turned out by it. Sahara was a young girl with champagne dreams and beer money, but considering what she came from she was doing okay for herself.

Sahara waved and Jada waved back. They knew some of the same people so they were cordial when they saw each other, but not Boots. She shot daggers at Jada as she passed to which she responded by throwing on her shades and switch harder. To Jada, Boots's was just one more sour face in a world of many.

Ever since Jada could remember she and her family had lived a world apart from their neighbors in the projects. With all the dirt they were involved in, it was the safest way to avoid an indictment. Jada was descended from a very long line of criminals. The Butler family notoriety went all the way back to her grandfather Jake, who in his heyday had been a leg breaker for Bumpy Johnson, but became the local numbers man in his later years. Up until the time of his death Jake had always had some type of hustle going on. It was a fixation that he passed on to all of his sons, but Jake Jr., or J.J. as they called him, showed the most promise. He was a beast when it came to his grind and his woman Gina was no slouch either. They were like the Bonnie and Clyde of the late eighties, and they lavished everything they took in on their baby girl, Jada.

Things began to go south when J.J. had gotten arrested for murder. He hadn't even been in Manhattan when the deed was done, but one of his close friends had told the police otherwise in order to save his own skin. Even though J.J. was innocent of the killing, because of his violent criminal history a jury would've more than likely gotten him fried so he copped out to a lesser charge and had to wear fifteen to life. The whole family was heartbroken when they lost J.J., but nobody took it harder than Gina. She slipped into a deep depression and the only thing that seemed to soothe her bleeding heart was cocaine. When she had snorted through most of the money they'd had in the stash, Gina started freebasing and it was all downhill from there. Social Services stepped in and had it not been for Jada's grandmother, Ms. Pat, taking her in, the little girl would've become a ward of the state.

Jada was only supposed to be with Ms. Pat until Gina successfully completed the rehabilitation program, but less than three months after she checked in, Gina fled the program. Sobriety had become too heavy a cross to carry so Gina went back to the oblivion of the pipe. Not long after her great escape they found Gina dead in Central Park. She had gone into cardiac arrest after one of her drug binges and collapsed in a secluded section of the park. Nobody really knew if it was that last blast that had killed her, or the fact that she lay in the freezing snow for almost thirty hours before somebody finally found her.

Ms. Pat had stepped to the plate and played the role of both mother and father to young Jada. Even with the constantly shifting cast of relatives that revolved in and out of the Butler house, Jada's grandmother made sure that Jada was never short on love. But for as loving as Ms. Pat was she made sure that Jada was under no illusions about the ugliness of the world they lived in. Ms. Pat did the best she could in the attempt to raise Jada right, but she was so busy with her own struggles that Jada was often left in the care of her aunts and uncles and it was from them that she really learned the ropes of what life was all about. Her uncles taught her to be hard and independent, while her aunts instilled in her ruthlessness and cunning. By the time Jada was a teenager she was an accident waiting to happen.

During her developmental years Jada stumbled through life making more than her fair share of bad decisions, especially when it came to men. Jada had always been a pretty girl so men were constantly coming at her promising everything but delivering nothing. She had to make trips to Planned Parenthood and the Free Clinic more often than she cared to remember, before she even got a clue as to sorting bullshit from the truth. For as hard as her aunts and uncles had made her mentally, there wasn't much they could do about her tender heart. The more she had gotten her heart broken the colder she became, until it reached a point where she just stopped feeling anything at all. By the time Jada was able to stand on her own she had become a predator and everything was food.

"What up, Jada?" Scar called from the stairs. He had his henchman Lloyd with him.

"About to turn it in because I'm tired as hell." She continued walking toward the building with the three stooges on her heels.

"I know that's right because you've been running through my mind all day," Lloyd said. He was a funny-faced dark-skinned kid with an overbite and a nervous tick.

"Oh, now that's one I never heard before," Jada said sarcastically. She tapped for the elevator and busied herself with her BlackBerry hoping they'd get the hint, which they didn't.

Scar stepped up before Boogie could hit her with another stupid line. "So what you getting into today?"

"My bed, I just told you that I'm tired." Jada rolled her eyes behind her shades. She silently wished that the elevator would hurry so she could get away from Scar. She'd known him for years, but he still gave her the creeps.

"Nah, I meant later on," he explained. "That new flick *The Last Outlaw* just came out and I'm trying to catch it on opening night. The shit is based on a book by that nigga K'wan and it's supposed to be off the hook!"

"Sorry, I saw the screening last weekend. The author's wife is a friend of mine."

Scar scowled. "Yeah, I forgot that you run in high-class circles."

"Because I'm a high-class chick. Ask about me," Jada said, waving her lollipop dismissively.

"A'ight, so if not the flick then let's go get something to eat," Scar pressed her.

The elevator was still nowhere in sight and Jada couldn't take it anymore so she decided to level with him. "Look"—she removed her shades—"Scar, you my nigga, but you know I ain't messing with you like that."

"And what's that supposed to mean?" he asked.

"Nothing, it just means that I ain't really got time for the bullshit you're putting down. Me and you live two different lifestyles."

"Oh, so now you acting all high off ya shit cuz you shining a little bit? I guess you too good to fuck with the hood niggaz anymore?" Scar asked defensively.

"Never that, you know my family is filled with some of the illest cats this project or any other has yet to produce. What I'm saying is that you still running around trying to game bitches outta their drawers with a bag of piff and a movie and that ain't me, duke."

"There you go with that bullshit." Scar sucked his teeth.

"No, there you go with that bullshit. Scar, you shit where you live so your dirt is out there for everyone to see. Why do you think that ain't nobody in the hood fucking wit you but them young bitches?"

"Jada, you know how the streets talk."

"Nah, I know how you move. Scar, me and you are peoples, but it ain't gonna never be much more than that," she told him just as the elevator finally reached the first floor. Jada stepped into the car without as much as a good-bye.

"Well, fuck you too then, bitch," Scar said after the elevator door had closed.

"Damn, I would love to have her work my dick like she be working them lollipops," Lloyd said.

"Jada ain't trying to fuck with you, nigga. You're a scumbag," Scar told him.

"Well, she ain't fucking with you either, so that makes *us* scumbags. And if Cutty ever caught wind that we was sniffing around his baby mama he might not appreciate it."

Scar looked at Lloyd like he was stupid. "Nigga, is you crazy? They gave Cutty the long walk. That fast bitch Jada ain't fit to be no prisoner's wife. If it ain't my cock that tames her, it'll be some other nigga that's out here getting it. Wit a bitch like Jada, you can fuck her six ways to Saturday, but if you ain't handling it ain't gonna get you no closer to your heat, because she ain't got one." Scar pushed past Lloyd and walked back outside. When he reemerged from the building Sahara and Boots were still sitting on the bench. He looked at the girls who were staring at him in anticipation and figured something was better than nothing. "What up, y'all trying to get high?"

Chapter 4

BY THE TIME JADA MADE IT TO HER DOOR SHE WAS TIRED, irritated, and starting to get musty. All she wanted to do was take a shower and crawl into her bed. She had longed for the peace and quiet of her bedroom for the last fifteen hours, and when she opened her front door she sighed heavily because she knew she wasn't going to get it there. The sounds of Lil Wayne's "Mr. Carter" blaring from the stereo speakers battled with the television, which was also turned all the way up, and tuned to The Steve Wilkos Show. Clothes were hanging on lines of rope that crisscrossed the living room, drying in the intense *project heat* coming from the pipes. Weeks-old newspapers were stacked on the coffee table and chairs, while toys littered the chipped tiled floors. In the center of all the craziness, ironing a dollar bill on a towel was the patriarch of the family, Patricia Butler.

"Hey, Grandma." Jada threw her purse on the plastic-covered couch.

"Umm hmm," Ms. Pat mumbled and continued her ironing. The smoke from the Kool cigarette dangling from her mouth wafted up over her glasses and over her stocking cap-covered head.

"What are you doing?" Jada asked, looking at the rows of pressed dollars.

"That lil Charlie done let me wash his pants without making sure he emptied his pockets first. Now I got to press all these damn singles 'cause you know I ain't wasting no change round here." She flapped the dollar in one of her meaty palms to sort out the wrinkles before placing another wet one on the towel to be ironed. "I wonder where the hell he was at to have all these singles anyhow."

"Probably the strip club," Jada commented.

"And speaking of whereabouts, where have you been?" Ms. Pat looked at Jada over the rims of her bifocals.

"Oh, I told you me and the girls were going out for drinks," Jada said innocently.

Ms. Pat stopped her ironing and looked at her granddaughter seriously. "Girl, that was two days ago, so don't come in here calling yourself being cute. Now I've been in here chasing behind your bad-ass kids and I done missed out on I don't know how much money because your wayward ass is hindering my movements."

"Sorry, Grandma."

"Sorry is a dog with three broken legs trying to crawl to a cool drink of water on a hot day. You're just trifling." Ms. Pat waggled the iron in her direction as she spoke. "Now you done had your fun so I think you best tend to your business before you try to pull another disappearing act." Ms. Pat went back to ironing the damp bill.

"Grandma, why don't you stop acting like that, you know I be making moves," Jada said, pulling the wrapper off another lollipop and sticking it in her mouth.

"Moves, my ass, I hope that lollipop was the only thing you were sucking on while you were out in them streets." Ms. Pat thought on it for a second. "As a matter of fact, don't even answer that. And while you're in the move-making mood, why don't you move your ass around the house and clean up after them kids of yours?"

"A'ight, Grandma." Jada waved her off.

There was a soft knocking on the door, two quick taps then a dead slap. Ms. Pat expelled the smoke through her nose and twisted her lips. Mumbling under her breath she put the iron down and shuffled to the door, pausing to check the small derringer she kept in the pocket of her floral duster. Pushing her glasses up on her forehead she peered through the peephole to see who it was before undoing the multiple locks on the door. Ms. Pat snatched the door open and immediately tore into the young man standing on the other side.

"What you knocking on this door for, lil nigga?" She tapped her foot impatiently waiting for him to answer.

"Ah, how you doing, Ms. Pat? I . . . ah," the boy stammered.

"What is that some new slang that y'all kicking these days? Speak English, boy. What the hell you want?"

The boy looked around cautiously before whispering, "I came to get some smoke."

Ms. Pat's eyes went wide. She peered down the hallways in both directions before snatching the boy by the front of his jacket and pulling him into the apartment. Ms. Pat shoved him against the wall and began patting the frightened boy down while Jada looked on in amusement. "You the police or something?" She ran her hands along his thighs, grazing his testicles one time too many.

"No, ma'am," the boy said, looking at Ms. Pat as if she'd lost it.

"Well, if you ain't the police then you must be a fool because everybody knows Ms. Pat don't sell weed, I sell advice. I got *kind words* for five dollars, *sound advice* for ten, and a *good talking to* for twenty. Now if you're really in need of help then you may be interested in the Ms. Pat special, where every half hour starts at fifty dollars." Ms. Pat was talking so fast that the boy looked baffled. "What are you special? What you need, boy?"

"Ah, I'll take some sound advice," he said, holding out a twenty-dollar bill.

"Bet." Ms. Pat snatched the money from him. She reached into her duster and gave the boy a ten-dollar bag of weed and a five-dollar bag. "Check it out, young'n, since I'm just opening up shop, I'll give you some sound advice, throw in that kind word and a box of slow death for the twenty and we square," she offered.

"That works," the boy said eagerly. He'd only intended on spending ten dollars with Ms. Pat, but with cigarettes being almost ten dollars in the store he couldn't pass up the play.

Ms. Pat went into the kitchen and popped open her deep freezer, where there were several cartons of cigarettes packed in with the food. She put one of the frosty packs of cigarettes in his hand, but held it for a minute and looked into his eyes. "I'm serving you this time, but if you ever pop up at my door again without an invitation we're liable to have a misunderstanding"—she patted the pistol in her duster—"ya dig?"

"My fault, Ms. Pat, I didn't know," he apologized.

"Don't worry about it, baby. Next time just hit me on the chirp." Ms. Pat waved her Boost phone. After giving the boy her information she ushered him out and relocked her door. "Some of these boys ain't got the good sense God gave 'em when they slid their black asses into the world," Ms. Pat said to no one in particular when she came back into the living room.

"Grandma, you better be easy with having people knock on the door like that. You know we already got issues with the city," Jada reminded her.

Ms. Pat looked at her seriously. "Child, I been getting it how I live for longer than you or ya daddy been alive, so don't come around her trying to tell me how to conduct my business, ya hear? And if we got any problems with the city it's because you brought them here, so don't get me started, Jada Butler. I've been in these projects for forty-six years and ain't ever had so much as a complaint filed against me with housing or nobody else."

"Because there isn't anybody bold enough to want a problem with your crazy self." Jada laughed.

"Call me what ya want, but you won't never call me no punk-bitch. I know you looked at ya granddaddy and my boys as the heads of the Butler family, but don't never forget it was the Butler women who gave them power."

Jada sucked her teeth. "Listen to you, like you were out there popping your guns with the fellas."

"Not at all, but I was sure the one getting rid of them when they came home dirty," Ms. Pat shot back.

Before the argument could go any further the sounds of tiny running feet filled the hallway. Three faces that looked much like Jada's came rushing into the living room and swarmed her. "Mommy!" they screamed in unison.

"Thank the Lord," Ms. Pat said under her breath.

Jada ignored her grandmother and hugged her kids. "Hey, I missed you guys." Jada beamed as she kissed each one of her kids on the forehead.

"It's hard to tell. The way you hang out all night you would never know that you were a mother, let alone had three of these little devils," Ms. Pat said.

It was true; Jada partied like a rock star while her kids spent most of their time with Ms. Pat or other relatives. It wasn't that she didn't love her kids, but she didn't know any other way to be. She had always watched her mother and father party while leaving her with Ms. Pat so she ended up repeating the cycle with her own kids. Ms. Pat was a godsend as far as keeping the kids out of harm's way, but with all the stuff she had going on out of the house she hadn't set the best example for her kids either.

"Where ya been, Mommy? We missed you," Jalen asked. She was the middle child and Jada's baby girl.

"Mommy was out with some friends," Jada told her.

"Grandma says you were out sacking," Davita capped. She was Jada's oldest, fourteen years of pure attitude.

"What's sacking?" Miles asked. He was Jada's youngest and the one who looked the least like her.

Jada cut her eyes at her grandmother, who was going about her ironing as if she hadn't heard a thing. "Sacking is just another word for partying," Jada told the little boy.

"When I get older I wanna go sacking just like Mommy," Jalen said proudly.

"And I'm sure you will," Ms. Pat offered.

"Okay, you kids go play while Mommy gets in the shower. When I come out I'm gonna make your breakfast," Jada told the kids.

Ms. Pat put her iron down again. "They had breakfast thirty minutes ago. Y'all kids go on and get ready for school." Ms. Pat shooed them out.

"I'm going to wash up," Jada said to no one in particular.

"Yes, wash them streets off yo ass. Jada, don't sneak outta here without coming to talk to me. There are some things I wanna say to you," Ms. Pat told her.

"Whatever." Jada shuffled down the hall. She unlocked her bedroom door and slipped inside, peeling her clothes off as she crossed it. She searched high and low for her lavender Donna Karan bathrobe but couldn't find it anywhere. Tiring of looking for it she wrapped a beach towel around herself and headed to the bathroom for her shower only to find it occupied. Ms. Pat was in the kitchen and her kids were gone so she knew it had to be one of the wayward freeloaders that her grandmother couldn't help taking in every so often.

Jada banged on the door like the police and it was almost a full five minutes before she finally heard the lock being undone. She drew her lips back, prepared to black out on whoever had been hogging the bathroom, but her jaw dropped when she saw who it was. He had put on some weight since the last time she saw him, but he still had that same scurvy hunch to his back, like he was always skulking. A green do-rag was tied on his head, with the flap hanging down his neck. Draped over his wet and naked body was Jada's Donna Karan robe.

"Oh, hell no!" Jada placed her hands on her hips.

When he smiled the bathroom light glistened off the gold tooth in the front of his mouth. "What's the matter, baby girl? Ain't you glad to see your Uncle Mookie?"

IF YOU LOOKED UP THE word *goon* in the dictionary you'd see a picture of Uncle Mookie, beaming like a kid at graduation. Morris Butler a.k.a. Mookie was the second oldest of Ms. Pat's sons and by far the biggest headache to fall off the Butler tree. He wasn't the largest man, standing at five-eight and weighing a shade less than 180 pounds, but his appetite for destruction was enormous. Mookie was a shifty man who was quick to violence and only played for keeps. Had it not been for Mookie's violent temper he might have actually been somebody in the streets, but he couldn't stay out of jail. Since he was a kid Mookie had loved to fight and stay in the mix. Beef was his drug of choice and he looked for any excuse to get high. When Jada's father was on the streets hustling, Uncle Mookie and his crime partner Fish had been right there in the trenches with him, dispatching enemies of the Butler family and intimidating other dealers in the area.

When Jada's father was sentenced it fell to Mookie to keep the operation going, but with his poor head for business it was only a matter of time before the well went dry. With his meal ticket gone Mookie did what to him was the most logical thing, picked up his pistol and robbed everything moving. Mookie and Fish hit the streets with a vengeance and demanded that all the dealers who now got money in what was once Butler territory paid a street tax to keep doing business. The smart ones paid and the not so smart wound up in the trunks of cars or local emergency rooms. It got so bad that the only time the dealers could get money untaxed was the period of time between Mookie's and Fish's prison stints.

"Somebody must've left the monkey cage open at the zoo." Jada snaked her neck and looked her uncle up and down.

"If I didn't know any better I'd think you were happy to see me."
Mookie bopped out of the bathroom.

"Mookie, if your ass escaped from jail again you better get outta
here. I got kids in this house and an ACS investigation going on, so
I don't need the police kicking Grandma's door in."

Mookie sucked his teeth. "Ain't nobody escape from nowhere,
I'm out on work release, so I swung by Ma's to take a shower, and
what the hell do you mean you've got an ACS case pending? Jada,
don't make me fuck you up for beating my nieces and nephews all
extra and shit."

"Please, ain't nobody beating these bad-ass kids, even though I
should from all the hell they give me. One of these hating ass bitches
was trying to be funny and called them on me. That's my word, when
I find out who it was imma slay one of these hos."

Mookie shook his head. "Just like a Butler, always ready to kick
ass first and take names later."

"You're one to talk." Jada rolled her eyes. "If I recall correctly
the last charge you caught was for assault."

Mookie downplayed it. "That wasn't nothing but a little misunderstanding."

"You call putting forty-two stitches in someone's head a misunderstanding?"

"Hey, if he hadn't pulled that pistol on me I wouldn't have had
to clobber his ass with it. The lil niggaz of this generation have a
serious lack of respect for the O.G.s."

"What the fuck ever, Uncle Mookie. And why do you have your
jailhouse ass in my robe? You know how much that shit cost?"

Mookie sucked his teeth. "A'ight, a'ight, don't get ya drawers in
a bunch." He slipped out of the robe and stood in the hallway as
naked as the day he was born. "I'm done with it anyway." He tossed
it to her and shuffled down the hall, leaving Jada holding the damp
robe with a disgusted look on her face.

Chapter 5

OF COURSE IT WOULD'VE BEEN TOO MUCH TO ASK FOR Mookie to have washed the tub out after ringing it with God only knew how many days' worth of street soot. Cursing under her breath, Jada washed the tub and opted for a quick shower instead of the long soak she'd planned. Even after scrubbing the tub thoroughly, the memory of the dirt ring soured her on the idea.

Moving as quietly as she could so that the kids and her grandmother wouldn't notice her, Jada slipped into her room and locked the door behind her. She tossed the towel she'd been forced to wrap herself in into the corner and stretched out naked on her bed, praying for the sleep that had eluded her during her binge. No sooner than her eyelids began to drop, her bedroom phone rang. Jada snatched the phone up and answered with attitude. "Yeah?"

"Thieving ass bitch, you gonna get just what your hand calls for," a muffled voice said on the other end.

"Eat a dick and die!" Jada slammed the phone down. She had started receiving the disturbing phone calls about a week or so prior, not long after her last blowup with Miles's father, Cutty, over some missing money. Even though the argument had happened weeks prior she still remembered his sharp words as if he had just said them.

SHE HAD BEEN DUCKING CUTTY'S phone calls for more than a week, but he caught her out there that time by having someone call her on three-way. The moment she had heard his gruff voice come over the phone an icy finger ran down her back.

"What the fuck is popping, Jada?"

"Damn, hello to you too," she said sarcastically.

"Yo, now ain't the time for ya fucking mouth, B. I've been trying to track you down for over a week and couldn't get through. What the fuck did you get that extra line installed for if you ain't gonna be around to answer it?"

"My fault, I've been busy."

"So busy that you've forgotten the ones who've taken care of you?" he shot back.

Jada looked at the phone as if she'd heard him wrong. "Cutty, don't come at me with that jailhouse bullshit because I've been taking care of me and these kids since you left. I've got a massive headache right now, so please don't add to it."

"If you stayed in the house instead of running out boozing all night then you might not have this problem."

"Cutty, I don't know who you've got on the line that you're trying to impress, but knock it the fuck off," Jada capped.

Cutty laughed. "Apparently you must've forgotten who I am?" Cutty was one of the fallen legends of Douglass Projects. Before the same streets they praise decided to betray them, Cutty, Rio, and Shamel had been like the Holy Trinity of the crack game, but even the best runs come to an end. Cutty received twenty-five to life, but he got off easy compared to his comrades. Shamel had fallen in the line of duty, and Rio fed himself a bullet after the accidental death of his girlfriend. There had been a number of heirs to the projects to come after them, but none were as well remembered as the trio.

"Ain't nobody forgot nothing, Cutty, but you can't eat a memory," Jada shot back.

"See you're gonna make me say some shit to you over this phone that might get me another charge."

"As if it would make a difference," Jada mumbled.

"Fuck all the smart shit you're talking. What happened to that thing you were supposed to do for me a few weeks back? You were supposed to meet up with my man's sister so you can settle that debt for me and you never called her."

"My bad, I had to go to Davita's school and when I tried to hit shorty back to reschedule I kept getting the voice mail. I'll get around to it," she said as if it was nothing.

"Jada, you know better than to come at me with that bozo shit. I'm in prison, not the streets. You can't really promise a nigga something in here and not come through. Behind the wall all you got is your word and Cutty's word is his bond."

"Sorry," she mumbled.

"So I'm noticing. You're not only sorry, Jada, but you're trifling too."

"What kinda bullshit are you talking about now?"

"I'm talking about after I couldn't get you on the line I had my mom go to the stash-account to take care of it for me."

Jada was shocked. "Your mother? I know you didn't let your mama have access to our bank account?"

"*My* bank account and yes, I did. What you thought I was gonna jam myself by only allowing you to have access?" Cutty laughed. "This ain't Casino, baby, and you ain't Ginger."

"Cutty, that's some real shady shit to say," Jada told him.

"Nah, what's shady is the punch line of this fucked up ass joke. My mom said that account is short."

"Cutty, I know that money is only supposed to be for emergencies, but I had to tap it to take care of a few things. Welfare don't hardly give you enough to make ends meet. Just last week I had to go to building fifty-five and—"

"Jada, if you say one more thing other than the truth, as God is my witness I'm gonna reach through this phone and rip your fucking lips off," he cut her off. "I'm missing almost twenty thousand dollars and I wanna know where the fuck it is?"

Jada was speechless at first. She had been tapping into the money here and there, but she hadn't expected the tally to be so high. "Cutty, you mother must have it wrong because—" she began, but he cut her off again.

"Jada, you're already insulting my intelligence so please don't insult my mother too. The bottom line is that I wanna know where my money is, and if you can't tell me that then you need to tell me how you plan to put it back."

"Nigga, I know you ain't trying to call me no thief?" Jada got indignant as she tried to spin a plausible lie in her head that would explain where the money had gone.

"I ain't *trying* to tell you shit. What I *am* telling you is that if you don't produce my bread, immediately, me and you gonna have a problem, bitch."

"Hold the fuck on. Who do you think you're talking to?"

"I'm talking to the trifling cunt that my dumb ass trusted with my life and my kid!" he raged.

"Fuck you, ya mama's a cunt! Cock-eyed old bitch!" Jada yelled back.

"Jada, I don't know what the fuck you're out there doing with my bread, but you better give me back what belongs to me or you're gonna be the sorriest black bitch in Harlem," Cutty warned her.

"I know you ain't trying to send no threats this way like I'm some punk bitch?" Jada's tone darkened. "Cutty, you know how the Butlers give it up so please don't take it there."

"Shorty, the way I feel right now, everybody in your house who didn't come outta my nuts can get it!"

Jada was hurt by the way he was speaking to her, but she wouldn't give him the satisfaction of showing it. "I hear you talking, gangsta. When I was running around out here for you making moves, and sucking your dick on the dance floor, I was your lifeline and now you're talking to me like I'm just some bitch you're fucking. We're gonna see how tough you talk when it's all said and done." Jada's mind immediately went to the shopping spree she was going to go on with what was left of Cutty's money.

Cutty laughed. "Bitch, I know you like I know my own dick, so you can rule out the petty ass bank robbery in your head. I already had my mom remove your name from the account and my lil man's and them from B.K. know not to put another dime in your hands. The ride is over, boo."

"So this is how you're gonna do it, Cutty? You're just gonna leave me and the kids out here with nothing?" Jada was emotional.

"My *kid* is gonna be straight. My mother is petitioning for custody so you should be getting the paperwork any day now."

"So how am I supposed to get by?" The tears had escaped and were streaking her cheeks.

"Get by on that punk ass twenty thousand you stole, whore. If you need to get ya ones up then here's a thought for you. Why don't you stop giving that washed-up pussy away so freely and try selling it?" It was a low blow and they both knew it.

With that statement Jada knew that it was the end of her and Cutty. "That's some cold-blooded shit, but I should've expected as much from a low-life convict like you. But that's alright, Cutty, you're gonna rue the day you crossed a bitch like me."

"Trust me, I already do. Outside of my money and my son we ain't got shit to talk about. Get my money, Jada."

"Well, here's a *thought* for you, Cutty. The night you got fall down drunk and me and J.C. had to carry you home, not only did I fuck him in your bed while you were laying there sleeping, I sucked his dick and let him cum in my mouth. See you in twenty-five years, ass-pirate!" She ended the call.

JADA HAD ALWAYS CONSIDERED HERSELF one of the coldest young chicks in the streets, but she had always had a tender heart for Cutty . . . a heart that had been stomped into pieces. True, she was guilty of tapping his bank account and skimming a little of what he had coming in, but Jada felt like she was entitled to it. When Cutty got knocked and everyone kept living their lives, Jada put hers on hold to ride with her baby daddy. From risking her freedom by visiting him with a vagina full of heroin, to bleeding other dudes so they could eat, and now he wanted to cast her aside like trash. With having the financial rug pulled from under them a lesser broad would've fallen apart, but Jada was a Butler and it would take more than idle threats for a dude doing two decades to break her spirit.

"Fuck it." Jada pushed the memories from her mind and nestled into her covers to get some long overdue sleep. No sooner did her eyes close than her cell phone rang. Without even looking to see who it was she flipped the phone open, prepared to get her spazz on, but the anger drained away when she heard who was on the other end.

"Oh, shit. What up, cousin, Gucci?"

Chapter 6

WHEN ARTHUR WEIS LIFTED HIS HEAD FROM HIS DESK HE looked like he had been hit in his face with a ball of flower. His cheeks and nose were a ruddy shade to match his heavily veined eyes. On his cluttered desk there was a hand mirror smeared with cocaine. As he peered down at his chalky reflection in the mirror he didn't see the successful attorney who had fought his way up the ladder into his own lucrative private practice, he saw the monster his greed had made him.

From the time when he worked as a legal aid in Manhattan Criminal Court, Arthur had made a name for himself as an attorney who would go above and beyond in his pursuit to win a case. Unlike some of his colleagues, Arthur didn't care to barter with the prosecution for reduced sentences, there was no money in that. Arthur knew to stick for the long bread he had to make a name for himself as a shark and only then would he be able to crawl out of the shitty position he was in. It didn't take long for Arthur's name to be circulated among the career criminals he helped beat the system and they all came to Arthur when they got in a jam and needed someone to look the other way.

When he was able to establish his own practice, clients flocked

to him like disciples, and carrying cash in barrels for his services.
The lifestyle that his clients led was so enticing to him that he often
found himself letting his career and personal life overlap. You could
often find Arthur in the back of the club popping bottles with notorious killers and bosses. He quickly became one of the darlings of
the underworld and reveled in the adoration he got from some of
the ghetto's most powerful organizations. For as sweet as the life was
for him, Arthur was mortal and therefore subject to the larcenies
that lurk in the hearts of men.

Arthur got greedy and instead of doing his job he just collected
money. Even if Arthur knew he couldn't win the case he would feed
the clients false hope just to get their money and march them to
their demises with a straight face. Quite a few of his former clients
didn't take kindly to being railroaded and had promised to settle
up with Arthur, but he knew none of them were stupid enough to
actually touch a lawyer as high-profiled as Weis. His biggest head-
aches were coming from the state, thanks to a sour client and some
sloppy money laundering. Arthur's life was slowly becoming a shit
storm and he was standing in the middle of it with a broken um-
brella.

When Arthur heard his door click open unexpectedly he jumped
out of his seat and knocked over his coffee on the brief that had
been sitting on his desk. Arthur was so focused on saving what little
bit of cocaine he had left that he had the mirror held up in plain
sight when his assistant walked in. She was a pretty young brown-
skinned girl with bright eyes and a nice shape.

"Jesus, what the hell are you doing just busting in here like that?
I told you to cancel my appointments for the day, I don't wanna see
any more clients!" he barked on her. Her mouth opened but no sound
came out as fear had made her mute. When Arthur saw the shadows materialize behind her he knew just what her fear was like because it crept into his heart too.

"I'm not a client, I'm the bitch you've been fucking for the last six months." Don B. walked in, draped in black leather and heavy jewels. He was flanked by several hard-faced men wearing murderous scowls. Don B. was anything but your typical rags to riches story. He had once been a ghetto superstar, handpicked and tutored by the old kings of Harlem, and on the fast track to being the next hood legend. He was a natural hustler, but more importantly he had a sharp mind. Don B. had seen the writing on the wall and knew that he could only bleed the streets for so long before they eventually bled him, so he set his sights on music and started Big Dawg Entertainment and the wheels of fate were set in motion. Seemingly overnight he watched Big Dawg go from a startup company to one of the most successful labels in the music industry. From the hottest upcoming rappers to R&B veterans, Big Dawg had it all. But nothing was without its price, which Don B. would learn over the years. True, Jah, Pain, Lex, the list went on so long that many of them had become little more than nameless faces, but the Don remained and so the show would go on.

"What's up, Don? I didn't see you on my calendar for today. Is everything cool?" Arthur asked nervously.

Don B. stepped forward and stared at Arthur from behind his black shades. He ran his finger across the saucer, then over his gums, pausing for a minute to feel the potency. "No, everything ain't cool, muthafucka. I don't appreciate being fucked unless you're a bitch that throws it like a porn star. Are you a porn star, Arthur, because you've surely fucked me?"

"Listen, if this is about that little thing with the guy Harold, I promise you that I'm working on it, brother." Arthur gave him a dopey smile.

Without warning Don B. smacked the cocaine-coated mirror from Arthur's hand. "First of all, I ain't ya fucking brother, cracker, and second of all you're a damn liar. You took my bread and left my lil nigga Fully for dead!"

During the production of the Left Coast's second album Fully had gone out drinking with some of the homeys and gotten into a fight with some guys in a bar. He hit one of the guys with a bottle and disfigured him. The situation looked bad for Fully but Weis had promised to get him off for the right price. Desperate to get the album finished Don B. went against the advice of his regular attorney and paid Arthur five hundred thousand dollars to get it done. In the end Fully ended up blowing trial and getting a flat twelve instead of the six to nine the DA initially offered.

Arthur adjusted his tie nervously. "Don, that wasn't my fault, it was that cunt of a judge and rotten luck! What are the odds that her son was killed five years ago by the same gang Fully belonged to? She had a hard-on for the guy from the time she read his jacket. It was outta my hands."

"Of course, because you needed your hands free to take my money, you fucking crook!" Don B. snapped.

"Hey, now that's not true. Don, I fought my ass off for Fully, and when I blew it I accepted responsibility for it and gave you a discount to get his appeal done. I know you're salty because it's taking so long, but these things take time with the red tape and all, ya know?"

"Yeah, we know all about *tape*." Don B. nodded to one of his henchmen who produced a roll of duct tape. "Weis, I may be a lot of things, but I ain't no fool. You never filed Fully's appeal because you knew he couldn't win the damn case in the first place. Now I gave you a half a ticket for the case and if you stack that on top of the appeal you never filed for and add interest, it puts you into me for about a million and change. Do you have my money?"

"Come on, Don, you know me, we go back. Listen, on my mother's eyes I put that paperwork in, I can even show you the e-mail confirming it." Arthur went to turn his computer monitor around but Don B. stopped him.

"That's not what I asked you," Don B. said coldly.

Arthur looked from the man holding the duct tape and smiling menacingly, back to Don B., and swallowed the lump in his throat. "Don, I didn't steal from you, man, I swear to Christ. Okay, if you wanna work something out I've got fifty thousand in my desk drawer and I can get you a little more in a few days. Let's say I kick you back the bread you gave me on the appeal and we're square, huh?"

Don B. removed his shades and glared at Arthur. "I gave you a million dollars which is what I expect back."

"Don, let's be reasonable about this, we're friends for Christ's sake!" Arthur began, but was cut off when Don B. stuck a gun in his belly.

"Friends don't fuck friends, Arthur." Don B. waved his men forward. Arthur struggled with everything he had but he was no match for the thugs who used the duct tape to bind him stomach-down across his desk. Using two pairs of handcuffs they clamped Arthur's ankles to the legs of the desk, forcing him to have to lie with his ass up.

"Don, what the hell are you doing, man?" Arthur struggled to crane his neck so he could see the men over his shoulder.

"It's like I said, kid, friends don't fuck friends, but when you took my bread that ended our friendship." Don B. hooked his thumbs through his belt loops and gave Arthur a look that made his blood run cold.

When Arthur started to get the picture he began thrashing wildly trying to get free of the tape. "Wait, wait, wait, you're going too far, Don B! I know I'm in the wrong because I owe you money, but this is fucked up on so many levels!"

Don B. frowned. "Arthur, you got me twisted. The Don only indulges in pussy, I don't play them games you hinting at." Hearing this made Arthur breathe a sigh of relief, but it was a short-lived moment when he heard Don B.'s voice again. "Yo, Herc," Don B. called over his shoulder. All 350 pounds of Herc lumbered forward licking his lips at the sight of Arthur bound and helpless. "Herc, until this piece of shit pays what he owes, he's property of Big Dawg. Enjoy, my nigga." Don B. patted Herc on the back and headed for the office door. Devil grabbed the secretary by the arm and followed.

"Don, you can't do this to me! This is inhumane!" Arthur shouted over the sounds of his pants and underwear being ripped.

Don B. stopped and looked over his shoulder. "Nah, this is the game you chose to play."

Don B. and Devil escorted the secretary into the reception area, leaving Herc and whoever else stayed behind to their devices. The girl was sobbing uncontrollably because she knew after what she had witnessed there was no way they would let her live.

Devil went around the girl's desk and retrieved her purse from the floor. He fumbled around inside until he came up holding her driver's license and a picture of her kids. He ran his thumb across the image of her teenage daughter and licked his chops. "What'd you see, baby?" he addressed her coolly.

"I didn't see nothing, I swear I didn't," she said between sobs.

Don B. pondered her answer for what seemed like an eternity before giving Devil the nod to cut her loose. "Come here, shorty." Don B. waved her over. The secretary took timid steps toward Don B., keeping her eyes glued to the ground. "Look at me." He forced her face up. In his hand he held a thick roll of money. He placed the money into her trembling hands along with a slip of paper that had a number scribbled on it. "Take a few days and get ya shit right, ma. Use that number if you want a real job, ya dig?" The girl was too frightened to answer so she just nodded dumbly and scurried out.

"How you gonna scare a chick shitless and then offer her a job?" Devil asked after the girl had gone.

Don B. smirked at him. "I was feeling kind. Besides, if I get her on the payroll I stand a better chance to sample that sweet little ass. Did you see the body on that bitch?"

The two of them laughed so hard at Don B.'s twisted humor that they had almost forgotten that they were at the scene of a crime. That changed when they heard Arthur's high-pitched squeal coming from the next room.

DON B. LED HIS ENTOURAGE out of the plush Fifth Avenue building as if they totally belonged, dressed in baggy jeans and jewelry. Devil drove Don B. in his Durango while Herc and the rest of the soldiers rode in the minivan. On the way to their vehicles they drew the occasional stare from the business types they passed but one set of eyes lingered on them longer than anyone else's. Hatred swelled behind the eyes and it took everything the watcher had not to move on Don B. right then and there, but the watcher was patient. The watcher had waited years to settle up with the Don so a few more days wouldn't change what was coming. Only when the men had climbed back into their vehicles and pulled off did the watcher take his eyes off the entourage.

"YOU NEVER CEASE TO AMAZE me with the levels of stupid shit you choose to pull," Devil told Don B. once they were safely away from the scene. "The plan was for us to come down here and maybe smack Arthur around a little to get him to pay back the money he owed; you never said nothing about no funny ass rape shit!"

"Sometimes plans change, my nigga," Don B. said as if it was nothing.

"Yeah, I should've known something was funny when you insisted on bringing Herc and the rest of them ass pirates along. My nigga, Arthur Weis is a scumbag, but he's still a fucking lawyer! We might've been able to get away with beating his ass, but there's no way in hell this shit is gonna ride."

"Sure he is. To a man like Arthur money is more precious than his pride. If he gives up what happened then all his shady shit comes to light and that's the end of his career and his lifestyle. Nah, he ain't gonna say shit."

"I guess you got it all figured out, huh?"

"Don't I always? That's why I'm the Don and these niggaz is soldiers," Don B. said smugly. His statement wasn't directed toward Devil, but the truth in it still stung a bit. "Now, on to the next order of business; did Animal make his flight?"

Devil shrugged. "He said he would, but the plane landed hours ago and I still ain't heard from him."

"See, this is the problem when you're dealing with these *Rain Man* ass niggaz. He knows we've got a lot going on and his ass is MIA . . . again. That's my word, B, if this nigga ain't on deck for the session I booked for him and Chip we gonna have an issue."

"Yeah right." Devil laughed. "You talk that shit now, but I know ya lying. Animal done put so much bread in ya pocket I'm surprised you ain't never tried to kiss the nigga in the mouth, *pause*."

Don B. chuckled. "Yeah, that crazy muthafucka is hella talented, he's just weird as hell. Did Shawna ever call you back and confirm our appointment with ol' boy?"

"Yeah, she said he griped about you wanting to do another walk-through, but eventually saw it our way and agreed."

"Fucking right he did for as much bread as I already dropped on this shit, just the licenses alone cost me a grip. Sal and them really fucked that club up and I don't even wanna talk about the back taxes." Don B. massaged his temples. "It's gonna take some work, but I know I can bring the beat back. The Zone might be dead, but Code Red is gonna be alive and kicking come the grand reopening."

Code Red was Don B.'s latest venture. The midtown club had had several different names, but the most recent had been The Zone. The cat Sal who had bought the spot had champagne dreams with *beer* money. The Zone had gotten off to a good start, but it wasn't long before Sal's poor business moves had him spending more than he was bringing in. Sal had lost everything and the city was about to seize the place before a friend of a friend introduced him to Don B. It was only supposed to be a loan until Sal got on his feet, but when Don B. saw the potential in the place he muscled his way in and just like that Sal now had a partner and his club a new name, Code Red.

Devil shook his head. "Don, I still can't believe you went through with it. That spot ain't jumped like that in damn near ten years. How do you figure you can do what the last five owners haven't been able to?"

Don B. just smiled. "Because I'm the Don. Now let's go see a man about a club."

BY THE TIME DON B. and his entourage pulled up on the corner of Ninety-sixth and Amsterdam Sal was already standing outside the spot. Sal looked like he was snatched from the cast of some B-rated mob movie dressed in a salmon-colored jogging suit and white sneakers. He was a sour-looking Italian man with thinning brown hair and a plump red nose that made him resemble W. C. Fields. Between his stubby ringed fingers he pinched a brown cigarette, which he took deep pulls on while watching Don B. through his fishbowl glasses.

"Sal, what's up, baby?" Don B. extended his hand and Sal reluctantly shook it.

"Don, I swear you're the biggest ballbuster I know. We've gone over this stuff a hundred times already so I don't see why I gotta rush outta my kid's basketball game to do this shit again?" Sal said bitterly.

"Because it'll make me feel better," Don B. told Sal and brushed past him into Code Red.

The outside of Code Red was made of black one-way glass allowing the partygoers to see out but keeping those outside the club blind to what was going on inside. That had been Don B.'s first decree when he came on board. Inside was a buzz of activity with contractors, electricians, and deliverymen moving every which way in preparation for Don B.'s party. The event was still a few days away but for what Don B. had planned they needed almost a week to get ready. Most of it was over the top, but that was how Don B. wanted it. Code Red was to be his newest baby and he planned on spoiling it like he did when he birthed Big Dawg.

"Looks good, man," Devil said, running his finger across the top of the twelve-foot-long glass bar. It was the longest of the three which would serve the patrons of Code Red.

"Like I keep telling your boy here, I got it under control," Sal said, looking at his watch. "The cases of liquor will be delivered tomorrow and I've already confirmed with the caterer that the food will be here the morning of the event. Are you satisfied?"

"And security?" Don B. asked, ticking off the checklist in his head.

"Yeah, yeah, I got some guys from my brother-in-law's company to handle the basics and a few friends of mine will also be here to handle any potentially messy situations," Sal assured him. "Now that just leaves us wit that last thing we talked about. I was gonna let it wait until later in the week but since you insisted on us meeting today we may as well take care of it now."

Don B. looked to Devil who produced an envelope from his pocket and handed it to him. Don B. extended the envelope to Sal, but held it short of his greedy mitts. "So this ensures that we ain't gonna have no problems with the police, right?"

"Don B., I told you the guy who set it up is a friend of ours, so why are you so fucking paranoid?"

"Sal, there's a difference between paranoid and careful. The Don has many enemies on the streets."

"Not a lovable guy like you?" Sal asked sarcastically.

"You're a real funny guy, Sally." Don B. tossed him the envelope. "Now if that'll be all youz guys can get outta here so my people can work and I might be able to get back to my daughter's game before the fourth quarter, not that I ain't gonna have to hear my wife bitching about me running out for the rest of the night."

"Yeah, go handle ya business. I got some moves to make too," Don B. said and led Devil back outside.

"This joint is looking kinda sexy, kid." Devil hugged Don B. playfully as they walked.

"Yeah, that's why I'm being so meticulous about this whole thing. Son, niggaz hated on me in the streets and in the rap game, but I've been able to fly under the radar and keep the bullshit to a minimum, but this club is gonna put me somewhere else with it. The larger I get the more malicious energy these niggaz gonna send at me and I'm trying to avoid Murphy's Law, smell me?"

"Who the fuck is Murphy?" Devil asked.

Don B. gave Devil a stupid look. "It's a saying; anything that can go wrong will go wrong. There are gonna be a lot of important people coming out to support this event and I don't need no bullshit souring my game."

As if on cue Don B. heard someone calling his name. Devil moved between Don B. and the man half shambling toward him, hand already reaching for his pistol, but he froze in mid-draw when he recognized his old partner. "Remo?" Devil asked in disbelief.

Remo had really let himself go. His clothes were expensive, but they looked like he had slept in them for the past few nights. His normally clean-shaven head was now covered in tight clumps of knotted hair and it had been a while since his face had seen a razor. When Remo smiled and showed his teeth that had begun to rot, Devil felt like his heart shattered in his chest.

"Big D, you slipping. I could've laid both of y'all down and been in the wind before you drew that rod!" Remo said jovially. "What, you just gonna stand there gawking or give me some love?"

Devil managed to snap out of it and embrace his old friend.

Remo smelled like he hadn't washed in a few days but Devil didn't shy away. "Damn, it's good to see you, homey."

"It's good to be seen. You know it ain't many of the old crew left," Remo said. His eyes drifted toward Don B. who was standing off to the side scowling at him. "What's good, nephew." Remo spread his arms.

"What up?" Don B. replied dryly and gave him dap.

Remo eyed him suspiciously. "I swear, boy, you and ya daddy always did know how to hold grudges better than anybody else in the family."

"*Family*," Don B. snorted, "now that's a word niggaz use way too freely."

Remo couldn't mask the hurt in his eyes. "Don, I know you're salty with me because I fucked up, but ya uncle is pulling it together, that's why I came down here to see you."

"Is that right?" Don B. asked in a very uninterested tone.

"Yeah, man. I heard through the grapevine that you got this big event lined up and I wanted to help out, maybe do some security work for you, nephew."

"I don't know if that'll be such a good idea, Remo."

"C'mon, Don, you know ain't nobody ever watch ya back as good as me and Devil when I was still rolling wit y'all. Just give me a chance to prove myself."

"I did give you a chance to prove yourself, and you proved unworthy. I can't trust my life to a crackhead."

"Is that all I am to you now?" Remo asked emotionally. "Don B, when you was out there handing out CDs and getting kicked outta clubs I was the one holding you down, not these new cats you've taken to running around with, who praise you like some damn pagan god!"

"You're right, but you fucked up what we had when you decided that your habits and these bitches came before business." Don B.

took his shades off and looked his uncle directly in the eyes. "Remo, you're fam so I'll always love you, but I can't fuck wit you," Don B. said sadly and walked off.

"Don . . ." Devil called after him but Remo stopped him.

"Fuck it, let him go," Remo said, wiping the tear from his ashy cheek.

"Remo, let me try and talk to him, okay?"

"Nah, Devil. It's gonna be what it's gonna be. I ain't gonna keep you because I know you got stuff to do. It was good seeing you though, family." Remo hugged his partner.

Devil took all the money he had in his pocket and placed it in Remo's hands. "Remo, you know that whenever you're ready to come in out of the cold I'm here for you."

"Devil, your heart is now and forever will be in the right place, so you'll always be my brother. Ya man though"—he scoffed and pointed at Don B.—"he's got a lot to learn about this here game. The faster you go up, the harder your black ass is gonna land when it falls from grace."

LONG AFTER DON B. AND Devil had pulled off Remo was still standing on the curb looking down at the toes of his scuffed boots. He had come to Don B. almost on his knees only to be brushed to the side like someone who had had nothing to do with building Big Dawg Entertainment. Don B. playing him off like a common smoker not only hurt Remo but it made him bitter. He stopped seeing his nephew as the little boy he had helped sculpt, and saw him as just another perpetrating ass cat who needed their ghetto pass revoked.

"What up, big homey?" a voice called from behind Remo, startling him. He cautiously started backing away as he didn't recognize the heavily tinted Acura sitting on shiny chrome rims. "It's me, son." The driver rolled the window down.

"Shit, youngin, don't you know better than to be rolling up all suspect and shit?" Remo capped as he ambled over to the car. "I heard you was dead."

"Nah, I ain't dead I'm just keeping a low profile after that thing, smell me? But fuck all that, I got something lined up that you might be able to help me with if you still 'bout ya cheese?" The driver popped open a suitcase full of money that was on the passenger's seat.

"For that kinda paper I'd tear a niggaz head off!" Remo said hungrily.

"Glad to hear it. Get in the car and let's take a lil ride while we talk."

Chapter 7

TIONNA TOOK A LONG GULP OF AIR WHEN SHE ASCENDED from the train station on Ninety-sixth and Broadway. It was about a thousand degrees beneath the streets of New York, but it was one of the fastest ways to travel if you didn't have a ride. She had been spending a lot of time on the subway lately, but didn't think she'd ever get used to it. How she longed for the days of hopping in and out of foreign cars, but she knew those days were over, at least until she found another come-up.

Once upon a time Tionna had been regarded as royalty in Harlem. She was thick in all the right places, with flawless chocolate skin and silky black hair that hung down her back. Every cat holding a few dollars was checking for her, but she belonged to Duhan. Since they were teenagers they had been dating on and off and even had two sons together. Duhan was on the fast track to stardom and she was at his side for the entire ride. Duhan was a sure bet to be a boss, but jealousy and the government threw a monkey wrench in his plans and hit him with five to life on a trumped-up kingpin charge.

With Duhan out of the picture and no real means to support herself Tionna wound up back on the block with her old friends and up to new tricks. For a minute it seemed like Tionna was returning to her former glory, but as they said, "What's done in the dark always comes to the light." In the end Tionna's ways had cost her Duhan and her last apartment. A mysterious fire had broken out that claimed everything she owned except the clothes on her back. Thankfully no one had been home at the time of the fire, but Tionna found herself completely assed out and back to square one. She knew who had been the catalyst for both, but had only herself to blame for even allowing herself to get caught slipping. It was a mistake she had no intention of making twice.

The months that followed were rough for Tionna. Her best friend Gucci's mother had let Tionna and the kids stay with her while Section 8 tried to find her another apartment, but that situation turned out to be a crazy one. Ms. Ronnie was cool, but she had too many damn rules for Tionna's taste, so it was a blessing when Tionna got the letter about her new place. Tionna had initially thought that the apartment would be in some renovated building like the one she had just been burnt out of, but it was actually in a nice section of Manhattan that boasted easy access and a great school system.

On her way up from the train station she grabbed two bags of piff from some of the local corner boys. Their haze wasn't the best in the world, but it was way better than anything else within a ten-block radius. Tionna often missed the convenience of living uptown, but she'd much rather deal with *so-so* weed than shoot-outs in front of the building. Her new hood was a far cry from the one she'd grown up in and not as upscale as the one she'd lost, but it would have to do for the time being and she was determined to make the best of it.

Tionna rolled into the smoke shop to grab two cigars and spotted a girl named Zada who lived in her building. Zada was a cool chick, but she had way too many problems and made it a point to share them with everyone, whether they wanted to hear them or not. Tionna started to turn around and go to another store, but Zada had already spotted her so she mustered a plastic smile.

"Hi, Tionna." Zada hugged Tionna and kissed her on both cheeks.

"Sup Z?" Tionna said.

"Not much. Just came to get a Dutch so me and Harv can smoke. You wanna burn one with us?" Zada offered.

"Nah, I got a lil piff so I'm gonna do me. Thanks though," Tionna said pleasantly.

What she really meant was that she didn't want to smoke the cheap shit they were about to put in their lungs. Zada and Harv would smoke damn near anything as long as it got them high. Tionna had standards with hers though. If it wasn't piff or chocolate she wouldn't smoke it.

"Well, if that's the case then I need to roll with you," Zada said shamelessly. Tionna liked Zada well enough, but her constant quest for the next blunt session got on her last nerve.

Tionna had to think fast or run the risk of Zada ruining what little bit of downtime she would have before the kids got in. "Ah, you can come by, but give me about an hour or so. I've got something I need to take care of right quick." Tionna gave her a wink.

Zada showed all thirty-two of her teeth. "Got a little shorty coming by, huh?" Zada asked, trying to get into Tionna's business.

"Just give me an hour and then you can stop by." Tionna hurried to make her purchase so Zada wouldn't press her any further. Tionna normally would've told someone trying to get all in her mix to go kill themselves, but she kinda liked Zada and didn't want to hurt her feelings. By the time Zada came by Tionna would've been high as a kite and better equipped to deal with her emotional ass. With her Dutch Masters secured in her purse, Tionna made tracks toward her new residence.

The Marquis was what they called *prime real estate*. It was a beautiful twenty-seven story building with round-the-clock security and was located within walking distance of six trains and four buses. From the huge supermarket in the courtyard to several different stores that shared the property, Tionna never had to go far for anything. Every time she woke up and looked out at her view of Central Park she wondered how for as much dirt as she did, she could still be so lucky.

When the building formally known as Westside Manor was sold, the new owners jacked the rent for new tenants to ten times what the old ones were paying. A good amount of the residents had inherited the apartments from their parents or grandparents, but every new tenant had to pay the piper unless they managed to hit the Mega Ball. The Mega Ball was a lottery the city forced the Marquis to hold every few years that gave government-assisted tenants a shot at getting into the building. Because of the circumstances surrounding how Tionna had lost her apartment they made an exception to the rule and gave her a two-bedroom that had just been vacated.

As soon as Tionna touched the foyer of the lobby the security guard, Angel, buzzed her in. He was a handsome Puerto Rican kid who wore his hair in a low cut that he kept freshly shaped. Angel was a good dude who had run into some less than favorable luck and ended up catching some short time. As a condition of his parole he ended up doing security at the Marquis. Unlike some of the other guards he wasn't a hard ass. Angel was easygoing and unless you were harassing the tenants or doing something to put his job in jeopardy you were cool.

"What is it, ma?" Angel greeted Tionna when she crossed the threshold.

"Chilling, just getting in from work," Tionna replied.

"Yo, how is that shit for you? Working at a law firm and all, I know you get the four-one-one on a lot of shit."

"It ain't even that serious, Angel. I just answer the phones and do a little filing. I do my job and come home, period," Tionna said.

She had been working at the law firm of Gould and Silva for over a year and still didn't know everyone there by name.

"I still wouldn't mind being a fly on the wall for one of those crazy muthafuckers who roll through there. I hear the broad's specialty is castrating niggaz," Angel half joked.

"Marlene isn't that bad, she's just good at what she does," Tionna defended her boss. She really thought Marlene to be too uptight, but she had to admire her. Here was a woman who had managed to claw her way up out of the same ghettos and managed to become a successful attorney. Gould and Silva practiced a variety of law, but their specialty was divorce. Marlene was like a freak of nature when it came to making sure her clients left their spouses with nothing. Some said that she was a scorned lover seeking to take her revenge out on all men, but whatever her motivation you couldn't deny the fact that Marlene Silva was one of the best at what she did. It was even said that on more than one occasion Marlene had reduced abusive husbands to tears in open court. Tionna figured if she could muster up a fraction of Marlene's determination she'd be all good.

"So you say. Just hope you don't ever come across her in a courtroom. My man Jose had to get two more jobs just to keep up with the payments she got his bitch of a wife," Angel said.

"She wasn't a bitch when he was laying with her now was she?" Tionna shot back. "Yo, if I'm fucking a nigga, washing his drawers and breeding his kids, then I need to be taken care of when we split the pie. What, you think the wasted years of that woman's life don't count for anything?"

Angel took a step back and raised his hands in surrender. "Damn, T, I wasn't looking for the cross-examination. You're starting to sound like your boss."

"Nah, I ain't sounding like Marlene. I'm sounding like somebody that's been through it. Angel, when you've given your time and your heart to somebody only to have them pull the plug and leave you with nothing but your sorrows then we can have this conversation again," Tionna said and headed for the elevator.

TIONNA STEPPED INTO HER APARTMENT and breathed a sigh of relief. After dealing with the bullshit at Gould and Silva all day it felt good to be home. The kids were still at school so she had at least another hour to herself. She planned to roll up a blunt and pour herself a glass of wine and soak in the tub before she did her homework. Since she had been working at the firm Tionna had developed a fascination with the law and decided to take some paralegal courses online. There was no way she was going to put herself through eight more years of school to try for the bar, but with the certificate she could push for a promotion or at least a pay raise.

She had just kicked her shoes off when someone started ringing the hell out of her doorbell. She cursed under her breath because she just knew it was thirsty ass Zada trying to get in on her blunt. She considered ignoring the bell, but Zada knew she was home because she had just seen her in the store. Tionna decided to just tell Zada that she didn't wanna be bothered and didn't care if she was hurt by it or not.

"Hold on a fucking minute!" Tionna shouted as the ringing increased. She snatched the door open with a four-letter-word pursed on her lips, but the curse fell away when she saw the dark sunglasses staring back at her.

"Why is it that no matter where you live I have to wait a hundred years before you answer the damn door?" Gucci said with a warm smile.

Tionna was so overjoyed to see her best friend that the only thing she could do in way of a response was to embrace her.

• • •

GUCCI HAD ALWAYS BEEN A pretty girl, but her time away from New York had done her good and it showed in the subtle glow her skin had picked up. She had put on some weight, all in her hips from the looks of it, and now wore her hair in a short feathered cut that showed off her face. She was dressed in a black skirt with a low-cut red blouse with a thin black Gucci scarf slung around her neck like she was going skiing. It wasn't cold enough for the scarf, but it looked good with the black and red print Gucci bag.

Tionna and Gucci had a friendship that went back as far as grade school. When Tionna's mother was off on her drug binges she often found herself spending the night with Gucci and Ms. Ronnie. Unlike the other kids, Gucci never made fun of Tionna having a crackhead for a mother and always went out of her way to make her feel like family. Gucci was a year or two younger than Tionna, but had an understanding of life that would rival that of a girl twice her age. They were more like sisters than best friends and you rarely saw one without the other.

By the time they hit middle school the call of the streets was ringing loudly in both their ears. They were both off the hook, but whereas Tionna's mother let her run wild, Ms. Ronnie didn't play that with Gucci. Ms. Ronnie gave Gucci enough rope to hang herself, but she always stressed the importance of school. Gucci managed to hang in there long enough to finish high school, but Tionna ended up getting pregnant with little Duhan and ended up dropping out. She eventually went back and got her GED, but she always regretted not being able to walk down the aisle as her friend had.

Over the years Tionna and Gucci still hung out, but Tionna slipped further and further into the role of a kingpin's wife while Gucci was searching for her own escape from the ghetto. When they closed the curtain on Duhan's movie, Gucci was right there to help Tionna pick up the pieces. It wasn't long before Gucci had her running partner back and the two girls hit the hood with a vengeance. It was during the brief resurrection when Gucci met Animal and things began to change.

Animal had been a guaranteed case of a kid who wouldn't make it very far into his twenties. The streets knew of him because he was a part of Tech's crew, but they feared him because of his Jones for violence. The letting of blood was like a high for him that he couldn't get enough of, so he let his gun go to feed his habit. Animal was a beast when it came to battle and even the heaviest hitters in the game didn't want to tangle with him, but the brute was only a portion of who he was. The side that few other than Gucci knew was a compassionate young man with a talent for music. It was because of his talent that he landed a record deal with Big Dawg Entertainment and ended up becoming an overnight superstar. His train out of the ghetto had finally come in, but it was an empty moment because he couldn't share it with the people closest to him. China lost her life during their last job and the police canceled Silk, but Tech was a victim of his own demons. The governing body of the New York underworld decided that Tech's bark was getting too loud and silenced him.

The courtship between Gucci and Animal was something no one had expected, especially Tionna. Gucci was someone who didn't give her heart easily, and definitely not so soon. Tionna tried to tell herself and Gucci that it was a phase, but the sparkle in both their eyes whenever she was around them said that it was real. Each of them had found something in the other that they felt was missing in their lives and they used it as the foundation of their relationship. Gucci always said that she wasn't with Animal for his money, but the large black diamonds in her ears said that she was reaping the benefits.

"You sneaky heifer, why didn't you tell me you were flying in?" Tionna rocked back and forth with Gucci still in her arms.

Gucci broke the embrace and smoothed over her outfit. "Because if it'd been up to you, I'd still be at the airport."

"True," Tionna agreed. "So what wind blows your country ass up this way?"

Gucci took off her shades so that Tionna could see her brown eyes. "First of all, I ain't country, and second of all, the last time I checked my driver's license said New York State."

"I can't tell, seeing how you spend more time in Plano than you do in Harlem," Tionna accused. Animal had a cute two-bedroom in a working-class section of town that Gucci shared with him from time to time.

"T, you of all people should know that my heart is and always will be on Seventh Avenue, a bitch is just trying to come up. And speaking of come up, this shit doesn't look like no government-assisted housing to me." Gucci admired Tionna's high-rise apartment.

"Girl, it was the luck of the draw, literally." Tionna went on to give Gucci the short version of how she'd come by the apartment. "I swear I didn't know what to do when my crib got burnt down, but God had a plan for me."

Gucci looked at Tionna suspiciously. "I know your ass ain't on no saved shit?"

Tionna twisted her lips. "As much as I love weed and dick, I don't think so. I just know a blessing when I see one. And it's a good thing too, because if me and my kids had ended up homeless then Don B.'s ass would've ended up missing," Tionna said venomously.

"T, you still running with the theory that Don B. was behind your crib getting burned down?"

"It ain't no theory, Gucci, it's a fact. Even if the police are too fucking stupid to figure it out I know it was Don B.," Tionna said, recalling his threat.

After their falling out Tionna threatened to go to the press with a story about Don B. taking advantage of her and he warned her that if she played with fire she was going to get burnt, she just didn't think he meant it literally.

"They say that all is fair in love and war," Gucci teased.

"Love didn't have anything to do with me fucking Don B. That was about business. And speaking of business, where is that workaholic boyfriend of yours? I haven't seen Animal since the first trip you guys took."

Gucci shrugged. "Hell if I know. He dropped me off and said that he had something to do."

Chapter 8

BY THE TIME HONEY FINISHED MAKING HER ROUNDS through the Jersey Gardens Mall they were among the last few people there. She went in every store from Level X to Zales making purchases as she went. Most of the stuff she bought she didn't really need, but she bought it because she could. That's how it was when your man was Shai Clark, the reigning Don of New York City.

"How many more freaking stores are you gonna go in?" Shai asked as Honey stood in front of a lingerie store having a staring match with the mannequin in the window. He and his best friend/bodyguard Swan were sitting at one of the rest areas surrounded by dozens of bags. Between Honey and Giselle they had nearly cleaned the mall out.

"Knock it off, Shai. You know you can't rush perfection," Honey said over her shoulder. She was trying to figure out if the teddy she was staring at went with the red pumps she had in one of her bags. Even after giving birth to her second child she still boasted a flat stomach and small waist. Men couldn't help but to give her a second look in passing, but they did it at their own risks. In New York Shai had almost as much authority as the mayor and he wouldn't hesitate to exercise it to protect what was his.

"You're rushing her now, but when her ass is prancing around the house in one of those sexy outfits you'll be glad you waited," Giselle added her two cents. She was a pretty Spanish girl who was thick in all the right places.

"Why don't you mind your business, Giselle?" Swan warned.

Giselle spun on Swan and snaked her neck when she spoke. "Nigga, you better stop talking to me like I'm Mara." Mara was their young daughter.

"At least she listens."

In response, Giselle give him the middle finger. She and Swan fought like cats and dogs, but there was no mistaking the love hiding behind the insults. They had been together since high school and had two kids together.

"I know one damn thing, if you don't hurry your ass up you're gonna be taking the bus back to New York," Shai threatened her.

"Considering how funny these buses run at this time of night, I'd catch the ride if I were you, shorty." The voice drew all their attention.

Animal stepped from behind a kiosk bringing with him an air of tension. His mane of wild black hair fell around his childlike face, partially obscuring one eye. When he parted his bowed lips to sneer at the startled group you could see the diamond and gold teeth hiding behind them.

"Little nigga, you must've lost your last mind rolling on us like this." Swan stepped forward and began reaching for his weapon. He'd taken two steps before he felt something pressed into the small of his back. Swan cursed under his breath because he had allowed himself to be caught slipping. Giselle looked at him with pleading eyes waiting for the signal to pull her .22, but Swan shook his head. He might die, but there was a chance that his lady may live to raise their kids. He turned his head slowly and saw Brasco's scowling face and the shotgun. Ashanti and Nefertiti appeared next and they too were armed.

Animal cast his cold eyes on Swan and grinned ever so slightly. "Swan, if you can't count on anything else you can count on the fact that you and me will butt heads sooner or later, but not right this minute. Now you be cool before I let my young boy *push* you."

"Let me push this pussy, Animal, come on, man." Brasco was almost pleading. He had a burning hatred for Swan and made no secret of it.

Animal studied the scene and for a minute it almost looked like he was gonna let Brasco off Swan. "Nah, when and if Swan's number is called his head belongs to me. I need a few ticks with Shai to discuss more immediate business."

"Just tell us what you want and get out of here!" Honey pleaded.

"Bitch, did anybody give you permission to speak?" Nefertiti barked.

Unexpectedly Animal grabbed Nefertiti by the collar and shook him like a rag doll. "You trump-mouthed little bastard, I should smack your head off your shoulders for disrespecting that man's wife. You been hiding down that rabbit hole so long that you don't remember the G-code? Apologize!"

"Yo, Animal . . ." Nef began and Animal shook him more violently.

"Nef, either you apologize for disrespecting this lady or we're gonna put this meeting on pause while I fuck you up," Animal said seriously.

"My fault," Nefertiti mumbled.

Animal shook his head. "And they call me an animal."

"What do you want, man?" Shai asked in a fearless tone. He knew better than to antagonize Animal with him having the advantage, but one thing his father always taught him was to never show fear when facing a wolf.

Animal spread his arms. "What any man wants. Justice. I think everyone here knows the reason for my abrupt departure from New York and let me be perfectly clear that it's never sat well with me.

First, some piece of shit who I don't even know sets the police on my ass to save his own sorry hide and then the closest thing I had to family got smoked by someone he considered a friend." He looked at Swan when he said this and the young man tensed. "Don't look so surprised, Swan. You think I don't know it was you who killed Tech?"

Just the mention of the name made Swan's heart ache. Tech had been a young boy who had balls the size of Yankee Stadium. He would bring it to anyone who wanted it and always played by the rules, which is the thing Swan admired most about him until he was ordered to take his life. Tech's was the one death out of them all that Swan regretted most. Had it been his call he'd have let Tech go with an ass whipping, but Shai was the boss. At the end of the day his personal feelings held no weight when it came to business.

"He was out of control, Animal. Even you knew that," Swan tried to reason.

"He was your brother, muthafucka. Or have you been eating out of your master's hand so long that you've forgotten your oath?" Animal rolled up his sleeve and showed them the fresh tattoo on his forearm. It was a portrait of a blindfolded woman holding a scale in one hand and a sword in the other. Sitting on her head like a crown was a five-pointed star. Written in script beneath her was the phrase *Blood out, Blood in.*

"Look, if you wanna kill me then go ahead, but don't involve my people in it," Swan said bravely.

Animal laughed. "The jungle creed only applies to those of us who decide to play the game. Unlike you, the word *honor* still means something to me. Killing you would be sweet as candy, Swan, but watching you spend your life, however long or short, looking over your shoulder amuses me. It's like the cat playing with a mouse that knows he's living on borrowed time, but isn't really sure when the cat is gonna get tired of playing and eat him. You broke my heart when you murdered Tech, but at the end of the day I know you were just playing the good soldier and following orders. Tech died by your hand, but it was not your will." He looked at Shai.

"So you plan to kill me for ordering the hit?" Shai asked.

"For as much as I've thought about it, no. It would thrill me to whack you, but it would complicate what I got going on by going to war with the Clarks. And even if I chopped your fucking head off it wouldn't balance the scales because you reacted as they expected you to, like a child trying to drive his daddy's car. Shai, I applaud you for trying to bring the peace back to Harlem, but you're hardly Poppa or Tommy Gunz for that matter. Neither of them would've allowed one of their capos to force their hands over a personal beef. I don't want no problems with you, Shai, at least not yet, but I am gonna take my pound of flesh out of everyone that's caused me pain, including Rico. I'm only telling you this as a courtesy because you're the boss of New York, even if it's in name only."

"You know Rico is one of my people," Shai reminded him.

"That's your bad, not mine, Shai. If you wanna lay your head on the chopping block for this nigga, I'm okay with that. Like they say, a bullet ain't got no name on it. But if you were smart you'd fall back and let me do what I gotta do and get outta your hair."

"And what if I say otherwise?" Shai asked, suspecting he already knew how Animal would respond.

Animal paused as if he was weighing it. "Then I'll take my chances going through you to get to him." Animal began backing away. When he was clear his three friends joined him. As an afterthought Animal called to Shai, "Get word to your people, Shai. The dog is back and he's hungry."

IT WASN'T UNTIL THE YOUNG hoods were gone that the realization of what had just happened set in. Honey began to sob uncontrollably drawing the attention of two police officers who had been eating in the food court. As usual they were too late to catch the perpetrators. It didn't matter though because neither Shai nor anyone with him would've talked to the police.

"I can't believe that little punk did that," Giselle said when they had made it back to the parking lot and the safety of Shai's armor-plated Suburban.

"These jokers got some big balls, but don't even trip. I'm gonna see Animal in the streets. Shai"—he turned to his best friend—"on everything I love I'm gonna gobble this nigga up." Swan checked the clip of his gun.

"Let it be," Shai said to the surprise of everyone in the truck, especially Swan's.

Swan looked at Shai as if he'd lost it. "What the fuck do you mean, let it be? Shai, if we weren't in that mall he probably would've tried to kill us."

"Swan, we both know how Animal is built. If he wanted to kill us it wouldn't have mattered if we were in a mall or a precinct, he would've let his hammer go. I can understand your anger, my nigga, but I can also understand that young man's pain. I was harsh in the sentence I passed on Tech, but I had to make an example of him for the shit he was pulling. If I'd let him rock, every one of these young niggaz would've been trying to come for a piece of the commission. That was a judgment call and that's what I tell myself so I can sleep with the decision, but if I had it to do all over again I would've let him live."

"We're gonna look like pussies if we let this go," Swan said heatedly.

Shai looked at Swan. "Swan, we're bosses, so I'm not concerned what it'll look like for us not to punish Animal. What I am worried about is waking up one night to find that crazy little bastard standing over my son's crib. Animal's face is plastered in every rap magazine in the country yet he comes at us in a public place, knowing that he was likely going to his death or a very long prison term. This tells us that he's past the point of logic and ain't gonna rest until this score is settled."

"Shai, do you seriously think that Animal would throw his life away over his man getting whacked?"

Shai thought on it for a minute. "How would you react if it had been Tommy?" Shai's older brother Tommy had been a mentor to all Poppa's young guns, but Swan was his favorite.

"You've got a point," Swan said, knowing full well he'd have charged into hell wearing gasoline underpants if it had been Tommy instead of Tech.

"Of course I do, which is why I say that as long as Animal doesn't come this way with that shit we don't have to erase him, at least not yet."

"Animal is outta his freaking mind going at Rico with just him and the three stooges."

"The fact that he has a death wish isn't anything new, Swan. Heads feared Tech, but it was Animal who gave them cold sweats at night because he would go where no one else was willing to." Shai weighed the situation. "Animal's lil homeys are a tough lot, but I think he'll save the prize for himself."

"You mean go at Rico alone? Even if he can get past Rico's soldiers, Changa is gonna do him filthy," Swan said of Rico's chief enforcer and bodyguard.

"Then Animal don't fear nothing short of God, and that's still up for debate. Changa is a monster, but Animal can be a very determined enemy. He's crazy enough to try it."

"Then I stand corrected. He doesn't have a death wish, he's trying to commit suicide." Swan doubled over with laughter, but Shai's face was serious. "Slim, you're not actually thinking that Animal might pull this off?"

"I hope not, because if he can get to Rico you never know who he might set his sights on next," Shai said seriously. "Nah, we're gonna fall back and make sure our asses are covered."

Swan was less than pleased with Shai's decision, but he was the boss. "So what about Rico?"

Shai looked at his friend and laughed. "Not much we can do besides hope his wife has taken out an insurance policy on his ass."

DETECTIVE BROWN WAITED UNTIL SHAI and his entourage had exited the mall before coming out from his hiding place. He had been behind a rack of clothing inside the lingerie store watching the exchange between Shai and Animal. He started to intervene when he saw Animal and his crew draw weapons, but decided that it would save him the trouble and the paperwork if he let him whack Shai. Unfortunately the confrontation ended without violence.

"Pussies," Brown snickered and whipped out his cell phone. "Alvarez, bring the car around to the north entrance and pick me up."

"If I scoop you we're gonna lose Shai. I just saw them come out," Detective Alvarez said on the other end. He was adjusting the lenses on his binoculars trying to figure out what Shai and Swan were arguing about.

"Don't worry about the youngest Clark. I've got a feeling he's gonna hightail it back to his estate and stay there for a while," Brown said.

"And what makes you say that?" Alvarez asked disbelievingly. He knew better than most how Shai and his crew loved to be seen.

"Because the boogeyman just rolled back into town." He ended the call.

Chapter 9

BESIDES THE STAFF AND A FEW LOCALS THERE WEREN'T
many people inside the little Spanish restaurant on 167th and Amsterdam. The young girl who was working the grill and the register
did the best she could not to keep people waiting while the rest of
their short staff attended to the men eating in the back of the restaurant.

Rico sat as he always did, with his back to the wall and his eyes on
the door. He had recently cut his thinning hair down to a buzz cut
with a sharp line, making him look several years younger. The sleeves
of his starched white shirt were rolled up, and his tie flipped over his
shoulder so he wouldn't stain it with the juicy steak he was devour-
ing. The cook was so gifted that he had twice offered her a position
on his staff, but she declined. Rico was thinking that the next time he
approached he would make her an offer she couldn't refuse.

Surrounding Rico were several of his lieutenants and his bodyguard, Changa. Changa wasn't much to look at, standing a shade
less than six feet tall and being of average build, but those who knew
him knew that he was not a man to be taken lightly. Before coming
to work for Rico in the States Changa had been a soldier of fortune
working for a powerful drug cartel in Mexico City. He took great

pride in his work, executing men, women, and children at the behest of his employers until the government finally caught up with them and took the crew down. Changa would've faced the firing squad with the rest of his unit had it not been for Rico and a well-placed bribe that got him out of the country. He had since been in Rico's debt and would do anything for him, which Rico made him prove time and again when he sent him to perform unspeakable acts on his enemies.

"So, how're we looking, fellas?" Rico addressed his lieutenants with a mouthful of steak.

"As good as ever," Lee said, sliding him a fat manila envelope. He was a light-skinned kid with a box-shaped head and hazy brown eyes.

Rico peeked inside the envelope and nodded in approval. "That's what's up."

The second lieutenant, Willie, slid him a folded newspaper that was also full of cash. That just left Ras, who was twirling his fingers in his dreads and looking off into space like he had something better to do. "What about you?" Ras reached under the table and produced a greasy-looking paper bag that he set in front of Rico. "What the fuck is this?" Rico looked at the bag as if he didn't even wanna touch it.

"It's your cut," Ras said as if it should've been obvious.

"I know *what* it is. I wanna know why the hell it looks like you took an order of ribs out before you put my money in?" Rico asked.

"Because I did." Ras laughed but no one else did.

"You need to take your life more seriously," Changa said, never turning away from the can of Pepsi he had been sipping. Though his eyes were covered with dark sunglasses everyone at the table knew they were locked on Ras.

"Chill out, Changa, I was just playing," Ras explained. Ras was an animal on the streets so it wasn't that he feared him, but he was smart enough to avoid a problem with him.

"That's your problem, bro, you play too much sometimes," Changa said.

Rico motioned with his hand for Changa to be cool. "Ras, how come every week we gotta have this conversation?"

"My bad Rico, man, I was just trying to make a joke and—" Ras began, but was silenced by a wave of Rico's hand.

"Fuck your joke. I'm talking about the way you do things in general." Rico hefted the greasy bag to make a point. "How many cats you know that will transport fifty thousand dollars like this?" Ras mumbled something, but Rico overtalked him. "None, that's how many. Ras, not only is this shit unsanitary, but it just looks stupid. Think about how crazy I would look if I was walking down the block wearing a five-thousand-dollar suit carrying a greasy ass paper bag."

"I didn't think about it like that, Rico," Ras reluctantly admitted.

"And that's the issue here, Ras, you don't think before you do shit. Besides Lee, my lil man Prince seems like the only one who can get it right," Rico told him.

"I don't see that nigga here with his bag," Ras said as if he was putting Prince on blast.

"That's because he dropped his bag and was gone twenty minutes before y'all got here." Rico wiped his hands on a napkin and pushed back from the table to address his team. "Fellas, what I keep trying to instill in y'all is that this ain't some nickel and dime operation we're running here. We've got too much bread running in and out of this organization to treat it like we're pitching *gee* packs on the block, and I suggest you all get it through your heads. Now that we've dealt with that let's address some of these more pressing issues like these cats from the projects making y'all look like pussies." He looked from Ras to Lee, who squirmed uncomfortably in his seat.

"Yeah, I heard ol' boy and them made y'all look crazy the other night," Ras teased him.

"I know you ain't talking with how ya man Ron got his shit split two weeks ago?" Lee shot back. "I heard he stomped that nigga unconscious."

"Why don't both of y'all shut up because you sound like idiots? This nigga is disrespecting your hood and your soldiers and instead of figuring out which way you wanna kill him you're in here arguing among each other about who he violated the most." Rico shook his head in disappointment.

"Man, do you think we ain't tried to whack this King James muthafucka a hundred times already? Little Snoopy from 115th shot this muthafucka and hit him with his car. The next day when he's going to the store King rolls up on him and beats him to death with a baseball bat. No matter how many times you lay this bastard out he gets back up and kills somebody. It's like he can't be killed."

Changa gave a throaty laugh. "Anybody can be killed, bro. It's all about the methods you employ."

"Then I welcome you to try it, because I'm tired of losing my boys," Ras said.

"Then maybe you should take a more hands-on approach with the situation," Rico suggested. Rico steeped his fingers and addressed his troops. "One way or another this King James muthafucka has gotta get dealt with because it looks bad when my guys get treated like third-rate hustlers when everybody knows we're connected."

Lee snorted. "Connected? Shit, I don't see Prince Clark sending nobody down to the slums trying to help out. He's tucked away in his castle counting money while we're down here in the trenches dealing with this fucking nut job. As I think on it, I can't remember Shai ever getting his hands dirty. The only reason he's the boss is because his daddy's in the ground and his brother is in the joint."

"You watch your fucking mouth!" Rico slammed his fist against the table so hard that Changa's Pepsi fell over and stained the white tablecloth. "Listen to me and listen good, young punk. Poppa Clark was a god to guys like me on the come up, when most of you were still swimming in your daddy's nut sack, so you get five more years of experience under your belt before you even fix your mouth to say his name. Furthermore, regardless of how you feel about Shai Clark, he's the boss and you never disrespect the boss, you understand me?"

Lee lowered his eyes and checked his tone. "You're right, Rico, and I didn't mean any disrespect, but I was only trying to shed some light on what a lot of us are feeling."

"And what are y'all feeling that I'm not already hearing regular complaints about?" Rico asked.

Lee looked at Ras who just shrugged. "Rico, we all know that Shai is the boss, nobody's disputing that, but that don't necessarily make it right. Dawg, it's been our crew out here holding it down and kicking dough up to Shai and them, but we don't get treated no different than anybody else when it comes to certain shit. When Danny Boy and his crew were waging war with the Bloods Shai stepped in and squashed that shit, so why do we gotta get our asses handed to us left and right with no support. All I'm asking is when Shai's gonna even the playing field?"

Rico didn't have an immediate response, because he knew that there was truth in his lieutenant's words. This wasn't the first time he had heard the grumbling of his troops over the uneven balance of power. Though he would never admit it publically it bothered him too. A lot of cats on the streets felt as Lee did, that Shai's default inheritance of the throne was unfair and the power should have shifted to a more seasoned soldier when Poppa Clark died and Tommy got locked up. But unlike some of the soldiers who wore their emotions on their sleeves, Rico always kept his game face and showed the proper respect for Shai. But this didn't change the fact that he was becoming more and more dissatisfied with the youngest Clark son and some of the decisions he was making, like the situation with Tech a while back. Little did Shai know Rico and some of his boys had planned on staging a revolt if he hadn't handled Tech accordingly. Shai ordering the young bandit's execution settled some of the unrest, but it didn't quiet the whispers about a more fitting boss running the organization, namely Rico.

"Just be easy for now, Lee. When the time comes for the power to shift, you and your boys just be ready to bust your guns," Rico told him.

"What the fuck are you looking at?" Changa asked the frail busboy who was eavesdropping from the corner. He had been watching them for a while but no one but Changa had noticed.

"Nothing," the boy said quickly and went to wiping down one of the tables. The way the man with the sunglasses looked at him made his flesh crawl.

"Leave him alone, Changa. The boy is the cook's nephew," Rico told him. "Come here, little man." Rico waved the boy over. The boy reluctantly approached the table, but he kept his eyes fixed on his shoes. "Look at me." Rico tapped the boy on the chin and forced him to meet his deadly stare. "Didn't anybody ever tell you that it was rude to listen in on grown people's conversations?" Rico motioned toward his men.

The boy wrung his hands together nervously when he spoke. "I'm sorry, sir. I didn't mean to stare, but I've never seen guys with such nice clothes. My auntie tells me that you're important, but she never says how. I figured you were movie stars or something so I was trying to see what shows I knew you from."

This got a hearty laugh from Rico. "Your auntie was right to tell you that we were important men, but we ain't no movie stars."

"Yeah, we're *block* stars," Lee added comically and all the men laughed.

Rico wiped the tear of laughter from the corner of his eye and pulled his bankroll from his pants pocket. He tossed a fifty on the table and stood up with his jacket. "Thanks for the chuckle, kid. That's for you." He nodded at the money. "Make sure you clean this table good and tell your auntie she needs to speak with me, okay?" Rico patted him on the cheek twice.

The busboy stood there smiling and nodding like an idiot until Rico and his men had left the restaurant. He dipped one of the dinner napkins into an abandoned glass of water and wiped his face where Rico's vile hand had touched him. After making sure nobody was watching, the busboy used the steak knife to pick the Pepsi can up off the table and dropped it into the pocket of his apron. It was the easiest five hundred dollars he had ever made.

"WHY ARE YOU ALWAYS MESSING with that thing?" Rico asked Ras, who was scrolling on his BlackBerry.

"It's how I stay connected with the world," Ras said, not bothering to take his eyes off the BlackBerry screen. "Oh, shit. Did y'all hear about this nigga getting killed in PA?" Ras held up the BlackBerry so they could see the news article he had pulled up on the screen.

"So what? Niggaz get killed every day. What's so special about that stiff in PA?" Changa asked.

"Because we know him!" Ras said excitedly. "Y'all don't remember that cat Rock Head from 140th?"

"You mean that dude who snitched on all those people? Fuck him, I got a cousin doing ten flat because of his rat ass," Rico said. "I think all snitches should be tortured and put to death."

"He was tortured alright. The cause of death is officially a cocaine overdose, but dig this. They stuck a knife in his ass and cut out his tongue!" Ras read the details of the article to them.

"Then it was a fitting death for his bitch ass." Rico sat on the floor. "Now instead of you chasing news articles like some fucking hard-up reporter I suggest you get back to your block to make sure the shift change goes smoothly. I'm gonna be spending the next few days getting ready for my niece's wedding, so I ain't gonna have time to babysit you mutts."

"Damn, that reminds me, I got a sacred union of my own that I need to get ready for in a few." Lee rubbed his hands greedily.

"Dawg, you're always chasing pussy," Ras said. He had seen Lee with chicks that looked like they'd stepped off the silver screen and he secretly resented him for it.

"If you'd seen this broad you'd be chasing her too," Lee replied. "And I know you ain't talking the way you and that hood-booger been hugged up lately. You getting all that cake on the block and your wife a project bitch!" Lee laughed at him.

"Watch you mouth, nigga. Mimi ain't no project bitch, she just lives there," Ras said.

Lee looked at him sideways. "Nigga, you know all them hos outta Taft is straight hood rats. You've had your head jammed so far in her ass that I'm surprised she ain't convinced you to flip Blood yet."

"Fuck outta here, that's her thing not mine. The only flag I'm waving is a green one for this paper!" Ras assured him.

"You better be careful, them gang bitches can be scandalous as hell," Changa warned.

"Nah, Mimi is different."

"Whatever, nigga. I'm getting outta here to go dive off in something. I'll holla." Lee walked off.

"Yeah, I'll catch you guys on the come around." Ras went in the other direction.

Rico shook his head. "Pussy is gonna be the death of both them niggaz."

PART 2

Welcome to the Jungle

Chapter 10

SAHARA WAS AS HIGH AS A KITE WHEN THE TAXI DEPOSited her on 124th and LaSalle. Scar had popped a bottle of Grey Goose and fired up two blunts of some of the stickiest weed she'd ever smoked and they were all feeling nice. When he'd thought they were all zooted Scar started getting touchy so Sahara concocted an excuse about having to leave to check on one of her aunts who was visiting from the Ivory Coast. She had been around the block far too long to fall into the trap he was trying to set. Scar was handling a few dollars but his paper was hardly long enough to get in Sahara's pants, which was more than she could say for Boots's thirsty ass. When Sahara had left, Boots was still sitting on the bed dreamyeyed while Scar fondled her breasts.

As she cut up the small path leading to building 3150 she spotted a white on white 750 easing to a stop at the bus stop on the avenue. The car was heavily tinted but she knew someone important was in it the way the young girls and guys began to flock around it. Three young cats got out and pushed the crowd back to make room for the driver to exit the vehicle. He was a brown-skinned cat who wore his hair in neat cornrows with a big red medallion hanging from his neck. The driver was familiar to her but she couldn't think of where she had seen him before until one of the girls shouted the name *Animal* just before she fainted into her friend's arms.

Sahara had seen Animal in videos, but he was far sexier in person. His three cronies talked shit and snapped pictures with the young groupies as if they were the ones that had an album coming out, but the Animal just smiled and nodded politely. From what Sahara remembered hearing about him from his days on the streets he was supposed to be some kind of monster, but he struck her as more of a bashful kid than anything. There was a childlike shyness to him as he stood there signing autographs in front of the projects that peeked Sahara's curiosity. She had just made up her mind to go over and try to cut into the star when the lobby door of 3150 swung open and out stepped the man she had come uptown to see, King James.

King was a brute of a man standing at nearly six feet four and weighing somewhere in the mid-two hundreds. He was dressed in a navy-blue tracksuit with a pair of white on white Nike Airs, and a tarantula pendant that was filled with so many diamonds that it was hard to look at in the right light. At his side was his best friend and watch dog Lakim, watching the crowd forming on the avenue like a hungry dog.

"What up, ma?" King greeted Sahara with a warm bear hug.

"Hey, baby!" she squealed as if she hadn't been plotting on another man thirty seconds prior.

"What's going on over there?" King nodded toward the crowd around the Beamer.

"I don't know, but son is shining real heavy," Lakim said. "Yo, ain't that the lil nigga from the third floor?"

King squinted his eyes and spotted little Ashanti in the crowd. "Yeah, that's Ashanti."

"Didn't that nigga get thrown in a boys' home for them bodies?" Lakim recalled.

King laughed. "You know they ain't built a kiddy jail that could hold that bad ass lil muthafucka." When the crowd shifted King caught a glimpse of the medallion the driver was wearing. "Hold the fuck on, I know that ain't who I think it is coming through my fucking hood unannounced. Come on, son." King started down the path with Sahara and Lakim on his heels.

"BLOOD, YOU SHOULD'VE LET ME push that nigga Swan. We know it was him that leaned Tech so I don't know why we playing with it," Brasco grunted from the passenger seat of the Beamer. They had just come back from Jersey and gotten off on the 125th Street exit of the Westside Highway.

"Because one life doesn't come close to evening the score for my brother's life. When the wind blows I want the whole house of cards to fall," Animal told him.

"Them niggaz was straight shook." Ashanti laughed from the backseat, where he was playing Nefertiti in 2K10.

Animal looked in the rearview mirror at Ashanti who was wearing a mischievous grin. "Is that what you think, that Shai and Swan were afraid of us?"

"Hell yeah, we had the drop on them and they bitches so they was short!" Ashanti boasted.

Animal shook his head at Ashanti's ignorance. "Lil brother, that wasn't fear, it was discretion."

Ashanti frowned as he didn't understand the word. "You mean he thought we were gonna cut him up?"

"That's dissection, idiot," Nefertiti teased.

"I got your idiot right here." Ashanti flicked the button on the controller and drained a three-pointer in the video game. Animal reached behind him and yanked the plug out of the Xbox. "What you do that for?"

"Because I need you to pay attention to what's going on and not some fucking video game," Animal said sternly. "Make no mistake about this, B; you don't survive as long as Swan has by fearing the next man. True, we would've laid them straight to rest if it had popped off at the mall but none of us really wanted it to go down like that. Shai's got too much going on legitimately to be banging out in public places. If a man like him wants you dead then he sends a hit squad to wipe your family out."

Ashanti tossed the joystick down on the leather seat. "So if he's so bad ass, then why would we risk going in there and threatening him like that?"

"I didn't threaten Shai; I simply told him what my position was on this whole thing. Niggaz tried to slay me and I ain't about to let it ride. Blood will answer for blood, homey."

"A'ight, let me see if I follow you. So, we know Swan was the one who laid Tech, but we're not gonna hit him?" Nefertiti asked.

"Not yet. Me and Swan are gonna lock ass, but it's gonna be on my terms and it won't be no all-out crew thing, just two predators vying for dominance," Animal said seriously.

"Man, I don't give a shit who we push as long as I get to put the lean on somebody soon," Brasco said.

Animal smiled. "All the pups will be fed when the time is right. Right now I just wanna kick back and enjoy the city." Animal's cell phone vibrated on the console where it rested. He looked down at the name that flashed across the caller ID screen and smiled. "What up, lil mama?" He put the call on speakerphone.

"You nigga! I thought you were gonna call me when you got up-town," the female on the other end quizzed him. She had a sultry voice with a rough edge that reminded you of a porn star talking shit during a shoot.

"My fault, I've been running around taking care of business," he told her.

"I hear that hot shit, you need to come take care of me before I catch an attitude."

"Slow down, baby, I got you."

"I got time for you if he don't," Ashanti said.

"Eww, who the fuck is that, one of them clown-ass Big Dawg niggaz?" she capped.

"Bitch, I'm a Big Dawg, but I ain't no rapper," Ashanti said slyly.

"That's *five-star* bitch to you, lil nigga," she checked him.

"I ain't know it was like that, ma." Ashanti took some of the base out of his voice, recognizing one of his own.

"Well, now you do, shorty. Anyway,"—she rolled her eyes on the other end as if he could see her through the phone—"Animal, what's good? A bitch needs to get tightened up so you need to come holla at me."

"I told you that I got you, boo. You gonna have that thing ready for me when I come through?" Animal asked.

"Baby boy, I've been playing wit that thing since you called me and I don't know how much longer I can hold out," she said seductively.

Animal smiled. "That's my girl. Check, let me finish up with these niggaz and I'm holla at you on the later side, ya dig?"

"Don't make it too long, daddy. You be safe out there and I love you," she said sincerely.

"I love you too, ma," he told her and ended the call.

"Let me find out," Brasco said accusingly.

Animal cut his eyes at him. "Let you find out what?"

"That you ain't as loyal to Gucci as you've been claiming to be."

"Let me tell you something, blood. Two things you ain't never gotta question are my willingness to push a nigga off this planet if the paper is right and my loyalty to Gucci. Don't read too deep into what you hear," Animal told him.

"Well, what I heard sounds like you about to get into some fresh pussy. I'm proud of you, son," Nefertiti said with a broad grin, but the grin faded when Animal's cold stare landed on him.

"Y'all muthafuckas got one-track minds. Can't a nigga be cool with a chick without trying to fuck?" Animal asked.

"No," the trio answered in unison.

Animal shook his head. "Well y'all need to take your minds off who I am or ain't fucking and get it on the business. There's killing to be done." That silenced everyone.

After another ten minutes of riding in silence Brasco finally spoke up. "So what's the game plan, homey? We gonna run down on this nigga Rico and eat his food or what?"

"We gonna carve that turkey up real nice, my nigga. I'm gonna stop his money and then his clock. Once we cripple his organization then when the time is right the main course will be served," Animal assured him.

Brasco nodded in approval. "That works for me. Since you ain't gonna let us lay hands on that yellow nigga Swan I'm gonna take Rico's head and mount that shit on my wall. On Blood I need to feast on something, cuz my ribs is touching."

"Son, Rico got like a thousand soldiers and a million guns; you really think we gonna be able to get at him?" Nefertiti asked.

"It ain't a question of *if* we can get at them, but *when* we gonna split them niggaz wigs. I won't be denied my vengeance," Animal said with ice in his voice. "But y'all don't have to dwell on that right now. I know when I put out the call to arms you'll answer like you always do. But now ain't the time for that. I'm home, my nigga, and I wanna feel these streets before they feel me."

"That's what I'm talking about. Let's get to this bottle popping to celebrate your return," Nefertiti said excitedly.

"Fuck all that, we need to hit the strip club or something," Brasco suggested.

"The both of y'all are bugging, let's go to the weed spot and see if we can pick up some hos on the strip," Ashanti countered.

Ever since Animal had picked them up that morning they had been arguing like siblings over their big brother. Their bickering used to annoy Animal to no end, but that day he welcomed it because it was just one more reminder of how much he missed his beloved Harlem and his little crew. From state to state Animal rolled with made dudes, in and out of the industry, and though they showed him love it was nothing like what he felt when he was with Brasco, Ashanti, and Nef. The young men riding with him were his brothers, and they loved him just as much as he loved them, if not more so.

"Y'all niggaz be easy," Animal said in his lazy drawl. He removed a blunt from his shirt pocket and lit it, knowing the weed would get them to calm down and listen while he spoke his piece. "I got a run to make right quick, then a studio session with Chip. When I'm done I'll come scoop y'all and we can do whatever you want."

"So fuck it, we'll come to the studio with you," Ashanti suggested.

"Not tonight, we gotta mix these songs down and if I take y'all with me I won't end up doing shit but getting too slopped to work. As soon as I'm done we'll kick it though. I promise." Animal steered the Beamer up Broadway and made two lefts on 124th. A group of girls who had been coming out of the liquor store watched the sleek automobile in awe, wondering who was inside.

"Yeah, I see you checking me out, ma," Ashanti called out the window.

"Is that little Ashanti?" one of the girls asked.

"Of course it is. You see how I'm rolling."

"Whose car y'all done stole?" the other girl asked.

"Stole? Bitch, don't be trying to play me like I'm some scumbag nigga. I'm rolling with my big brother, Animal!"

"Chill, son," Animal whispered. He wanted to keep as low a profile as possible so he could move around the city freely.

"That ain't no Animal," the first girl disputed. Before Animal could stop him, Ashanti rolled the window all the way down so the girls could see inside. When they spotted the rapper their eyes got wide with shock. "Oh, my God!"

"Fucking Ashanti," Brasco cursed as they pulled into the bus stop with the girls damn near running to catch up to the car. From the way they were squealing and carrying on it didn't take long before a small crowd had gathered around the car.

"Ashanti, I could kill you for this shit," Animal said, cringing as a not-so-attractive girl pressed her face against the driver's side window.

"You're a superstar now, son, what did you expect? You might as well get out and greet your adoring public," Ashanti said proudly.

"Or at least see if some of these hood rats are trying to fuck," Brasco added before sliding from the car, followed by his crew.

Brasco, Nefertiti, and Ashanti worked crowd control as Animal stood beside the car and signed autographs for the people that had gathered around to praise him. One girl didn't have any paper so she asked Animal if he could sign her baby's diaper, but from the way it smelled he had to decline. It was hard to believe that not so long ago people would've been running away from him, but now they flocked to him like some teen idol. It wasn't the first time it had happened to him since the release of the video but he still hadn't gotten used to it.

"Come on, B, y'all niggaz know y'all can't be bringing all this unwanted attention to my hood," King said as he parted the crowd.

"King, what's good? I heard you were home." Ashanti gave him dap.

"Yeah, and I heard your little ass was locked up?"

"Again," Lakim added.

"Come on, y'all know how I do it. If they wanna keep me caged they're gonna have to throw me in a super max and put me under twenty-four-hour guard, but even then they probably couldn't do nothing with me," Ashanti boasted.

"I hear that hot shit. I've been to a few spots that would straighten your little ass right out," King told Ashanti. He turned his dark eyes to Animal who was busy trying to keep a girl's hands out of his hair. "What up, you can't speak?"

Animal looked up and a broad grin immediately crossed his face. "Oh, shit. What up, my nigga." Animal hugged him. "Damn son, you got big than a muthafucka!"

King flexed. "You know it ain't but three things you can do when you're locked down for twenty-three hours a day: read, eat, and lift weights."

"Looks like you could lift damn near the whole building," Animal teased him.

Ashanti looked from King to Animal with a confused expression on his face as he had never heard Animal speak of the terror of the General Grant Houses. "How do y'all know each other?"

Animal grinned. "It's a long story."

Animal and King had a relationship that went back several years. Back in the days King had been the young protégé of Animal's older brother Justice, a notorious killer and the right arm of one of Harlem's most ruthless kingpins K-Dawg. Under K-Dawg the Road Dawgz crew had terrorized Harlem laying low anyone who went against them, including the district attorney assigned to prosecute them. One of K-Dawg's young boys had blown his head off during a press conference in broad daylight on the courthouse steps. K-Dawg and his crew feared nothing, but their reign eventually came to an end when they orchestrated a mass suicide that took the lives of almost a dozen police officers. The police never did make a positive ID on K-Dawg's corpse, but they reasoned that it was highly unlikely that even someone who seemed as invincible as he did could've survived the explosion.

As a teen King had been a small fish taken under the wing by the hardened Justice, but when he was sent off to prison at the age of sixteen he became more of a monster than Justice had been during his run on the streets. In a strange twist of fate King and Justice had ended up in the same prison for a time. Being that King's family never came to see about him, Animal and his aunt would often pull him down too when they went to see Justice. Animal enjoyed listening to King talk during the visits. They were just about the same age, but King had a maturity about him that made him seem far older than he was. Eventually Justice was moved to another prison and Animal was so caught up in the streets that he stopped going to see King, but every so often he would send him letters of a few dollars here and there. He had heard through the grapevine that King was home and making quite a name for himself but this was the first time he had seen him since he was a teenager.

"So, how's big brother?" King asked him.

"He's good. I ain't seen him in a while, but I write him at least once a week," Animal said.

"That's what's up. Yo, when you speak to that nigga tell him to get at me. I got some bread put to the side for him."

"He's straight. If I don't do nothing else I make sure his commissary is right."

"I know you do, superstar, but I still wanna do something for him from me. Son took care of the God when he was on the streets and in the joint," King said honestly.

"Wow, I didn't know you know famous people," Sahara interjected. She was tired of playing the sidelines waiting for Animal to notice her.

King gave her a wicked look. "Ma, don't play ya self. My whole team is stars."

"Ya heard," Lakim added.

"King, cut it out. You know I didn't mean it like that." Sahara stroked his beard tenderly.

King made the introduction. "Animal, this is my lil young thing, Sahara."

"How you doing, sis?" Animal shook her hand.

"I'm good," Sahara said in a seductive tone. She caught King glaring at her so she fixed it up. "I loved the mix tape you and Don B. put out. 'Child of the Ghetto' is my joint!"

"Thank you. I'll make sure I drop a copy to King for you the next time I swing this way," Animal said.

"I heard you live in Texas now. Are you in New York for business or pleasure?" she asked.

"A little bit of both."

"Well, if you get some time you should come and hang out with me and King. I got a girlfriend that I think you'd like."

"Sorry, but I got a lady," Animal told her, not sure if he liked the way Sahara was staring at him. He had seen that look in the eyes of many a woman and it always led to trouble.

"Oh, you're married?" Sahara asked as if she cared one way or the other.

"Not yet."

"Then I don't see nothing wrong with just hanging out, right?"

"All depends on what kind of hanging you mean."

"Ask ya man, King. He'll tell you how me and my girls get down." She licked her lips. It was a simple gesture, but watching her do it made Animal feel dirty.

"Sahara, this man is a star so what the fuck he look like going in on some hood rats?" King clowned her.

"I know you ain't trying to play nobody because you can't keep your nose out of this hood rat pussy!" she shot back.

King's nostrils flared letting Sahara know she had overplayed her hand. Before she could apologize King had her by the arm, shaking her. "Sahara, you better take your sack-chasing ass in the building and wait for me before I bust ya shit for trying to style out here." He shoved her toward the building.

"A'ight, damn. You ain't gotta be pushing nobody," Sahara mumbled as she made hurried steps toward the building. She made it a point to switch extra hard so that Animal could see what she was working with.

"You gotta excuse that, my dude. You know how these lil broads can be," King said by way of an apology.

"Yeah, I be knowing," Animal said to King, but his eyes followed Sahara to the building. He had never cheated on Gucci, but Sahara was definitely eye candy. "But yo, I ain't gonna keep you, I just rolled through to drop these niggaz." He motioned toward the stooges. "I gotta bust a move."

"Yeah, I gotta *bust* something too," King said, looking over his shoulder at Sahara who was peering through the lobby's glass window watching them. "But it was good to see you, T. I know you're a big superstar now so you've left the streets alone but if you ever need some dirt done you know you can holla at ya boy!"

Animal smirked. "Appreciate it, King, but just because you take an animal out of the jungle doesn't change the fact that he's an animal." There was something about the way he said it that made everyone around him uneasy.

"True indeed, God, true indeed. In any event, if you need me you can find me here holding court any day of the week. Now that I'm back on top I gotta work twice as hard to hold my kingdom and I don't plan on letting up on these niggaz for one second," King assured him.

"My nigga is gonna be the king of all of this shit, word is bond," Lakim added.

"King James, huh?" Animal smirked. "If you like it then I love it, my nigga. I'm outta here."

Animal gave everybody dap and hopped back in his whip. He threw his hood up through the sunroof and peeled away.

Chapter 11

"I SEE Y'ALL LIL NIGGAZ ON A COME UP," KING SAID AS HE watched Animal pull away.

"We trying to get it how we live like everybody else," Ashanti said.

"Stop fronting, you ain't getting it like nothing, you little pissy dick muthafucka." King playfully threw a combination of light jabs at Ashanti, who weaved most of them and came back with a few of his own. "I see you're still on your footwork."

"You gotta stay on your toes when you're constantly trying to duck the beast, god. They're trying to throw the key away on niggaz out here, feel me?"

King nodded in agreement. "Indeed I do, which is why I always find myself wondering why you keep throwing stones?"

"What you mean, King?" Ashanti asked as if he was ignorant to his own antics.

"Check, every time you turn around your lil ass is getting arrested or carted off to kiddie jail. They're just slapping your wrist now because you're so young, but in a minute you're gonna be sixteen and they're gonna show you how the devil really gets down. They took eight years of my life that I can never get back."

Ashanti pondered King's words and chose his own carefully when he spoke. "King, you were only a year or two older than me when they locked you up for killing that kid back in the days, but when you came home the whole hood laid down at your feet because they knew your were a real nigga."

"Ashanti, I didn't know it at the time but I was a *real nigga* long before I had ever taken a life. I got sent away for trying to protect myself from a man who was trying to harm me, not for paper, turf, or stripes. The things I saw and participated in while I was away stole my innocence and turned me into the monster that my enemies have nightmares about when they lay down with their wives and children."

"And that's why the hood pays homage," Ashanti shot back. "Man, niggaz in the hood love the King James from 3150 more than they do the one who wrote the Bible."

"Ashanti, that ain't love, it's fear. When I touched down I had already made up my mind that I was gonna go harder than the next man on these corners and take what nobody wanted me to have. I don't have shit so I don't have anything to lose."

"And what I got?" Ashanti asked seriously. "My family abandoned me and when I didn't have a pot to piss in it was my niggaz who sheltered me and the streets who fed me, so please try to help me to understand what the fuck I got to lose if I get locked up or die out here?"

King found himself at a loss for words. When he looked down into Ashanti's glassy brown eyes he saw the same combination of anger and fear that had greeted him every time he looked in the mirror when he'd first gotten to prison. He could've spent all night trying to get Ashanti to see his point, but he knew it was useless. The streets had him and only death would break their union.

"So be it," King said in a defeated tone. "I can't knock ya hustle, Ashanti, you just make sure you take care of yourself while you're out here."

"He's gonna be okay. His family has got him," Brasco assured King.

King held Brasco's gaze and saw nothing in his eyes. It was the same lifeless expression that he was running into more and more as he dealt with the new breed of hustlers. They had nothing to lose and everything to gain. "You make sure y'all do," he told Brasco. "We out, La." He motioned for Lakim to follow him to the building.

"That nigga King is always trying to preach to somebody. I ain't trying to hear that fake ass God-Body shit," Nefertiti said when King had disappeared into the building.

"Nah, King is a good nigga. A lot of cats could take a page from his book," Brasco said, reflecting on King's words. The truth in them hit very close to home, but he would never admit it in front of his crew.

"Man, fuck all that, we need to see about getting some more trees since Animal peeled off with the good shit," Ashanti suggested.

"I got a bag of Arizona on me," Nefertiti said.

"You about a stashing ass nigga, Nef, why you just now saying something about it?" Brasco asked.

"Because I didn't feel like hearing y'all clown on me in the car. You know every time Animal comes around with that good shit y'all start acting like y'all don't smoke green no more."

"We gonna smoke it today. Roll that shit up, son," Ashanti told him.

"I'm two steps ahead of you." Nefertiti produced an already rolled blunt from his jacket pocket.

"That's what I'm talking about!" Brasco declared.

No sooner than Nefertiti lit the weed he heard someone shout, "Squally!"

A brown Buick came out of nowhere and screeched to a stop directly in front of where they were standing. Ashanti didn't even think twice when he hopped the fence and took off running through the projects. Nefertiti and Brasco thought about running too but the hard-faced black cop closing in on them, with his weapon drawn, gave them pause.

"Please run so I can pop you," Detective Brown said while pointing his .357 at the two kids. His hard face was twisted into his signature scowl as he rolled up on Brasco and Nefertiti. "Grab the fence, cocksucker!" he ordered them. Brasco and Nefertiti slowly turned around and placed their hands on the short black gate. Brown placed his gun to the back of Brasco's head and began to pat him down roughly.

"C'mon, son, why you fucking with us over a blunt?" Brasco asked.

"Because I can," Detective Brown said before slapping him in the nuts.

"It must be Christmas in the hood because instead of two turtle doves we got two shit-birds," Detective Alvarez joked as he joined his partner. The tall Puerto Rican detective was dressed in blue jeans, boots, and a bubble vest. "What's up, Lawrence?" he addressed Brasco.

"Alvarez, tell this nigga to chill. We wasn't doing nothing," Brasco told him.

"Bullshit, you two shades are always doing something." Alvarez shoved Nefertiti into the fence and searched him. When they were satisfied that the two youths weren't carrying weapons they allowed them to get off the fence. "What's popping, Blood?"

"Like I said, ain't shit popping. We was just standing here when y'all muthafuckas rolled up on us on some A-Team shit," Brasco replied.

"Oh, I seriously doubt that," Alvarez told him. He looked down at the ground and saw the still burning blunt Nefertiti had dropped when they rolled up. With a mischievous smile on his face he picked up the blunt. Alvarez took two short tokes and frowned. "Damn, y'all must really be doing bad to be smoking this bullshit." He tossed the blunt into the street.

"Man, you're the police; you ain't supposed to be doing that," Nefertiti pointed out, which got him slapped in the back of the head by Detective Brown.

"Bitch nigga, the fact that we're the police means we can do what the fuck we want and the only person you can tell who might halfway care is God." He laughed at Nef, then turned his attention to Brasco. "I don't know why you little thug keep thinking you got rights. When are y'all gonna get the memo that a street nigga ain't shit in the eyes of the law?"

Brasco hated Detective Brown and his eyes betrayed this. "You can't be the law forever, son. One day you gotta lay that badge to rest and when that time comes you'll be a regular citizen, subject to the laws of the jungle."

Detective Brown shoved Brasco roughly against the gate and grabbed him by the front of his hoodie. "You threatening me, lil nigga?"

Brasco slowly looked from the hands pinning him to the eyes of the enraged cop and spoke very slowly and very seriously. "Detective Brown, no matter how ignorant you may think I am, I'm not stupid enough to threaten a cop. But what I will tell you is that if you don't take your hands off me I'm going to jail or the morgue tonight." Brasco saw Detective Brown's finger trembling near the trigger of his gun, but he refused to show his fear.

Sensing that the scene was about to take a turn for the worse Alvarez placed a calming hand on his partner's forearm. "Cool out, partner. You know better than to give a scumbag like this home-court advantage." He tugged at Brown a bit and his partner allowed himself to be led away and let Alvarez deal with Brasco. "Brasco, we didn't come over here to bust your balls. If I wanted to do that I could get word to your parole officer and tell him that you crossed state lines without his permission. Now how do you think that would look?"

Brasco turned away. "Dude, I don't know what you're talking about. I haven't left Harlem since I got outta jail."

"Then explain this to me." Alvarez pulled up a picture on his digital camera and held it up for Brasco to see. It was of all of them coming out of the mall earlier that day. "Brasco, let's keep it one hundred between us. We know that Animal is back in town, and though I'm pissed off about him getting off for all that dumb shit that I *know* he was involved in, I'm not holding a grudge over it. If the system is cool with letting that sociopath run around unchecked then so am I. What I do have a problem with is bodies popping up the moment he sets foot back in my city, especially after all the work me and my partner put in to get things quiet again after Tech got wasted."

Detective Brown laughed. "I hear they did that boy so filthy that the mortician had to pad his suit because there wasn't enough left of him to keep it from caving in." Brasco took a step toward Detective Brown, but Alvarez held him where he was. "I wish you would." Brown raised his gun.

"Brasco, you and my partner going at each other all afternoon ain't gonna do nothing but get somebody hurt, and I'm trying to avoid unnecessary bloodshed. Look, you saw the pictures so you know that we know that Animal is here for a reason. We've got an idea why, but we need you to connect the dots before somebody else gets hurt."

Brasco's face was serious when he responded, "Who's Animal?"

Detective Brown reached over to slap Brasco for his blatant lie, but Alvarez held him back. "A'ight, if that's how you wanna play it, *Lawrence,* I'm wit it. Put your hands behind your back," Alvarez ordered Brasco.

"This is some bullshit, how you gonna lock my man up?" Nefertiti asked.

"We ain't locking him up, we're locking *y'all* up." Detective Brown shoved him against the gate and placed the handcuffs around his wrist.

"What's the charge?" Brasco asked.

Alvarez tightened the cuffs around Brasco's wrists. "So far it's possession of narcotics and trespassing, but I'm sure we'll think of some more shit by the time we get to the precinct."

"That's a punk ass charge and you know it. The judge ain't gonna do nothing but give us court dates and cut us loose," Brasco said.

"Yeah, but ain't no telling when you're gonna get to see the judge. You know the Bookings are overcrowded as it is." Alvarez smirked at him.

"Yeah, it could be days before they finally find your paperwork after we misplace it," Brown added. "Unless of course you guys decided you wanted to tell us why Animal is here?"

Brasco just shrugged. "Sorry, I can't help you."

"Fuck it, we'll do it your way." Alvarez steered Brasco toward the car, while Brown escorted Nefertiti.

Brasco looked over at Nefertiti who looked shook, but he was holding it together like a true soldier. "Yo, Nef, looks like we're partying in the Tombs tonight, huh?"

Brasco laughed as he was pushed into the police car.

DETECTIVES BROWN AND ALVAREZ HAD just pulled up in front of their precinct when Brown's phone rang. He picked it up and listened as the caller on the other end began rattling off something that his partner could hear pieces of through the phone. When Brown ended the call he had a worried expression on his face.

"What's up?" Alvarez asked.

"That was the captain. We gotta hurry up and drop these clowns off, then get down to Brooklyn," Brown told him.

"Shit, man, can't one of the local squads handle it?" Alvarez was anxious to start interrogating Animal's people and going to Brooklyn would cut into the maximum time they had to hold the duo.

"No, the captain wants us to check into this one personally. They say the corpses were fucked up . . . real fucked up," Brown told him. Suddenly Alvarez realized what his partner was hinting at and looked in the backseat at Brasco and Ashanti.

"Don't look at us. We've been with you guys for the last hour and a half fighting traffic." Brasco chuckled.

"Any witnesses?" Alvarez asked his partner.

Brown looked at him seriously. "Knowing our boy, I doubt it."

Chapter 12

ANIMAL ARRIVED ON THE QUIET BLOCK IN BED-STUY Brooklyn almost a full twenty minutes before the taxicab pulled up in front of the brownstone at the other end of the block. From the backseat spilled a beautiful brown-skinned woman wearing a wide-brimmed hat. The woman was dressed in a long leather coat and a pair of black thigh-high stilettos. The cabdriver almost stumbled from the cab when he hopped out to get her bags. From the looks of the symbols on them she had been burning down Fifth Avenue. The exotic dream accepted the bags with a predatory smile and tipped him a five before climbing the steps of the brownstone.

Animal waited an additional ten minutes before getting out of his car to retrieve the black shoulder bag that he had spent nearly a half hour checking and double-checking before packing it away. Instead of going inside the brownstone the woman had disappeared into, Animal entered the one next door. Months ago he had had a home girl of his rent an apartment in it and show her face once or twice a day to make it look good, but no one actually lived there. He entered the third-floor apartment and did a brief check of the rooms to make sure the apartment was deserted as he had instructed. Once it was secure he pulled a coverall and shoe covers from the bag and slipped them on over his clothes and boots. After tucking his hair snugly beneath a stocking cap he went back out the door and headed for the roof.

The space separating the two brownstones was only two feet so Animal had no problem clearing the ledge. In the center of the adjoining brownstone roof there was a skylight that looked down into the master bedroom. Peering down he caught a glimpse of the woman just as she was coming out of her clothes and smiled. Her body was smooth with perky breasts, nicely rounded hips, and a small rose tattooed on her right shoulder. Animal kept his eyes glued to her until she grabbed a towel and disappeared into the bathroom.

It was no trouble for him to pop open the left pane of the skylight since he had removed the screws when he arrived in New York that morning. Lowering himself through the glass as far as he could, he dropped the rest of the way onto the bed, scattering the rose petals the woman had laid out over the comforter. On both nightstands and around the bed scented candles flickered in the breeze created by the missing windowpane. She had obviously planned a romantic evening for her and her lover, but even the best laid plans could go wrong and Animal had every intention of making sure that's what happened.

When the woman came out of the bathroom she was so focused on drying her hair that she didn't even notice the menacing eyes staring at her from the shadows behind the bathroom door. She tossed the towel on the back of the chair in front of the vanity table and sat down to do her makeup. It wasn't until she looked up at the mirror to apply her lipstick did she realize she wasn't alone. By the time she opened her mouth to scream it was already too late.

Animal clamped his hand tightly over her mouth and jerked her head roughly to the right. "If you make a sound I'm gonna break your pretty neck. Keep your mouth closed and you might live to

tell your girlfriends how you escaped the boogeyman. Do you understand?" The girl nodded and Animal removed his hand. He spun
her around in the chair and glared at her from behind the stocking
cap. "Where is it?"

"Where is what?" she asked in a frightened voice.

Animal sighed and slapped her across the face. "Bitch, don't play
me for lame, you know what I'm talking about! You and your boyfriend took something that didn't belong to you and we want it
back. Where's Rico's money?"

The girl's eyes widened. She had never met Rico but she knew
his reputation well from the stories her man whispered to her at
night. "I don't know nothing about no money or no Rico."

Animal grabbed the girl roughly by the hair and flung her onto
the bed. He straddled the frightened woman's body and placed the
barrel of his gun against her forehead. "Bitch, either you're gonna
come correct and give me Rico's bread or I'm gonna leave a nasty stain
on these pretty satin sheets." Animal ran his finger over her crotch
with his free hand.

"Please, I don't know anything about Rico's money, but I've got
about five thousand in the house and some jewelry that you can take.
Please don't rape me." The woman pleaded with tears streaking down
her cheeks.

Animal reached out and touched her face tenderly. She was too
terrified to move away. "Baby girl, I'm a lot of things, but I ain't no
rapist. Quit that crying." He wiped her tears away with his thumb.
"Since you say you don't know anything about Rico's money I'm
gonna take you at your word, but I'm gonna need you to do something for me in return for letting you live."

"What do you want me to do?" Her voice trembled.

"Same thing you were doing when I busted in on you. Get ready
to receive your man."

• • •

LEE WAS HAPPY TO GET away from Harlem and back to the solitude of his Brooklyn hideaway. He hated the fact that he always had to go uptown to meet Rico, but you didn't make waves with someone who was allowing you to get more money than you'd ever seen in your life.

He looked at his watch and saw that it was eight-thirty, which meant he would be right on time. Ever since he had met the brown-skinned chick at the strip club they had been partying like rock stars. It had gotten so deep that he even started letting her stay at a brownstone he owned in Brooklyn rent-free. As a show of her appreciation, in addition to their normal sexual romps she treated him to something especially nasty once a week. His fiancée was starting to get suspicious about his weekly disappearing acts but brown skin's pussy was so good he didn't even care. Last week he found her dressed like a runaway slave and he got to be the plantation owner who took her virtue. He couldn't wait to see what she had planned for him that day.

As soon as Lee entered the brownstone he could smell the sweet smell of chronic, barely covered by the scented candles burning all over the house. "Baby, where are you?" Lee called.

"I'm upstairs," she called back.

He rounded the corner leading to the stairs and saw a trail of discarded clothing, starting at the ground floor and leading up. "That's what I'm talking about," Lee said and started removing his own clothes as he climbed the stairs. There was a trail of candles leading up the stairs and to the bedroom door. He could see the candlelight flickering in the darkened bedroom, highlighting his lady's nude silhouette stretched across the bed on her stomach, waiting to receive him. Both her hands were bound to either side of the bedposts by silk scarves.

Lee swooped down and began to let his hands explore her nakedness. He planted soft kisses on her back and ass while whispering what he was about to do to them. His hand slipped between her legs and explored her box with its two longest fingers. She was soaking wet and it only served to make Lee's dick harder. He was so overwhelmed by lust that it never occurred to him that it was impossible for her to have tied her own arms to the bed.

"Yeah, I've been waiting on this all day." Lee mounted her from behind. He pushed his throbbing penis against her lips softly, going just a little deeper every time. She was so wet he was able to easily tap the back of her walls with each ecstasy-filled stroke. "Feels like you've been waiting on it too, huh?"

"Umm hmm," she moaned. Lee was hitting her spot, but the fear of the third party in the room kept her from enjoying it.

"Damn, this shit is warm." Lee breathed against her back and sank into the hidden compartments of her love. He tried to keep his slow even rhythm but her pussy was so good he found himself speeding up. Lee's chest heaved like he was running the hundred-meter dash as he pounded her, feeling himself about to blast off. "Damn, I'm 'bout to bust . . . I'm 'bout to bust . . ." Just as Lee was climaxing a plastic bag was slipped over his head.

"That's right, I want you to struggle." Animal held Lee in a headlock as he thrashed about. Animal waited until Lee looked like he was about to pass out before ripping a hole in the bag. Lee collapsed on the floor and gasped in the sweet air like he was breathing for the first time.

"Man, what the fuck is this all about? Do you know who I am?" Lee coughed.

Animal looked at him pitifully. "You know, the bad guy in the movie always asks that dumb-ass question when he finds himself on the short end, but the answer never changes anything." Animal casually screwed the silencer onto his gun. "Yes, I know just who you are and what you are. A fucking thief."

"You must be outta your mind, chump. I'm getting dough in them streets, I'm with Rico!" Lee declared as if dropping his boss's name would increase his chances of living.

"Yeah, y'all are getting a lot of bread working under Rico, which is why he's so disappointed in you for stealing from him, Lee," Animal lied.

Lee suddenly realized the seriousness of his situation. "Man, that's bullshit. I've been loyal to Rico from the day he put me down. Ask him!"

"Ain't no sense in asking at this point. What's done is done." Animal shot Lee in one kneecap and then the other.

"MUTHAFUCKA!" Lee screamed, holding his knees. "You can't do me like this. This is fucked up!"

Animal started to shoot him again, but had a better idea. "You're right. This ain't no way for one of Rico's boys to go out." Animal reached into the shoulder bag and pulled out a small Louisville slugger. "Since you niggaz under Rico are supposed to be such stand-up dudes I'm gonna make it so you can't stand up." Animal laughed before he tore into Lee with the bat. He struck him all over, paying special attention to his back and legs. After a while the pain got so intense that Lee couldn't do much but lie there and twitch.

"Please stop!" the woman sobbed from the bed.

Animal looked over his shoulder. "Don't talk," he told her. "It fucks with my concentration." Feeling creative Animal plucked a few hairpins from the woman's vanity table and knelt with them and a candle beside Lee's prone body. "You still with us?" Animal slapped Lee until he finally started to groan. "Good, I can't have you blacking out on me. If you're not awake it takes the fun out of what I'm about to do."

"Please . . ." Lee whispered, but Animal ignored him and continued his preparations. He held the hairpins over the candles until the tips turned red and began to smoke.

"Growing up I've always been fascinated by something my granny used to say." Animal placed his forearm across Lee's throat so he couldn't turn his head. "An eye for an eye." He slipped one of the hairpins into Lee's eye, drawing a high wail from the semiconscious man. When the hairpin cooled he heated another one and worked on the other eye. By the time he finished Lee was no longer conscious. Animal had feared that he'd accidentally killed him, but was pleased when he felt the faint pulse at the base of Lee's throat. Leaning in he whispered, "Remember, this is what happens when you cross Rico." When he was done drilling Rico's name into Lee's subconscious he walked over to the nightstand with his shoulder bag. From inside he produced a Pepsi can wrapped in a Ziploc bag. So as not to smudge the prints he used a pencil to remove the can from the bag and set it on the nightstand.

"Okay, you've done what you came to do so I can go, right?" the woman asked.

When Animal looked into her eyes he saw not one ounce of remorse for betraying her man. He had not met the woman before that day, but he hated her. Animal tapped his finger against his chin as if he was deep in thought. "It seems that we have ourselves quite a dilemma here, sis. Rico says that I'm supposed to kill everybody in here, but I ain't no monster. Let's make a wager, shall we?"

"A what?" the woman asked nervously.

"A wager. A bet," Animal explained.

He ripped off two strips of the duct tape, placing one across her nose and the other across her mouth. "If you can manage to get this tape off with your hands tied then you have your life." He laughed and left Lee and his whore for dead.

ANIMAL WAITED FOR FIFTEEN MINUTES before he placed an anonymous call to the police to report screams coming from the brownstone. By the time they got there the girl had suffocated, but Lee was still alive . . . barely. In addition to the gunshot wounds he had two broken legs and severe spinal damage. With his eyes burned out he would never be able to see again, but his mouth worked just

fine. During the ride to the hospital in the ambulance he just kept
babbling incoherently, but the three words they were able to make
out were *Rico* and *double cross*, which was all they needed to start
putting the pieces together.

Chapter 13

TIONNA FELT LIKE SHE WAS FLYING FIRST CLASS AS SHE reclined in the passenger seat of Gucci's Lincoln Navigator. The truck was snow-white with blood-red seats sitting on red 24s with the chrome lips. The dashboard was lit up like Christmas, but Gucci didn't know how to work much other than the air conditioner and CD player, though she looked damn good doing it. Animal had gotten the behemoth for her as a birthday gift, but she would only accept it if he agreed to let her take over the car note.

They coasted up Seventh Avenue, blasting an unmixed version of Animal's LP, setting off the car alarms of almost every vehicle they passed while people looked on in envy. Chicks hated and dudes clocked the two shorties in the big ride. When they reached the light on 136th and Seventh a red Beamer pulled up beside them with the music blasting. Both the driver and the passenger were cute and rocking heavy jewels, but Gucci wasn't moved.

"Damn, shorty, it's like that?" the driver of the Beamer asked.

Gucci looked down at him over her shades. "It ain't like nothing. I'm just trying to save me the headache and your people the trouble of having to visit you in the hospital."

The passenger of the Beamer gave her an agitated look. "What, you think we some chump ass niggaz or something?" He and his partner were getting quite a few dollars uptown and were known to bust their guns.

"No disrespect to you, fam. I'm quite sure you're about your business but I can't afford to take that risk. My man is a lil *extra*."

The two men in the Beamer shared a laugh before the driver responded to Gucci's statement. "Nigga got you scared to live, huh?"

At that Gucci chuckled. "Nah, just smart enough not to risk dying. The license plate says it all, boo. One." Gucci peeled through the green light.

The driver was about to follow, but his partner stopped him.

"Didn't you read the plate?" the passenger asked.

The driver looked at him like he was stupid. "Fuck does the plate have to do with that bitch styling on us just now?"

"It read ANIMALS," the passenger pointed out.

The driver let it roll around in his head for a minute before the light of recognition went off in his head. "As in *The* Animal?"

"You wanna find out?" the passenger replied.

The driver thought on it for a minute. "Nah, I'm good. Let's roll through Fourteenth and see who's on the stoop."

"DAMN, GUCCI, WHY YOU PULL off so fast?" Tionna asked, craning her neck to see if the Beamer was following. Tionna had seen them around some heavy dudes so she knew they were handling, but had never been introduced. Gucci pulled off before she even had a chance to exchange numbers and she wasn't feeling it.

"Because I love my life," Gucci said, never taking her eyes from the road.

"Sometimes I hate the fact that you're in a relationship. I miss having my road dawg running the streets with me," Tionna said sadly.

"We all gotta grow up sometime, T. When you were heavy with Duhan I let you shine, right?" Gucci reminded her.

"I don't mean it like that, G. I'd never try to hate on your happiness, but I ain't got nobody to hang with anymore." Tionna faked pouting.

"Stop it. You still got Tracy and Boots," Gucci said.

Tionna's face became serious. "Bitch, please. Boots is out here losing it fucking with them lifeless bitches from her hood and I don't even wanna get into Tracy. I'm hearing some real funny-style shit about her."

"Funny style like how?" Gucci inquired.

"Mommy, I didn't know Auntie Tracy was a comedian," little Duran said, rubbing the sleep from his eyes. He and Duhan had been so quiet that they'd forgotten the kids were in the car. Duran had slept through most of the conversation but Duhan was all ears. The cattish stare he was giving Tionna reminded her of the way his father used to look at her when he knew she was up to no good.

"Boy, you better learn to stay outta grown folks' business," Tionna warned little Duhan.

"But I didn't even say anything," he said.

"I don't give a damn, you were thinking it. Don't let me have to bust you in your little smart-ass mouth, understand?"

"Yes, Mommy," Duhan grumbled. It seemed like the older he got the more rebellious he seemed to become. Tionna had known his father since they were kids so she knew the signs when she saw them. It was the subtle changes in her kids that really made Tionna get on her job with getting them off Fortieth.

"Tionna, you need to leave them kids alone. How you gonna trip and you're the one talking in front of them?" Gucci said.

"She's got a point, Mom," Duhan added.

Tionna spun in her seat to face him. "You ain't too big to get that ass tapped, so keep playing if you want to Duhan."

Gucci swung a wide right on 140th and Seventh nearly clipping a parked Buick in the process. Even three buildings away she could feel the hate bouncing off her sunglasses. She welcomed the negativity and leaned even harder in the seat. Tionna peeped her game and dipped her seat back a little farther, watching the envious stares from over the dashboard. Figuring they had punished them enough Gucci pulled the car into a vacant spot beside where the Senate had their card table set up.

"Look-a-here, look-a-here," Cords sang as he watched Gucci and Tionna slide from the Navigator. He slicked his dried perm back while licking his lips hungrily.

Cords was wearing a browning yellow dress shirt under a worn overcoat, but you couldn't tell Jerry "Cords" Holloway that he wasn't the shit. At the height of his game he had a number one record on the charts and women throwing themselves at his feet on the nightly basis. Then doo-wop died and so did his star. Cords had cut a few solo records after the fact, but none lived up to the success of his group efforts. Now he was just a man living in the shadow of what he used to be.

"Good afternoon, gentlemen," Gucci said, grabbing Duran out of the backseat. Duhan chose to hop out on his own and took off up the block.

"Yes, it is a good afternoon and it just got better," Cords said slyly. He was giving Gucci his best seductive look, which got him a giggle.

"Old nigga, why don't you give it up? That girl don't want nothing to do with your washed-up ass," Harley ribbed him. As usual he had a Newport 100 dangling between his lips.

"Harley, why don't you quit being such a hater?" Cords shot back.

Harley and his partner Rayfield looked at each other comically. "You hear this nigga trying to sound hip?" Harley laughed.

"He sounds retarded," Rayfield capped. He was the ex-hustler who had squared up due to health issues. The doctor told him that the next dose of lead he took would be fatal, so Rayfield came in off the streets and became a square. He often reminisced on his heyday of getting money in Harlem, but had no desire to get back in the game. The game was the same, but the players and the rules were different. Sonny had seen man after man fall to the new fad of snitching for shorter sentences and it turned his stomach every time he thought of it.

"You know Cords thinks his ass is still the shit, even though he ain't put a record out in a hundred years," Sonny said in his southern drawl. He had been living in New York for years but still carried himself like a country boy dressed in overalls and work boots.

These four men were known as the Senate, unofficial keepers of the block and gatherers of information. Day after day, rain or shine, they congregated around their rickety old card table swapping stories and being nosey. They were as much a fixture on the block and the old peach tree and everyone knew them in one way or another.

"Hey, guys." Tionna stepped onto the curb and greeted them.

"Hi Tionna, ain't seen you in a minute." Harley smiled warmly.

"Yeah, I've been busy with work and school."

"Work?" Cords chuckled. "I never thought I'd see the day when you'd be working somebody's job."

"If that ain't the pot and you ain't had a gig since 'seventy-two." Harley checked him. "T," he addressed the young girl, "I think it's a good thing that you're working and going to school. We need more young ladies like you out there trying to better themselves instead of fucking their lives up." He cut his eyes at his niece Karen, who was standing across the street behind McDonald's with her boyfriend Craig. Both of them were barely into their twenties but looked to be much older because of their heavy drug use. Let Karen tell it they only used recreationally, but anybody with eyes could tell they were addicts.

"We gonna play cards or what?" Rayfield asked, trying to take his friend's mind off his wayward niece.

"Yeah, it was on me," Sonny spoke up.

"The hell it was, me and Ray won that last book!" Cords barked.

"Nigga, you crazier than a muthafucka, I trumped yo punk ass queen!" Harley added his two cents. It would most likely be hours before they got around to finishing the game, but this was the norm with the Senate.

"THESE MUTHAFUCKAS ARE TOO MUCH," Gucci said, stepping away from the table and taking a seat on the stoop.

"That's an understatement." Tionna joined her. Though she had spent most of her life ripping and running up and down that block she felt out of place being back there after trying her best to avoid it since she'd left for the final time. One Hundred Fortieth Street held twice as many bad memories for her as it did good ones.

"Yo, my lung is on the gate. Let's hit five-six and get some of that super weed," Gucci suggested.

"Gucci, you're bugging, that block is hot as hell. I don't even like to pass through that muthafucka let alone buy drugs. I think they got some green on the Ave."

"Please, I'd rather go without than to smoke that dirt they're trying to pass off as Haze."

"Oh, I forgot you're too good for regular weed now that you've joined the ranks of the rich and famous," Tionna teased her.

"It ain't even about that, T. I've been smoking that Cali bud with Animal for so long that regular weed doesn't even get me high anymore." Gucci snapped her fingers as an idea formed in her head. "I know who to call to get that fire." She pulled out her cell and punched in a number.

"Auntie Ronnie!" Duhan said and ran up the block toward the two approaching women.

"And Grandma!" Duran took off behind him.

As usual Ms. Ronnie had on something crazy. She was outfitted in a tight-fitting black dress and high-heeled green shoes with a silver blouse. She looked crazy, but you couldn't tell her that she wasn't the baddest chick on the streets. Close on her heels, fidgeting uncomfortably with her skirt, was Yvette, Tionna's mother.

Yvette looked cute in her gray skirt suit and flat shoes. Her braids needed to be done over, but Ms. Ronnie had whipped them into a nice style. From the look on her face you could see that she was beginning to get her weight back, but her eyes still had that sunken look about them. Tionna couldn't look her in the eyes for too long because she saw too much of herself in her mother.

It had been a minute since Tionna had seen Yvette other than in passing. Growing up they had a great relationship, but as the drugs got hold of Yvette and the streets got hold of Tionna they seemed to grow apart. On more than once occasion Yvette had cleaned herself up long enough to play the role of mother to Tionna, but it was never for more than a few months at a time. After a while life without Yvette in it seemed more normal than life with her and Tionna numbed herself to her mother's bullshit. Over the years Tionna learned to accept her mother's addiction for just what it was, a sickness, but the pain she carried with her since she was a little girl still lingered. She and Yvette had developed a decent relationship when she was older, but she had never been able to shake that feeling of abandonment that she had carried since being a child.

"Girl, look at you. Somebody's ass is in trouble at service tonight!" Gucci sang, admiring Yvette's outfit. She and Yvette had always been close, sometimes closer than she was to her own mother. Ronnie had always been good to Gucci, but she didn't have her finger on the pulse of the streets like Yvette did. There were things Gucci could talk to Yvette about that she wouldn't dare mention in front of Ronnie.

Yvette blushed. "Gucci, I'm going to church to worship not chase men."

"Speak for yourself." Ronnie fluffed her weave. "It's some fine, and employed, Negroes in the house of the Lord. If I got to be saved to combat being single then so be it, hallelujah!" Ronnie stomped her foot for emphasis.

"Mommy, you're going to hell," Gucci said, embarrassed.

Ronnie looked Gucci and Tionna up and down. "At least I'll have plenty of company."

Yvette broke the ice. "Hi, Tionna."

"Hey," Tionna said slightly above a whisper.

"Been a minute since I seen you, what's been going on?" Yvette asked warmly.

"Not much, trying to make it from day to day like everybody else."

"So how's them studies coming? I know working and going to school is kicking your ass."

Tionna look surprised. "How'd you know I started going to school too?"

Yvette winked. "You know ya mama always got her ear to the streets. You better keep your nose in those books and outta these streets. Some of those paralegal courses are no joke."

"And how would you know that?" Tionna asked.

"Because I got certified in 1984," Yvette shot back, shocking her daughter.

"I didn't know that," Tionna admitted.

"There's a lot you don't know about your mama, which is why you need to come by and visit her more often," Ronnie butted in.

"I know I should, but you know I be super busy with the kids," Tionna said. As if on cue Duhan and Duran came running up.

"Grandma, Grandma," they sang in unison, rushing Yvette for hugs.

"And have my two boys been behaving themselves?" Yvette rubbed the tops of their heads lovingly.

"Hell no, you know they stay in something." Tionna cut her eyes at her sons, who were staring at her mockingly from behind their grandmother.

Yvette smiled. "Tionna, you better leave my babies alone."

"Your babies need to stop working my nerves. They need to have their lil asses in church too," Tionna said.

"I ain't trying to be sitting up in no church clapping and praising." Duhan imitated someone catching the Holy Ghost.

"Boy, don't be poking fun at the Lord." Ronnie shook Duhan. "As a matter of fact it might do y'all little asses some good to come to service with us tonight."

"Ronnie, we can't just kidnap Tionna's kids, she might've had plans," Yvette said.

"Take em!" Tionna blurted out, drawing a disapproving look from Ronnie. "What I meant is that I don't have anything planned. Me and Gucci were just gonna ride around for a while in her new truck. Besides, I know Mommy wants to spend some time with them. Ain't that right, Grandma?" Tionna smiled devilishly at her mother.

"I think I've got a couple of hours to spare," Yvette teased. She was actually thrilled to be able to spend some time with her grandsons considering both she and Tionna were too busy running the streets to make sure they visited.

"Now that that's settled we'll be on our way." Gucci pulled Tionna by the arm.

"Hold on, heifer. We got one more piece of business to settle first." Ronnie held her hand out.

"What?" Gucci looked at the outstretched hand.

"Tramps, we doing y'all a favor by taking these lil demons into the house of the Lord in the first place. The least you could do is throw me some money for gas and a Dutch."

"You are so thirsty," Gucci said before handing her mother a twenty.

"I don't know why you acting like you ain't got it. I just saw Animal's video. My son-in-law looked good on that TV," Ronnie said.

"First of all, we ain't married yet. And second of all his money is his money and my money is mine," Gucci said with conviction.

Ronnie grabbed her by the shoulders and looked her in the eyes. "Who are you and what have you done with my baby?" she joked.

Gucci broke loose. "Get off me and stop acting crazy."

"I can't lie, I seen the video too," Yvette admitted with a smile. "You and that pretty lil thing fucka is gonna have some fine babies."

Gucci checked them. "See, now I know y'all are speeding. Me and Animal ain't having babies no time soon, if ever."

"Gucci, you better come on wit it I don't wanna be no old ass grandma. Catch me while I'm still young and fine." Ronnie gave Yvette a high-five.

Gucci rolled her eyes. "Anyway, if y'all are done trying to plan my future me and my girl are about to spin Harlem. Come on, T."

Tionna kissed her kids then hugged her mother. "Thank you, Mommy."

"You know that's what grandmothers are for. I ain't been around much, Tionna, but I'm gonna try and do better." Yvette kissed her on both cheeks.

"I know, Ma."

"Listen, before y'all two get all caught up in the bullshit you need to remember that service is over at ten, so have your asses where we can find you when we come back. Ain't nobody trying to be babysitting, ya hear?"

"Yes, Ms. Ronnie," Tionna agreed.

"Ma, would y'all go ahead already," Gucci said.

"Just remember what I said," Ronnie warned before they left to get in her car.

"Now that we've got that out of the way let's hit the liquor store and hit the bricks," Gucci said.

"Where should we go?"

Gucci tossed her keys in the air and caught them. "Anywhere we want but I suggest we head to the projects and get some bud."

"I ain't been to Douglass in a minute. I wonder what's going on down there."

Chapter 14

SCAR LAY BACK ON THE TATTERED BAR STOOL BLOWING
rings of smoke through his nose and watching them dissipate into
the air. Between his legs Boots knelt on a sofa cushion staring up at
him with weed-slanted eyes. In one hand she held a twenty-two-
ounce of St. Ides and in the other his cock.

"You know I don't be doing this kinda shit, right?" she asked,
taking a sip of her beer.

"I know, baby, and that's why I'm gonna make sure you're taken
care of," Scar assured her, gently running his fingers through her
sloppy weave.

Boots hesitated for a minute before she finally allowed him to
guide her head down to his waiting penis. When she closed her
mouth around the head he hissed like a rattlesnake that had just
been disturbed from an afternoon nap. She teased the rim of his
penis with the tip of her tongue, occasionally licking down the base
of his shaft.

"Damn, this shit is good," Scar panted. "Jay, come get some of
this."

"Nah, I'm good." Jay stood in the corner looking like he was about to audition for *American Idol*. He was a young boy, who wasn't much older than Solomon, but dying to prove to the older cats that he belonged.

"Let me find out this nigga is scared." Lloyd snickered from the kitchen table where he was weighing coke and baking soda that had to be cooked.

"Fuck you, man. I ain't scared," Jay said in a very unconvincing tone. He had never been with a woman, but he wouldn't tell them that and leave himself open for further ridicule from his new friends.

Scar continued to manipulate Boots's head and regarded Jay with a critical eye. "Shorty, I know you ain't in here talking scared business? You talked all that shit about getting money on the block and you scared to tag some pussy?" Scar shook his head. "Maybe you ain't ready to play with the big boys."

"Nah, I'm ready to get it with y'all," Jay said.

A tremor went through Scar as Boots took all of him in her throat and tickled his balls with her tongue. "If you're ready then you need to get over here and handle your business." Scar tossed Jay a condom.

Jay stood there staring at the condom and the huge brown ass hiked up in front of him. The prospect of mounting Boots made him so nervous that he felt his bowels shift. He looked from Scar's judgmental expression to the golden tunnel in front of him and knew what he had to do. With trembling hands Jay slipped the condom on and eased behind Boots with his pants around his ankles. When he entered her from behind the heat of her vagina radiated through him as if someone had trapped a little piece of the sun and stuck it up in her. As Jay stroked her, he fought to keep his cool, but it was a losing battle and he ended up blowing his wad in less than five minutes. Jay got up and duck-waddled to the kitchen.

Boots took Scar's dick from her mouth and looked over her

shoulder at Jay who was cleaning himself with a wet paper towel. "Damn, either my pussy is just that good or your little ass is a virgin."

"Bitch, I ain't no virgin," Jay said heatedly.

"Hey, watch your mouth," Scar told Jay. "And you stop fucking wit my little man and get back to work on my big man," he told Boots and shoved his cock back inside her mouth.

"Don't trip, Jay. Even the best of us come up short sometimes." Lloyd brushed the coke from his fingers. "Let a real nigga show you how to handle a bitch."

Lloyd was so thirsty and stupid that he didn't even bother with a condom as he shoved himself roughly inside Boots's box and tried to pulverize her intestines. Between his pounding her and Scar trying to gag her she was in a world of pain and neither of the men seemed to care. With a grunt Lloyd pulled out and squirted off all over Boots's ass, thighs, and calves while Scar continued to fuck her throat.

When she heard Scar's moans become louder she knew what was about to happen and tried to move her face, but he held her firmly in place by her hair. With a grunt Scar's dick exploded in a stream of cum that soaked Boots's face and hair.

"You dirty muthafucka," Boots cursed him as she wiped cum out of her eyes.

Scar chuckled. "My fault, Boots. I couldn't hold it." He dug into his pocket and peeled some bills from his bank roll and placed them on the table. "Good looking out. That was some of the meanest head that I ever had. No wonder Bernie ain't left your trifling ass yet."

"What the fuck ever, Scar." Boots picked the bills up and counted them. She looked up at Scar and frowned. "There's only a hundred dollars here."

"Yeah, you said you wanted a buck to get down," Scar replied.

"I meant a buck apiece, Scar!"

An expression of fake confusion crossed Scar's face. "Oh, I thought you meant a buck for the team. Don't worry, I got you the next time." He tossed Boots her jacket.

"I swear I don't know why I fuck wit y'all." Boots stormed toward the door.

"Because money talks and bullshit runs a marathon," Lloyd taunted her on the way out. Boots slammed the door so hard that the peephole cover was still spinning after she'd gone.

Jay laughed. "Shorty was mad as hell."

"Fuck that alcoholic bitch," Scar said, checking a text message that had just come through on his cell. "Yo, let's roll downstairs so I can meet this nigga Prince and give him this money." He led them into the hallway and locked the apartment behind them.

"So what're we getting into after we meet Prince?" Jay asked. After getting his first nut off he was ready to run a marathon.

"I'm not sure what I'm getting into, but your little ass is gonna play the building and work off that debt you owe. You ain't been on the job but a week or so and you're already fucking up money." Scar shook his head. "That ain't good, man."

"I know you're mad, Scar, but Shakes ran off with the package. It wasn't my fault," Jay tried to explain.

"It is your fault because you should know better than to leave a base head with your drugs unattended," Scar scolded him.

"Word up, Jay," Lloyd added.

"And you ain't no fucking better, because I told your stupid ass to hold him down," Scar barked on Lloyd. "I swear, y'all two muthafuckas is like the blind leading the blind."

The elevator finally came and when it opened Shakes was leaning against the wall in a half nod. When he noticed Scar and his crew standing there his eyes got as wide as saucers.

"Shit!" Shakes said, frantically searching for an escape but there was none.

"Shit is right, nigga." Scar snatched him by the front of his jacket and yanked him from the elevator. "I'm about to show you what we do to thieving ass crackheads."

SCAR AND HIS CREW HAD slapped Shakes around and forced him to the rooftop of 845 where they stripped him of all his clothes. He stood there as naked as the day he was born, freezing his ass off and trying to think of a fitting excuse to save his life. Normally Shakes was a wizard with words, but the cold stare Scar was giving him had him at a loss for words. He knew it was a bad idea to rob dealers in the hood where he laid his head, but the monkey that had been clawing at his back forced him to act irrationally and now his decision had come back to bite him on the ass. Shakes had fucked up . . . royally.

Scar just stared at him for a long time before finally breaking the silence. "You know you fucked up, right?"

"I know, man, but I'm sure we can work this out," Shakes said, rubbing his arms more out of nervousness than seeking warmth.

"Ain't shit to work out, homey. I don't knock you for taking advantage of this green ass nigga over here"—Scar motioned toward Jay—"because that's what base heads do, they get over on people. But the fact that you knew it was my work and still had the balls to take it is what doesn't sit right with me."

"C'mon, lil man, you know how I get sometimes when I'm sick," he told Jay. "Sometimes these drugs make you do stupid shit, but I ain't mean no harm. I knew you since you was a shorty." He tried to gain sympathy from Jay, but the boy turned away.

"Which only makes it worse," Scar said as he slowly began to circle Shakes's trembling form. "If you can rob somebody who you watched grow up then you is a piece of shit that needs to be dealt with. The only question is: what would make a fitting punishment for what you've done?"

"You know in some countries when you get caught stealing they cut off your hands," Lloyd said.

Scar smiled. "What you think, Shakes? Should I cut your hands off?"

Tears began to run down Shakes's ashy cheeks. "Scar, please don't do me like this. Let me work it off."

"These niggaz might've been stupid enough to put a package in your hands but I ain't. We're gonna have to think of something else." Scar scratched his chin and suddenly had a malicious idea. "I've got it, since you flew off with my package let's see if you can fly for real."

"Oh, hell nah." Shakes tried to run, but Lloyd grabbed him in a chokehold and dragged him back.

"Get his legs," Scar ordered Jay.

"Huh?" Jay asked, shocked.

"Don't huh me, muthafucka. I said get his legs!" Scar barked.

Jay reluctantly approached the squirming Shakes. Jay was saddened by the pitiful look in Shakes's eyes, but he was frightened by the look in Scar's. He and Lloyd carried Shakes to the roof's edge while Scar looked on like a proud father. Jay silently prayed that Scar would change his mind but the taunting look on his face said that it was already a done deal.

"You got any last words, Shakes?" Scar asked.

"Don't do this," Shakes pleaded, crying like a baby. Piss ran down his leg and onto Jay's hands. It was a disgusting feeling but he was too afraid to let go.

"Toss this muthafucka!" Scar ordered.

Shakes closed his eyes and said a prayer as Lloyd and Jay swayed him back and forth building momentum and let him go. "MAMA!!!!!!" Shakes screamed over and over as he soared. He had screamed his throat raw before he realized that he hadn't fallen twenty stories to his death, but only a few feet to his embarrassment. Instead of throwing him off the roof, they threw him on the ground of the rooftop.

"Shakes, do you really think that I would risk a murder charge over a piece of shit like you?" Scar asked.

"Thanks, man. Thank you." Shakes wiped his eyes. He was cold, scraped, and pissy but at least he was alive. "Scar, I promise I'll never do nothing that stupid again."

"I'm sure you won't." Scar picked up a large cinder block. "Hold him. Spread-eagle," he told Jay and Lloyd. This time they moved without hesitation and stretched Shakes's arms out.

"Hold on, you said you weren't gonna kill me." Shakes looked up nervously.

"I'm not, but I am going to teach you a lesson," Scar told him before he crushed Shake's right hand with the cinder block.

Chapter 15

MALIKA WAS DEAD ON HER FEET BY THE TIME SHE CAME up out of the train station on 103rd and Broadway. She had been out since that morning pounding the pavement and filling out job applications with anyone who said they were hiring. She'd been at it at least four days a week for the last month or so and still hadn't landed anything.

Having to take care of herself and Solomon, Malika was feeling the pinch of the dwindling economy and what little she got from Public Assistance wasn't doing much to ease it. The only reason she still bothered with them is because it kept her rent next to nothing and the food stamps kept her freezer stocked. Thinking of her stamps made her remember that she still hadn't gotten anything for dinner. As bad as her feet were hurting the supermarket on 104th seemed like it was miles away. She decided that it would be easier just to grab some sandwiches and call it a night so she headed for the corner deli.

As Malika was approaching the deli she spotted a familiar face unloading some crates off a delivery truck. She started to turn around and go the other way, but before she could move he had already spotted her. He was ruggedly handsome with chocolate skin and wavy black hair that blended nicely into his neat beard. His name was Teddy, and he was one of the guys who made the weekly deliveries to the local bodega and another impulsive decision Malika regretted.

She and Teddy had flirted heavily for about a month or so before they started officially seeing each other. Teddy was slightly older and therefore a bit more seasoned and had Malika open with things like Broadway plays and nice dinners. Being as inexperienced with life and men as she was, she found herself falling for Teddy and giving her body to him. When they had sex Teddy took her body to heights that Suede had never even come close to, and she lavished as much of her young pussy on him as he could stand. After a while Malika began noticing subtle hints that something was wrong, when it became harder to get him on the phone and his visits became less and less frequent. When she'd started hearing the rumors of him having another chick on the side she tried not to feed into them, but she couldn't deny the writing on the wall. Malika wasn't foolish enough to wait around until the other shoe dropped so she cut Teddy loose and changed her number. She still bumped into him from time to time when he was making deliveries but she always kept the conversations short and sweet.

"What's good, stranger?" he greeted her with a warm smile. Teddy had to have paid a grip for his teeth because they were perfect and white.

Malika shrugged shyly. "Same old, same old. I can't really complain," she said and reached for the door, but he stopped her by placing his hand against it.

"Damn, it's like that?"

"It ain't like nothing, Teddy. What are you talking about?"

"I'm talking about how you just left a nigga hanging with no real explanation. I thought we had something?"

"We did have something, but you didn't want it unless it was on your terms, remember?" she reminded him.

"It wasn't like that and you know it."

She folded her arms. "So, what was it like, Teddy? Come on, I'm a big girl so you ain't gotta lie to me. You wanted to do your thing so I gave you enough space to do it."

Teddy sighed. "Malika, I ain't gonna front like I wasn't doing my thing, but you know you were always special to me." He pulled her in for a hug.

Malika tried to push him away, but he held fast. "Don't start this shit, Teddy." She breathed deeply of his scent. His was a little musty from working all day, but she could smell the sweetness of baby powder lingering beneath.

"I ain't trying to start nothing. I'm trying to finish it. Why don't we go to dinner tonight and talk?"

For an instant Malika considered it, but quickly pushed the thought from her mind. "Nah, that ain't gonna work." She broke the embrace and walked into the store.

Malika greeted the old man sitting on a crate by the front door and shouted her order to the dude behind the counter. Teddy was in the back having the owner sign for the deliveries so she wanted to get her stuff and get out as quickly as possible. She could feel Teddy's eyes on her as she tried to decide between onion and garlic chips or barbecue, but she wouldn't give him or her loins the satisfaction of looking up at him. She didn't trust herself, especially her eyes. The eyes would always be the giveaway. Pushing the silliness out of her head she grabbed her snacks and headed to the counter where the young man was just finishing up her sandwiches. Living in the hood may have had its disadvantages, but there was nothing like a heated roast beef and cheddar from the corner store.

"Twenty-two seventy-five all together, Miss," he told her.

Malika peeked over her shoulder to make sure Teddy wasn't watching, before pulling her Quest card out of her purse and sliding it through the machine and punching in her pin. The young man at the counter looked down at the machine and after a few seconds frowned.

"It didn't go through. Maybe you try it again?" he suggested. Malika swiped her card again but it still didn't work. "I don't know," he said with a shrug.

"That's impossible, let me try it again," she said in a soft voice.

"You already tried it twice and it didn't work. You gotta either pay cash or I can't help you."

Malika fished around in her purse and only came up with six dollars. Even if she put all the snacks back she still wouldn't have enough to cover the sandwiches. She felt like melting into a puddle of shit because she had no idea what they were going to eat until she had a chance to find out what was going on with her card the next morning. She felt someone hovering over her and turned to see Teddy. The incident had gone from bad to worse.

"Here you go, ock." Teddy handed him a fifty. "Just give my change to the lady." He strode for the door.

Malika looked from the total to Teddy's parting back. Reluctantly she snatched the fifty-dollar bill and caught him at the door. "Nah, I'm good." She tried to hand Teddy the money back, but he refused.

"It's all good, Malika. Just get ya stuff," he told her.

"I ain't no charity case!" she blurted out and immediately regretted it when she saw the pity in his eyes. "What I mean is I don't like owing nobody nothing."

"And I don't like to be owed, which is why it was a gift," he replied and continued walking out of the store toward his truck.

Malika wanted to let it go, but her pride told her that there was more to say so she followed. "It's never nothing for something. Even doctors get paid to save lives. I really appreciate what you're doing, Teddy, but if you don't let me pay you back then it's gonna bother me."

Teddy thought on it for a minute. "Okay, if you insist on paying me back let's hook up tonight."

"I don't think that would be a good idea," she said.

"Stop acting like that, Malika. I ain't asking for no ass. I just wanna hang out for a while. I miss you, ma," he said sincerely.

Malika entertained it briefly then caught herself. "Nah, besides, I've got little man."

"If not tonight then maybe tomorrow, or the day after?" he pressed.

"Teddy . . ."

"Malika, you said yourself that if you owe me it's gonna bother you." He smirked.

Looking at that perfect white smile took Malika somewhere else. "I'll think about it and get back with you on it."

"A'ight, fair enough. So let me get ya number and . . ."

"Stop it, I said I'd call you."

"Okay, okay, I ain't gonna twist ya arm about it, sis." Teddy climbed into his truck and rolled the window down to conclude their conversation. "I know you said you can't make it out tonight, but I hope you change your mind. It's veal night at Carmine's and you know how you love that spinach."

"Whatever, Teddy." She smiled. "I'll call you."

"Make sure you do that, ma. Make sure you do that." Teddy winked and pulled the cube truck out into traffic.

Malika stood there until the truck had disappeared up Amsterdam Avenue and only when she was sure he could no longer see her did she smile. Teddy could be a snake like the rest of them, but he always made her feel special when they were together and that's what she dug the most about him. She doubted that she would take Teddy up on his invitation, but it still felt good for someone to offer. After getting her sandwiches she made her way to her side of the projects. She replayed the conversation over in her head, holding on to the small moment of elation. Her heart told her that nothing could ruin her day, but when she made it to the front of her building she knew that her heart had been wrong . . . again.

SOLOMON GOT OFF THE TRAIN at 103rd Street and Central Park West and bounced up the stairs to the avenue. When he emerged from the station he gave a cautious look around to make sure no one saw him for fear that they would tell his mother. She had only recently started allowing him to travel by his self via public transportation, and that was only after he promised to only take the bus to and from school. She was fearful of all the craziness that went on in the subway stations, but all the cool kids from his school took the train and he didn't want to be the square.

Along his walk up to Manhattan Avenue it seemed like Solomon must've waved hello to at least a dozen people before he finally crossed over into the projects. He and his mother were very well liked among most of the residents because they treated everyone with respect no matter what walk of life they came from. Malika had always instilled this trait in her son and she would go upside his head whenever he strayed from it. When he rounded the corner of his building he saw his friend Jay posted up in the building with Scar. Solomon pushed his pants down slightly off his ass and threw an extra bop in his walk as he approached.

"You see, lil nigga, that's the kinda shit you gotta do to niggaz to get them to stop playing with you. You gotta be heartless out here or these fools are gonna walk all over you," Scar was telling Jay when Solomon walked up.

"What up, y'all, what's going on?" Jay gave everyone in front of the building dap.

"Ain't nothing, just schooling ya lil man on the laws of the jungle," Scar said proudly. "What popping though?"

"Ain't nothing, just coming from school," Solomon said in his hip voice. "Where it's at?"

"Where it's at is upstairs for you, lil one. You know ya mom would trip if she caught you out here with the hard-legs," Prince told him. Prince was the elder statesman among the young homeys on the Columbus side of the projects. His crew supplied Scar and several other low-level players with the poison they slung in the hood. Prince was a quiet man who practiced love over war, but his name had been tied to a few bodies.

Solomon looked at the other heads that were snickering and addressed Prince. "Come on, man, why you acting like I'm doing something wrong by standing in front of the building I live in?"

Prince saw that Scar and the others were watching so he was mindful of his words so as not to bruise young Solomon's ego. "Sol, I ain't trying to stop your shine, but you know what we do out here, so the block is always hot. The police could roll up at any given moment and cart us all off to the slammer."

"Damn, Prince, all you talk about is getting knocked. I'd be more worried about clocking that bread than the police," Lloyd said boastfully.

"Which is why your simple ass is always getting pinched for something stupid," Prince shot back. "My nigga, with all the shit they're building up and down Columbus how long do you think they're gonna let you be out here reckless with it? It ain't like when Rio was out here making it jump. Nah, the block is twice as hot and the money is half as long."

"Well, if it's like that then how come you still hustle, Prince?" Solomon asked.

The question caught Prince off guard so he decided to answer it as honestly as he could. "Because it's all I know. Look, we get it how we live because these are the cards society dealt us, but you come from something else, Sol. Your mom makes sure you're taken care of so you ain't gotta be out here playing yourself."

"Man, that lil bit of money we get from Welfare ain't doing nothing. There's gonna come a time when I gotta step my game up, yo," Solomon said.

"Then you step ya game up by sticking to the plans your mother has laid out for you instead of trying to get caught up out here with these niggaz," Prince said a little more sharply than he'd intended to. Seeing the hurt in the boy's face he softened his tone. "Sol, I ain't trying to come down on you, I'm just trying to let you know what's popping."

"Shit, he live in the projects like the rest of us so I'm sure he know what it is out here. Let the lil nigga be." Scar sucked his teeth. He hated when Prince started preaching.

Prince shot him a dirty look then turned his attention back to Solomon. "My G, stay a kid for a while and leave this here business to the grown folks."

Malika stormed up. "Solomon, what are you doing hanging out in front of this building?"

"What up, Malika?" Scar greeted her with a smile.

"Not now, Scar," Malika said, never taking her eyes off her son who was standing there nervously. "Solomon, I asked you a question."

"I was just chilling for a minute, Ma," Solomon mumbled.

"Chilling my ass, I told you I don't want you hanging in front of this hot ass building!"

"Malika, he only been here for a second or two and I was just sending him upstairs." Prince tried to advocate for Solomon which turned her anger on him.

"Prince, you stick to telling the rest of these lil niggaz what to do and I'll handle my own child, thank you very much," Malika said with attitude. "And does your aunt know you're out here?" she turned to Jay.

Jay shrugged. "I don't think she'd too much care if she did."

Malika sighed. "Let's go, Solomon." She snatched the door open. As Solomon walked into the building he cut his eyes at her and was rewarded with a hard slap in the back of the head. "You roll them eyes at me again and I'll pluck them outta your damn head." She shoved him. Prince and the others could still hear Malika yelling at Solomon long after the heavy door had closed.

"Yo, she straight spazzed on that lil nigga." Scar laughed and gave his boys dap.

Prince looked at him and shook his head. "Scar, you ain't shit for laughing at son like that for his moms going in on him. I keep telling you that it's bad business to have these young boys out here with you."

Scar sucked his teeth. "Man, why you coming at me like I'm making these little dudes stand around out here? If they wanna play the block and get a lil change then that's on their parents to tell them different. Me, I'm trying to let everybody eat who wants to get a dollar."

"Which is why one of these chicks is either gonna call the police on you or cut your fucking throat over their kids," Prince warned.

"Well, I don't recall you kicking that save the children shit when you gave me my first bundle," Scar shot back.

"We're a different breed of cats, Scar. We took to the streets because we were starving and this was the only way to feed ourselves."

"And what do you think is going on with the next generation?" Scar challenged. "Damn near every broad in the hood is either on Welfare or Social Security, getting peanuts a month, so their kids look to the streets to get their ones up. If you wanna blame somebody then blame they mamas for lying on their asses collecting checks instead of trying to work somewhere."

Prince shook his head. "You just don't get it, do you?"

"Nope," Scar said smugly.

"Fuck it, I'm out." Prince gave Scar dap. Lloyd extended his hand but Prince looked at him as if he was stupid and walked off.

"Hating ass nigga," Lloyd said once Prince was out of earshot.

"Man, the only reason Prince is acting all concerned over that lil nigga is because he wants to smash Malika," Scar said scornfully.

"Shorty do got a phat ass. I had thought about cracking that myself," Lloyd said.

"Please, that uppity bitch ain't trying to give your project ass no pussy. For as long as she's been living here I don't know not one nigga that she let beat."

"Maybe she likes girls," Lloyd suggested.

"Maybe, but once she get a shot of this horse cock she gonna come back over to this side." Scar grabbed his crotch. He suddenly noticed Jay giving him a disturbing look. "What, you tight because I'm talking about ya man's moms?"

"Nah, I'm cool," Jay lied. He really wanted to bust Scar in his head for talking about Malika in such a way. Ever since he and Solomon had become friends Malika had treated him as if he was her own son. When his mother would go on her drug binges it was Malika who would take him in and make sure that he was fed and off the streets.

"Yeah, you're cool alright. Now get your cool ass to work and get that money up you let Shakes burn you for. I'm bout to shoot uptown right quick and get something to eat."

"Yeah, I'm hungry than a muthafucka too," Lloyd said.

"Then you better go up the block to Benny's and get a special because your ass is staying out here with Jay. I don't need no more fuckups."

"Why I gotta stay out here with him?" Lloyd complained.

"Because I said so. Now stop crying like a little bitch and let's get this money," Scar told him before walking off.

"DAMN, WHY THAT NIGGA ALWAYS so serious?" Jay asked once Scar had gone.

"Because this shit ain't a game out here, which is what we keep trying to teach silly lil muthafuckas like you," Lloyd snapped. "Dude, if you plan on living long enough to see a dollar you better wise up to what the fuck is good in the streets. The fact that your ass is out here pitching in front of the building says that you're behind the curve already."

"But you're out here with me, so where does that put you on the curve?" Jay shot back.

"You a real funny cat, you know that." Lloyd leaned against the fence and lit a cigarette. He took deep drags off his square, ignoring Jay, and scoped the scenery. When his eyes landed on the two figures creeping toward him he choked on the smoke. "Shit," he began coughing.

"You good?" Jay asked in a genuinely concerned voice.

"Hell no, nigga. Let's take a walk," Lloyd urged.

"Hold on, playboy, don't dip off just yet." Mookie's voice froze the fleeing dealers. He was dressed in a forest-green sweat suit and matching suede Filas. The flap of his dou-rag blew in the breeze like a flag. On his heels was his brutish partner Fish. Fish looked like a walking mailbox with a nappy afro and a lazy eye. He wasn't the sharpest knife in the drawer, but deadly in combat.

"Oh, shit, what up, Mookie? I didn't even see you," Lloyd lied.

"Umm hmm," Mookie said, sucking his teeth and eyeing Lloyd suspiciously. "What the business is, youngster?"

Lloyd chuckled nervously. "Nothing much, man. Just out here chilling, ya know?"

Fish snorted. "Looks like they out here *clocking* to me, Mook."

Mookie raised an eyebrow. "Is that right? Y'all lil niggaz out here getting rich? If that's the case then let me hold something."

Lloyd patted his pockets and shrugged. "I ain't got it."

Mookie's eyes narrowed to slits. "Y'all out here selling crack from sunup to sunup and you ain't got no bread? That shit sound kinda funny to me." Mookie sucked his teeth. "Real funny." Mookie looked from Jay, who looked like he would piss himself at any moment. "A'ight, so we gonna play a little game called all I find all I keep."

"Yo, Mookie, I ain't gonna have you out here patting me down like I'm still ten years old. This is a new day," Lloyd said defiantly.

Mookie raised his sweat shirt so that Lloyd could see the butt of the .45 he was carrying. "New day, same nigga. Now grab the muth-afucking ceiling before I disrespect you out here," Mookie ordered and began patting Lloyd down. From Lloyd's pocket he produced a wad of bills. "Umm hmmm, thought you ain't have it?"

"Come on, man, that's the pack money," Lloyd said.

"It was the pack money. Now it's a street tax for you lying to me." Mookie laughed at him. "Now where the stones at?"

"If Lloyd got the bread then this lil dude is probably holding the stones." Fish shoved Jay toward Mookie.

"What's up wit it?" Mookie asked Jay. Jay looked at the floor and said nothing. "Lil nigga, I'd hate to have to split them big ass lips of yours to prove a point. Cough up them rocks," Mookie barked. Keeping his eyes on the ground Jay handed over the Ziploc bag full of crack rocks he had stuffed in his pants. "What's this about a G-pack?" Mookie tested the weight. "Yeah, this is nice. Looks like we gonna have us a good old welcome home celebration tonight, Fish."

"Sho nuff, Mookie, sho nuff," Fish said happily.

"Mookie, you know we ain't gonna let this shit ride," Lloyd told him.

Mookie gave him a comical look. "Pussy, you ain't gonna bust a grape in a fruit fight. And if that scar-faced sissy you work for wants to make something of it, I'll be right in 865 smoking yo rocks." Mookie bopped off with Fish in tow. As an afterthought he turned to Jay. "Shorty, if I were you I'd find a better class of friends to hang out with because these niggaz are gonna fuck around and get you murdered. Find yourself another game because you damn sure ain't got the heart to play this one."

Lloyd continued staring up the block long after Mookie and Fish had disappeared into the building. If he'd had a gun he would've shot Mookie dead, but since he wasn't strapped all he could do was stand there and fume, wondering how he was going to break the news to Scar that they'd taken another loss.

Chapter 16

THE FIRST THING RICO NOTICED WHEN HE WALKED INTO his plush Queens home was the smell of pork chops frying. He had expected his wife Carmen to still be out shopping, but from the way the food smelled he wasn't mad at the fact that she'd come home early.

"Is that you, Ricardo?" Carmen called as she came out of the kitchen, wiping her hands on her apron. She was an olive-skinned woman who wore her thick black hair ratted. Her face was nearly as beautiful as it had been when Rico had met her fifteen years prior, but she was beginning to put on a little weight.

"Hey, baby." Rico kissed her on the cheek. "Did you miss me?"

"No, I had my young black lover to keep me warm inside while you were running the streets," she joked.

"You better watch that. If I ever caught you giving my stuff away I'd make the front page of every damn newspaper in the city." He slapped her on the ass playfully.

"Oh, stop doing that in front of company. How are you today, Changa?"

"Fine, thank you." Changa smiled.

"Will you be staying for dinner?"

"With the way that food smells how could I not stay?" He rubbed his stomach greedily.

"That's all you guys ever do is mooch off me," Rico kidded him. "Oh, I picked these up while we were out." Rico handed Carmen a plastic bag.

She peered inside and smiled at the healthy-looking steaks. "Good, I'm going to season them now so we can have them for breakfast in the morning with some eggs."

"Jesus, I wish I had someone at home to cook for me every day," Changa said.

"Changa, I keep telling you that you should come to church with us. There are some nice girls there that I'm sure would go for a successful guy like you."

"No, I don't think I'd be very welcomed in God's house. But thank you," Changa said politely.

"Nonsense." Carmen snapped him with the dish towel. "Everyone is welcomed in God's house, even the sinners." She looked from Changa to Rico and back again. "Now you go in the living room and make yourself comfortable, the food will be done shortly."

"Okay, Carmen." Changa headed toward the living room, glad to escape one of Carmen's campaigns to get him into church. He knew that she meant well, but it irritated him.

"Why don't you fix us a couple of drinks while you're out there, Changa? I need to speak with Carmen for a few," Rico called after his bodyguard and followed his wife into the kitchen.

"So, what brings you home so early today?" Carmen asked as she went about the task of washing the dishes.

"I couldn't wait to get home to my lady." He hugged her from behind and kissed her on the cheek.

"Ah, only if that were true." She reached around and patted Rico on the ass. "I'm glad you're home early though. Did you stop by the tailor so he could fit you for your tuxedo?"

"No, I'll take care of it though," Rico said.

"Rico, you've been telling me that since last Tuesday. Rosa's wedding is next week and you know she's depending on you to walk her down the isle," Carmen reminded him.

"Carmen, didn't I tell you I'd take care of it? I've been running around all day and I'm tired, so the last thing I want to have my wife bitching at me about is some wedding that we've got plenty of time to get ready for," Rico huffed.

"You watch your mouth in my house, Ricardo. Don't you go talking to me like I'm one of your hoodlum friends." Carmen waggled her finger at him. "That's your problem, you're always running the streets and neglecting your family!"

"Carmen, are you serious? You live in a big ass house and spend your holidays in Saks and I'm neglecting you." He shook his head. "If the streets don't drive me crazy you sure as hell will."

"So I'm gonna drive you crazy because I'm worried about you, Rico? You should be glad your wife cares about you because your flunkies sure don't. Every time you leave this house I hold my breath hoping that I don't get the call from Changa or one of the guys telling me that something has happened to you." She crossed herself.

"What's there to worry about, baby. I'm just a humble supermarket owner. Nobody wants to bother with me," he assured her.

Carmen dried her hands and turned to look at him seriously. "Rico, save that kind of talk for the police or one of the little girls who haven't known you since you were on the corner selling nickel bags. The streets are getting dangerous, Papi."

Rico sighed and rubbed his temples. "Carmen, I've been doing this for twice as long as we've been together, so please don't try and tell me about my business. I'm a boss, and nobody is gonna fuck with a boss."

"That may have been true ten years ago, but today the word *boss* is just that, a word when you are dealing with wild animals," she shot back. "Just today, I read in the paper how a thirteen-year-old killed a girl who was just walking along the street, and all for what, to prove that he had balls? Ricardo, I look into the eyes of these little boys who operate the streets and see only two things: despair and hate, and it makes me afraid for you because these are the broken souls you deal with day in and day out." Carmen took his hand. "You are the man of this house and as your wife I'm going to support you as I always have, but as your wife I have to ask that you at least think about what I'm saying to you."

The look in his wife's eyes tugged at Rico's heart strings. Carmen had been his voice of reason throughout his whole climb of the ladder to hood success so he valued her wisdom, but she didn't understand. Rico had enough money to step away and still live a decent life, but when you were that deep in it ceased to be about the money, and became about the addiction to the lifestyle. To put an end to the conversation Rico simply kissed her cheek and said, "I will."

CHANGA WAS JUST FINISHING THEIR drinks when Rico came into the living room. "Yo, the Knicks are playing the Heat." Changa pointed at the big screen television.

Rico sank into his recliner. "Fuck the Knicks."

Changa came from around the bar and handed Rico a glass of cognac, then took a seat on the couch to the left of him. "I decided not to hit you with a chaser, because for you to say fuck the Knicks your day must've just taken a turn for the worse."

"Nah, I'm good." Rico took a light sip of his drink. "Just growing pains of marriage."

"And that's just why I'm never getting married." Changa laughed.

The melodic doorbell sang through the house, irritating Rico further. He hated that damn door chime, but Carmen loved it so he dealt. "Baby, can you get that!" he called down the hall. "Probably one of her fucking friends," he told Changa. "I swear these neighborhood broads come over here at least three times a week to eat my food, be nosey, and drink up my booze."

"Maybe you should put them to work," Changa joked. He and Rico laughed at it for a short second, but the smirks turned to looks of concern when they heard raised voices in the foyer.

"You can't just come into my house like that!" Carmen shouted loud enough for Rico and Changa to hear her and take action.

In a flash Changa was on his feet with his gun drawn, moving toward the foyer. He disappeared into the hall and within seconds he was backpedaling into the living room with his hands in the air and the gun hanging harmlessly around his thumb. Moving with him into the living room, with his gun pointed between Changa's eyes, was Detective Brown. Following shortly behind him was Detective Alvarez, with half a dozen blue uniforms behind him.

"Looks like somebody got caught with his hand in the cookie jar," Brown said, carefully disarming Changa.

"I've got a license," Changa said.

"Muthafucka I'd bet a week's pay that you ain't even got a green card, let alone a license to carry a firearm in an English-speaking country." Alvarez laughed at him. "Grab the bar before I let these eager public servants jump off in your ass. You too, Ricky," he told Rico.

"That's Rico," he corrected him.

"It's gonna be Rachel where you're going." Brown shoved Rico against the bar next to Changa and began patting him down.

"You can't just barge in here like this, where's your warrant?" Carmen wanted to know.

Brown paused from his frisking. "We don't need a warrant when in pursuit of a suspect that's fled into a domicile."

"That's bullshit, nobody has run in here," Rico told him.

"Sure we did, two roaches stole a bread crumb from the local bakery and ran under your door," Brown said sarcastically. He shoved a piece of paper in Rico's face. "This here says that we've come to snag your asses for murder."

"Murder? You've got to be out of your fucking mind!" Rico told the detectives.

"The hell we are." Alvarez stepped forward. "There's a lady dead and a crippled guy singing soprano about how you orchestrated the whole thing."

Rico laughed. "It's his word against mine, it'll never stick."

"Maybe not to you, but he's fucked." Alvarez pointed at Changa. "We've got his prints at the scene."

Rico glared at Changa and told him without words what would come of him bringing heat to not only Rico's organization but his home.

Changa's jaw dropped. "You're trying to set me up." He tried to rush Alvarez but the officers tackled him to the ground and cuffed him.

"The both of you know that I'm too long in the tooth to walk into something this fucking idiotic." Rico allowed himself to be cuffed.

"Maybe, maybe not. We'll get it all sorted out at the station." Detective Brown shoved Rico toward the door.

"Carmen," Rico called over his shoulder, "call the lawyer and tell him what went down." Rico and Changa were escorted out the door. Changa continued to profess his ignorance to the murder, but Detectives Brown and Alvarez didn't come for you unless they were sure. Everybody in the hood knew this about the cops. Rico had no idea what was going on, but what he did know was that before it was all said and done heads would roll.

Chapter 17

GUCCI FELT WHAT COULD ONLY BE DESCRIBED AS *EXHILA-ration* as she pushed through Harlem in her shiny new toy, with her best friend riding shotgun. Animal denied her nothing and she lived like a queen when she was in Texas, but it failed in comparison to just being able to toll through her old haunts uptown. The spirit of Harlem's call was so powerful that most of its natives always found reasons to come back to take a dip in the Fountain of Swag, and she was no exception.

"Bitch, are you smoking or sightseeing?" Tionna brought her back to the here and now.

"Here you hype." Gucci flicked the ash and handed the blunt to Tionna. "And watch my seats."

"Ain't nobody gonna fuck up ya lil ride so be easy," Tionna said.

"Damn, I miss Harlem!" Gucci exclaimed as she looked out her window at the passing sights.

"I don't know why because ain't shit going on now that wasn't going on when you left." Tionna dumped the ashes out the window and handed the blunt back to Gucci.

"It ain't just about the people and what they're doing, it's about

Harlem. Tell me you don't get a chill every time you pass 110th Street, or hit Fifty-fifth on a hot summer day?"

"Can't say that I do," Tionna said flatly.

Gucci shook her head. "Then maybe you need to try getting out of New York once in a while so you can see what I'm talking about."

"Please, I got two bad-ass kids, no man, and between my job and school, no life. Where the fuck am I going?"

"Come down to Texas, it ain't like we've never invited you," Gucci reminded her.

"And what do you expect me to do with those two little demons of mine?"

"Bring them with you, T. We got a big ass backyard for them to run around in to burn off some of that pinned up energy. Stop acting like we ain't family and pack your shit."

Tionna thought on it for a minute. "Nah, I don't think so, Gucci. You know I miss my sister from another mister, but I don't wanna cramp your style."

"What do you mean by that?"

"I'm saying, you're down there doing you with your boo. I don't wanna be no third wheel."

"Tionna, if you're a third wheel then we'll be a tricycle. I don't give a fuck who I'm with, you will always be welcome. Besides, I could use the company. I'm always in New York because this nigga Animal is always running around doing this and that leaving a bitch on stuck. Every time you turn around him and that damn Soda gotta make a move."

"Who, the little cat with the big chain? Homebody can get it!" Tionna admitted.

"Yeah, right between the eyes. All he does is smoke weed, sip syrup, and chase bitches. I keep telling Animal that if I catch him dirty I'm gonna leave him, right after I body his ass."

Tionna sucked her teeth. "Gucci, you're tripping. Animal's nose is so open for you that I couldn't even see him looking at another broad."

"Yeah a'ight, that's because you haven't had to live through these shameless ass groupies that follow these rappers around like shadows. I had to bust this bitch in the mouth one day when we were in the mall."

"Say word?"

"Word to everything, T. Ol' girl was pressing my man like she didn't even see me standing there and when I tried to brush her off politely she had the nerve to roll her eyes."

"No, she didn't."

"Yes, she did, and I ran straight up in her mouth."

"Harlem." Tionna gave Gucci a high-five. "Shit, I didn't know it was like that."

"Yeah, and it's gonna get worse when the album drops," Gucci said in a defeated tone.

For the first time in a long time Tionna saw what could've passed for doubt on Gucci's face. "You think Animal might jump out the window?"

Gucci thought on it for a while. She had replayed the question to herself over and over in her head, but hearing someone add voice to it made it seem slightly realer. "I'd like to think not, T, but I guess only time will tell." Gucci dipped a little lower in her seat and manipulated the wheel with one hand, while she hit the blunt with the other. She hit a deep pothole and ended up getting ashes on herself.

"You might wanna keep your eyes on the road, sis."

"You know I'm an expert driver, T, which is more than I can say for your ass. Yo, do you remember when that trick-ass nigga Happy let you hold his Jeep and you got drunk and crashed it?" Gucci slapped the steering wheel laughing.

"I don't know what you think is so funny about it seeing how it was you who gassed me to drink that cheap ass vodka. That shit is right up there with White Star Moet on my DO NOT DRINK list."

"I thought Happy was gonna beat your ass for crashing his whip, but he was more concerned about the cut on your forehead than the forty grand he lost on the car. And to top it off, when he came to pick us up from the hospital you threw up in his Lincoln. I heard that the suede interior stunk so bad that he had to rip everything out. Speaking of Happy, what's up with that fool? I haven't seen him since that ass whipping he took at Mochas."

"He's still around doing shit to people and getting away with it. His ass has started hanging around with that dude Levi," Tionna informed her.

"Levi Brown?" Gucci shook her head. "As my grandma used to say, that is one of God's surliest creatures."

"You ain't never lied, Gucci. You ever notice how he looks at you when you're walking past him? It's like he can see through your clothes."

Gucci rubbed her arm. "Stop, you're giving me the creeps, T. So is Happy still trying to see how far he can shove his head up your ass?"

"You know that. I had to change my number three times messing with his clingy ass." Tionna huffed.

"Three times, why so many?"

"Because somehow he was able to get my number every time I changed it and it started getting on my fucking nerves. The first time he got it was off the Internet and the second time that dizzy bitch Boots gave it to him on her funny shit. When I checked her about it she tried to act like she didn't know me and Happy wasn't rocking no more. That ho just wanted to cause a situation."

"Boots's ass is so trifling," Gucci said.

"Like we don't all know that. Did you know that she still won't come clean about letting Happy pop her head off."

Gucci nearly sideswiped a parked car when she heard that. "She fucked Happy?"

"You didn't know? I always suspected she was playing foul because of she used to try and be up under him all the time, but my lil home girl from 112th confirmed it. She peeped Boots coming outta Happy's building on some five in the morning shit. I started to run up in her trap over the shit, but I decided to be the bigger woman and just asked her if she was fucking him."

"Of course she denied it," Gucci said.

"You know she did. Boots looked into my face and went into the whole script of how we're all like sisters and she'd never do that to me, but I know Boots's style. I didn't press her about it, I just let it be but best believe that I feed her with a long-handled spoon, ol' washed-up ass!"

Gucci raised an eyebrow. "Let me find out you had more feelings for Happy than you let on."

"Fuck Happy. He wasn't nothing but an ATM that I let smell my pussy from time to time when I needed a few dollars. I could care less that she fucked Happy, but the fact that I'm supposed to be her girl and she lied when I asked her is what got me tight."

"That's ya home girl," Gucci said sarcastically.

"Like you don't fuck wit her too."

"Only because *you* do, Tionna. I been told you that broke bitch wasn't to be trusted, but you stayed fucking with her. When Tracy wanted to pound her out for stealing that half a bottle of perfume out of her crib, you were the first one to get in between them."

"Gucci, you and I both know that Tracy would've slaughtered Boots if I had let it go down. Shit, it would've been a closed casket funeral."

"Tracy is a beast when it comes to combat," Gucci agreed. "What's up with her anyway? It seems like every time I try to call her she's either rushing to get off the phone or sending me to the voice mail."

Tionna's face suddenly became very serious. "I see her from time to time, but we don't really hang no more. The streets are saying some real crazy shit about Tracy and her boo, Remo."

"Like what?"

"Like that habit got them on some Bonnie and Clyde shit for a blast. I didn't really pay the talk no mind at first, but when I saw her for myself I had to take a step back and ask what was good. I was coming outta Pathmark late one night and I spotted her on Lex by the train station looking twenty pounds lighter and dressed real suspect. She had on some bullshit plastic cats suit that was split down to the crotch under a dusty black trench coat. Yo, I almost didn't recognize our bitch out there."

"Did you call her on it?" Gucci asked.

"You know I did, but she tried to play it like it was nothing. She said her and Remo had just come from the club and she was trying to be sexy for him, meanwhile this nigga is leaning against the chicken spot halfway in a nod. Remo looked like a decent gust of wind would've blown his ass over."

"Now that I can believe. Animal told me that Don B. fired him, but wouldn't say why. Now you know when your own nephew fires you, your ass ain't 'bout shit!" Gucci said.

"As if that slimy muthafucka Don B. is any better," Tionna said harshly.

"Damn, I can't believe Tracy is out here caught up in that shit and we're riding around having a good time," Gucci said in a guilty tone. "Maybe we should try to get her into some type of treatment program?"

"Been there done that." Tionna waved her off. "I tried to hint around about it a time or two and she just tried to downplay it talking about she's just having fun with it."

"And you believed it, seeing that she was twisted?" Gucci asked.

"What was I supposed to do? Drag her to Phoenix House kicking and screaming? Gucci, you know just as well as I do that an addict has to wanna get clean before they actually do. Look how long we've been trying to get my mother straight and all she keeps doing is fucking up."

"Tionna, you know you're wrong for that," Gucci told her.

"The truth is the light, baby girl. Yvette has been chasing that dragon since we were kids."

"But she's clean now, and has been for a while, Tionna."

"A temporary arrangement. You mark my words, as soon as we let our guards down that trick will be back at it," Tionna said with a roll of her eyes.

Gucci abruptly pulled over and threw her hazards on. She removed her shades and gave Tionna a serious look. "Tionna, we've been friends for longer than I can remember so I ain't gonna pull no punches, I'm just gonna come out and say it. I love you, but sometimes you can be a miserable bitch."

"Me?" Tionna asked in disbelief.

"Yes, *you*. Look, T, I know Yvette has done some fucked-up shit over the years, but she's never stopped trying to be a mother to you. Even when she was smoking she never let you see her high or getting high."

"So because she tried to keep it a secret that makes it okay?"

"Of course I'm not saying that, but what I am saying is that Yvette was a better mother to you on drugs than a lot of mothers are to their kids sober. I can't ever remember her not making sure you had stuff on Christmases and birthdays. Shit, still to this day she bakes you a cake every year even though your fat ass doesn't need it," Gucci joked and Tionna flipped her off. "But in all seriousness, Tionna, Yvette is doing good. The road to sobriety is a long and hard one, but I think with some well-placed support she can make it." Gucci patted Tionna's leg tenderly.

When Tionna looked up at Gucci her eyes were misty. "We'll see."

"Stubborn ass." Gucci laughed and pulled back into traffic. As they sped down through Harlem Tionna did a double take at a luxury car that had stopped at what looked like a dice game. Her eyes zeroed in at a familiar profile but before she could make a positive ID of the dude in the red, Gucci bent the corner and took them out of sight.

Chapter 18

"FIVE HUNDRED IN THE BANK, ALL MONEY DOWN IS A BET and everything is good."

Bruiser shook the dice in his meaty palm. He was a hard-faced man who everyone on the block knew as a career criminal and general troublemaker. He was surrounded by a few of his henchmen who were watching the dice game as well as the players. When dealing with them it wasn't unheard of for an innocent dice game to turn into a stickup.

"Shoot fifty," one onlooker called.

"A hundred over here."

"Twenty he four or better!" someone offered a side bet.

Bruiser tossed the dice against the broken steps of the stoop and watched them spin. Two of the dice skipped and came up showing fives while the third bounced off the foot of a kid who was watching the game and landed on a one. The men who had their money down reached to collect their winnings but Bruiser stopped them.

"Hold on, I gotta roll that again," Bruiser said, picking the dice back up.

"What you talking about, son? You aced," a kid wearing a black Champion hoodie voiced.

"Ace my ass. That shit hit son's foot and he ain't got no money in it so the roll was no good." Bruiser began shaking the dice again.

The kid in the hoodie frowned. "Nah, son, we ain't even gonna have all that." He reached for the money and Bruiser stopped him midreach.

"My dude, if you touch that bread then me and you are gonna have an issue out here." Bruiser's eyes had a playful glint to them, like a kid anticipating a schoolyard fight.

The dice got so quiet that you could hear a pin drop as everyone looked on wondering what was going to come of the situation. The kid with the hoodie knew Bruiser and how he gave it up, but he had already laid the gauntlet and couldn't afford to lose face. With a gulp, he closed his hand around the crumpled bills and the shit hit the fan. Bruiser's strike was so swift that even the people watching barely saw him swing. The kid wearing the hoodie rocked once on his heels before falling sideways and smacking his face against the curb. He looked like a dead roach lying there with his feet and legs curled in the air.

"Somebody drag this fool outta here so we can finish the game," Bruiser said, shaking the dice. "Now like I was saying, five hundred in the bank."

"I got it stopped!" a voice called from somewhere behind the crowd of onlookers. The crowd parted like the Red Sea as several men stalked toward the dice game in a wave of diamonds and braids. Dangling from the leader's neck was a thick link chain with more diamonds than necessary in the cross hanging on the end of it. His wrist looked like it had been dipped in rock candy as he adjusted the bracelet wrapped around it. His ever-present blacked-out sunglasses sat lazily on the bridge of his nose, while red-rimmed eyes peered over them at the players of the game, soaking in Bruiser in particular.

"Oh, shit, it's Don B.!" someone shouted. The knockout and dice game was forgotten as everyone flocked to the self-proclaimed Don of Harlem.

"Well, well, if it ain't the hometown hero," Bruiser said with a sneer. "What you doing back in the hood? Slumming?"

"I see you still got jokes, lil fella," Don B. said sarcastically. "You know I gotta stay among my people, because without them I'm nothing." He laughed sarcastically and adjusted his chain.

Bruiser looked him up and down. "I hear that hot shit. A *real* man of the people, huh?"

"You know how the Don does it."

"That's funny because all of your so-called people were at Born and his mother's funeral except you. What up with that?" Bruiser put Don B. on blast.

Born had been Don B.'s right-hand man and original partner in Big Dawg Entertainment, before catching a lengthy prison sentence. When Born came home Don B. had offered him a position in the organization, but Born wanted to be a boss and tried to muscle his onetime best friend. Not long after they'd had a very public falling out, Born and his mother were gunned down on their way to church one Sunday morning. Don B. was never formally accused of playing a part in the murder, but the streets whispered that the order had come from his lips.

Don B. smiled, but there was no warmth in it. "Unfortunately I was unable to make it because I was always on business, but if you keep your ears to the streets like most niggaz at your level do, then I'm sure you heard that I not only paid for the services but I turned over a percentage of the company to his son. Lil nigga is a millionaire and he's only ten, smell me?"

"Ya new video is so fly, Don B." A big-breasted girl inched closer to the rapper. Her eyes told the whole story without her having to say a word.

"You know how we do it on my side, baby, it's all about eye candy." He did a little spin so she could check his gear.

"Candy? You rappers niggaz kill me wit ya silly shit." Bruiser sucked his teeth and went back to shaking the dice. "What's good, B., ain't nobody shooting no more? I know y'all niggaz ain't scared of this lil five hundred?" Bruiser addressed the crowd but most of them were now focused on Don B.

"I said I had it stopped, what happened?" Don B. asked.

"No bet to you, Don," Bruiser said.

"What, my money ain't no good?" Don B. pulled out a large bankroll and began fanning through the bills in front of Bruiser. The look in Bruiser's eyes was a murderous one, but Don B. knew that he wasn't stupid enough to try him with Devil hovering so close. Bruiser was a tough guy, but Devil was a seasoned killer.

"Nah, I ain't trying to take your money, Don. I hear niggaz who eat outta your hand come up dead?" Bruiser said slyly.

Devil had finally tired of Bruiser's mouth and stepped forward but Don B. waved him back. "Yeah, I lost a few homeys but they lived like kings when they were here," Don B. shot back. "Now, you gonna keep running ya yap or throw them bones? Imma take that bum-ass weed money you stunting with a trick it off at the strip club." This drew snickers from everybody who was watching.

Bruiser's ego finally got the best of him. "Fuck it, *superstar*, I'll take ya bet." He threw the dice and they showed two threes and a four. "Four is always a fighter."

Don B. snatched the dice in his jeweled hand and began to shake them. "Blow on these for me, love." Don B. held the dice out to the big-breasted girl.

"I'll blow on anything you need me to," she said slyly before blowing on the dice.

Don B. did a funny two-step move and threw the dice underhanded against the stoop. When the dice finally stopped spinning they all came up with the same number, five. "Trips, nigga, you know how them fives ride." Don B. snatched up the money.

Bruiser stared angrily at Don B. with murder mounting in his heart. He was so mad that his brown face began to turn a ruddy plum color and thoughts of murdering the smug rapper flooded his mind. "You got that," Bruiser said barely above a whisper.

"Oh, you don't wanna play no more? I got plenty more cake to lose, my G. That change we just shot for ain't 'bout nothing." Don B. shook the dice in a taunting manner.

"Nah, I'm good," Bruiser said and motioned to his crew that it was time to go.

"Good?" Don B. laughed. "You looking kinda sour to me, kid. Nigga, I know you sick because you came out here and gambled away your re-up. Maybe you should've listened to Hov's verse about fraudulent Willie's, son!"

"Chill, you won so leave it alone," Devil whispered, but Don B. ignored him. He had an audience so he intended to give them a show.

"Bruiser, you know you my nigga so stop acting like that," Don B. said sarcastically. "Check it out"—Don B. peeled off a hundred dollars and dropped it on the ground—"take that so you can get back in the game. It ain't about me needing your money, it's more about the thrill of seeing you lose it."

"Talk that shit, gangsta. Imma see you on the come around," Bruiser promised.

"Whatever, ya bum ass nigga. Just remember that a pup ain't never gonna be able to fuck with a dawg!" Don B. called after him. "This nigga Bruiser just blew my fucking high, I'm going to the store to get a Dutch."

"I'll walk with you, Don. I got something I need to holla at you about anyway," the big-breasted groupie said suggestively.

Don B. pushed his sunglasses down and gave her the once-over. "That might not be a bad idea. Shorty, hold the bank down for me." Don B. passed the money and dice off to a teenaged boy. "Devil, watch my bread and make sure these niggaz don't get light-fingered."

Don B. walked off with the girl.

• • •

FIFTEEN MINUTES LATER DON B. was sitting in the back of his Escalade with the girl working at his zipper. The girl finally managed to retrieve his thick penis and marveled at the curved muscle. "Damn, baby." She stroked him to an erection.

"You know we do everything big on my side," he told her, before steering her head toward his lap. When the tip of her tongue touched the head of his penis it was like an electrical charge went through his body. She worked the rim of his dick with just her tongue for a few seconds before sliding him into the back of her mouth and flexing her throat muscles around the head of his penis. The two of them exchanged moans as she deep-throated him, while he jammed his fingers in and out of her tight vagina. The girl's juices dripped down Don B.'s hand and wrists as he explored her. It seemed like the more feverishly he jammed his fingers into her, the more vigorously she sucked him. Just when Don B. felt himself about to cum she stopped and squeezed the head of his dick, holding him back from ejaculating.

When Don B. felt like he was about to black out he snatched her head away and took a minute to breathe. "Damn, girl, you've got the meanest shot of head I've ever had!"

"If you think these lips are the bomb"—she ran her finger across her mouth—"wait until you taste these lips." She slid her hand into her pants and began fingering herself. The girl scooted back on the last row of the SUV and wiggled out of her jeans and panties, exposing her hairy and unkempt pussy. One after the other she took turns sliding her fingers into herself and then licking them. "Boy, stop playing and come get this pussy."

Don B. almost killed himself when he tripped over his jeans trying to get to the girl. His exposed dick was so hard that it dripped pre-cum on his leather seats when he crawled between her legs. Balancing himself with one arm he dug around in his pocket for a box of condoms but came up empty. "Damn."

"What's the matter, baby, you don't want none of this honey?" she breathed in his ear, reaching between her legs and jerking Don B.'s dick.

"I ain't got no jimmys, ma," he said defeated.

The girl bit her lip and thought on it for a minute. "Come on, take it anyway. You rich so I know you ain't got nothing. Just don't cum inside me, okay?"

Don B. looked down at her and smiled his devilish smile. "If you like it then I love it," he said before plunging into her sweetness, and how sweet it was. Missionary was cool, but the Don needed to be in control so he flipped her over and hit it from the back. They started out at slow measured strokes, but it wasn't long before Don B. lost himself and tore off into it. Wrapping his arms around her waist he lifted the girl partially off the seat and began to thrust deeply into her. Spewing obscenities, he exploded inside the girl and fell back against the opposite door.

Don B. lay on his back on the opposite end of the row, panting and starting at the girl across the truck, who had soaked her inner thighs as well as the seat beneath her with both their juices. Lying there playing with her dripping pussy she didn't seem too upset about Don B. cumming inside her, not that he would give a shit anyhow. Just like he could pay to have the sex washed from his seat he could pay to have her washed from his life if she forgot her position. Don B. laughed to himself as he reached for the pack of cigarettes he'd dropped on the floor of the truck and it was then he saw someone standing outside his window.

It only took a split second for Don B.'s street instincts to kick in and propel him to the opposite door, and it took less time before the bullet shattered the window and pierced his shoulder. Don B.'s shoulder instantly went numb, and left him to fumble with the other door with one hand. He had almost undone the lock when another shooter came to that side of the truck and joined in the shooting, trapping Don B. in the middle. He lunged for the big-breasted girl, who was now screaming, and pulled her on top of him as he fell to the floor of the SUV. Bullets ripped through the girl's helpless body as Don B. held her there like a human shield.

Don B. stayed huddled beneath the corpse of the girl, bleeding like a stuck pig and begging God to spare his life long after the shooting had stopped. He could hear people outside the truck screaming, and sirens in the distance, but couldn't will himself to move from beneath the bullet-ridden corpse. Above his head the backseat door was snatched open and a pair of hands tugged at him. Don B. fought with everything he had, but it was useless with him just having one arm available. As Don B. lay on the street corner in front of the bodega he decided that if he was going to die, he would look into the eyes of his killers before he did so. When he opened his eyes he realized that it wasn't the shooters who had pulled him from the truck, but the police.

"Sir, are you hurt?" The officer was kneeling over him checking his wounds. The bullet appeared to have gone clean through, but he had several cuts and bruises on his face and lower body from the glass. He was laid out with his pants around his ankles but the embarrassment was a small price to pay for his life.

"They shot the Don!" someone shouted.

"I didn't know he was holding like that," one girl said of his exposed privates.

"Is he dead?"

Don B. heard it all, but none of it moved him. All he could do was stare at the girl he had blazed not two minutes prior. Gone was the cute young dime who had pressed him at the dice game, replaced by a mess of flesh, blood, and stolen dreams. Bullet holes riddled her back, with one even making it through the back of her skull and busting one of her eyes, the other eye stared accusingly at Don B. He knew that if he lived to be a thousand he would never forget the look on the girl's face.

"Let me through! I'm the bodyguard!"

Devil shoved his way through the crowd teary eyed. It was his job to protect Don B. and he'd allowed his charge to get caught up. If Don B. had gotten hurt Devil would've never been able to face his uncle, Remo.

"Don, speak to me, tell me what happened?" He knelt over the shocked rapper.

Don B. turned and looked at him through his broken sunglasses. There was a look of fear in his eyes that Devil had never seen. Don B. had to swallow before he could build up enough moisture in his mouth to talk.

"Yo, these niggaz tried to take my head."

Chapter 19

"YEAH, THEY TRIED TO TAKE MY HEAD. THESE PUSSY NIG-gaz tried to take my head," Animal rapped lazily into the microphone. The small booth was so full of smoke that all you could really make out of him was the ruby flooded Muppet bust hanging from his chain. He and the character bore a striking resemblance. He was so at peace wrapped in the comfort of his music that the stress of Lee's murder, and all the other bodies that would drop before it was all said and done, bled off into nothingness leaving behind only him and the music.

Manning the control board was Chip, one-third of the group The Left Coast Theory and executive producer on Animal's album. The Left Coast Theory had been composed of Chip, No Doze, and Fully. Some say that they were the purest hip-hop group to come along in a long time and they seemed destined to win, but destiny sometimes has a way of throwing you curve balls as they would soon learn. No Doze's heavy drugging had finally caught up to him and one day they found him running down Wilshire BLVD butt ass naked with a crack pipe in his mouth. His family checked him into a treatment facility to get help but that only made things worse with them substituting one drug for another. No Doze had lost his desire to make music and now spent his days staring out the window at his mother's house. Fully, the resident menace of the group, couldn't seem to stay out of trouble and eventually ended up getting handed a dime by the state of New York for a bar fight gone horribly wrong. All that remained of one of hip-hop's most promising groups was Chip.

The thin Lebanese immigrant looked completely out of place at times with the Big Dawg crew, but he felt right at home among them. Since Animal had come aboard Big Dawg, he and Chip had worked closely together so it wasn't unusual for him to find himself in a nest of vipers during their studio sessions. Initially it had made him uneasy, but after a while he'd gotten used to it. He and Animal would lock themselves away in various recording studios perfecting a sound that not even Don B. totally understood. The two made quite the odd pair, but no one could deny their chemistry as damn near everything they touched was a hit.

"A'ight, we're good," Chip said into the intercom, but Animal continued rhyming. Even after the music had been shut off he kept going. Chip had to bang on the glass to let him know to stop.

"That muthafucka be in a zone," Soda said from the love seat he was lounging on with two big butt young females that he had picked up God only knew where. Soda was to Stacks Green and his Texas crew what Animal was to Big Dawg, a star in the making. Though he didn't have quite the lyrical finesse that Animal did he had a star power about him that only came along once every few years. Though he was a small young man who couldn't have weighed more than 120 pounds on a good day, he carried himself with the air of a giant.

"Yeah, when Animal is in the booth he doesn't see anything but the beat," Chip told him while playing with the knobs on the board.

"What's with all that see the beat shit you and this nigga Animal always talking?" Soda asked.

"It is just what it sounds like," Chip told him, but Soda's face said that he still didn't get it. "See, most people hear music, but we can see it, every snare, horn, rift, we see them in big beautiful colors. It's like tripping acid and looking through a kaleidoscope."

Soda shook his head. "Y'all niggaz are weird."

"Weird and paid," Animal said, stepping out of the booth. He was topless and covered in sweat with his hair pulled back into a bushy ponytail. Tattooed across his back was the word *"Harlem"* with curved wings at each end like quotation marks. "You ready to go in and lay your vocals, Soda?"

"In a minute, my G. I gotta get my mind right first," Soda said, lighting the blunt dangling between his lips.

"Dude, it seems like you spend more time getting your mind right than working. We gotta get this shit done."

"Chill out, Animal. I know we're on the clock, but you can't rush perfection. Besides, this was just supposed to be a mix session; you're the one who decided he wanted to add another song to the album at the last minute."

"Creativity strikes us where it pleases." Animal winked at Soda and took the blunt from him.

"Wow, you're so 'prolittic,' " the light-skinned girl sitting next to Soda said.

"So what?" Animal asked, not familiar with the word.

"Prolittic," she enunciated. "You know like when you just keep coming up with material."

Animal and Chip looked at each other. "The word is *prolific*." Chip shook his head. "Soda, where the fuck did you find these broads and why are they even here?"

"Chill out, Mexico. These is my muses," Soda told him.

"I'm not Mexican, I'm Lebanese!" Chip corrected him for what felt like the hundredth time.

Soda waved him off. "What the fuck ever, Mexico. I don't know why you all up in my mix instead of doing what the fuck we pay them for which is to work them boards! So what you need to do is keep your nose in that music and outta my business."

"And what you need to do is watch how you talk to my friend, Soda," Animal said with a blank expression on his face. "I think we might be losing perspective here so let's make this a closed session. Soda, show your company out please."

"Come on, Animal, don't be like that. A'ight you got it, I'm about to go in the booth kill this shit right now," Soda assured him.

"That's dope, but I think it would still be a good idea if the ladies cut out. You can hook up with them after we're done," Animal suggested.

"Uh-uh, how he just gonna try to kick us out when you invited us here, Soda? Who do he think he is?" the dark-skinned girl said indignantly.

"I'm a nigga who respects a *lady* enough to be polite, but doesn't mind disciplining a *bitch* when she gets beside herself. Which category do you fall into, ma?" The temperature dropped ten degrees when Animal posed the question. The girl looked like she was gonna say something fly, but Soda wisely intervened.

"A'ight, time to go." Soda ushered the women toward the door, ignoring their complaints.

"Soda, this is some real crab shit. I'm gonna un-follow your ass on Twitter," the light-skinned girl threatened.

"My heart bleeds. Beat it, bitches." Soda slammed the door in their faces. "My fault, Animal."

"No apologies needed among friends, Soda." Animal gave him dap. "Now, go up in there and get ya murk on so we can wrap this session up."

"Bet." Soda strode into the booth confidently and slipped on the headphones.

"I swear I wanna slap that kid sometimes," Chip confessed to Animal after he started the music in Soda's headphones.

"Soda is a good dude. He just needs direction sometimes." Animal expelled smoke from his nose. "Soda's brah at times, but you could learn to lighten up too, Chip."

"Me? I'm the most easygoing dude in the world!" Chip declared.

"Yeah, you my muthafucking dawg, but you can be very uptight when it comes to making music."

Chip ran his hands through his wild hair. "Here we go with this. I want your little buddy to stop trying to make porn clips on the sofa and work like the rest of us and I'm uptight? If I'd been in here eating mushrooms instead of getting the music right you'd be the first one throwing a hissy fit, but I should go easy on him? This is a race thing, right?"

Animal laughed. "Chip, your ass is shot out."

"Yeah and you're greedy. Pass the weed, dude!"

Animal gave Chip the blunt and grabbed a towel from the couch to wipe away the sweat on his back and chest. His BlackBerry vibrated on the console with the word *unavailable* flashing across the screen. He didn't recognize the number so he started not to pick it up, but something in the pit of his gut told him to answer the call. "Yeah?"

"Hold on, I got Brasco on the other line," a female voice said.

Animal let out an aggravated sigh. If Brasco was calling him on a three-way then he had to be locked up somewhere for God only knew what. He had given them all specific instructions to be easy and not do anything stupid while he was in the town, but of course they didn't listen. In his mind he could see the three knuckleheads sitting in a holding cell somewhere, pointing the finger at each other trying to figure out who was to blame for the latest mess they'd gotten themselves into. Regardless of who was at fault Animal would do what he could to get them out, but he had every intention of giving them hell before he did.

"You still there?" the female voice came back.

"Yeah, I'm here."

"What is it, big homey?" Brasco's voice came over the line.

"Y'all niggaz got the hardest heads in the world. What the fuck did I tell y'all when I dropped you off?"

"Big homey, before you even go there let me run down to you what happened. Five minutes after you skirted Black and Brown rolled up on some bullshit," Brasco told him. By Black and Brown Animal knew he was talking about the notorious detectives Alvarez and Brown. They had a hard-on for Animal that he couldn't understand and had been subtle pains in his ass since he'd left New York.

"What the fuck they want?" Animal asked.

"Dudes was pressing us about some animals that escaped from the zoo. Of course we told them that we didn't know what they were talking about, but they locked us up anyway."

Animal shook his head. "Some dudes are just poor ass losers. I know you and Nef are probably down at the Tombs or on your way, but where did they put the lil one?"

Brasco laughed. "Me and Nef are the only ones twisted, the lil homey grew wings when they rolled."

"A'ight, don't sweat it, as soon as y'all go before the judge I'll have somebody waiting with the bail money."

"I don't think that'll be necessary, my nigga. They ain't got shit on us but a little bit of weed, so we'll probably be out tonight or tomorrow."

"We hope!" Nefertiti shouted in the background.

"Nef shut the fuck up and go ask the C.O. if we're gonna see the judge tonight or not," Brasco barked. "My fault." He turned his attention back to the phone. "All the extra theatrics are because we wouldn't help their pussy asses. I just wanted to give you the heads-up about these cocksuckers pounding the turf."

"Good looking out. Is there anything I can do for y'all while you're in there?" Animal asked.

"Yeah, if we don't make it to the party put a *gum* in something for ya nigga!" Brasco cracked up laughing.

"What? Nigga, what the fuck you mean put a *gum* in it?" the female voice came back. "I'm burning up my phone bill making three-way calls for your ass and you got the nerve to be on there talking greasy? See that's why I hate your scandalous ass, Brasco—"

Animal hung up and left Brasco and his lady to it. It was disturbing to know that his cronies were locked in, but more disturbing was the fact that Brown and Alvarez were on his heels again so soon. He'd known that they were pissed about not being able to connect him to the massacre that had claimed the life of his lover China White and led to Tech's execution, but he didn't give a shit because they didn't have anything on him. Still he knew that the detectives were the best at what they did and hadn't intended on drawing their ire just yet, but he couldn't let Rock Head slide. With the snitch being out from under police protection Animal figured he could kill him and no one would particularly care, but he had been wrong. Rock Head's murder occurring around the time that he came back to New York for the promotional tour was all the persistent detectives needed to reopen old wounds and continue their witch hunt to catch Animal dirty. He was more than confident in his ability at stealth, but he was hardly foolish enough to think that the detectives wouldn't be a problem. Alvarez and Brown were very poor losers and would go above and beyond the law to try and jam him. But this would not deter Animal from his course of action, only detour him a bit.

"Everything cool?" Chip asked, noticing the worried expression on Animal's face.

"Yeah, I'm good," Animal lied. Before Chip could dig deeper the studio phone rang.

Chip answered it and listened intently to the caller on the other line. From the look on his face Animal knew it wasn't good news. When Chip hung up he cut the music and hit the intercom. "It's a wrap for right now, Soda. We'll finish tomorrow."

"What the fuck, man?" Soda whined.

"What's good?" Animal asked.

"That was Devil. Don B.'s been shot."

"Is he okay?" Animal asked.

"Yeah, but he ain't happy. He wants us all to meet him at Harlem Hospital for an emergency staff meeting."

Animal put his shirt back on and grabbed his gun. First the detectives were asking about him and now Don B. had gotten shot. It seemed like lately he and New York were a recipe for drama. But drama or not, he had come too far to let anyone or anything stray him from the path he had set for himself.

"Looks like we got our work cut out for us, big homey," Animal said to the air before following Chip and Soda from the studio.

Chapter 20

THE SOUNDS OF TWEET'S "SOUTHERN HUMMINGBIRD" played softly on the portable CD player, while Malika sat on her tattered living-room couch staring out the window at the twinkling lights of the projects. She was going to bust out the Wii fit and do some yoga, but she was too drained so she decided to sip some tea and sort through the old mail she'd found in the kitchen drawer.

"Bills, bills, bills," Malika muttered as she tossed the envelopes into the trash can one by one. Halfway through the pile she came across an envelope addressed to her from the State of New York. It was a letter from the Welfare notifying her that she had to come in for recertification or risk her benefits being cut off. The deadline for her to come in had been two days prior, which explained why her EBT card no longer worked. She knew that she hadn't gotten the letter out of the box, which meant it had to be Solomon's handiwork. Just thinking about all the drama she would have to go through to recertify sent her pressure through the roof, and she was about to give Solomon's little ass hell.

Solomon almost jumped out of his skin when Malika stormed into his room unannounced. He was lying across the bed with his hand in his pants and watching something on his laptop that he didn't want his mother to see.

"Don't you know how to knock?" Solomon asked, flipping the screen closed.

"I pay the bills in here so I don't have to knock. Solomon, when did this letter come?" She tossed the envelope on the bed.

"I don't know," Solomon said and cut on his Xbox.

"What the hell do you mean, you don't know? You got it out of the box didn't you?"

"I guess." He shrugged and went about the task of loading Madden X. Malika stepped between Solomon and the television, blocking his view. "What's your problem, Ma?"

"My problem is that your irresponsible ass got our food stamps cut off because you didn't give me this letter. Now I gotta go up-town and sort all this shit out tomorrow."

Solomon looked at her quizzically. "So what's the big deal? You should be a pro at this by now."

Malika reached down and ripped the wires of the Xbox from the television.

Solomon bolted upright. "Chill before you break my game!"

"You don't own shit because you don't buy shit in here, Solomon. Your attitude has been really twisted lately and I don't like it."

"I ain't got no attitude, Ma. You the one acting like a crazy woman in front of my friends." Solomon folded his arms.

"Who, that degenerate ass Scar? Boy, you can't be serious. And you know damn well that the reason I *went in* is because I told you not to be posted up in front of the building with Scar and them."

"I wasn't chilling with Scar. I was with Jay."

Malika laughed. "As if his ass is still *innocent* little Jay. I don't know why you and Jay can't just hang out here and play video games like you used to instead of getting caught up in these projects."

"Ma, you can only play video games for so long. Nobody wants to be stuck in the house all day long. You don't let me go outside the hood, and when I go in front of the building to get some air you scream on me. I can't win for losing."

Malika took a deep breath and sat on the edge of the bed. "Solomon, why can't you understand that I'm trying to keep you out of harm's way? Every time you turn around somebody is either getting locked up or killed messing around in the streets, it seems like you can't turn on the news these days without seeing a grieving parent. A mother's worst fear is losing their child to this bullshit and I'm trying to spare you that."

Solomon sat up and folded his arms. "Come on, Ma, I know what time it is on the streets, that's why I don't mess around with the stuff Scar and those guys are into. Just because you may see me with them doesn't mean that I'm out there doing what they do."

"That may be, Solomon, but the police aren't gonna care if they swoop down on you. It won't matter if they're Scar's, Jay's, or your drugs, the police will divide them among the three of you and take all of your asses in."

"Not me. If the police roll on the spot I'm getting up outta there," Solomon said as if he had it all figured out.

"Boy, are you out of your damned mind? Don't even run from the police, all that will do is give them a reason to shoot you."

Solomon waved her off. "Ma, you don't know what's up out there."

"Little boy, I've probably forgotten more than you will ever learn. I became a mother when I was only a few years older than you are now when I found out that I was pregnant with you. During my pregnancy and after I have always been the rock that holds this family together, so you can't tell me anything about knowing what's up out there in the world, it's you who hasn't got a clue."

"I'm good, Mommy. I can take care of myself."

"Solomon, you can barely wipe your ass let alone survive out on your own. Stop being a smart ass and listen to what I'm telling you," Malika said.

"Okay, Ma." Solomon went back to his video game.

Malika stared at her son for a long time and said nothing. She could see that same determined look in his eyes that Suede had had whenever he was plotting and this is what scared her. Malika had bent over backward to make sure that her son was raised right, but for as good of a mother as she might've strived to be she was flawed because she was a woman and therefore it was impossible for her to really teach him how to be a man. It was times like those when she wished that she had had someone in her life to provide a positive example of manhood for Solomon, but she didn't, so until the situation changed she would have to wear both hats.

Malika got up off the bed and headed for the door. "The leftovers from dinner are in the microwave. I've got my key so don't go to the door."

"Where are you going?" he asked, as if he paid bills in the house.

"Out," she said over her shoulder before slamming his bedroom door.

MALIKA WELCOMED THE COOL AIR that ran across her face when she came out of the building. She loved the tranquility of her cozy little apartment but sometimes it felt like the walls were closing in on her, especially when she was having problems with Solomon, which seemed to be more and more frequent the older he got. Sometimes he stressed her so bad that she wanted to put her foot in his ass, but the guilt she carried for the fact that he was growing up fatherless stayed her anger.

Solomon, like most kids, didn't ask to be born but God had saw fit to bring him into the world anyhow. As parents they had a moral obligation to the children but not everyone held up their end of the bargain, which was the case with Suede. When things got bad in the house she sometimes questioned her decision to have a child so young, but every time she looked at him the doubt evaporated. She

loved Solomon more than anything and would go above and beyond to protect him, which is what Scar and his little crew needed
to get into their ignorant little heads.

"Just breathe, Malika," she told herself. She took stock of her
surroundings and realized that she had walked all the way to 109th
Street. She was now not only aggravated and confused, but almost
a half mile away from the apartment she was in no rush to get back
to. For as much as she loved Solomon she couldn't deal with him at
that moment. She spent all of her time taking care of him and that
night she wanted to be taken care of. After digging a quarter out of
her pocket she found a pay phone and called Teddy.

SOLOMON GAVE MALIKA ABOUT A fifteen-minute head start
before slipping into his jacket and heading for the door. He stopped
in front of the mirror to give himself the once-over before slipping
out the door. He knew his mother would try and kill him if she
found out that he'd gone out after dark which is why he had no in-
tentions of getting caught.

By the time Solomon made it from the elevator to the lobby door
his whole demeanor had changed. His happy schoolboy jaunt slowed
to a bop and a scowl melted over his face. The drop in the temperature had sent most people indoors, but the few who made their lives
in the courtyard remained. Nodding to a few heads he knew Solomon ambled from the building over to the bench where Lloyd and
Jay were applying their trade.

"Oh, shit, my nigga 'Love LockDown,'" Lloyd ribbed Solomon
as soon as he walked up. He was sitting on the backrest of the bench
passing something to an older guy that Solomon had seen around.

"What's good, son?" Solomon gave Lloyd dap and then Jay.

"Sol, ya moms is gonna flip if she catch you out here." Jay looked
around nervously as if Malika would spring from the bushes at any
moment.

"Nah, she gone for a while." Solomon took a seat on the bench next to Jay. "What's good wit y'all fools?"

"Out here chasing a dollar. Fuck is good wit you?" Lloyd asked in an accusatory tone as he twirled a cigar back and forth between his fingers.

"You know how I keep it," Solomon said in a hip tone that made Lloyd scoff.

"Yeah, which is why I'm trying to figure out what you're doing out here after the streetlights have come on?"

"Come on, B, stop trying to play me like I'm one of the lil niggaz from behind the center or something," Solomon said. It always irritated him when the older heads made fun of his mother's tight yoke on him, but Lloyd especially.

"Don't wet that, Sol, Lloyd is just playing," Jay said in an attempt to ease the discomfort he knew his friend was feeling.

Lloyd just scoffed and proceeded to split the cigar down the middle. "So where'd ya moms go to have you feeling frog enough to be out here hanging with the scumbags?"

"I don't know." Solomon shrugged. "She broke out on some fake mad shit a lil while ago. She's probably up the block at Jada's or something."

"Yo, that is one bad bitch!" Jay said excitedly.

"Yeah and she's out of your league, lil stud," Lloyd said, shooting him down.

"The way I hear it she's outta anybody's league unless it's Cutty's," Solomon added his two cents.

"See," Lloyd began as he lit the blunt he'd expertly rolled, "that's the problem with y'all cats, you always got ya mouth in grown folks' business and don't know what you're talking about."

"Man, everybody knows Jada is Cutty's BM and the nigga is straight crazy over her," Jay said.

"That ain't the word on the street." Lloyd exhaled a fog of smoke into Jay's face. "Cutty got a bitch uptown that he's claiming as his wife so Jada is up for the highest bidder. My nigga Scar been sizing that up for a minute." Lloyd handed the blunt to Jay. The boy tried to hit the weed like a champ and damn near choked to death.

Solomon looked at Lloyd quizzically. "Jada is a serious ass broad and only fucks wit boss cats, if anything I'd think she'd be trying to set it out to Prince if anybody."

"Prince ain't the boss of shit!" Lloyd said sharply. "All that nigga does is go between us and the man holding the yay. Solomon, you see for yourself every time you come out here it's us on the money. This hood and all the money that passes through it belongs to us. You better ask ya man, shorty."

"He ain't lying," Jay said and pulled a knot of money out of his pocket to prove it. "We be getting stupid paper outta these buildings, Sol." He waved the money proudly. The wad was money from the drug package, not Jay's, but Solomon was naïve enough to be enticed.

Jay tried to pass the blunt to Solomon but he declined. "I'm good."

Lloyd laughed. "Relax, it's only some *green*. What, you think we gonna give you dust or something on the sneak?" He tried to loosen him up but Solomon was still hesitant. "Jay, I told you this nigga was a square."

Solomon sat on the bench feeling like every set of eyes in the entire projects were focused on him. In the back of his mind he could hear his mother giving him a speech about gateway drugs, but it was drowned out by the mocking stare he was getting from Lloyd and his desire to belong. "Fuck it," Solomon said and took the weed.

MALIKA WASN'T SURE HOW IT had happened but she ended up at Teddy's apartment in the Bronx. She had called him just to shoot the breeze and try to burn off some steam before she went back home, but the more she talked the more she opened up about what was going on with her. The next thing she knew she was crying and

Teddy was pulling up to the corner in his Durango. They rode around for a while and talked while they sipped vodka and smoked green. She hadn't even realized that they'd left Manhattan until Teddy was parking the truck on 184th and Valentine. It was a tastefully decorated studio with a big screen television and a futon. He'd claimed he only needed five minutes to grab his wallet and change his jacket, but that five minutes turned into a half hour because TV1 was showing *Sparkle* and it was both their favorites.

Malika was at peace, lying across the futon watching Lonette McKee working the sexy red dress across the stage. She didn't get this kind of solitude with Solomon's antics and staring at the drab yellow walls of her apartment and it felt good. Without even realizing she had done so she snuggled closer to Teddy.

"I miss this," Teddy said, sealing the ends of the joint he was rolling.

"What, *Sparkle?*" Malika looked up at him.

"No, this." He motioned to them. "Remember when we used to do this all the time, lay around and watch movies?"

"Yeah, it would be nice until your phone would ring and you'd go in the bathroom to take the call." Malika sat up. "Teddy, I didn't really come over here to go down memory lane. I have enough negative stuff running around in my head already without adding our failed little romance to it."

"Malika, how can you call something that was never given a chance to work failed? When things were good between us they were really good. Don't you miss it?"

"Yeah I do," she admitted, "but I'm not willing to pay the price tag you're trying to hang on it. Yo, men continue to baffle me with the way they move. Y'all can have something that's priceless and you still want more. Why can't you ever be satisfied with just one chick?"

"Because we're greedy," he said honestly. "Now before you go all Shirley Chisum on me, let me explain. Men, we're like animals, meaning we move off instinct instead of thoughts. No matter how much a dude loves his girl, he's always gonna lust after other chicks, it's just how we're wired. But this doesn't mean we always gonna act on it. Our base desire to conquer women is why it's so hard to be faithful, but it's not impossible to be with one woman."

"So then why did you make it seem so impossible?" she asked.

"Because back then I didn't have that kind of discipline." He gave her a sincere look. The pain Malika saw behind his eyes caused her to turn away but he made her look at him. "I'm a different man now." He kissed her lips softly and ran his hand down her back.

"Teddy, don't." She pulled away, but it was halfhearted. It had been so long since she had been touched by a man that it felt almost electric. She wanted to give herself to him, but she was afraid.

"Malika, you don't have to carry your burdens anymore." He kissed her again and this time she kissed him back. "Let me help you carry them."

Time wrapped in on itself blurring the lines between seconds, minutes, and hours. It felt like Teddy had one thousand hands as he seemed to touch her everywhere at once, lighting small fires under her skin and deep in her gut. She floated down onto the futon and let him command her body. Teddy slipped between her legs, kissing her neck and stomach while he worked her pussy moist with two fingers. His penis felt heavy in his hand when he pulled it out and tried to glide it inside Malika. He had almost penetrated her when she stopped him.

"I know you got a condom?" She looked up at him with intoxicated eyes.

"Come on, baby, you know me." He pleaded, feeling like he was going to cum prematurely.

"Teddy, I'm already feeling like this is a mistake, so if I were you I'd wrap this pickle before I change my mind." She reached down and stroked his thick penis, dripping pre-cum onto her thigh.

Teddy grumbled something and rolled off her and walked to the bathroom with his rock-hard dick slapping his thighs. A few seconds later he came back holding up a Magnum package for her approval.

"That's more like it," Malika said with a smile.

Teddy rolled the condom over his throbbing manhood and lowered himself on top of Malika again. She was tight, so tight that even with her own moisture and the lubricant from the condom he couldn't get it in without hurting both of them. Teddy parted her legs and lowered his face to her vagina where he proceeded to work his tongue inside her, sending jolts of pleasure through her limbs. Malika dragged her nails across the back of Teddy's scalp while he worked her to a nice lather. She stared up at the ceiling as spots danced before her eyes while Teddy continued to lap her like a thirsty kitten. Her heart screamed "no," but her body barked "yes," and she tried to shove Teddy's whole face inside her. All of her fears and apprehensions faded away leaving only the longing to feel Teddy inside her and she let him know by reluctantly pulling his face free of her vagina.

Teddy's goatee was slick with Malika's juices as he looked down into her hungry eyes. He knew just what she wanted and intended to give it to her. Now that she was wet enough it was a little easier to enter her. Teddy slipped a little of him at a time into her tight glove, silently calling on God and every other saint he could think of. Malika's pussy was like a beam of sunshine shining down on his face on a summer day. With every pump inside her sweetness Teddy could feel her walls tightening around his shaft, making him want to go deeper. He held out for ten minutes before the buildup became too much for him and he exploded inside the condom. Teddy continued pumping as the cum kept spurting from his dick, eventually spilling out over the rim of the condom and dripping onto the futon. When he felt the last of it and his strength faded he collapsed on top of Malika, sucking his thumb like a baby.

Chapter 21

MS. PAT BLEW INTO THE LIVING ROOM LIKE HURRICANE Katrina. She was dressed in a deep purple skirt with a purple and yellow top, accented by the matching wide-brimmed purple hat. From behind her purple bifocals she glared at everyone assembled. Mookie and Fish sat at the coffee table trying not to look guilty of whatever they were up to. By their glassy eyes and stiff jaws, everyone in the house already had an idea. Miles and Jalen ran around the living room screaming and throwing socks at each other and bumping into Ms. Pat's china cabinet, while Davita lounged on the couch, texting on her phone like she didn't notice.

"Y'all don't hear the door?" Ms. Pat asked.

"No, Mama," Mookie said with a glassy look to his eyes. He and Fish had been sitting there stuck on stupid since they'd walked in almost an hour prior.

"I know it ain't for me, so why bother?" Davita rolled her eyes and went back to texting on her phone. Her little brother and sister never broke their stride as they continued running around the coffee table, knocking one of Ms. Pat's glass figurines to the floor and shattering it.

Ms. Pat's glasses fogged up as she walked calmly into the kitchen and came out with a glass of water, which she sipped gingerly. She snatched Davita's phone, mid-text, and dropped it into the glass of water, then tossed the water and phone onto the table between Mookie and Fish. Without missing a beat she tripped the running Jalen and snatched Miles by the back of his shirt and flung him on the couch next to his sister. Now that she had all their attentions Ms. Pat spoke.

"Heavenly Father you have surely blessed me with a house full of the laziest, most useless creatures you have ever seen fit to breathe breath in." Ms. Pat shook her head. "You lazy souls eat, sleep, shit, and pluck my nerves rent-free and I can't even get you off your asses to answer the door?" Davita opened her mouth to say something but Ms. Pat silenced her with a pointed finger. "I wish you would open your smart-ass mouth so I can send them rotten-ass teeth on an all-expenses-paid trip down your throat." Davita folded her arms but didn't say anything. "See"—Ms. Pat took slow steps toward Davita—"that's ya problem now, your mouth spends more time open than ya ears. If you'd spent as much time paying attention in school as you did talking slick you might not be getting left back."

"Again," Mookie added.

"And you." Ms. Pat turned her attention to her son. "I don't know what you and that extra thick Negro sitting next to you are planning, but it had better not go down in my house or in my hood. Y'all know I'm getting money outta this house and you always bringing the law calling. Shit, you probably didn't answer the door 'cause you was scared it was them warrant boys," she scoffed.

"Again," Davita mumbled.

"Shut up before I come across your mind, Vita," Ms. Pat warned as she headed to answer the door. She was still mumbling to herself when she opened the door to find Gucci and Tionna. "Oh, damn, let me get my winter coat," she said, looking Gucci up and down.

"What's that supposed to mean?" Gucci asked.

"If you're coming by my house then it must be snowing in hell so I gotta dress warm," Ms. Pat said with a smile. "Bring your narrow ass in here and give ya auntie a hug." Ms. Pat grabbed Gucci in a warm embrace. "Girl, you looking good." She spun Gucci around and slapped her on her ass. "And look at all that junk in your trunk. Animal must be knocking the lining out that young stuff. Ask his pretty ass if he got a brother."

"Auntie, your ass is still crazy as hell." Gucci laughed. "Oh, you remember my girl, Tionna, don't you?"

Ms. Pat peered at Tionna over the top of her glasses. "The hustler's wife. How could I forget?" Ms. Pat had never too much cared for Tionna because of the way she had carried herself when she was doing slightly better than everyone else. No matter how well off Ms. Pat and her husband were back in the days they never acted like they were above their neighbors because they knew that the same people you saw on the way up were the ones you saw on the way down. This was a lesson Tionna had to learn the hard way.

"How are you, Ms. Pat?" Tionna asked.

"I'm fine, child. I was just in here getting after these no good ass offspring of mine. Y'all come on in out of the hallway." Ms. Pat stepped back to let them inside.

"Is that my baby cousin?" Mookie got up and smiled at Gucci.

"Hey Mookie," Gucci said, giving him a halfhearted wave.

"That ain't no way to greet your big cousin. Come here." Mookie embraced her. There was something about the way he was running his hands up and down her back that made Gucci feel violated so she pushed away from him. "Girl, you look good, and I see you shining something fierce." He examined her jewels.

"I'm doing a'ight," Gucci told him, running her hands up and down her arms from the chills his stare was giving her.

"Um hmm." Mookie sucked his teeth sneakily. "Looks like you doing better than a'ight. I see Big Dawg's newest pup is taking care of cuz-o."

"All them chump ass niggaz is shining like new money," Fish said in his slow drawl. "Them boys getting all that scratch in Harlem but ain't kicking nothing back to the house. I don't know how I feel about that, how 'bout you, Mookie?"

Mookie took his time before answering. "I don't know, Fish. Seems to me like common sense would tell them that a full wolf is a lot less of a headache than a hungry one, but you know what; I think Don B. is a reasonable man who if we sat down with we may be able to get him to see things our way." He turned to Gucci. "What you think, cousin?"

Gucci took her shades off and stared at him with unwavering eyes. "I think that if you fuck around with my man or his peoples auntie will be saying her good-byes through a box because there ain't gonna be enough of you left for an open casket funeral."

Mookie's cheek twitched once, before a lazy smile appeared on his face. "That's how you know you're my blood, because you're loyal to your man. She get that from you, Ma," he told Ms. Pat.

"Boy, please, the only thing Gucci got from me is this damn seat cushion." Ms. Pat slapped her on the ass again. "All that predatory cunning come from her mama and them. Veronica and her sister Peaches used to have these boys out here fighting like cavemen. They're the reason they closed down that crack spot we were around the corner from when we lived on 113th and Lenox."

"What crack spot?" Gucci asked.

"You know the one in the candy store around the corner, Nuclear." She tried to jog Gucci's memory.

"Do you mean *Nucleus*?" Tionna corrected her. "Ms. Pat, that was a weed spot, they didn't sell crack."

"*We don't believe you, you need more people,*" Ms. Pat sang. "Little girl, I'm a weed smoker and that shit wasn't kosher. One time I bought two nickel bags of that shit from them foreign bitches and had to go to the emergency room after I blazed the first one. There ain't no way you supposed to be that high for five dollars.

Now what brings you ladies of the evening into the abode of this old woman?"

"Their habits," Jada said as she appeared in the living room. She had traded in her birthday suit for a pair of jeans and a turtleneck. She had pushed her weave back into a ponytail that showcased her pretty face. "Gucci, your ass called me this afternoon and you're just getting here?"

"Cuzo, you know I had to touch the town right quick before we came down." Gucci embraced Jada.

"Tionna, what's good?" Jada greeted Tionna.

"You." Tionna looked her up and down. "You sure don't look like a kid with three kids!"

"You know the Butlers are naturally blessed with figures," Jada said.

"We sure nuff are," Ms. Pat said while adjusting her large, saggy breasts inside her bra. "Now, if y'all have come down for more than my company then you might as well carry ya asses back to where you came from, cuz ain't nothing popping."

"Auntie Pat, what you mean ain't nothing popping? This is ya niece!" Gucci declared.

"Shit, I got a bunch of nieces, but that don't change the fact that I can't go to church tonight with a transaction tainting my soul." Ms. Pat adjusted her hat in the dingy mirror hanging next to the front door.

"Auntie, it's Thursday," Gucci pointed out.

"And? Ain't no rule that says you can only worship the Lord on Sundays. Me and Ms. Martha attend night service up in the Bronx on Thursdays."

"Smelling like nothing but the chronic," Davita said as she passed.

Ms. Pat threw her hands in the air and uttered a prayer. "Father God, merciful God, please put a clamp on my granddaughter's mouth and spare me a one to three in prison for assaulting this wench, amen!"

"Davita, you better watch your fucking mouth," Jada warned. Davita just rolled her eyes and kept going into the bedroom, with her brother and sister hot on her heels.

"Don't tell her nothing, Jada. She got one more smart thing to say and it's gonna be *Wrestlemania* fifty in this piece," Ms. Pat said. "Fooling with these damn kids done got my pressure up," Ms. Pat said, fishing around in her wig and producing a wrinkled joint. "One of y'all kids give me a light."

"Mama, didn't you just say you was going to church and said you didn't wanna be tainted?" Mookie asked.

Ms. Pat eventually found a lighter and lit her joint. She took a deep pull and expelled the smoke through her nose before answering Mookie. "I said tainted from a *transaction,* I ain't said nothing about consumption. Now stop minding grown folks' business and hand me the ashtray."

Gucci took one whiff of the pungent smoke and knew that her aunt was blowing some serious green. "Auntie, why don't you let ya niece hit that one time." Gucci reached for the joint, but Ms. Pat snatched it away.

"Little girl, we cool, but we ain't friends. Ain't no way in the hell I'm gonna be in here smoking with you. But if you wanna buy some bud that's a horse of a different color."

"Mama, you said you wasn't selling no bud before church," Mookie reminded her.

Ms. Pat flicked her ass in a soda top and glared at her son. "Boy, why don't you stop telling me what I said? You say a lot of things that you don't stick to. I'm gonna get a job, Mama; I'm gonna take better care of my kids, Mama; I ain't going back to the pen, Mama; nigga please. Instead of signifying you and Simple Jack," she motioned toward Fish—"need to start getting yourselves ready to go; I gotta get off to church."

"We was just gonna kick it around here for a lil while," Mookie said.

"Mookie, you know ain't no way I'm leaving two crackheads in my house while I ain't here. Do like Big Tymers and *get ya roll on*."

"A'ight, Mama. Let's go, Fish," Mookie said and reluctantly headed for the door.

"Bye, Auntie." Fish kissed Ms. Pat on the cheek. For as brutish as he was he had always had a soft spot in his heart for the Butler clan.

"Take care, Fish, and make sure Mookie gets back to the half-way house before curfew because I sure as hell don't want the police coming around here. I got too much going on for y'all criminal activities to be cramping my style," Ms. Pat told them as they were leaving. "I love them boys but Lord knows they ain't got a whole brain between them. Now what you heifers want?"

"I need some of whatever it is you're smoking right there." Gucci pointed at the joint.

Ms. Pat went to her china cabinet and knocked twice on the bottom shelf, revealing a hidden compartment. Using a key that hung around her neck she undid the lockbox inside the space and retrieved her stash. "I call this here Spider Man," Ms. Pat said as she laid several bags on the coffee table. The buds were a bright shade of green with orange fuzz.

Gucci picked one of the bags up and could smell the weed without opening it. "Damn, this is that bomb," Gucci said, smelling the bag. "How come you call it Spider Man?"

"Because that shit is so good you'll be climbing the walls after you smoke it."

"If that's the case then give me a twenty." Gucci placed a twenty on the coffee table.

"Me too." Tionna added her twenty to the pot.

"Yes, yes, all money down is a bet." Ms. Pat picked up the money. "Since I fucks wit y'all I'm gonna give you a play and let you get three for fifty."

"That sounds good to me. Jada, you got the extra ten?" Gucci asked.

Jada patted her pockets and shrugged. "I'm tapped out."

Ms. Pat shook her head. "Granddaughter, you've gotta be the brokest whore I know. If I ain't taught y'all girls nothing else it is to not come home with a wet pussy and an empty pocket, but apparently you were sleeping in class."

"Leave that girl alone, Auntie. Don't worry about it, Jada, I got the extra ten." Gucci handed Ms. Pat the bill.

After serving the two girls Ms. Pat grabbed her purse and headed for the door. "I'm off to church so I'll see you hussies later."

"Okay, love you, Auntie." Gucci kissed her on the cheek.

"Grandma, what time are you coming back?" Jada asked.

Ms. Pat stopped short. "I didn't realize that you had pushed me outta your womb."

"I was asking because I wanna go out with Gucci tonight. You know I don't get to hang with my cousin often enough." Jada smiled innocently.

Ms. Pat's eyes narrowed to slits. "Jada Butler, don't try to game me like I'm one of these slow ass young boys you got jumping outta windows. If you wanna go out, I suggest you find a babysitter or a church that will keep them little demons until you get done shaking your ass."

"But, Grandma, I ain't got no money to pay a sitter tonight."

"That sounds like a problem between you and your pockets. I'll put it to you like this: I do what I do like I'm doing it for TV and that's all you need to know. Deuces." Ms. Pat threw up the peace sign and left.

Jada flopped on the couch. "She gets on my damn nerves."

"It's all good, Jada. We didn't have any plans for tonight so it's cool if we kick it here with you." Gucci dug in her purse and pulled out a pint of cognac. "We'll make our own party."

"Hey." Tionna snapped her fingers.

"Then let's get the party started." Jada turned on the radio.

Jada picked her ringing cell phone off the coffee table and looked at the caller ID. She recognized the area code as PA, but didn't recognize the number. She started to loop, but remembered that she had met a dude from Philly who seemed like he was handling and figured it might've been him.

"Yo," Jada said into the phone.

"Bitch, I'm gonna cut your fucking face when I see you!" a female voice threatened on the other line.

Jada sighed, as it was the third call she had gotten that day. "I keep telling y'all lil hos about playing with me. I hope the dick is worth the headache that comes with it."

"I got something for you to catch, J-ho. You gonna get a stitch for every dollar you owe, so I hope you got a good plastic surgeon on standby. You better watch your back every time you walk outta 865, you bum ass project bitch," the caller taunted her.

"Well, if you know where I live then you know where to come pick up this ass whipping. And tell that faggot ass nigga Cutty that if he keeps having muthafuckas play on my phone I'm gonna slap a harassment charge on him right before I have one of my young boys run up in him on the way to Chow." Jada banged it.

"Damn, those sound like fighting words," Gucci said when Jada was off the phone.

"I'm gonna do more than fight if one of these lil bitches come around here playing." Jada pulled a small handgun from between the cushions on the couch. "The Butlers sling coke and iron, so don't get it fucked up."

"Ya heard." Gucci gave her a high-five.

"Jada, you keep guns laying out like that for your kids to accidentally get hold of?" Tionna asked in shock.

"My kids know that guns ain't toys and they should only touch them in case of extreme emergencies, like if a nigga is whipping my ass and I can't get to the hammer. Shit, Grandma made sure I knew how to pop that thang when I was thirteen."

"And that's real," Gucci added, remembering how she cried the first time Ms. Pat tried to teach her how to shoot. Ronnie flipped out when she found out what her daughter had been subjected to, but it went in one of Ms. Pat's ears and out the other. "So what's that all about anyhow?"

"Cutty and his bullshit," Jada said and went on to give the girls the short version of their breakup.

"Holy shit, you stole twenty thousand dollars from Cutty? It's no wonder he wants to kill your ass!" Gucci said.

"I didn't steal shit, I appropriated it," Jada said as if that made it less wrong.

Tionna gave Jada a serious look. "I've pulled a lot of stunts on my man, but I always knew not to play with paper. I knew his kids and his money were the only two things he would kill me for. That's a dangerous game to play, Jada."

"Ain't no game about it, Tionna. I'm out here taking care of his kid and him. That's my husband, so that money was entitled to me," Jada said confidently.

Tionna shook her head. "Jada, unless y'all got married you ain't his wife, you're his wifey. A lot of chicks throw that word around but it won't give you a leg to stand on in court. It's because we stay wifeys instead of becoming the wife why we always getting shitted on and left with nothing when it's all said and done." Tionna recalled her own drama with Duhan and having to start from scratch with no help.

"You ain't never lied." Jada gave Tionna dap. "And we don't make it no better. We're having too much fun living off their mercies to make sure our asses are covered when they pull the rug out from under us. We endure the kids, prison visits, and other women only to end up stressed out and on welfare."

"Somebody should write a book about this shit our sorry asses," Tionna said, pouring them all a light shot in the nickel plastic cups on the table.

"And what would they call it?" Gucci asked sarcastically.

Tionna pondered the question and a title materialized in her mind. "Welfare Wifeys!"

"I'll drink to that." Jada raised her glass.

"Welfare Wifeys," the girls said in unison and touched glasses before downing their cognac.

Just then the radio DJ announced that it was time for the "Top Eight at Eight" on Hot 103.7. Before Flex did his thing Ms. Info came on with her celebrity drama report. She had a few juicy pieces of information, but it was the story she promised to come back with at nine that got everyone's attention.

"When keeping it real goes wrong. Mega rapper and Harlem native gets shot at a dice game. Hello, don't millionaires usually gamble in casinos and not on street corners? We'll be back with details on an update on Don B.'s condition at nine."

To everyone's shock Tionna fell over laughing.

"Damn, T, a man gets shot and you're laughing? That's cold," Jada said.

Tionna finally composed herself to respond to Jada's statement. "Don B. ain't no fucking man, and I hope they bodied his ass." She tossed a Dutch Master on the table. "Now, one of y'all roll something up so I can be good and high when Ms. Info comes back with the details."

Though Tionna found it amusing, Gucci did not. She knew that whenever Don B. was on the chopping block someone other than him ended up suffering the consequences. Her thoughts immediately turned to Animal.

Chapter 22

BY THE TIME THEY PULLED UP TO HARLEM HOSPITAL IT was a madhouse. News vans were double parked up and down Lenox Avenue while journalists floated around talking to people and trying to find ways to get past security and into the hospital. There were hundreds of fans camped out outside the barriers erected to control traffic, holding candles and signs wishing Don B. a speedy recovery and the police tried their best to control the madness.

"Look at all these muthafucking people. I don't think I've seen this many niggaz in one place since they started bussing people into Houston from Katrina," Soda said from the backseat.

"Shit, Don B. is like the fucking John Kennedy of Harlem!" Chip said.

Animal ignored his chattering passengers and found a parking spot on Fifth Avenue. He secured his gun and made sure he didn't have anything on him before starting the trek back to Lenox. As soon as the trio rounded the corner they were blinded by the flashbulbs of the media and the crowd. Animal and his crew were assaulted by a flood of questions ranging from whether Don B. was dead to when the new material was coming out. He acted as if he didn't even hear them as he elbowed and shoved a path to the entrance, where they were immediately stopped by the police.

"Hold on, fellas. No one gets inside the hospital without proper ID and I need to know which patient you're going to visit?" a beefy black cop said, sizing them up.

"We're here to see Donald Bernard," Chip said, handing over his driver's license.

"Only police and immediate family are allowed upstairs," the cop told them.

"I'm his brother. Can't you see the resemblance?" Chip asked with a smile.

"Okay, wiseass, keep it moving." The cop handed him his ID back.

"We're part of the record label," Animal spoke up. He was hoping to have as little interaction with the police as possible but he didn't have time for the holdup.

"I wouldn't care if you were his wet nurse. Only authorized personnel are allowed upstairs and you ain't authorized, pretty boy," the cop said slyly.

Animal chuckled. "Pretty boy. I didn't know they were allowing homosexuals in the academy these days? Check it, since you're obviously just a grunt why don't you go get your superior officer so we can clear this up?"

The cop's eyes flashed anger and he took a threatening step toward Animal. "Why don't I *clear you up* for talking slick?"

Animal took his hands out of his pockets and let them dangle loosely at his sides. "You're welcome to try it, player. But if you put your hands on me I can guarantee you that Don B. is gonna have some company in there. Make your move, big man."

"What's going on out here?" An officer with sergeant's bars on his sleeves came out.

"About to clear the streets of this trash," the black officer told his superior, keeping his eyes fixed on Animal. Most young men were intimidated by the uniform, but he could tell that he would have to make a believer out of the wild-haired young man.

"He's with us," Devil said as he came out of the exit behind the sergeant. His eyes were red and filled with emotion, but his face was hard.

The sergeant looked from the young men to Devil. "Look, guy, it's crazy enough as it is with the fucking circus your boss getting shot has turned my district into without adding to it with this constant flux of traffic. We're already over the allowed number of visitors upstairs. I can't have this."

Devil sighed and tried to keep his cool. "Let me rap with you for a minute, boss." Devil led the sergeant off to the side. "Look, I appreciate the hassle you guys have gone through to accommodate us, and so does Big Dawg Entertainment. So much so that we'd like to make a donation to the Police Benevolent Association." Devil stuffed an envelope into the sergeant's coat pocket.

The sergeant patted his pocket to test the thickness of the envelope. "Okay, but they ain't all going up. I'll allow you one more visitor upstairs, but the rest of these jokers gotta wait in the lobby."

"Fair enough," Devil agreed. "Yo, Animal, come on." He waved him over.

"Fuck is up with this? Don't these pigs know we all made niggaz?" Soda said hostilely.

Devil grabbed young Soda by the arm and whispered to him, "This ain't the time or the place to let that weed and syrup talk for you, Soda. There's a lot going on right now, so I need all y'all to keep it cool. Kick back down in the lobby and we'll let you know what the deal is in a minute."

"You got that, Devil," Soda said reluctantly.

"Good man." Devil slapped him on his back harder than he needed to. "Let's go, Animal."

• • •

THE FIRST FACE ANIMAL SAW when he got off the elevator was Tone's. Tone was the cat that Don B. had come up with during his hustling days in Harlem. He was just as much a degenerate as the rest of them, if not more so, but Tone had a mind for business that couldn't be ignored, which is why Don B. brought him on as his manager. Tone was thumbing away so furiously on his Black-Berry that he didn't notice Animal until he was almost right on top of him, which was very unlike Tone. One of the things Animal liked most about Tone was the fact that no matter how expensively he might be dressed, he had never lost his killer edge. He was just as reliable in a gunfight as he was in a conference room.

"How is he?" Animal asked, giving Tone dap.

"Shit, you ain't got ears?"

Animal hadn't noticed it at first, but there was shouting coming from the hospital room.

"What part of fall the fuck back don't you niggaz understand? A'ight, let me say it to you in English: get the FUCK out!" Don B. was barking on somebody.

When Animal and company came into the room it was crowded with nurses and two hospital security officers. He was sitting up on one of the beds topless, with his arm in a sling. Don B. had some nicks and cuts, but the bandages going from his neck to his shoulder looked like the worst of the injuries.

"Mr. Bernard," one of the nurses began in an even tone. "You're recovering from a gunshot and still suffering the affects of the shock, so you need to rest. We can't have all these people in here."

"This shit is a scratch." He motioned toward his bandaged shoulder. "The Don is Teflon. Furthermore, if y'all would give me and my fam some privacy, everybody would be able to be on their way and y'all could do ya jobs properly."

"My dude, having all these people up here is not only against hospital policy, but it's a security risk. We need them to leave so we can do our jobs, feel me?" the dark-skinned security guard said in a hip tone.

Don B. gave him a blank look. "No, I don't feel you. How are you gonna protect me and you ain't even got a gun? Fuck outta here. Yo, can I get somebody with some sense in here so we can make heads or tails of all this shit?" Don B. looked around the room.

Seeing the hospital staff clearly irritated with Don B.'s treatment Tone decided to step in. "Okay, okay, let's all be adults about this. If you guys can give us ten minutes I promise we'll clear the room and let you work."

The nurse weighed it for a minute and finally agreed. "Okay, but let's make it five minutes and that's nonnegotiable," she said before leading the staff out of the room.

"These niggaz need to get their etiquette up." Don B. slouched back on the bed and rubbed his shoulder. "Yo, thanks for coming, Animal." He and Animal gave each other a complex handshake, which they ended with a military salute.

"You know, I was in motion as soon as I got word," Animal told him. "Police got Chip and Soda downstairs and it's niggaz on high alert in the streets. It's crazy out there."

"As is should be. You can never lay hands on a king and expect his subjects not to react. I'm in here strategizing my next move and these nurses is all up in my mix, B. They need to go somewhere with that dumb shit," Don B. fumed.

"Don, you can't keep wilding out in here like this, especially when the people you're flipping on are responsible for your life," Tone told him.

"I know, T, but I'm just tight! I can't believe these niggaz had the nerve to try and come at me cross-eyed. Cocksuckers act like I ain't got no power uptown? We gonna see about this shit. I'm putting something to rest personally." Don B. slammed his fist against the wall sending a jolt of pain through his shoulder.

"You need to take it easy, B., and let the wolves deal with this," Tone said.

"That's what I keep trying to tell him, man," Devil added.

"How the fuck can I take it easy when these niggaz tried to lay me in my own backyard?" Don B. looked around the room waiting for someone to answer the question. "I was born and raised on these Harlem streets and I pumped bread back into when I came up, I'm supposed to be untouchable north of 110th Street," he said emotionally.

"Anybody got a reason to hate you?" Animal asked. If it wasn't for the sincere expression on his face Don B. might've taken him for trying to be sarcastic. It was common knowledge that Don B. had countless haters due to both his accomplishments and wrongdoings.

"Not outside the usual dick suckers, but there was that lil thing with Bruiser right before the shooting went down. Don B. cracked him for some bread in the dice game and he wasn't happy about it," Devil recalled.

"Bruiser from 123rd?" Animal flipped through his mental Rolodex. "His gun definitely goes off, but I can't see somebody like him shooting first, especially over a dice game and in broad daylight. His heart ain't there."

"It don't matter where his heart is at because I'm about to put it on a sidewalk," Don B. said.

"You don't even know it was him who tried to get at you!" Tone tried to point out.

"It don't matter, fam. Bruiser and whoever else I know that has a problem with me is gonna get seen, B."

"So you just gonna murder seventy percent of the dudes in Harlem?" Animal asked. "Blood, we ain't gotta revisit my pedigree for you to know it's the gospel when I tell you it's a bad move to go about it like that."

"Then what would you suggest I do? Wait until they make another play for me and ask who they're working for? That ain't gonna work, lil homey. I need somebody touched."

"Then touch 'em, but make sure you touch the right muthafucka," Animal replied. "Let them people you pay do what they do and you just get low until this shit blows over. We can cancel the party and the promo tour and go back to recording."

Animal's approach came as a bit of a surprise to everyone in the room who knew him, because he was a notorious hothead whose reputation and methods for dispatching his enemies preceded him.

"Cancel the party? Are you crazy? No, too much has already been invested for it to go down. Besides that, it'd look bad on us if we turned tail. Let this party send a message out to all these niggaz that Big Dawg is still popping," Don B. said.

"So, you'd put your life at risk just to prove a point?" Tone asked disbelievingly.

"To hold my throne I'd be willing to put the lives of everyone in here at risk," Don B. said seriously. "They won't fold me and they won't fold Big Dawg. We're having this party." Their conversation was interrupted when two police officers walked into the room. "Come on, what happened to my five minutes?"

"Mr. Bernard, I'm Officer Rizzo and this is my partner, Officer Vasquez. We need to interview you about the shooting," the dark-haired officer told him.

"My story is the same as the one I told you when they were loading me in the ambulances. I don't know nothing," Don B. told the officer.

"Mr. Bernard," the blond cop began in an even tone, "we can do this the easy way or the hard way, and it's all the same to me. But if you don't help us then we can't help you."

"Help me?" Don B. gave him a crazy look. "My G, I could've used your help when these niggaz was trying to Rambo III me uptown. Right now all I need you to do is leave me alone until my lawyer gets here, cuz I ain't got shit to say."

"Fellas, I think we're done with the questioning right now. When our lawyer gets here he'll be able to provide you with all the information you need," Tone intervened.

The dark cop took in Tone's ensemble of a bow tie and sports coat and laughed. "Look, Farrakhan, we have a procedure to follow when it comes to gunshots so don't try to tell us how to do our jobs."

"Let me tell you something, nigga, I will knock . . ." Tone began, but was cut off by a well-dressed Hispanic man who had just entered the room. He was tall and handsome with playful eyes and a thin mustache. Watching his back was a bulldog of a man, who scowled at the whole Big Dawg crew, but his eyes lingered on Animal.

"No need for name calling, Tone." Detective Brown walked into the room. His badge swung from his thick neck like a warning. "Why don't you guys take a crack at this?" he told the uniformed cops. "You can still get credit for the pinch if anything comes of it."

The two officers were more than happy to turn the interrogation over to the detectives. "Good luck with this asshole," the tall cop capped on his way out.

Alvarez looked Don B. up and down and let out a high whistle. "Damn, looks like they really fucked you up, kid."

Don B. chuckled. "It's only a scratch. Listen, if you're coming in here to question me about the shooting let me save you some time. I don't know who shot me."

"You got us fucked up, kid. We don't give a damn who shot you because you're still alive, we care about who you're gonna have shot because knowing you they ain't gonna have that kinda luck," Brown told him.

"We don't score nothing off the attempts, bro, it's the successful ones we get points off," Alvarez added.

"Come on, y'all know I've put my street ways behind me. I'm just a businessman now," Don B. said sarcastically.

"Horse shit and you know it!" Brown snapped. "Regardless of what those asshole journalists write about you, I know what time it is, *Donald.* You ain't nothing but a low-life gangsta who made himself a grip for getting on the radio and promoting dumb shit. They call you a Don uptown now, but I call you a poor son of a bitch who has an unmarked grave waiting for him to lay down and take a nap."

Don B. stared the detective down. "Flattery will get you everywhere. Antonio," Don B. called to Tone, "please make sure you send a bottle of champagne to the detective's house for him and his wife. Oh, and include an Xbox 360 for that handsome young son of his. Little Rudy will get a kick out of the new Halo."

Detective Brown couldn't hide his contempt at Don B. for striking so close to home. "What? You trying to bring my family into this, you piece of shit?" He took a step toward Don B., but Tone was there to meet him. Detective Brown stared up at the slightly taller man with trouble in his eyes. "Fuck you gonna do?" he challenged.

Tone let several different scenarios play over in his head before answering the question. "Not a thing, Detective. You got it; I just wanna make sure everything is done legal."

"Legal? What the fuck do y'all know about legal?" Alvarez looked around the room as he spoke. "Each one of you is guilty of something. Some of you we've caught." He looked at the faces he was familiar with. His eyes lingered when they landed on Animal. "And some of you we will. What's up, Animal?"

Animal shrugged in the way of a response.

Detective Alvarez crossed the room and stood a few feet away from Animal. He looked into the young man's eyes and saw nothing, not even his own reflection. "So this is the Animal? Funny, from the things I've read about you I would've thought you'd be a lot . . . I don't know, scarier? The way the streets tell it, you're the man without fear."

Animal's lips twisted a fraction of an inch, but not enough to even be considered a smirk. "My granny used to tell me that the only reason we fear things is because of the stories we're told about them. Take away the stories and fear is crippled, and I'd bet on me against a gimp any day." Animal laughed at his own joke.

"They told me you had a very different sort of sense of humor," Alvarez told him. "You know it's funny that my partner and I should run into you tonight, seeing how we've been cleaning up your messes all day long."

Animal gave him a bewildered look. "I'm afraid I don't know what you're talking about."

"You know just what we're talking about," Detective Brown told him and placed two photos on the bed. "They found this one in Pennsylvania." He tapped the picture of Rock Head. "And this woman was found out in Brooklyn next to what was left of her boyfriend." He tapped the picture of the murdered woman. "One guy was missing his tongue and the other had his eyes melted out. What are you some kind of collector?"

Animal chuckled. "I collect art, gentlemen, not body parts."

"And I'm gonna collect your ass!" Detective Brown threatened.

Don B. laughed. "Yo, that shit sounded wild *homo,* son!"

Brown glared at Don B. "Shut up before I put another bullet in you. And you," he addressed Animal, "I can't tell you how long I've been waiting to look into your eyes, the eyes of the man they say kills without remorse."

Animal shrugged. "They also say that all cops are racist cocksuckers, but you can't believe everything you hear, right?"

"Wrong, shit-bird! We've already got the name of the guy who gave the order and from the way the bodies were done up we've figured you as the doer. Why don't you make this easy on yourself before the situation gets uglier and you become a candidate for the death penalty?"

Animal shrugged. "Afraid I don't know what you're talking about."

"Okay, let's see what your buddies have to say about it. We picked up two of your *yes*-men this afternoon."

Animal shook his head at the statement. "See, that's how I know you've got the wrong guy. My men don't say *yes* they say *who*. I'd heard through the grapevine that the two of you were on a witch hunt for something that didn't exist, but my days are a bit too full to chase incredible stories." His phone vibrated on his hip. "Now if you'll excuse me." Animal stepped off to the side and answered his phone.

"Hey, baby, I heard what happened and almost fell out. Are you okay?" Gucci asked on the other end.

"I'm still in one piece, love. That was Don B.'s madness. I was in the studio making the doughnuts."

Gucci let out a relieved breath. "I'm so glad, baby. Where are you?"

"At the hospital with Don B."

"Is he okay?"

Across the room Don B. was still going back and forth with the detectives so he stepped off to the side so he could better hear her.

"Yeah, just a few scrapes. He'll live," Animal told her. "What's good with you? Are you still uptown?"

"Nah, I'm in the projects with these heifers. Why, you trying to meet up?" Gucci asked in anticipation.

Animal looked up at the detectives who were both watching him. "Nah, I may be tied up for a while."

"Awww, I was hoping we could get into some gangsta shit tonight," Gucci whined.

Animal gave the detectives his back so they couldn't read his lips. "My gangster shit is gonna start long before I even think about making it to the crib. Will you wait for me, goddess?"

"I'll wait for you on the highest peak in heaven or at the lowest point in hell," Gucci replied proudly.

"And let nothing short of God change that."

• • •

WHEN ANIMAL RETURNED TO DON B.'s bedside to join the rest of the crew he noticed that Detective Brown was still watching him. It wasn't a curious stare like the one he'd been getting from Alvarez off and on since they entered the room. This one was a look of pure hatred.

"So why don't you tell us what happened, Don? And I don't mean the bullshit stories you fed those two rookies who were here a few minutes ago. You know you can keep it funky with me," Alvarez assured him.

Don B. sucked his teeth. "Dawg, I don't know what happened. I was in my truck talking to a lady friend when the shooting started. I didn't look to see who, what, or where, I just ducked."

"So is that what we should tell the little girl's mother?" Brown asked.

"My nigga, it ain't on me to figure out what you should tell her moms, that ain't on me," Don B. said nonchalantly.

"Oh, this is all on you." Brown shoved a picture of the girl's bullet-riddled body in his face. "You take a good look at what your bullshit got this little girl, shit-bird." He was so angry that the veins on his neck looked about ready to pop. He had a daughter close to the victim's age and he couldn't help but to see her every time he looked at the picture. "If she hadn't been in the car with your snake ass then she might still be alive."

"Yo, Brown, I'm saddened by what happened to her, but that wasn't on me that was on God. If you wanna make a complaint about what happened I suggest you find a church."

Brown couldn't contain his rage any longer. Before anyone realized what was going on Detective Brown was across and swooping down on Don B. Alvarez was too far away so all he could do was watch as his partner was about to do something that would surely get both of them kicked off the force.

Animal watched the events unfold in what seemed like slow motion. The rational side of his brain told him to leave it alone and let it play itself out, but before he could send the signal to the rest of his body, he was already moving. Detective Brown was so focused on Don B. that he didn't even notice Animal coming from his blindside. Animal could've knocked him out with little effort at that angle, but he chose just to step in enough to knock Brown off course. The detective crashed into Animal and bounced off the bed onto the floor. In a flash, he was on his feet and his anger was now fixed on Animal. He grabbed Animal by the front of his shirt and shoved him into the medicine cabinet, shattering the glass. Animal didn't bother to try and move when the detective came with an overhand left, but when he tried to follow with the right Animal slipped under the punch and locked his arm at the shoulder. He snaked his arm around Detective Brown's neck and began applying pressure.

"You little bastard, if you don't get your hands off me I'm gonna . . ." Brown began, but Animal cut his air off.

"You're gonna what? Die in my arms like a fairy tale?" Animal whispered into his ear. "Yeah, the noble prince gets the shit choked outta him by the wicked ogre." Animal pressed a little tighter. "I hate you and every *Chicken George* cop like you, Brown. Not because you a cop, but because you ain't grow balls until they presented you with that badge and gun, lil sweet bitch." Animal kissed him on the cheek. "You think the hood will throw me a parade if I waste you, Brown?" Animal tensed when he felt the cold bite of steel against the skin behind his ear.

"If you don't let my partner go then they're gonna have a nasty mess to clean up off that wall," Alvarez told him seriously. Animal smirked and released his grip on Brown. No sooner than the detective was loose he spun around and punched Animal in the face.

"Muthafucka I should kill you." Brown reached for his gun, but Alvarez stopped him.

"Cool out, man. He ain't worth it," Alvarez told his partner.

Brown thought about it. "You're right, but he's going to jail. You just assaulted a police officer, boy." Brown advanced on Animal with his handcuffs drawn.

"If that's the case then we're both going in because you sure enough tried to take my jaw." Animal rubbed his chin.

"And we all saw it," Don B. cut in. "I wonder how much the city is gonna offer us to settle when we sue y'all?"

"You think anybody is gonna take the word of you low life criminals over a public servant?" Brown laughed at them.

"No, but they'll take my word for it." A dark-skinned woman entered the room. She was dressed in a gray pant suit and a pair of stylish flats.

"Marlene Silva." She handed him a black business card with the words *Gould and Silva* etched above the line that read *Attorneys at Law.*

Detective Brown looked down at the card and snorted. "Damn, Don B., you must be real desperate to call in a divorce lawyer on something criminal."

"He didn't call her. I did," Tone spoke up. "And for your information my sister is fully licensed to practice criminal or any other kind of law."

"Yes, I just specialize in divorce because I like giving men dick and leaving them broke with bad credit instead of them always doing it to us." Marlene winked. "Now, what we have here appears to be a Mexican standoff, Detectives. If this young man is getting arrested then I'll have to insist that your partner be taken into custody too and all that will leave us both swamped with is paperwork until the Chinese New Year. Or we can get both parties to call it even?" She looked at Animal, who just shrugged. "Detective?"

Detective Brown shot daggers at Animal and he shot them right back. Prior to that meeting they had just been adversaries working on opposite sides of the law, but blood had been spilled which always changed things. This wasn't over and both of them knew it. "Whatever," Brown said grudgingly.

"Great, glad we could work that out." Marlene gave him her predatory smile.

"So am I. Now everyone can get out. This is a hospital, not Madison Square Garden!" a doctor barked upon entering the room, with hospital security hot on his heels.

"Cool it, Doc, we're the law"—Detective Alvarez flashed his badge—"and this beautiful soul over here is his lawyer." He thumbed at Marlene, who was in the corner whispering to Don B. and Tone. "We've got some questions we need to ask this guy and we'll be out of your hair."

"Then I suggest you do it quick," the doctor shot back. "Now," he addressed everyone else, "if you're not a cop or legal representation, get out of my hospital."

"I'm outta here. Holla at me when you can, blood." Animal gave Don B. dap.

"I got you, my nigga. Y'all hold ya head out there. Get wit y'all when they cut me loose," Don B. told his crew.

As the men exited the hospital room Detective Brown had some parting words for Animal. "I've got my eye on you, *blood*," he said sarcastically.

Animal stopped and gave Detective Brown a cold expression. "I hear you talking, Brown. You ain't got nothing to worry about for as long as I'm in your line of vision, it's when you don't see me that you better clutch that rosary a little tighter. Enjoy your night, *Detectives*."

"That guy gives me the creeps," Marlene confided in Tone after Animal had gone.

Tone looked over at Detective Brown, who tried to keep his game face on, but you could see the worry in his eyes. "You ain't the only one, sis."

Chapter 23

IT WAS AFTER 3:00 A.M. WHEN ANIMAL FINALLY MADE IT back to his apartment. The adrenaline of the day's excitement had bled off and fatigue was starting to set in. Normally he would've taken a shower before going to bed, but he was too tired. All he wanted to do was crawl under the blanket and go to sleep.

When he entered his bedroom he found Gucci sleeping soundly in his bed. As quietly as he could he slipped out of his clothes and slid in next to her. At first she didn't stir, but when she felt him planting soft kisses on the back of her neck she squirmed a bit. Still kissing her softly, he slid his hand under the covers and began working her panties down. They got caught somewhere around her hips, so she lifted herself off the bed slightly to help him out. Using his thumb as a guide he slipped inside her juicy vagina.

Animal lay there inside her for a minute or two appreciating her warmth before he started pumping. She was tight, but eventually loosened up as they got deeper into the act. Gucci arched her back and pushed her ass against Animal so he could go deeper still, and let out a slow whistling of wind as he hit her spot. When she tired of the spooning position she rolled him onto his back and mounted him. They called her lover the Animal in the streets, but she was the one in beast mode as she grabbed two fists full of his hair and began to buck and thrust her hips this way and that so he could touch every inch of her insides.

"That's right, tear these fucking walls down," Gucci snarled as she leaned in and began to nip at his neck. The bites were playful at first, but the pressure increased as she came closer to climaxing. Animal had already released himself, but Gucci was still riding him wildly.

"Goddamn, goddamn, goddamn," Gucci chanted over and over as she felt herself getting wetter. "Whooooooooooo!" Gucci bellowed as she got her nut off and collapsed onto Animal.

The room was now silent save for the sound of both their rapidly beating hearts.

"DAMN, I LOVE YOU," GUCCI said after she was able to compose herself.

"Do you love me, or do you love these ten inches of dick I drop off in your drawers?" Animal asked playfully.

Gucci rolled off him and slapped Animal on the chest. "Nigga, don't flatter yourself. You ain't holding no ten inches of dick . . . nine and a half, maybe. So how is Don B.?"

"That nigga is good. Somebody tried to pop his head off, but as usual he survived. But a girl got killed," Animal said sadly.

"Wow, I'm so sorry to hear that. Man, it seems like Don B. has more lives than an alley cat."

"Tell me about it," Animal said, reaching for the blunt clip in the ashtray. He fired the weed up and watched the smoke rings float to the ceiling.

"So I guess the party is off now?"

"Nah, from what Tone told me Don B. still wants to do it." Animal expelled smoke from his nose and passed the blunt to Gucci.

"After somebody tried to kill him that crazy muthafucka still wants to be on Front Street like that?" Gucci shook her head. "Some people just don't learn."

"You know how Don B. is when his mind is set to something. He's stepping out like that just to show the world how gangsta he is. Don B. might be rich in money, but he's as poor as a shit farmer in common sense."

Gucci laughed. "Boy, you're crazy. So I guess I can still bust out that red dress I bought from the Lenox Mall when we were in Atlanta. We're gonna crush 'em when we walk up in the spot!" she said excitedly, but Animal had a worried expression on his face. "What?"

"Gucci, I was thinking that maybe you shouldn't go to the party."

"See, this is that bullshit. What you think I'm gonna fuck up your groupie action if I tag along?" she accused.

"No, it's not like that at all. Listen, baby, anybody that knows Don B. knows that they made a big mistake by letting him live. As we speak he's got every wanna be in the hood pounding the pavement to find out what went down. The shooter ain't gonna be safe until Don B. is in the ground and everybody knows that. If they had the balls enough to try to push him back on a crowded block I doubt if they'll have any reservations about getting at him in the club. If something jumps off I don't wanna risk you getting caught in the cross fire." He reached for her, but she pulled away.

"So, it's cool for you to place yourself in the line of fire?"

"I'm not gonna be in the line of anything and security is gonna be extra tight. I can take care of myself if something pops off, but I won't be able to be at peak efficiency if I gotta worry about you too. Besides, I got a nasty rash that I need to shake."

"Fuck you mean a rash? Boy, if you've been out there sticking your dick in them nasty video hos it's on and cracking!"

"Not a real rash, Gucci, I mean the police. They got at me when I went by to check on Don B.," he told her.

Gucci sat up. "For what?"

"Just some bullshit that they're trying to hang on me, ain't nothing that will stick," he said as if it was nothing, but he had been thinking about it more than he let on.

"Animal, I know you ain't out there cutting up in them streets with Brasco and them again? See, I knew it was a bad idea for you to let your crew know you were back in town." Gucci folded her arms.

"Calm your ass down, Gucci. I ain't cutting up and Brasco and Nef are in jail. The police picked them up for smoking weed outside."

"I swear them two muthafuckas act like they ain't got half a brain between them, and Ashanti ain't no better. You know the whole hood is talking about him escaping from that boys' home so when you speak to him you better tell him to lay low."

"Ashanti is gonna be alright. He's built for tougher stuff than dudes twice his age," Animal said proudly.

"Whatever. So what did you do today besides go to the studio and the hospital?" Gucci asked him. There was something about her tone that made him look up at her.

"Nothing, just passed through the hood to see what was popping," he lied.

"You're gonna get enough of the hood and your hoodlum ass friends one of these days. I keep telling you that if I find out you're back at it I'm leaving you. I ain't fucking with no street nigga, Tayshawn." She used his government name to let him know she was serious.

"I ain't at nothing and you ain't going nowhere. We're soul mates, remember?"

"Like ol' girl said Soul Mates Dissipate, so you better act like you know," Gucci told him. "Listen, baby, I don't mean to sound like I'm riding you, but I worry sometimes." She took both his hands in hers. "Animal, in this time we've been together I've come to know your heart as intimately as I know my own, so I know what it means for you to be back in New York. Sometimes being in the center of where it all jumped off can stir old feelings, maybe even old grudges."

"Most of my enemies are dead and the ones who aren't know enough to steer clear of me."

"Maybe"—she kissed him on the chin—"but do you know enough to steer clear of them? Daddy, don't let that noble heart of yours fuck up what you're building for yourself." She slid out of the bed.

"Where're you going?" Animal propped up on one elbow and watched her supple ass peeking out from beneath the bunched pink nightgown.

"To pee. Why? Do you wanna wipe my pussy?"

"Clit to booty, baby," he capped and tossed one of his socks at her.

Animal lay on his back reflecting on Gucci's words. For as much as he hated to admit it she truly knew his heart, but it was his soul he feared she would never understand. For as much joy as his success and his lady brought him, Animal's spirit was still restless and until the life of his mentor was repaid it would remain so. Animal clipped the weed and rolled over on his back with his hands folded behind his head. As his weary eyes began to droop his last thoughts were of how he was going to kill Rico.

Gucci felt like she was pissing a river as she sat in the darkened bathroom. She was a lightweight so the drinks and weed she'd put away hit her harder than most. When she was done using the bathroom she took a quick shower and went back into the bedroom naked to see if Animal was up for another round, but in typical man fashion he was fast asleep.

She started to wake him, but he looked so peaceful that she decided against it. Animal had been going so hard trying to get his career off the ground that it was rare for him to get a good night's rest, especially with Gucci. Careful not to wake him she slid into bed and snuggled next to him.

"I love you so much," Gucci whispered and kissed him softly on the lips.

GUCCI FELT LIKE A NEW woman when she woke up the next day. She looked over at the clock and realized that it was half past ten. She reached for Animal to find his side of the bed cold and empty, but there was a white rose with a card on the pillow. "Aww." She smiled and read the card.

> Had an early session with Chip.
> I'll call you when I get a break
> Love always
> —Tayshawn

Gucci sniffed the sweet rose and smiled. She was still a little upset about him telling her not to come to the party, but the rose and the sex from the night before took some of the sting out of it. She knew that Animal was only trying to keep her safe and just wished that he would allow her to do the same for him.

She got out of bed and slipped on her robe to go in the kitchen to make herself a light lunch. On the way she tripped over Animal's jeans, which were still on the floor with the rest of his clothes from the night before. "This nigga here," she said, collecting his clothes to drop in the laundry hamper. The clothes stunk of weed, but there was something else that she couldn't quite put her finger on. Gucci pressed his shirt to her face and inhaled.

"Groove," she said. It was one of her favorite scented candles but she hadn't bought any in months, which raised the question of how did Animal get the scent in his clothes?

PART 3

Hood Politics 101

Chapter 24

BY THE TIME SOLOMON ROLLED OUT OF BED MALIKA WAS already dressed and had breakfast on the table, which he thought was strange since they were both notoriously dysfunctional in the mornings and hated waking up. What he didn't know was that she had never gone to sleep. She'd prepared a hearty meal of pancakes, eggs, and of course turkey sausage. Malika's parents had never fed their children pork and she never gave it to her son.

"What's up with you this morning, Mom?" he asked Malika as she was washing the breakfast dishes.

"What do you mean?" she asked, doing the two-step in front of the sink to Raheem DeVaughn's "Bulletproof."

"I mean why are you so happy? You've been floating around this kitchen like Mary Poppins or somebody all morning."

"Boy, you're tripping, I'm just in a good mood. Life ain't all about being sour," she said, drying her hands on the dish towel.

Solomon placed his hand on her forehead. "You sure you not sick or something?"

"Boy, get outta here and get your coat and bag so you can catch the bus and I can go handle my business." She shooed him.

While Solomon went off to get his stuff Malika took a minute to reflect on her evening with Teddy. The first round was the bomb, but a little uncomfortable because it had been so long for her, but rounds two and three were out of this world. She and Teddy had gone at it until the wee hours of the morning before he finally took her home so that she would be there to get Solomon ready for school. Part of her felt guilty for backsliding and letting Teddy hit it and reopening the door for his bullshit, but she promised herself she wouldn't get caught up this time. For as much as she was feeling Teddy she knew she had to play the situation between them just like it was; friends with benefits. As long as she didn't let her emotions get involved she'd be okay, or at least she hoped as much.

"You ready?" Solomon came into the kitchen startling her.

"Oh, yeah let's go." Malika grabbed her purse and her coat.

"Ma, are you sure you're okay?"

Malika paused, then smiled. "Sure am, son. In fact, I haven't felt this good in a while. Now let's go catch your bus."

MALIKA PUT SOLOMON ON HIS bus, then headed over to the train station so she could get to 125th Street to see her case worker. From past experience she knew that calling wouldn't do much more than frustrate her so she decided to deal with the matter in person.

She arrived at building fifty-five at about 9:15 and could already tell that the day was gonna be one big headache. She got there early to beat the crowd only to find that there was some kind of staff meeting so the circus was delayed by an hour anyhow. Malika had to fight through a throng of rude security guards, loud women, and whining babies before she was finally able to speak to someone and tell her what she was there for.

The woman behind the desk seemed to have a nasty attitude when she flung the stack of paperwork across the table to Malika and ordered her to take a seat until her name was called. Malika's first reaction was to curse the woman out but that would only delay the process so she just took the paperwork and went to find a seat.

The waiting area was filled almost to capacity with men, women, and children who all seemed to have an issue. She managed to find a seat in the corner near the window and went to the task of filling out the papers. The process was even more irritating than the first time she'd gone through it, with the million and one questions they asked you on the forms. Some of the information wasn't even necessary; it was just the state trying to get in your business.

Halfway through the paperwork Malika found her space invaded as two children ran past her coming close enough to almost step on her foot. Bringing up the rear was a girl who couldn't have been more than twenty if she was a day. Her short hair was hastily slicked into a greasy ponytail and held in place by a child's pop-bow. Malika looked from the stroller the girl was pushing to the bulge under her shirt and shook her head. She was just one of many little girls who were trying to grow up too fast.

"Anybody sitting there?" the girl asked Malika. Without waiting for Malika to answer she squeezed into the empty space. As she was trying to get her child out of the stroller one of the bigger kids she'd come in with bumped into it as he ran by.

"Peanut, Ray-Ray, I'm gonna bust y'all asses for you if you don't stop running around in here like y'all ain't got no home training!" she shouted across the room, drawing distasteful stares. "I don't know what y'all looking at? You need to tend to your own damn kids and don't worry about how I talk to mine."

"Are all of them yours?" Malika hadn't meant to ask, but she couldn't help herself.

The girl gave her an offended look. "Hell no! Ray-Ray is my other baby daddy's son, the rest are mine. Humph, ain't no way in the hell I'm gonna be running around with *five* kids," the girl said as if the idea was that far-fetched.

"Sorry," Malika said and went back to her paperwork.

The girl nudged her. "You got a pen? They always want you to fill some shit out but ain't never got nothing to write with."

"Here you go." Malika handed the girl one of the pens from her purse. She looked for her iPod to avoid the conversation the girl was surely about to start up, but realized Solomon had taken it.

"You know every time I come in here this place is overcrowded," the girl continued. "It seems like there's always more people than there are workers. You would think that with all the money the city makes they could hire somebody to come in here and help out, you know what I'm saying?"

"Yeah," Malika said and focused on her paperwork.

"They put us through all this bullshit for that little bit of change they expect us to live on and think that we just supposed to smile and take it. I say fuck all that shit, the only reason I even put up with these nasty attitude bitches is because I get almost seven hundred dollars in food stamps every month. If it wasn't for that I would've told all these bitches to kiss my ass!"

"Can you keep your voice down please?" a plump Mexican woman wearing a name tag shouted from across the room.

"If you wasn't over there trying to be nosey then your ass wouldn't hear what me and my home girl were talking about!" the girl shot back. "These bitches be killing me the way they run around up in here like they the Queen Bee or some shit, you feel me, girl?" She held up her hand for a high-five but Malika just looked at her. "Oh, I know you ain't in here trying to be cute after I just stuck up for you when that Spanish bitch tried to check you?"

"I wasn't trying to *be* anything, I'm just sitting here filling out my paperwork like everybody else."

"Ex-act-ly." The girl snapped her fingers three times while she enunciated the word. "Your ass is in here trying to get on Welfare like everybody else so I don't know why you're trying to front like you're better than us, flinging your dreads and shit like you're cute, you fake ass Lauren Hill."

"Little girl, I've had about enough of your mouth." Malika stood up and the girl stood with her.

"What, you got some frog in you? I'll get it popping up in this bitch!"

"Miss, are these your kids?" one of the security guards had Peanut and Ray-Ray by the arms.

"Yeah, those are my kids and you need to take your hands off of them before I sue you and this whole muthafucka!" she said indignantly and snatched her children out of the guard's grip. "Y'all bring ya asses over here. That fat fuck didn't touch you, did he?"

"No, Mama," the boys said in unison.

"Good because I'd hate to have to go up-top in here. What were you doing to my kids?" she snapped at the guard.

Unlike Malika the guard didn't have a whole lot of patience. He kept smiling for anyone who may have been watching, but his tone was sharp and direct when he spoke. "First of all I wasn't doing anything to these bad-ass kids of yours; second of all they stuffed paper towels in the urinals and flooded the men's room. Now if you don't keep a leash on these monkeys and curb that nasty ass mouth of yours I'm gonna see to it that you get thrown out of here today and every time you come back I'll fix it so you're the last person seen for the day. Y'all have a good one," the guard capped and walked away.

"Fake ass flashlight cop," the girl mumbled as the guard walked away. "And I don't know why I can't never go nowhere without y'all acting a fucking fool and embarrassing me." She gave both boys a good slap. "Now go sit your asses down before I let Social Services have you the next time they come to the house."

Malika knew for a fact that she couldn't endure the ignorant young girl or her kids for a moment longer, but thankfully she didn't have to because they were calling her name.

• • •

BY THE TIME MALIKA FINALLY left the Welfare building at 3:30 she was ready to pull her hair out at the roots. As if the ordeal with the girl hadn't being trying enough, the hoops they made her jump through to recertify her for food stamps were too much. After filling out the stacks of papers, and running back and forth to the copy place on the corner to Xerox the documents they needed, Malika was informed that her case worker had already gone for the day and she would have to come back tomorrow. It took all of her resolve to keep from spitting on the girl behind the counter for not telling her that in the first place. Now she found herself standing in the middle of 125th Street aggravated, broke, and she still had to find a way to come up with dinner for her and Solomon.

As she passed a small pawnshop she looked down at the bracelet her mother had bought her for her sixteenth birthday and paused. She cherished the tennis bracelet but at that point eating took precedence over material things. With a lump in her throat she went inside and pawned the bracelet. They only gave her a quarter of what it was worth, but at least she and Solomon would be able to get by until she got things straight with her case worker. Malika was beyond disgusted with not only the way her day was going but with how her life was playing out. She had considered throwing herself into traffic, but decided against it because her life insurance had lapsed and she couldn't bare the thought of leaving Solomon worse off than he already was.

Malika was too depressed to go back home and stare at the walls so she figured she would walk the streets for a while until she thought of something, this is when Teddy's invitation came to her. Before they had parted company he had invited her to meet him that evening at the bowling alley on Fordham Road for some after-dinner drinks. She had intended to blow it off but after the day she had had a good strong drink was just what she needed. The clock on the side of the bank read 4:00 P.M. so she figured if she hurried she would still be able to meet Teddy at the bowling alley by five. Adding pep to her step, she headed toward the D train.

Chapter 25

THE POOL HALL WASN'T MUCH TO LOOK AT BUT THE ATmosphere was cool and the drinks were potent. Teddy introduced Malika around to his three best friends June, Smitty, and Sean and their ladies. For the most part everybody was cool, except June's wife Marsha who Malika kept catching dirty looks from while they were setting up their tables.

"Don't pay her any mind," Teddy whispered in Malika's ear as he brought two pool sticks and two Coronas to the table he had booked for him and her. "Marsha is always like that around new females."

"Oh, so you bring a lot of chicks around her?" Malika asked, leaning on her pool cue.

"Only the special ones." Teddy winked and leaned over the table to break, but Malika laid her pool stick across his.

"Whatever happened to ladies first?"

"You're right, where are my manners?" Teddy gave her a mock bow and stepped out of the way. He watched intently as Malika bent over the pool table, giving him the perfect view of her perky little ass. She must've felt his eyes on her because she wiggled it flirtatiously as her pool stick collided with the cue ball.

"Not bad," he said as he watched several of the balls scurry into holes.

"You could learn a thing or two from me." Malika sauntered over to the other side of the table and leaned over to take her next shot.

"I could probably teach you a thing or two." Teddy pressed himself against her taking away Malika's concentration.

"So now you gonna cheat to win, huh?" Malika pushed her ass into his waist as she tried again to align the stick with the cue ball. Feeling his hardness through his jeans made her smile wickedly.

"I'm down to do whatever it takes to win the prize, ma," he said seriously. Teddy looked behind him to see June and Smitty watching him. June gave him a wink, which Marsha caught and punched him in the ribs. "You gonna cause a situation in here, baby," Teddy whispered to her.

Malika looked over her shoulder and saw the girls glaring at her and whispering among themselves. "Some chicks don't have anything better to do than hate," she said and sank her next shot.

Teddy flashed June a stern look to check his wife, to which he just shrugged his shoulders. "If I were a chick I'd hate on you," Teddy told her jokingly.

"For what? I wear jeans and sneakers most of the time and I don't bother with makeup or a hairdresser so there's nothing glamorous about me." She sipped her Corona and looked for her next shot.

"That's just it, you shine without trying to," he said. "Malika, I know chicks that take hours getting themselves ready to go out, but you can roll out of bed and still look better than them."

"Oh, now this is a first." Malika took her next shot.

"What, someone paying you a compliment?"

"Nah, a dude still talking sweet after he got the pussy." She laughed and leaned over the table to drop the two ball in the side pocket.

"You stay with the jokes." He shoved her playfully and made her miss the shot.

"You gotta laugh at something or you'll cry over everything," she told him before sinking the next shot. For the next hour or so they sipped and flirted over two games of pool with her winning the first and Teddy barely winning the second.

"You're a lot better at pool than you let on, shorty," Teddy said, tapping his pool stick on the floor.

"You got lucky the last game," Malika boasted.

"So then let's shoot the tiebreaker, double or nothing."

Malika sized him up. "I didn't realize we were gambling."

Teddy invaded her space and whispered directly onto her lips, "Everything in life is a gamble."

The scent of liquor mingled with desire on Teddy's breath made the hair on the back of Malika's neck stand up. "I gotta use the bathroom," she said, backing up. "Rack 'em, I'll be back in a second."

Malika made hurried steps toward the bathroom trying to put as much distance between her and Teddy's charismatic ass as possible. Between the liquor and the magnetic attraction between them her mind was starting to go places it had no business going and voyeurism had never been her thing.

When she got in the cramped ladies' room Marsha and the other girls were having an intense discussion. When they noticed Malika everyone got quiet. Malika rolled her eyes and cut through the sea of scornful glares into the stall where she slammed the door and squatted over the bowl to relieve herself. Through the stall door she could hear the humming of their voices like worker bees so she focused talking about who she assumed to be her.

"That shit is just so trifling," she could hear Marsha saying.

"Look, as long as it ain't ya man, leave it alone," one of the other girls told her.

"Fuck that, I'd tell. If that creep-ass nigga is doing it and they're all friends there ain't no telling what they're doing in their spare time," a third girl chimed in. "I know if I ever catch Smitty trying to move like Teddy his ass belongs to me, ya hear?"

Having heard enough Malika wiped herself and came out of the stall with her head held high and a hard switch in her stride on the way to the bathroom sink. She took her time washing her hands and watching the girls through the mirror as they watched her. Malika dispensed a few of the rough brown paper towels and dried her hands calmly before addressing the girls. "Is there something I can help any of y'all with?"

"No, it seems like you've helped yourself to enough," a dark-skinned girl, whose name escaped Malika, said.

"And what is that supposed to mean?" Malika poked her chest out. She had never been a fighter and the thick dark-skinned girl looked like she would mop the floor with Malika, but her dad had always taught her to stick up for herself and she wouldn't let the girl know she was scared.

"Nothing," Liz said, trying to avoid what she saw coming. The little yellow girl was as much a brawler as her friends, but she would be damned if they would have her in the streets scrapping in her new shoes.

"Oh, because I was feeling like there was some type of problem." Malika rolled her eyes, letting the drinks pump courage into her. This was all it took to set Marsha off.

"You know what? There is a problem and that problem is little hot in the pants bitches sticking their pussies where they don't belong."

Malika backed up and looked at her. "Excuse you? Look, you don't know me or nothing about me so you're way out of line for trying to judge me."

It was Marsha's turn to take a step back. "I'm out of line trying to judge you? You're out of pocket for even being here right now! See chicks like you get the shit beat out of them because they ain't got no boundaries and no class. I wish I would catch you trying to rub up on June like you're doing that foul ass nigga Teddy. I'd rock you the fuck to sleep, bitch."

"Bitch? Ya mama's a bitch!" Malika shot back and took a step toward Marsha but the other two girls jumped in the middle.

"Marsha, chill, it ain't ya place to check the situation," Liz cut in. "We too grown to be fighting in bathrooms over dick y'all."

"Tell your miserable ass home girl that!" Malika said indignantly.

"Slow up, shorty, because I really don't know you like that and you're already starting off on the wrong foot," Liz checked Malika. "Malika, you seem like you crazy cool but you're confused about a lot of shit and you need to be easy. You in here trying to defend Teddy like he's your boo is like trying to fit circles into squares."

Malika sucked her teeth. "If you've got something to say then you need to spit it out."

Liz raised her hands in surrender. "It ain't my place or my business. All I'm gonna tell you is, you need to make sure you know who your enemies are before you fire those shots."

"Whatever, I'm good on the riddles. Since it seems like me being here is causing problems then maybe I need to get up outta here," Malika said.

"Yeah, you should probably do that, before reality sets in and you realize how much of a fool Teddy is making of you," Marsha said venomously.

Malika sized Marsha up. "Well, a wise bitch would never argue with a fool because you can't tell one from the other from a distance. Y'all be easy." Malika flung her hair and stormed out of the bathroom.

Marsha stood there shaking her head with her nostrils flaring. "Bitches can be so stupid."

"True indeed, but we were all young and stupid at one point. Now let's get back out there and keep our eyes on *our* men."

• • •

WHEN MALIKA EXITED THE BATHROOM a small crowd had gathered around the entranceway, undoubtedly having overheard the shouting between the girls. In the center of the pack, wearing a confused expression, was Teddy.

"Everything okay?" Teddy asked, but Malika ignored him and kept walking. He caught up with her near the door. "What's good with you?"

"I should be asking you the same question, Teddy." She looked him up and down. "I was having a fucked up enough day already without your home girls making me feel like I'm some kind of skank."

"Malika, what are you talking about?"

"I'm talking about those cackling ass hens that were in the bathroom making me feel like I'm some kind of home wrecker or something. Teddy, I did that *other woman* shit when I was a teenager and I'm not trying to go through it again." She took a step but he stopped her.

"Malika, you could never be the other anything. Chicks like you are one of a kind. I don't know what Marsha and them bitches said to you in the bathroom, but if it didn't come outta my mouth it ain't the gospel."

"So you don't have a girl?" she asked.

Teddy's eye ticked, but he kept his face even.

"Is that what this is all about?" He smirked as if it was nothing. "Malika, I wouldn't even insult your intelligence by telling you that I've been keeping it in my pants since the last time we were together. Yeah, I got a lil situation that ain't really working out, and Marsh and them know shorty which is why they're trying to throw shade on you, but don't feed into that."

"Teddy, you could've just kept it one hundred and told me that you were dealing with someone and let me decide for myself if I still wanted to see you tonight."

"For what? You said yourself that there was nothing more to

this than two old friends hanging out so it never crossed my mind to get that deep into it," he said swiftly. "Malika, we can go back up in there and I'll make Marsh and them tell you what it is," he faked for the door.

"No, you don't have to do all that. I've had all the drama I can stand in a twenty-four hour period. Just take me home."

"You sure, we could go get some dinner or something?" he suggested.

"Nah, I appreciate it, but I'm good. I just wanna get home to my son."

Chapter 26

TEDDY DROPPED MALIKA OFF IN FRONT OF HER PROJECTS and told her he would call and check on her in a few to which she just responded with a grunt. She hadn't meant to be so snippy with him, but she was still pissed about what had gone down at the bowling alley with the girl Marsha. Malika wasn't used to excessive amounts of drama and it had her drained. All she wanted to do was get upstairs to her apartment and crawl under the covers.

As usual the knuckleheads were loitering in the courtyard. Lloyd shuffled back and forth in front of the building directing the fiends to the bench at the far end where Jay was sitting, looking around nervously. It was obvious to a duck what he was up to. Malika started to say something to him about it, but decided against it. She could barely deal with her own child, let alone add her two cents in the business of someone else's. She had always liked Jay but she knew at that moment that would be the end of his and Solomon's friendship. The last thing she needed was her son getting caught up in their bullshit. Posted up in front of the building were Scar and Prince who were overseeing the operation.

"What up, Malika?" Scar greeted her with his larcenous smile.

"Hey, Scar," she said in an uninterested tone.

"Damn, you look like somebody kicked your dog," Prince said jokingly.

"It sure feels like it, Prince," Malika said with a sigh.

"You wanna talk about it?"

"Not really, I just wanna get upstairs and into my bed."

"You need some company?" Scar asked.

Malika looked at him crazy. "I don't think so. Prince, have you seen Solomon? I've been calling him for the last hour or so to see if he made it in from school yet but he didn't answer."

"Yeah, I saw him go in the building about an hour or so ago."

"Thanks," she said, continuing into the building.

"Malika, if you change ya mind you know where to find me," Scar called after her, but Malika ignored him.

When Malika got into her apartment she tripped over Solomon's book bag that he had dropped in the middle of the floor, which she had constantly asked him to stop doing. Talking to him was about as effective as talking to a wall and it was getting on her nerves. She snatched the bag off the floor and stormed toward his bedroom. Solomon's room was a mess with dirty laundry and dishes on the floor. The boy lay across the bed playing a video game as if he didn't even notice the filth.

"Solomon, how many times do I have to tell you about cleaning up behind yourself?" She threw the book bag on the bed.

"My fault," he said nonchalantly.

"And where the hell have you been? I've been trying to call you for an hour?"

"I got here a while ago. I saw your missed calls on the caller ID," he told her, never taking his eyes off the video game.

Malika stepped between him and the television. "Then why didn't you call me back?"

"Because the phone is cut off one-way, and so is the Internet and the cable!" he said with attitude.

Malika cursed silently. She had gotten the notice about the

interruption of services from Verizon, but she couldn't pay them and still have carfare to get back and forth to her appointments. She intended to call them and try to get an extension, but with everything going on it slipped her mind.

"Damn, I'm sorry. I'll call them in the morning and take care of it," Malika said.

"With what?" he asked sarcastically.

"You let me worry about that. Did you do your homework yet?"

"I'll do it later."

"Solomon, you know the rules; no video games or television until you've done your homework." She turned the game off.

"Damn, you didn't even give me a chance to save my season!" he barked.

"You'd better watch your mouth, before I bust you in it," she warned. "I don't know what this chip is you've been carrying around on your shoulder the last few weeks, but you'd better get it together before we have a problem."

"Wouldn't want that. We've got enough problems as it is," he said and opened up his book bag to do his homework. Malika started to get in his ass, but someone knocking at the door saved him.

Malika went to the door and looked through the peephole where she saw two men wearing blue coveralls. "Yes?" She opened the door a crack.

"How are you, ma'am? We're from Rent-A-Center. We've come for the television and entertainment system you were renting from us." He looked at the clipboard to double-check the information. "You're late on your payments."

"Oh, yeah . . . Listen, I meant to call you guys about that. I know I'm a little behind, but if you'll give me another week I'll mail you a check," she lied, hoping he would buy it.

He didn't.

"Sorry, but you haven't made a payment in three months so we gotta collect the stuff."

"C'mon, just give me a little more time and I promise, promise, promise that I'll straighten it out," she pleaded.

The man looked at her sympathetically. "I wish I could, lady, but I could lose my job if I don't collect this stuff. I'm really sorry."

Malika sighed. "Not as sorry as I am." She opened the door to let them in. As the repo men were coming in to collect her entertainment system Solomon bumped past them into the hallway. "Solomon, where are you going?"

"To the store, I'll be back," he said without stopping.

"Solomon, get your butt back in here and do your homework," Malika called after him but he kept going. "Boy, do you hear me?" Malika thought about following but the sound of something breaking in the living room distracted her.

Fifteen minutes after they had come, the repo men had left with half of Malika's living room. Solomon still hadn't come back from the store and she didn't have the strength to go out and look for him. Malika's hollow living room was a reflection of how her soul felt at that moment. She was so distraught that she threw up in the wastebasket. Feeling defeated and broken, Malika sat in the empty space left by her entertainment system and cried.

"LOOK AT THIS MUTHAFUCKA." SCAR motioned to Solomon who was coming out of the building with his face twisted up.

"What up, son? You good?" Jay asked, sensing that something was wrong with his friend.

"Yeah, I'm a'ight," Solomon lied. Jay knew him well enough to see through it, but he wouldn't pry in front of Scar. "So what up, where it at?" Solomon leaned on the fence next to Lloyd, who has hitting a blunt.

"Shit, just doing what we do." Lloyd gave Solomon dap.

"And what we do is illegal, so you need to keep it trucking before ya mother comes out here and call the police on us for trying to corrupt you." Scar shooed him.

"Stall him out, Scar. The lil nigga is a'ight," Lloyd said, exhaling weed smoke through his nose. "What up, lil homey, you ready for round two?" He extended the blunt. To everyone's especially Scar's surprise Solomon hit the blunt like a champ. He damn near choked to death but they appreciated his zeal.

"Lil man trying to grow up, huh?" Scar said, looking him up and down.

"Ain't no men in my house, so I guess the job falls to me," Solomon told Scar.

"Where the fuck did you pick that up, on a Lil Wayne CD?" Scar laughed, but Solomon didn't.

Scar narrowed his eyes. "What you got cooking in that big ass brain of yours?"

"A come-up," Solomon said seriously.

"Sol, I heard that Guarded Riverside is paying to tutor little kids. As smart as you are I know you could land the gig," Jay told him.

Solomon gave Jay a blank stare. "My dude, do I look like I'm trying to bust my brain for the shorts they're giving out? Nah, I need to get some real money." He looked at Scar.

Scar waved him off. "Fuck outta here with that lame shit you talking."

"Scar, I'm dead-ass serious. I'm stepping to you on some G-shit out of respect because this is your block, a bird nigga would've just tried to come out with his lil work and hustle around you, but I ain't off that."

Scar laughed. "You hear this square ass nigga?" He stepped directly in front of Solomon in an attempt to intimidate him. He could tell the boy was scared but he wouldn't back down. "Son, this ain't Summer Youth. This is the trap."

"It's also where the money is," Solomon told him. "Dick, y'all have known me almost all my life so you know my story. Me and mama-love are barely getting by and I'm tired of sitting on my ass watching her struggle. I need to make a play, big homey."

The hunger behind Solomon's eyes drew a broad smile to Scar's face. He reached in his pocket and pulled out a few loose bags of crack, and tested the weight in his hand. "You really trying to get out here and get it up?"

"Come on, Scar, you know Sol don't . . ." Jay began, but Scar silenced him with a look.

"I asked you a question, B." Scar shook the cracks in his hand. In response Solomon held out his hand. "Bet." Scar dropped the bags in his hand. "Let me see how you handle yourself with getting those off and we'll talk." Like a trained soldier Solomon spun on his heels and walked toward the building. Scar watched him comically and shook his head.

"Scar, do you think that was a good idea. If he gets knocked his moms is gonna go through the roof," Jay pointed out.

"If he gets knocked he ain't got nobody but himself to blame, he asked for those rocks, I didn't offer them to him," Scar said.

"Son, you crazy for putting that nigga down, Prince is gonna wild the fuck out when he finds out." Lloyd shook his head.

"Man, who the fuck is out here holding this down, me or Prince?" Scar snapped. "If a little nigga wanna feed his people, who the fuck am I to stop him if I got enough food on my plate for everybody to eat? Lloyd, I don't know why you and this little bitch nigga Jay worrying so much for anyhow; after about twenty minutes of standing in that lobby Solomon is either gonna get spooked or tired and run back upstairs."

"You ain't never lied." Lloyd nodded behind Scar at Solomon who was coming back out of the building.

"What's the matter, you heard somebody getting off the elevator and thought it was them D-boyz?" Scar teased him.

"Nah, I'm finished, let me get a few more." Solomon held his hand out.

Scar gave him a disbelieving look. "How the hell did you get off fifteen bags in sixty damn seconds when I didn't even see anybody go in the building?"

"Because I know two people on the first floor who smoke, they just keep it quiet. They bought six a piece and shorty from the fifth floor is waiting for me to come back with the three more 'cause she wanted five. Let's get this money."

Chapter 27

ALMOST TWENTY HOURS AFTER HE WAS PICKED UP, RICO was released from custody. His lawyer petitioned to have him released from the precinct but of course Brown and Alvarez saw that that didn't happen. Rico was processed and sent through Central Bookings before appearing before a judge and being released on bond. Changa was not so fortunate.

From what the lawyer told him someone had broken into Lee's house and tried to murder him and his girlfriend and for reasons Rico didn't understand Lee was convinced that he was behind it. The police had rousted him for hours but Rico had airtight alibis that accounted for almost every minute of that day, and receipts from the different places he had stopped to back it up. The police didn't have anything to link him to what happened other than Lee's word and he was in and out of consciousness. Once he got lawyer'd-up the detectives couldn't touch him, unfortunately the same couldn't be said for Changa.

Apparently the police had found a soda can at the crime scene with Changa's prints on it. How they got there was a mystery to Rico and everybody else. Rico wanted to arrange a meeting between him and Changa, but the lawyer advised against it. As it stood they didn't have enough to charge Rico with a crime but the prints gave them a fist full of Changa's balls. It was best if he cut himself loose from the situation while he could and help Changa from a distance, if he decided to help him at all. If Changa was guilty of what the police were saying then he was in violation because he had killed a member of Tito's family, and it was an offense that called for death. The threads of the situation had to be unraveled without haste and Rico knew just who to holla at.

Before he was even released Rico had set the wheels in motion, but it was a task that was easier said than done. He had Carmen place a call to a third party that would connect him to the source. There was some reluctance because it was such short notice, but after a brief explanation of the seriousness of the situation the source agreed to see Rico and the meeting was set to go down at Katz Deli off of Houston.

Rico instructed his driver to pull up in front of the fire hydrant and to keep the engine running, as he hadn't planned on staying longer than he had to. Attending him were two hired thugs named Mud and Dirt whom he kept on retainer for sticky situations like the one he found himself caught up in. They were a shabby pair who didn't put much stock in physical appearance, but they were thorough when it came to causing mayhem. He had tried to get a hold of Ras to let him know what was going on, but kept getting the voice mail. Knowing Ras's irresponsible ass he had probably let the battery die, as he was known to do regularly. Rico promised himself that after he took a hot bath and got a good night's rest he was going to tighten up his ranks.

With Rico leading the pack the trio breezed inside the deli and headed straight for the back. Already seated at a booth in the far corner was the man he had come to see, Shai Clark. The young Don sat slouched in the chair reading a tattered copy of *Hip-Hop Weekly*. To his left and right respectively sat Angelo and Swan. Two tables to the left young Doc sat with two hard-faced men, picking over a corned beef sandwich. He spared Rico and his people a brief glance when they initially walked in, but other than that he didn't acknowledge him. Seeing Shai out in full guard at a friendly meeting made Rico suspect that he may have already had an idea of what was going on and who was behind what.

Rico stopped Mud and Dirt before he reached Shai's table. "Y'all go get ya selves some sandwiches or something from the counter while I talk to this dude. I won't be long," he told them before joining Shai at his table.

Shai took his time closing his magazine and smoothing the faded cover. "What's up, Rico?"

"I was hoping you could tell me. Shai, I know you already know the gist of what happened so I ain't gonna bore you with the details of what I've been through, but what I will ask is if you could help me with what's going on?"

"Rico, all I've gotten through the ghetto grapevine so far is that Changa tried to push Lee's shit back and fucked it up, now Lee and anybody with ears is fingering you because they know Changa's your dude."

"But, Shai, that's crazy. Lee made a lot of money for me on the streets and he always came correct with it, it'd be stupid to kill him. And even if I did want Lee dead why the hell would I send my personal bodyguard to do it?"

Shai shrugged. "Rico, that's a discussion for you and your fam to have, you know we don't get involved unless it affects the business of the Commission as a whole."

"If somebody is trying to frame me then it will affect the Commission if I'm not here to earn!" Rico shot back.

"Rico, I've known you long enough to know that you're a lot of things but never sloppy, especially when it comes to homicide. Maybe Changa and Lee had a beef you didn't know about and it got to the point where there was no more to be said," Shai suggested.

Rico let Shai's statement seep in and analyzed it before

responding. "Yes, I had thought about it like that since his prints prove that he was there, but it doesn't sound like Changa. For one thing he's very meticulous when it comes to killing, so there's no way he would've been foolish enough to leave his prints. The other thing that was bothering me was the way it was done." Rico went on to give Shai the details of the crime as he had received them, which caused Shai to raise an eyebrow as he hadn't heard the whole story.

"Damn, they took the boy's eyes and paralyzed him?" Angelo shook his head. "There ain't too many who twist shit up that disrespectfully and I don't break bread with none of them."

Shai gave Angelo a concerned look, then turned back to Rico. "I don't know, dawg. You need to put a lid on whoever is trying to cramp your style so you can get this heat off you and get back to business. I'm taking a hell of a chance even meeting you here knowing you're fresh out on a murder charge, you're as hot as a firecracker. Whatever is going down I hope you get a lid on it soon, because these internal strifes with the families ain't good for business."

"So what am I supposed to do, send hit squads at everybody who I have an issue with in the streets?" Rico asked sarcastically.

"No, just the ones who got balls enough and guns enough to actually succeed in putting a tag on your toe," Shai told him seriously. "But I say again, this is a conversation you should be having with your men, not me. You let a weasel loose in your henhouse and it's on you to get him out." Shai pushed away from the table and stood up. "Rico, if I hear anything I'll make sure I get word to you. In the meantime, stay low and regroup, my dude. I'm sure before it's all said and done you'll have it all figured out." Shai dropped the copy of *Hip-Hop Weekly* on the table in front of Rico on his way out.

"YA BOY RICO SURE LOOKED scared," Swan said once they were outside the deli.

"I might be too if I had his kind of problems. The thing about niggaz like Animal is that they never stop. You can beat them, stab them, or shoot them but if you don't kill them you'll always have to worry about them," Shai said.

"Then how come we haven't put his brains on the wall yet?" Swan asked. "Shai, you said yourself that if Animal can get to Rico he might start getting big ideas. Why do you allow him to live knowing what kind of problem he represents?"

"It's simple. Animal knows that I could have him whacked out whenever I got the notion to, but I gave him a pass. If he actually comes out of this alive it's a courtesy he won't forget. If Animal kills Rico then we promote someone who isn't so much of a headache and all is quiet again; if Animal gets pushed we don't have to worry about him, either way it's a win for us."

"If that's the case then why didn't you just tell Rico that it was Animal who went in on his people?" Angelo asked.

"For the same reasons that my father never sat me down and told me what it would take to walk a mile in his shoes. None of us have passed the test of fire with someone whispering the answers on the sidelines. If Rico is smart he'll put it together and if he isn't then he's dead, simple as that," Shai said.

"You know, if I didn't know any better I'd think you were getting pretty good at this crime boss thing," Swan said, holding the back door of the black SUV open for Shai to get in, while Angelo watched the street for trouble.

Shai looked back at his friends and smiled. "Because I had the best teachers."

"HOW'D EVERYTHING GO?" DIRT ASKED, taking the seat Angelo had abandoned. Mud also joined them.

"It was a waste of fucking time because Shai didn't tell me anything I don't already know," Rico said heatedly. "Shai is out here rolling five or six deep, then his ass is nervous about something too, so maybe I ain't the only one with an invisible enemy. I wouldn't be surprised if this whole shit was done by somebody trying to upset the balance of power and all them muthafuckas are taking precautions."

"You ain't lying, Rico. I heard on the streets that a few cats that's getting it up out there all decided to take week-long vacations outta New York at the same time, like they knew something was coming before anybody else. This shit has gotta be connected," Mud suggested, while he flipped through the pages of the discarded magazine on the table. "With the way everybody jetting out this party that Big Dawg is supposed to be throwing is probably gonna be whack." Mud tapped the advertisement for the grand opening of Code Red.

Rico treated Mud's statement like white noise at first, but that was before his eyes landed on the photo collage that featured all of the big stars who were supposed to be in New York for the event. He snatched the magazine from Mud and looked closely at one picture in particular.

Thanks to the ad his enemy now had a face.

Chapter 28

IT WAS CHILLY OUTSIDE, BUT ANIMAL HAD HIS WINDOWS rolled down letting the wind whip through his hair. He needed it to wake him up as he had had little sleep the last few days. He felt bad about telling Gucci the little white lie, but he reasoned it was for the best. If he had told her where he was really going then he would have to also tell her why he was going there and it wasn't a story he was quite ready to tell.

The old Damu Ridas cut "Shoulda Been a B-Dog" blasted so loud through his speakers that he had to adjust his rearview mirror twice from the vibration. He rode past Columbia University and watched as multicultural kids moved back and forth on their way to class or just shooting the shit. Most of the students were oblivious to the fact that their school sat on the border of one of America's many urban ghettos, and those who did know what time it was could often be found skulking around in the hood trying to score their vice of choice. At 110th Animal made a left and headed east toward his destination. To his surprise and relief he was able to find parking on Columbus Avenue so he didn't have far to walk back. He took a minute to pop a mint into his mouth and spray Febreze before getting out of the car and disappearing into the block.

As soon as Animal stepped into the building he could smell whatever solution they had used to clean the floors. It smelled like oranges soaked in ammonia, but he would rather smell that than the sickly odor it was used to cover up. Behind the desk in the lobby sat a heavyset dark-skinned woman dressed in a nurse's uniform. How brows were tightly knitted as she concentrated on the magazine on her lap. Feeling that someone had entered the room she looked up and her thick lips parted into a wide smile.

"Now I know I'm seeing things, get your narrow ass over here and give me some love." She came from around the corner and hugged him tightly. "Boy, I haven't seen you in so long! Where have you been?"

"Here and there." He smiled warmly. "How you been, Mrs. Brown?"

Mrs. Brown sighed. "Well, I got my health so I can't complain."

"I know I was supposed to call first but . . ."

"No need to explain. You've been a busy man." She smiled.

"You don't know the half, Mrs. Brown. This new job I've got has taken up a lot of my time."

"You don't have to tell me, I've got ears and eyes." She held up the magazine she'd been reading. It was a copy of *Hip-Hop Weekly*, with the page folded back on the interview he'd done with them two months prior. He remembered how he had been initially against doing the interview because of the photo they wanted to use. It was a picture of him standing in a cage scowling at the camera, with teeth of sharpened steel instead of gold. Strewn around the cage were the dead bodies of several people dressed like tourists, with the caption "Don't Feed the Animals" spray-painted in graffiti. Animal didn't like the picture because he felt that it gave off the wrong image of him and his music, but Don B. thought it would be great for publicity, and of course he was right. The picture was now one of the most downloaded wallpapers on the Internet.

"We're all very proud of you, *Animal*."

Animal could feel himself blushing at Mrs. Brown calling him by his street name. "Thank you," he said like a shy child who had just won the class spelling bee. There was a long pause before Animal finally got around to the question he had come to ask. "How's she doing?"

Mrs. Brown's face darkened a bit, but she kept her smile. "Up and down, but God is good, baby. Come on and let me take you to her." She took Animal gently by the arm. "I'm sure she'll be glad to have a visitor, especially a celebrity."

Animal followed Mrs. Brown down the pale hallway with his eyes fixed on the green tiles under his feet, mindful not to look into any of the rooms on either side of the hall. Animal had visited the nursing home dozens of times, but the trips never got easier. He always felt like the residents of the facility were watching him with accusatory eyes. It was as if the residents being so close to the end of their lives could see the shadow of death that he wore like a cloak around his shoulders.

Mrs. Brown stopped at a room at the end of the first-floor hallway and peered inside. "She's awake, good. Come on." She led Animal into the room.

It was a sparsely decorated room with only a bed and a small table that could be used for writing or eating. The television mounted on the wall was tuned to an old episode of *Murder, She Wrote* but there was no sound coming from it. A large wing-backed chair sat in the corner facing the window with an old woman looking out at the sunset. Her skin looked as thin as parchment and was ghostly pale from lack of direct sunlight. She had a mane of silver hair that fell around her thin shoulders in two long braids. It pained Animal to look at her, yet he couldn't turn his eyes away.

"Hanna, it's Maggie," Mrs. Brown called out to her.

She turned her milky white eyes in the direction of Mrs. Brown's voice and smiled. "I'm blind not deaf, girl. I heard you when you came in, but I also heard two sets of footsteps. Who've you got with you?"

"Hey," Animal said softly.

Hanna's face suddenly became very serious. "Tayshawn?" She stepped forward slowly with her hands extended.

Animal cringed, but didn't move away when she began exploring the lines of his face. Tears sprang to the corners of her eyes and traced thin lines down her cheeks. "Oh, my Tayshawn." She wrapped her withered arms around him and squeezed as tight as she could. "Dear God, how long has it been?"

"Too long," Animal said, fighting back tears of his own.

"Well, I'm gonna leave you two alone so you can catch up. I think there's some lemonade in the kitchen if anybody is thirsty," Mrs. Brown offered, but neither Animal nor Hanna gave any indication that they heard her so she quietly left the room.

"It's been so long since I've had a visitor," Hanna said.

"Sorry I haven't come by in a while. I've been pretty busy," Animal said.

"I know how it is with you young people, always on the go. My grandson was the same way." When Hanna made the statement Animal was glad that she was blind so she couldn't see the change in his facial expression. "Lionel was always running like he had the devil on his heels, and it's a shame that death was the only thing to make him slow down. He was all that I had left, you know, and now I'm just a lonely old lady." Hanna began to weep.

"Don't cry, Hanna." Animal put his arm around her. "As long as I'm here you'll never be alone."

Hanna wiped her eyes with the back of her robe. "My Tayshawn is always there for his Hanna. I'm glad that you were my grandson's friend and I just wished some of your goodness would've rubbed off on him while he was alive."

The statement hit Animal in the chest like a fist and it took all of his will to keep him from breaking down. "Lionel was a good kid. He just had a lot of demons riding him."

"Demons." She laughed. "There's something about Lionel and

demons in the same sentence that seems to just fit. But let's not speak ill of the dead, Tayshawn. Come and sit with me." She motioned for Animal to help her back to her chair by the window. Still holding her tiny hands in his Animal took the chair opposite hers and studied the old woman. The worry lines around her eyes were deeper than he remembered, and her hair had begun to thin on the top, but she still carried herself with the same nobility as she had when she was twenty-something.

"So, tell me all about it," Hanna said, snapping Animal out of his daze.

"About what?"

"Come on now. You think that I haven't heard about your new-found success? You've been the talk of everyone here for the last few months. And might I add how popular you've become with the young nurses." She winked.

"It's okay, I guess," he said modestly.

"Tayshawn, becoming a star is more than just okay. I can remember back when I was still touring the circuit. When I took the stage and looked out at all those people in the audience it was like I was being transported to another world." She closed her eyes and reflected. "And all the boys followed me around like I was the Pied Piper. Hand me that picture." She pointed to her nightstand where she kept a five-by-eight photo. It was a black-and-white picture of a much younger Hanna and a jovial-looking black woman. "That picture was taken in 1951 at the Blue Room in Detroit."

"Wow, you were sexy, Hanna," Animal said playfully.

"You bet your ass I was."

"Who's the pretty brown-skinned girl?" Animal asked, wondering why her features were so familiar to him.

"Ms. Willie Mae Thornton."

Animal's eyes widened. "Big Mama Thornton?"

"The one and only." Hanna smiled. "It was the first time that the Blue Room had ever allowed a black and a white singer to share the same stage. It didn't go on to make much noise in the way of the news, but it was a great boon for colored singers. She and I went on to become great friends, but we lost contact when my second husband and I moved to Paris for a few years. I was so sad when I found out that she'd died in 'eighty-four."

Animal shook his head. "I would've given anything to see her perform; she was one of my favorites."

"Then take the picture."

"Hanna, I couldn't . . ."

"Nonsense." She cut him off. "I'm blind so I don't need it. Besides, I knew her in life and though my memory is a little hazy these days, I still have clearer pictures of her in my head than any old photo could produce. You take that picture and put it in a pretty frame for me." She patted his hand.

Animal's phone vibrated. He looked at the screen and saw the word *Kismet* flash across the screen and knew it was Gucci, but he hit the ignore button.

"Take your call if you have to," Hanna said, having heard the vibration.

"Nah, it can wait. Catching up with you is more important right now. So have you been getting the money I've been sending to Mrs. Brown for you?" he asked.

"Yes, thank you. Not that I have much need for it in here." She tried to laugh but it came out as a raspy cough.

Animal sprang to his feet and moved to attend to Hanna. "Are you okay? Should I go get Mrs. Brown?"

"No, just get me some water." She waved at the pitcher on her nightstand. Animal filled a glass and helped Hanna take a few sips through the straw. When she handed the cup back to Animal the straw was stained with what looked like blood.

"Hanna, are you sure you're okay?" he asked.

"I'm fine. It's these damn dust bunnies that are doing it. I've complained about the lazy cleaning girls forgetting to dust in here thoroughly, but it keeps falling on deaf ears."

Animal wasn't convinced. "Hanna, you know we don't keep things from each other. Please don't lie to me."

Hanna's face saddened. "It's nothing more than what they've been saying for years. There's a problem with this, that's blocked, those are wearing down. If I had a dollar for every time the doctors told me I was gonna die I'd be a rich woman."

"Hanna, if there's anything I can do . . ."

"Tayshawn, it's in God's hands. I don't worry about it so neither should you. Now, tell me about this new life you've created for yourself."

Chapter 29

GUCCI SAT IN HER TRUCK WITH SADE'S "SOLDIER OF Love" playing, hoping that it would help to assuage the throbbing in her temples. She was supposed to be enjoying her time back in Harlem, but instead she was refereeing a battle between her heart and her instincts. It had taken everything she had not to call Animal and give him the third degree about the scent in his clothes, but she grudgingly held her insecurities in check. Her mind told her that it was probably nothing, but her gut told her it was *something*. The mystery of the scent in his clothes was driving her crazy and she knew she'd only end up frustrating herself if she stayed in the house trying to solve it, so she decided to hit the streets. She didn't really have a destination when she set out but she eventually ended up back down in the projects waiting for Jada, who at last check was twenty minutes late.

"Gucci, Gucci!" a voice snapped her out of the daze she was in. She looked up expecting to see her cousin Jada, but it was Boots.

"Oh, shit, what's popping?" Gucci got out of the truck and gave Boots a hug. Boots smelled like sex masked by perfume, but Gucci didn't complain. She was happy to see a familiar face.

"Damn, I ain't seen you in a minute, Gucci. What's good?"

"You know me, ma, just trying to live like everybody else," Gucci said modestly.

Boots looked Gucci up and down taking in every stitch of clothing and a piece of jewelry. "If this is trying to get by then I'd be damn happy to struggle. Gucci, you look fabulous! I guess the life of a star's wife is really paying off for you."

"I have no complaints. Animal takes good care of me, but I take better care of myself."

"And speaking of Animal, how is he? I hear he don't come to NY much anymore," Boots asked innocently, but Gucci knew she was fishing for information. Outside of Tionna none of Gucci's friends knew the real reason Animal fled New York.

"Animal is good. He spends so much time working that he doesn't have a lot of free time these days. You know how these niggaz get when they're chasing a dollar," Gucci said.

"I wish. All Bernie does is get drunk, smoke weed, and play video games with his friends all day, what kinda fucking man is that?"

"Well, you're the one who decided to lay up and have all those kids with him."

"Only two of them are Bernie's and the reason I went through with the first one was because he was actually about something back then. Just think I could've been a ballplayer's wife and this clumsy fucker blows his knee out and there goes *our* dream."

"Boots, if I recall correctly he messed his knee up chasing you!" Gucci laughed.

"Yeah, Bernie wanted to beat my ass that day, but you know I've always been the fastest chick in the projects." Boots ran in place jokingly. "Man, those were the good old days, what happened to them?"

"We grew up and the realities of life set in," Gucci said seriously.

"Cuzo, what the deal?" Jada walked up. She looked Boots up and down and reluctantly greeted her too. "Hey."

"You think you had me waiting long enough?" Gucci asked, looking at her watch.

"You know you can't rush perfection." Jada tugged at the waist-line of the tight jeans she was wearing.

"And it's a little early for those." Gucci nodded to the fuchsia pumps she was wearing.

Jada gave her a disbelieving look. "Baby girl, the streets are always watching, so a top-notch bitch like me can never be caught at less than her best. Anything else is not only beneath me, but will most likely become the next topic for discussion on the bench." She looked over at Boots who was wearing a pair of faded jeans and scuffed shoes. "So you ready to roll?" she asked Gucci.

"Yeah, let's bounce. Boots, what you about to get into?" Gucci asked.

Boots shrugged. "Nothing, just trying to see what's going on out here."

"You wanna roll with us?"

Boots looked over at Jada who was giving her a disgusted look. "Nah, y'all go ahead. I think I'm gonna play the block until later. I'm waiting on the mailman anyhow."

Gucci could tell the girl was lying. "You sure?"

"Gucci, didn't you hear her say she was good. Come on already?" Jada said rudely.

Boots looked like she wanted to say something, but she let it ride. "Nah, I'm good, Gucci. But if you come back through the hood holla at me."

"That's a bet. Give me your new number because I don't have it in this phone." Gucci raised her rhinestone-decorated BlackBerry.

"Why don't you give me yours? I don't have any minutes on my phone right now, but I'm going to buy a card in a few," Boots lied. While Gucci rattled off her number Boots's eyes kept going to the shiny truck and she felt herself getting sicker and sicker by the second. Her friend was doing it big, but instead of being happy for Gucci she was secretly resentful.

"Make sure you get up with me soon, okay?" Gucci hugged Boots.

"I got you, Gucci." Boots gave her a fake smile and walked off.

"Dusty bitch," Jada said when Boots was out of earshot.

"Jada, you need to stop being so damn bitter all the time," Gucci said.

"I ain't bitter, cuzo, I just can't stand that bitch right there. She's sneaky and she's trifling."

"And this coming from a woman who looted twenty-stacks from her man's bank account?"

"*Appropriated*, I keep telling you bitches." Jada laughed.

A car came speeding down Columbus and slowed as it approached Gucci's truck. Both girls watched the car curiously as the back window rolled down slowly. "You bum ass bitches!" someone screamed before tossing a bottle at them. The glass bottle broke on the ground a few feet away from them and they immediately recognized the smell of urine.

"Fuck you!" Jada shouted after the car as it sped away.

"Damn who the fuck was that?" Gucci checked her Louboutin flats to make sure pee hadn't splashed them.

"Just another hater in a world of many. Let's get off this dead-ass block and go have some fun." Jada climbed in the passenger's side while Gucci climbed behind the wheel. "Gucci, I can't think of the last time we hung out two days in a row, this has gotta be some kid of record."

"Why can't I just wanna kick it with my little cousin?" Gucci asked innocently.

"I'm only six months behind you! But seriously, when you called to tell me you were coming down you sounded like something was wrong."

"Ain't nothing, I just wanted to get out of the house for a while and Tionna is at work so I figured I'd come scoop you," Gucci told her, but it was only half true.

"Wow, so I'm coming off the bench, huh?" Jada looked at her.

"I'm sorry, cousin. I didn't mean it like that. You know you're my ride or die chick too."

"I'll ride with you, but I ain't dying with you! So what're you doing with so much free time on your hands? I thought sure you were gonna be laid up with your man today since you ran the streets all day yesterday?"

"He had some *business* to handle," Gucci said sarcastically.

Jada shook her head. "Niggaz kill me with that shit. They rip and run all day, but get mad when we try to step out."

"Nah, me and Animal got a pretty good understanding. We're both free to hang out as long as the sun doesn't catch us coming in."

"One of the many drawbacks of being locked down."

"Sup Jada?" Scar rolled up on the truck and startled the girls as neither of them had seen him approaching.

"Boy, didn't anybody ever tell you it's dangerous to roll up on people's rides like that?" Gucci asked with attitude.

From where Scar was standing he couldn't see the .22 she had popped out from the secret compartment. Had he not called Jada by name she would've probably shot him.

"My fault, ma." Scar drank Gucci in with his eyes. "Damn, you don't hang with nothing but bad chicks, huh, Jada?"

"You know we move in packs, Scar," Jada told him.

"So what's your name, shorty?" Scar asked Gucci.

"My name is *taken*," she replied.

"Scar, if I were you I would back up off my cousin, because her man gets major psycho when it comes to his," Jada warned him.

"I ain't no sucka."

"Ain't about you being no sucka, Scar. I just don't want your blood on my hands if Animal catches you sniffing around," Jada said.

Scar immediately recognized the name and the crimes associated with it. Not long ago one of his homeys had fallen victim to

Animal and his young pack. "So you're the Animal's woman, huh?" he asked Gucci. There was something about the shift in his mood that made her uneasy.

"I'm my own woman, but The Animal is what they call the man I love," Gucci shot back. She didn't want to give Scar too much, but she would never deny who her heart belonged to. "Look, I ain't trying to brush you off or nothing, but we gotta make a move." Gucci put the car in gear and pulled away from the curb.

"Yeah, Imma see y'all around," Scar said, rubbing his hands together.

"THAT NIGGA SCAR IS ALWAYS trying to press somebody with his old thirsty ass," Jada said once they were away.

"What's his story?" Gucci asked.

"Scar ain't nobody but a wannabe Nino Brown like the rest of these niggaz. He ain't about nothing." Jada waved him off. Just then her cell phone rang. When she saw that it was her grandmother's number she frowned. "Damn, what the hell could those kids have done that quick?" Jada answered the phone, "Yes, Grandma."

"This ya uncle, Mookie."

"Mookie, what do you want?"

"Hold on, I got Cutty on the other line." Before Jada could warn him not to, Mookie clicked over and patched Cutty's call through.

"What up?" Cutty's gruff voice came through the phone.

"Fuck you want, jailbird?" Jada snapped.

"You got that situated yet?"

"I ain't got shit situated. And you've got a lot of nerve calling me after all that shit you popped and having your little chicken heads calling me!"

"You I ain't call to hear ya bullshit, Jada. You know I'm trying to make moves in here and I got some people that I need to get squared away before I have to push one of these niggaz back," Cutty explained.

"Cry me a river, nigga. You should've thought about it before you started talking to me like Super Thug."

Cutty sighed. "So this is what it's come to?"

"Like you said, I'm dead to you. If I'm dead to you, then your ass is sure enough a bitter memory to me."

"Jada, you're my son's mother so I still got a little bit of love for your ass, even if you ain't shit. If you do me like this I close my heart to you and you become my enemy. Don't do this to yourself or my son. Think about it before you make a choice that you can't take back."

Jada gave a dramatic pause. "Thought about it, and the answer is still 'fuck you'! If you want your money then take it in blood, nigga." Jada ended the call.

"Jada, do you think it's wise to antagonize Cutty like that?" Gucci asked once she was off the phone.

"Fuck Cutty." Jada folded her arms and turned to the window so Gucci couldn't see her eyes watering up.

"Jada, I know you're fucked up by what happened between you and Cutty and it's okay to be upset, but you ain't gotta play the hard rock with me."

Jada turned back to her cousin and her eyes were filled with tears. "I gave my soul, my body, and my loyalty to this nigga and he can just cast me to the side like I'm trash? I ain't nobody's trash, Gucci."

"Of course not, you're a Butler. Jada, y'all are mad at each other right now but give it some time and maybe you can work it out, if not for the sake of your relationship then for the sake of Miles. Cutty is still his father."

"As far as I'm concerned, Miles doesn't have a father anymore. Cutty ain't never gonna see his son again if I have anything to do with it."

"See, now you're talking crazy. Jada, you're my family and I'll ride with you in any and all things, except this. Keeping a child from his father is wrong, especially when the father wants to be involved. There's too much of that going on as it is."

Jada sucked her teeth. "Women raised us and we came out okay."

"But we're not little boys, Jada. A boy needs his father."

"And a real father wouldn't have left his son and his baby's mother out here to fend for themselves. Gucci, you should've heard the things he said to me on the phone. I can never forgive Cutty for that," Jada said emotionally.

Gucci had never seen her cousin this emotionally distraught before. Since the girls had become old enough to date Jada had always been the one in control of the situation, bending men to suit her but that all changed when she hooked up with Cutty. Outside of her father he was the only man she had ever loved and it was apparent by the pain in her eyes.

"I hear you, Jada. But let's not get all depressed in here. The day is young and we're younger, so where you wanna go first?"

"Well, we can start by hitting the liquor store on 105th and Columbus," Jada suggested.

"Damn, the sun is still up and you're ready to get it in?" Gucci asked in disbelief.

"Look, you're the one who called me talking about she wanted to hang, and this is how I hang. Now let's do this."

Gucci crossed Hundredth Street and came up Manhattan Avenue along the back of the projects. As she passed the corner store she saw Happy with a young girl leaning in the window of his car while his hand explored her ass. She just shook her head and kept trucking around to the liquor store. When they got to the liquor store Gucci opted to get out and go inside because she knew if she sent Jada she was likely to come out with something way too strong for that hour of the day. She grabbed two cold bottles of Arbor Mist and a Lotto ticket and rolled out of the store. On her way back to her truck she spotted a familiar license plate on the back of a white

Beamer. If Animal was supposed to be at the studio with Chip then why was his car parked near the projects? After what happened during Tech's attempted takeover of the projects she knew he wouldn't be down there hanging out so he had to be up to something.

Gucci pulled out her cell and called Animal, but the phone just rang before going to voice mail. She tried him again and this time the voice mail picked up automatically. "So that's how you wanna play it, huh?" Gucci stuffed her phone back into her purse and got back in the truck, slamming the door behind her.

"Damn, what the hell is up with you?" Jada asked.

"Nothing," Gucci said, rummaging around in her purse for her wallet. "Jada, you feel like stepping out this weekend?"

"After that bullshit with Cutty, hell yeah. But I'm broke and ain't got nothing to wear," Jada said.

"I didn't ask you about all that. Just hop on the phone and secure your babysitter for Friday night. We're about to go shopping," Gucci told her as she pulled her wallet out.

"Gucci, I told you I don't have any money."

"Don't worry about it, cuzo. It's on Animal." Gucci held up his credit card and smiled wickedly.

Chapter 30

ANIMAL WASN'T SURE WHETHER HE FELT BETTER OR worse after visiting Hanna at the nursing home. He felt better because he hadn't seen her in so long, but worse because he knew that he was the cause of her condition.

Many years ago, when Animal first got heavy in the game, Tech had accepted a contract on the life of a guy who had run afoul of one of Shai's capos. Eager to prove himself Animal begged Tech to let him take care of it. He stalked Lionel for nearly a week before finally getting the drop on him one day at his house. Lionel didn't even hear Animal creep up on him until the first bullet was whistling through his cheek. As he was leaning in he heard a noise behind him so he spun with his gun raised and reacted. The bullet struck Hanna in the head as she was coming into the kitchen to see what was going on. Thankfully she lived, but she had lost her sight because of Animal.

For years the guilt of the accidental shooting rode him like a dark horseman, which is what prompted him to begin his masquerade as a concerned friend of Lionel's. Tech had called him a fool for playing it so close to the crime, but it was something Animal felt like he had to do. When he got his weight up Animal began funneling funds through a dummy company to pay for Hanna to be moved into a prestigious care facility, and made sure that she was at least comfortable in the twilight of her life.

Visiting with Hanna often took Animal through a series of extreme emotional highs and lows and the blunt he was steaming in the car only added to the emotional imbalance. When he looked up at his reflection in the rearview mirror he noticed tears dancing in the corners of his eyes. *"The living have no need of your tears, you have promises to the dead to keep,"* the face in the mirror said to him.

"You're right," Animal whispered.

He was too wound up to go home so he decided to spin for a while until he could get right. Animal cut across 125th Street to cop some reading material for him and Gucci. He selected a book called *Eviction Notice* for her and *Soledad Brother* for himself. He had read the book twice already, but it was one of his favorites and he had lost his copy at the airport. On the way back to his car he signed a few autographs for some high school girls who had recognized him from the video. The love he got lifted his dark mood a bit, but the sourness came back when he spotted the two CD vendors posted up in front of the gyro stand.

"CDs, DVDs, one for five and five for twenty. Check 'em out," one of the vendors was accosting people as they passed him, while his brutish-looking partner stood vigil for police.

Animal's eyes zeroed in on the stack of CDs baring his likeness on the top row of the rack. "I see y'all got that new Big Dawg shit, huh?"

"You know we do." The vendor grabbed two CDs and held them out for Animal to inspect. "I got that 'Welcome to the Jungle' and 'Dog off the Chain' by that kid, Animal."

"Word, I didn't know The Animal's CD was out?" Animal took the CD and examined it. It was a photo-shopped picture of him wearing a dog chain.

"Yeah, yeah, we got the exclusive B," the vendor said proudly.

Animal tightened his grip on the bag of books in his hand. "A'ight, let me get all of these." Animal waved the CD.

The vendor looked at him to see if he was serious. "All of them?"

"Yeah, I'll take every copy of this CD you've got."

The vendor zipped open his roll-on and did a quick count of the CDs. "I got a hundred joints so that's gonna be about five hundred dollars, but since you spending big with me I'll let you have them for four-fifty."

"Four-fifty? I got a better idea. How about I'm gonna take them all and not give you shit," Animal said seriously.

Hearing the threat the other vendor stepped up. The knife he held in his hand glistened in the sunlight menacingly. "Shorty, you better get the fuck up outta here with that shit before you catch a bad decision out here."

"Can't be worse than the decision you two made by calling ya selves bootlegging," Animal told him, moving to keep both the vendors in his line of vision as they tried to surround him.

The first vendor laughed. "Who the fuck you think you are, Super Fly?"

"No, I'm the muthafucka your pirating ass calls yourself stealing from," Animal told them with a smile. "Now y'all can either give my shit up or I can take it. What you trying to do?"

Animal already knew how it was going to play out so it was no surprise when the vendor with the knife made a move. The strike was a novice one which Animal easily blocked and countered with the bag of books. The novels connected with the bridge of the vendor's nose, breaking it and splattering blood on both of them. Animal followed with an overhand right that rocked the armed vendor to sleep before he even hit the ground. The second vendor landed a sucker punch and busted Animal's lip. The taste of blood in his mouth only served to fuel Animal's already mounting anger and he attacked the vendor viciously with a series of rights and lefts. The vendor tried to sag to the ground but Animal held him up by the front of his shirt.

"Muthafucka you must be stupid." Animal smacked him with the books. "I put my heart into this shit." Animal smacked him with the books again and this time he let the vendor hit the floor. The vendor was barely conscious, but this didn't stop Animal from stomping him mercilessly over and over, cracking his skull and cheekbone. A crowd of spectators had formed around him, but Animal couldn't see anything but the blood running from the vendor's head onto the cracked pavement.

"Leave that man alone. You're gonna kill him!" a woman shouted.

"Fuck that nigga up!" someone else added.

"Let me get my camera phone so I can YouTube this shit," a girl chimed in.

"Ain't that The Animal?" Another voice was added to the mix.

Hearing his name struck a cord in Animal's mind and brought him back to reality. At his feet the two vendors lay twisted and motionless. Animal looked around at the faces that only moments before had been praising him, but now they wore horrified expressions like he was Frankenstein's monster. He was suddenly overcome with a feeling of vertigo and he staggered through the crowd toward his car. Just before he reached it he felt someone behind him and spun with his gun drawn, ready to pop. His finger froze on the trigger as he found himself staring into the frightened eyes of a young boy, holding one of the bootleg CDs.

"Fuck is you rolling up on me like that for?" Animal snapped.

"Sorry, I just wanted to get your autograph." The boy nervously held the CD out.

Animal signed the CD and handed it back. "Here ya go, shorty."

"Thanks, man. When I grow up I wanna be just like you, blood!" the boy said excitedly.

Animal looked down in embarrassment at his bloodstained clothes. "No, you don't," he said and hopped in his ride.

Animal had driven almost ten blocks before the adrenaline had finally begun to fade. He was mad at the vendors for selling his CDs but he was angrier with himself for the way he had handled the situation. He had let his emotions think for him and as a result he had almost killed two men in front of a hundred people on 125th Street. Even when he was still putting in work his sloppy behavior would have been unacceptable, but the fact that his face was plastered on billboards and magazines across the country made the move even stupider. It seemed like every other week he was reading about a rapper fucking up his blessing and landing in prison for something stupid and he had come very close to joining that number.

"Dude, you bugging," Animal told himself.

There was only a few hours left before he was to meet Don B. and the crew at Code Red so his best bet was to push back to the crib and lay low until then, but first he wanted to swing by the liquor store and get something to sip until then. A stiff drink was just what he needed to calm his nerves.

ANIMAL PUSHED THE BEAMER UP Broadway knocking the new Styles P. joint and feeling himself, as everyone watched his car. It felt funny riding up to 145th Street as a civilian considering all the dirt he'd done up that way over the years. There was a time when Animal would only venture that far up Broadway to buy drugs or kill someone, so he made sure to stay on point for people who might've had old scores that needed settling or general haters.

When Animal pulled into the bus stop outside the liquor store it seemed like every eye on the block landed on him. When he slid out of the vehicle his heavy jewels drew positive and negative attention. Those in the know could smell death on the fresh-faced young man so they wisely gave him a wide berth, and those who didn't know what it was would find out if they tried to press him. Three minutes after he'd entered the liquor store he came back out, clutching the black bag to his chest like it was the game-winning football and jumped back in his ride. The Hennessy and Nuvo would provide him a nice buzz, but the additive he'd stashed in the car would make the ride a truly dreamy one.

When he got to the top of the block he happened to look out his window and notice a mural painted on the wall. It was of a fresh-faced, brown-skinned youth wearing a Gucci bucket and gold crucifix. The birth and death dates put the young man at about twenty-two years old. When Animal closed his eyes, he could hear the shots and smell the acidic bite of gun smoke as if he were living the moment all over again. The boy had made the misfortune of running afoul of a member of the Commission. It was never made clear what the offense had been, nor did it matter to Animal at the time. When the money was dropped the boy's life was forfeit.

A car beeping behind him snapped Animal out of his daydream. He looked in his rearview and saw a tinted blue BMW 335i flashing its high beams and beeping the horn hostilely.

"Fuck is wrong with you, move ya shit!" he could hear a female voice shouting at him. Animal shook off the ghosts of his past and rolled through the light just as it was turning yellow. On the next block he pulled over at the bodega to grab a few Dutches before he went home. As he was getting out of the car the BMW that had been flashing him pulled to an aggressive stop behind his ride. Sensing trouble he dipped his hand into his back pocket where he had put his .380. The car was tinted but he could see two chicks in the front, but there was no telling who could be lying in wait in the backseat. No one knew better than him how trifling females could be.

"Ain't you that kid Animal?" the driver called out. She was a pretty Spanish girl with chinky eyes and silky black hair that she wore in a ponytail.

"That all depends." He squinted, trying to see through the tints. His body was tense, poised to spring into action at the first signs of something shady.

"Damn, baby, why you all uptight? I'm just trying to get an introduction. Come here and let me holla at you."

Animal gave her a comical look. "Shorty, what the fuck I look like to you?"

"Get out the car and go talk to him," the dark-skinned girl on the passenger side urged the driver. She and the driver went back and forth for a minute before the driver finally got out of the car and when she did Animal had to do a double take. She was about five feet five with a slim waist and hips that curved almost perfectly. As she moved toward him he let his eyes roam from her angelic face to the tight blue jeans that hugged her thighs like a second skin.

"You can eighty-six the hammer. I ain't got nothing on me that can hurt you," the pretty girl said when she stepped on the curb. To prove her point she turned in a slow circle so Animal could check her out.

"That's a matter of opinion," Animal said slyly with his eyes locked on her ass. "So, what you want from me, ma? An autograph or something?"

"Stop it five, I'm a fan, but I ain't no groupie. You can save the autograph, but I'll take an introduction. My name is Kelly," she told him. When her lips moved it was like watching two rose pedals blowing in a soft breeze.

"As you already know, they call me The Animal." He shook her hand. Her nails were freshly done with a fly airbrush design on them. "It's a pleasure to meet you, Kelly."

Kelly held his hand a little longer than necessary. "Nah, the pleasure is all mine. Since we've got the introductions out of the way how about you slide me your number so we can continue this conversation at a time when we're not double parked and at risk of getting tickets."

"I don't give my number out like that, shorty," Animal told her.

"Isn't the female supposed to be the one to say that?"

"Baby, you got jokes. But to keep it one hundred with you, I got a girl and a chick as fine as you is liable to cause a situation," Animal said honestly, not believing the words coming out of his mouth. Tech was probably rolling over in his grave at that moment.

"That's good to know. That means you won't turn into one of them clingy ass niggaz on me." She smiled. Her teeth were almost perfect except for the slight gap in the top row. "Check it out, daddy. I ain't trying to marry you, just trying to make a new friend. I don't wanna scare you."

Animal chuckled. "I don't fear nothing but God, shorty. I'm just trying to let you know what's good with me."

"And I'm letting you know what's good with me." Kelly pulled a business card from the pocket of her jeans and handed it to Animal. "I ain't gonna take up too much of your time because I know you're a busy man, but you might wanna make your next move your best move. Take care, Mr. Animal," she said and sauntered back to her car, where her friend was giggling like a schoolgirl.

Animal stood there for a time still trying to make heads or tails out of what had just happened. He loved the shit outta Gucci, but Kelly was a bad bitch and for a minute he thought about jumping out the window.

His cell going off letting him know he had a text message snapped him out of his lustful fantasy about Kelly. The text was from his lil home girl and though it was only one word it spoke in volumes.

Food.

Chapter 31

RAS'S LEXUS LOOKED LIKE A SHINY WINDUP TOY DOUBLE parked on the corner of 131st and Seventh. He had just got the sleek black car detailed and applied two extra coats of polish to the rims so that everyone would notice him when he rolled through the hood. He sat on the hood in his gangsta lean looking like new money, dressed in a Gucci jacket and crisp jeans cuffed over his Gucci shoes. His heavy gold chain swung from his neck with the sun bouncing off the clear diamonds in the medallion. He checked the hour on his gold watch for the fifth time in as many minutes, wondering what was taking his shorty so long to come down. As if on cue he spotted her making her way through the projects.

Mimi turned every head when she came strutting down the pathway to the avenue. She was a tiny thing of five-five with porn star curves and pouty pink lips. She was dressed in a black leather miniskirt that strained to hold her shapely thighs and the matching jacket with high red boots. Her long, plum-colored hair blew in the wind when she moved like Julia Roberts in *Pretty Woman*. The shirt she wore beneath the leather ensemble was cut so low that you could see the five tiny stars tattooed across her breasts. Ras couldn't help but to smile at the sight of Mimi and the larcenous stares she was getting from the guys. They could look all they wanted, but they would never be able to touch because she belonged to him.

"Hey, daddy." Mimi stood on her tiptoes and wrapped her arms around Ras's neck. She kissed Ras passionately while his hands explored her ass, not caring who was watching.

"I missed you, baby," Ras said tenderly.

"Not as much as I've missed you." Mimi gave him another peck on the lips for good measure. "You be so busy lately that I never get to see you, so I look forward to the little bit of time that you make to spend with me."

"I know, baby, but I'm working on it. Once I find some trustworthy guys to replace the ones I lost in the last raid I can kick back for a minute," he said, thinking of the lieutenants he had been meaning to replace for the last few weeks. With Ras overseeing everything and not having to pay lieutenants it meant extra money in his pocket, so he was taking his time about hiring help just yet.

"If you want, I could reach out to some of the guys in my hood. I know them niggaz are always thirsty for a come up," Mimi offered.

"Nah, boo. I don't want you fucking around out there in them streets, you ain't from that and I wanna keep it that way," Ras said in an attempt to be noble.

"Damn, you're so protective when it comes to me." She blushed.

"Of course, you know what you mean to me."

"Awww." She batted her eyes. "I'm ya lil mama?" she asked with a devilish grin.

"Haven't you always been?" Ras smiled. "Now let's go so we can catch this flick. After we leave the movies we've got dinner reservations at this joint downtown." Ras held the door for Mimi as she oozed into the Lexus.

Feeling someone watching her, Mimi looked up and spotted some dudes she knew from her neighborhood. She could tell that they were up to no good from the way they were sizing Ras and his car up. Mimi waited until she had established eye contact with them and gave them a half grin. It was a look that most people knew too well, and enough to convey her message to them. The boys saluted her and stalked off, mumbling with themselves about having to find another victim. Ras looked like fresh meat, but it would be less of a headache for them to find another victim than to tangle with Mimi over something she had already laid claim to.

NORMALLY THEY WOULD'VE GONE TO the movies downtown, but Mimi insisted they drive out to Queens instead. When Ras complained about the distance she told him that it was one of the few that were still showing *Avatar* in 3D and she didn't want to be cheated out of the effect as it would be her first time seeing it. The theater Mimi selected was a beat-up-looking movie house in a run-down part of town. Ras didn't like it and had even considered going back to the car for his gun, but Mimi was already pulling him inside so they could catch the beginning of the movie.

When they walked into the screening room their eyes and noses were assaulted by the heavy stench of weed smoke and alcohol. The crowd was made up of mostly young, rowdy kids and a few working-class-looking people scattered here and there. Navigating the sticky floor Ras and Mimi made their way down to the front/center row where they settled in to watch the coming attractions. Ras gave a cautious look around to make sure nobody was watching before drawing Mimi's attention to the heart-shaped box he pulled from his jacket.

"What's this?" Mimi looked at the box curiously.

"Just open it," he urged her.

Mimi opened the box and inside there was a beautiful white gold necklace with tiny diamond stars between the links. "Oh, my God, this is so beautiful! What did I do to deserve this?"

Ras had been preparing this speech in his head for a week, but when the time came he drew a blank so he just spoke from his heart.

"Well, we've been seeing each other for a while now, but I want it to be official. I want you to be my girl, Mimi." He kissed her.

"Of course I will, daddy." Mimi planted kisses all over his lips and face. "Help me put it on." She turned her back to him and lifted her hair. The necklace looked beautiful on Mimi, stopping just short of the tattoos across her breasts. "I love it."

"And I love you," Ras said with moist eyes. It was a good thing that the lights went out for the movie to start or Mimi might've seen the tear slide down Ras's cheek.

Mimi snuggled close to Ras and kissed him softly on the throat. "You know I kinda feel bad that you've blessed me with this nice gift and I don't have anything for you."

"You just being here with me is enough, Mimi," Ras told her.

"Nah, it's not enough for me. I might not have a nice piece of jewelry to give you, but I've got something I was supposed to give you a long time ago." Mimi popped the buttons on his shirt and started kissing him from his neck down to his stomach. She undid his pants and played with his dick until it was hard. "You want this?" she asked, licking gently around the head of his dick.

"You know I do," he panted, forcing her head down. Mimi began to work him expertly with her mouth, locking her thumb and index finger around his shaft and jerking it slowly. Her tongue danced under his balls sending a shiver so intense up his back that Ras had to pull her head away. "Damn, hold on."

"What's the matter? You don't like it?" She kissed his neck and continued jerking him.

"I love it."

"Then let me work," she told him and pushed him back. Mimi popped the top off her large soda and slurped up some of the ice. "You're gonna love this," she said, dipping her head back into his lap. With the ice in her mouth Mimi began to suck him off at various speeds, spitting down the side of his shaft to keep it slick. She was having so much fun getting Ras off that she could feel her own juices soaking through her thong. Mimi stimulated herself with her finger and kept her focus on Ras.

"Damn, this is great!" Ras hissed.

"It's about to get better," Mimi said through a mouth full of ice. She worked her head back up Ras's stomach, leaving a trail of moisture from her mouth. She ran her hands through the fluid and traced lines all over Ras's face. "Does this feel good, daddy?"

"Umm hmm," he moaned as she nibbled at the vein in his throat.

"Good." She flicked her tongue along the roof of her mouth. "Now that you're all relaxed, it's time for your real present."

"And what's that, baby?" Ras asked with his eyes closed.

The soft brush of her tongue across his neck turned into a searing pain and Ras's eyes snapped open. In the dim light of the theater he could see his bloodstained shirt and the cold eyes of his lover. Mimi's chin was smeared with blood and a razor was pinched between her lips. Feeling his hurt over her betrayal numbed Ras to the pain and he made a mad lunge for her, but Mimi slipped over the chair and was crouched behind him. She locked her arm around Ras's neck and used her weight to apply pressure to the wound, causing the blood to flow more rapidly. Ras tried to stand and it was then he realized that during her seduction Mimi had handcuffed his belt to the cup holder in the arm of the chair.

"My homey, Animal, wanted you to have this," Mimi whispered in his ear and pulled the razor from one side of his throat to the other.

Chapter 32

ANIMAL WAS SURPRISED WHEN HE CAME IN FROM A STU-
dio session at 11:00 A.M. to find Gucci still in the house. Lately she
made it a point to spend more and more time away from the apartment. If she wasn't out with her mother she was up to God knew
what with Tionna. It was as if she was purposely avoiding Animal
and it bothered him.

For the last few days Animal had noticed a change in Gucci. They
weren't drastic changes, in fact they were quite subtle. A change in
the way she kissed him, the way she parted her hair, very small things.
The only reason he noticed them at all was because he had spent
the majority of their relationship studying her. The way he studied
her wasn't unlike the way he studied his prey before he took them
off the streets, minus the malicious intent. Animal paid close attention to Gucci so that he could learn her and understand better how
she needed to be loved. With normal people love was something that
flowed naturally and didn't need to be dissected but Animal was
anything but normal.

Animal reasoned that the reason Gucci had been acting so different was because of the time he was spending in the studio. The
pressure of being back in New York had started to become too

much for him and he found himself becoming more of a killer than a predator and it bothered him. Not really trusting himself to be out and about he stayed locked away in the studio recording music with Chip. At the rate they were going the second album would be almost done by the time he left New York, which couldn't come soon enough. Animal had thought him coming back to New York would've been a blessing, but the unfinished business made it a curse. Once Rico was dead he was on the first thing smoking back to Plano.

Gucci came into the living room dressed only in a short robe and head scarf. When she bent over to pick up the dirty socks Animal had left on the floor he got a clear view of her freshly trimmed nest. Most of Animal's body was tired but his soldier felt wide awake in his jeans. Peeling himself off the couch he eased behind Gucci and pressed himself against her.

"Don't start something you can't finish," she said over her shoulder.

"I never do." Animal ran his hands over her shoulders. "Let's get one right quick."

"Boy please." She shrugged him off her and walked toward the bedroom. "I've been laying here in thong damn near every night and you don't give me so much as a second look before you're passed out."

Animal followed her into the bedroom and flopped on the bed. "I'm sorry, baby, you know I be tired after those studio sessions."

"If you would lay off the weed and sip maybe you'd have some energy left for me when you came in," she said sharply.

"Gucci, you know I don't fuck around like that no more." He tugged at the strings of her robe, but she pulled away.

"Nigga, please, you came in here with the damn Sunkist bottle in your pocket the other night! Animal, I ain't trying to ride you because you're grown, but that shit ain't nothing to play with. What do you think it would do to me if you died over a fucking buzz?"

"Gucci, it wasn't like that. Me and Soda was fucking around with this record the other night and—"

"Animal, don't tell me about you and somebody else because I'm not sleeping with Soda, I'm talking about what you're doing."

"A'ight, you're right, Gucci," he said, more to shut her up than anything. Gucci had a very good point, but he didn't want to hear it at that moment.

"Tell me anything just to shut me up, huh?" Gucci called him on it. She pulled a pair of jeans from a shopping bag she had tucked in the closet and began taking the tags off.

"Where you off to?" he asked, examining the snug sweater she had laid out to go with the jeans.

"I got a hot date," Gucci said sarcastically and plucked a pair of bebe heels from the box.

"Gucci, don't play with me. You know I'd paint this city with a nigga's blood if I thought you was tipping," he said seriously.

"Yeah, and I'd slap a double coat on it with your blood and the bitch you called yourself laying up with. Never underestimate a woman scorned, my nigga." When she began to walk past him, Animal pulled her down onto the bed.

"You know that it's only you my eyes see and only for you does my heart pump blood." He planted soft kisses on her face. Animal worked his hand between her legs and flicked her clit.

"Stop it, Tayshawn. I can't be getting all nasty with you and I gotta meet Tionna in a little while."

Animal sighed. "Oh, Lord, what are you two up to now?"

"We ain't up to shit. She wants to treat me to lunch. It's nice that somebody wants the honor." Gucci looked him up and down.

"Baby, I know I've been MIA, but it was a necessary evil," he said sincerely. "But I do wanna spend time with you, ma. As a matter of fact, why don't I treat you and Tionna to lunch?"

"You ain't gotta do it because you feel like you have to, I want you to do it because you *want* to," she said.

"I do *want* to." He kissed her. "Let me jump in the shower right quick and we can skate." Animal peeled off his jeans, which he left in the middle of the floor, and went into the bathroom.

Gucci waited until she heard the shower come on before grabbing his jeans and beginning her inspection. In his wallet there were only business cards and a few back receipts, which Gucci took a second to examine. Satisfied that he hadn't made any unusual withdrawals or deposits she moved to the prize, which was his Black-Berry. She checked the time and amount of times called from the numbers she didn't recognize to see if anything looked funny. His call log seemed to be clean, but his texts were a different story. There was a text from someone listed as Lil Mama that simply said *Food*. She wasn't sure what it was in reference to, but before it was all said and done she would find out.

ANIMAL TOOK THEM INTO BROOKLYN for a late lunch and some drinks at a spot called Mojitos. It was a nice Cuban restaurant that sat out of the way just off Flushing Avenue. The food was great and they made original Mojitos with the actual sugarcane. When the waitress was taking them to their seats they passed a table full of well-dressed women who were also enjoying a late lunch. One of them did a double take like she knew Animal from somewhere. Animal acted like he didn't notice, but Gucci did.

"I like this place, Animal. How'd you find out about it?" Tionna asked as she took her seat. The restaurant was dim and had a very romantic feel to it.

"Some friends and I had a meeting here once," Animal said, purposely avoiding making eye contact with Gucci who was scowling at him.

"I'll bet," Gucci said, studying her menu.

A thin waitress wearing too much eyeliner and steel-toed boots approached the table. "Hello, I'm Francine and I'll be your server. Is this your first time at Mojitos?"

"He's been here before." Gucci cut her eyes at Animal.

"Oh, maybe that's why you look so familiar," Francine said pleasantly, which got her a dirty look from Gucci. "Well, today's specials are—"

"Ah, I already know what I want," Gucci cut her off. "I'll have the steak, with the red beans and yellow rice. Tionna, you ready?" Gucci looked at her friend who had a puzzled expression on her face.

"Ah, I guess I'll go with the chicken," Tionna said awkwardly.

Francine did her best to overlook Gucci's attitude and kept it professional. When she took Animal's order she did so with a smile. "And what can I get for you, love?"

"The coconut shrimp please, sis," Animal said, trying to hide his embarrassment.

"Okay, I'll be right back with your orders." Francine took their menus and went off to place the orders.

"What's good with you and ol' girl?" Gucci asked.

"Excuse me?"

"I don't know, I just felt like there was some kind of connection between y'all. Like you knew each other or something."

"Gucci, I ain't never met that broad a day in my life," Animal declared.

"Why don't y'all cut it out and play nice?" Tionna interjected. "So, Animal, how do you like being a big star?"

Animal shrugged. "It ain't really about nothing. Like . . . I don't feel any different. Mad people know me now, but to me I'm still Animal. The only part I'll probably get used to is people recognizing me wherever I go. I'm used to moving in silence, ya dig?"

"You know I know," Tionna said, recalling some of his exploits. "But not for nothing, I'm really proud of you, Animal. Not many get that hand up outta the hood and the ones that do more often than not fuck it up."

"Yeah, Animal still does stuff that he ain't got no business doing, but for the most part he keeps his head where it's supposed to be." Gucci rested her hand over his on the table and it drained away some of the tension.

"I've got a strong lady behind me." Animal placed his other hand over hers. Just when it seemed like all was right with the world the girl who had been staring at Animal walked over to their table. She was short and thick wearing a navy-blue business suit.

"Hi, I'm sorry to bother you but I wanted to catch you before your food came out. I was wondering if you could sign a few autographs for me and my friends? We're huge fans of your music." The girl gazed at Animal dreamily.

Tionna cleared her throat to get everyone's attention. "Hello, don't you think it's a little rude of you to come over here asking for an autograph when you see us having a family meal?"

"It's okay, T," Animal told her and got up from the table to sign a napkin for the girl. Tionna started to get up too, but Gucci gave her the signal to be easy. It started with just the girl in the suit but within minutes Animal had a small line of people pressing around their table. Finally having her fill of the bullshit Gucci got up and left, with Tionna on her heels.

"Gucci," he called out to her but she kept going, leaving him to the constantly swelling crowd of fans.

"HOLD ON, GUCCI!" TIONNA CAUGHT up with her as she descended the ramp of the restaurant.

"Let's go, T," Gucci called over her shoulder.

Tionna finally got close enough to Gucci to grab her arm and slow her down. "Damn, what's your problem?"

"You didn't see that shit in there, T? You didn't see them bitches flirting with Animal?" Gucci fumed.

"Yes, I saw it, but I didn't see him flirting back. Gucci, you need to relax for a minute."

"Fuck was that all about?" Animal came out of the restaurant.

He came down the ramp and stood directly in front of Gucci. She tried to give him a defiant look but her eyes betrayed her hurt. "Gucci, I was only gonna sign a few autographs then break the crowd up. Why'd you run out like that?"

"I don't know, I guess the whole thing with you not wanting me to go to the party and then the groupie bum rush in there made me snap a little." Gucci wiped the corners of her eyes.

Animal cupped her face in his hands so that she would have to see the sincerity in his eyes when he spoke. "Baby, I don't want you at that club tonight for safety reasons, not because I'm hiding anything from you. All that Animal shit that people are feeding into is just a job. At the end of the day you're a part of my real life, not Big Dawg and not the industry, just you!" He pulled her close to him.

"I know," she said into his chest. "I'm just so scared you're gonna come home one day and tell me that you've found something better in this new life of yours."

"It's this life of *ours* and ain't nothing here or there better than what I already got." He rubbed her cheeks softly and planted a tender kiss on her lips.

"Maybe we should do this whole lunch thing another time," Tionna suggested.

"I'm sorry for being a basket case and fucking everything up, guys," Gucci told them.

"Gucci, you know I love you even if you ain't playing with a full deck." Tionna hugged her.

"I second that emotion," Animal agreed.

"Well, it's still early so I'm gonna find something to get into. What's good with y'all?" Tionna asked.

Animal put his arm around Gucci and snuggled against her. "I think I'm gonna go home and spend some time with my lady."

• • •

WHEN ANIMAL AND GUCCI GOT back to their apartment they made love into the night and fell asleep in each other's arms without a care in the world. When Animal woke up it was after eight in the evening and he had twelve missed calls on his phone, all from Don B. and various Big Dawg employees. Don B. had the entire evening planned; they were going to do a photo shoot wearing some of the latest of Big Dawg's new clothing line, then they would dress for the club. Don B. hadn't trusted them enough to dress themselves so he brought in professional stylists and tons of clothes for them to work with. Once the crew was dressed they would be shuttled over to the club in a caravan of three black on black Maybachs. Don B. had spared no expense on this one.

Animal sat on the side of the bed and woke Gucci up. "Baby, I'm about to boogie."

"Okay, have fun and be safe," she said sleepily and kissed him.

Grabbing his keys and his gun Animal slid out the door with a smile on his face knowing how big he and his team were about to do it. It would've been nice if Gucci was there, but considering how crazy it was sure to get it was probably best that she didn't come.

AS SOON AS THE DOOR clicked closed Gucci's eyes snapped open. She rolled over and grabbed her cell phone so she could put the roll call out to her girls. Tionna refused to be a part of it because of her personal feelings about the whole thing, but Jada was down and so was Boots. It was hard convincing Jada to play nice, but she eventually went along with it so they'd be three deep when they crashed the building. If Animal thought that he was going to go party on some Hollywood shit and leave her at home waiting he had another think coming. The headline of his movie would read "Co-starring Gucci."

PART 4

Beauties & the Beasts

Chapter 33

MALIKA LAY ON TEDDY'S FUTON WATCHING *MARTIN* RE-
runs on TV while sipping a glass of white wine. She had found
herself spending quite a bit of time with him over the last few days.
As soon as Teddy had heard what happened with Malika's entertainment system he was on the scene the next day with a brand-
new one. Malika tried to refuse the gift but he insisted, pushing his
way into her apartment and showing the delivery guys where to set
up. Solomon was like a kid at Christmas when he saw the high-tech
stereo set and television. When she'd left the house he was still sitting in front of the big screen playing video games. Teddy had even
gone as far as getting Malika's phone and Internet reconnected.
Teddy was turning out to be the only bright spot in her dark days
and because of this she found herself open all over again.

"Yo, I'm about to run to the store right quick, you need anything?" Teddy asked, slipping his jacket on.

"Yeah, bring me back a Pepsi and a bag of onion and garlic
chips," Malika told him and rolled back on her stomach to watch
her show.

"And what're you gonna give me for it?" Teddy slapped her
across the ass playfully.

"I thought you were done for a while after round two, big boy," she said, playfully running her foot over his crotch through his jeans.

"I can never get enough of that sweetness you got between these thighs." Teddy spread her legs and stuck his face in her crotch.

"You're so nasty." She rolled to the other side of the futon and out of his reach.

"You ain't seen nasty yet. Wait until I get you to Puerto Rico in a few weeks. I'm gonna really show you nasty then."

Malika frowned. "Teddy, why do you play so much?"

"Ain't nobody playing, I'm serious. You've been having a rough time of it lately, Malika, and you deserve for someone to do something nice for you every once in a while. I've got some time off coming and I think Puerto Rico would be a great place to spend it, but it'll be even more special if I had someone to share it with."

"And what am I supposed to do with my son while we're traveling the coast?" Malika wanted to know.

"He's a big boy and we'll only be gone for a weekend. Couldn't you get one of your friends to check in on him from time to time while we're gone?"

"Teddy, I'm not gonna just leave my son like that, especially not in the projects we live in. I don't play those types of games."

"A'ight, so maybe we take him with us? You said you've been worried about him being on the block, so why not get him out of the hood for a weekend to open him up to something new. The culture will do him good."

"I don't know, Teddy. You and me doing us is one thing but it may be a little soon to be bringing my son into it," Malika said. One thing she didn't do was bring men around her son who she was still unsure about.

"Damn, treat a nigga like a stranger why don't ya?" Teddy shook his head.

"I'm sorry, baby. I didn't mean it like that." Malika crawled up on her knees and hugged him. "Teddy, you've been a godsend to me and I don't know how I would've made it through some of this stuff without your shoulder to cry on, but there's more than just me to think about in this equation. I've got my son to think about, and you've got *situations* to deal with."

"See, I knew you fed into that bullshit Marsha and them were kicking at the pool hall," Teddy said hostilely.

"First of all, you need to calm down." Malika snaked her neck. "And second of all I didn't feed into shit, I'm just calling it like I see it. Teddy, you said yourself that you've another situation that hasn't been completely resolved so it doesn't make any sense to get too deep into another situation before you've cleaned up the first one."

Teddy clutched his head like she was giving him a headache. "Malika, I want you to trust me but you gotta be willing to let me in. Don't answer me about Puerto Rico now, give it some thought, then get back, okay?" Malika nodded. "Good. Now I'm going to the store." Teddy left the apartment.

Malika lay there for a minute and contemplated Teddy's offer. For as bad as she would've loved an all-expense-paid trip to Puerto Rico she knew the timing was wrong. Solomon seemed to be becoming more belligerent by the day, questioning her when she told him something and hanging in front of the building every time her back was turned. The neighbors were even whispering that Solomon might be selling drugs, but she didn't believe her son had slipped that far yet. Solomon was feeling himself and she needed to find a way to slow him down. Thinking of Solomon made Malika realize that she hadn't spoken to him in a few hours. Teddy had left his cell phone on the table so she decided to use it to call Solomon. As Malika was flipping the phone open another call was coming through, so she ended up answering the phone by accident.

"Hello? Hello?" she could hear a feminine voice coming over the line. She looked at the caller ID screen and it read "home." "I hope this ain't one of Teddy's bitches playing on the phone. I keep telling you little bitches about staying in your lane, but I can see that I'm gonna have to show you . . . again. Is anybody there?" Not really sure what to do Malika hung up the phone.

For a long while Malika just sat there holding the phone. She had completely forgotten that she was supposed to be calling Solomon as her mind tried to make heads or tails out of the situation she had allowed herself to walk into. She shouldn't have been surprised by something like this going with Teddy, especially after the things Marsha and the other girl were saying to her. The phone rang three more times, twice were from home again and once from a blocked number. Malika just ignored it and slipped her clothes on.

Teddy finally came back from the store looking like he had run both ways. Dropping the bags on the floor he began to search the room. "Looking for this?" She held the phone up and as she did it started ringing again. She looked at the word *home* on the caller ID and handed the phone to Teddy. "It's for you."

"Malika, I can explain . . ." he began, but she didn't want to hear it.

"No need, Teddy. I know just how this movie plays out," she said emotionally.

"Malika, it ain't like you think."

She looked at Teddy as if he had lost his mind. "What the fuck do you mean it ain't like that? Teddy, you had the number stored as HOME in your phone. I might not have gotten my degree, but I'm not an idiot. Teddy, just say that you live with a bitch!"

"Okay, I live with a broad, but it's complicated, Malika." Teddy tried to plead his case, but Malika didn't need to hear it.

"Trust me, boo, I know all about it. You and shorty are on the outs and it's looking like y'all are headed for a breakup, right?"

"Malika . . ." he began.

"Teddy, please stop. Anything else that comes out of your mouth is gonna be a lie so save your tongue and my ears the speech," Malika said, calmly pulling her dreads back into a ponytail. "I told you from the gate that all you had to do was keep it one hundred with me, but you couldn't do that, could you? Men amaze me because they'd rather lie and risk a problem than telling the truth and letting the chips fall where they will."

"So you would've still fucked with me if I had told you that I was living with another chick who I'm not fucking?" Teddy asked.

"No, because that shit sounds crazy. Teddy, we had fun, but I guess at the end of the day it is what it is."

"So you're just gonna walk out on what we have without even giving me the benefit of the doubt?" Teddy called after her.

"Teddy, what do we have except a bunch of problems and lies? I've got enough problems of my own without you adding to it, man." Malika felt herself getting emotional so she cut it short. "It's been fun, Teddy, but I deserve better than what you're offering."

"Hold on, Malika. It's late, so at least let me give you a ride back to your block." He grabbed her by the arm trying to stop her.

Malika jerked away and gave him a look that made Teddy take a step back.

"Teddy, please don't pick now to start acting like you care about me. I'll be fine on the train." She closed the door softly behind her.

WITH THE WEEKEND SUBWAY SCHEDULE it took Malika over two hours to get home. She didn't mind the ride though because she needed the time to clear her head. The way things played out with Teddy stung because she was really feeling him, but it could've gone a lot worse. At the end of the day she knew to take it for what it was, a good time. Malika might not have had a fancy job or any degrees but she had a good heart and because of this she knew good things would come to her. When the time was right a man would come along that only saw her and no one else, and until then she would just learn to be happy with herself.

When she crossed Manhattan Avenue the first thing she noticed was the eerie silence. It was a relatively nice night and no one was on any of the corners. When she crossed the street on 102nd she spotted Scar and Jay skulking through the parking lot, with Scar whispering in his ear about only the devil knew what. Tucked under Scar's arm was a rolled-up paper bag.

No matter how far down the rabbit hole Jay slipped Malika still saw him as the little boy who used to come by the house to play with her son. Seeing what Jay was becoming made Malika thankful for Solomon. He could be hardheaded and had mannish ways but at least he wasn't out committing crimes like the rest of the kids in the neighborhood. Malika knew she raised her son better than that and felt bad about turning a blind eye to little Jay. She was going to make it her business to go and have a talk with Jay's aunt about the things he was getting into.

When Malika rounded the corner toward her building she found the courtyard just as empty as the avenue. As she walked along she noticed that several of the streetlights had been busted out as well as the ones in front of her building. She almost didn't see Prince until she was right on top of him.

"Damn, you scared me." Malika jumped when Prince peeled from the shadows.

"I'm sorry, Malika, but I've been trying to find you all day," Prince said. There was something in his tone that made her uneasy.

"Prince, what's wrong?"

"Some shit went down out here earlier between Scar and some niggaz from the other side of the projects. There was a shooting and Solomon got caught up in it," Prince said with a heavy heart.

"Oh, my God, please don't tell me my baby is dead?" Malika grabbed Prince by the shirt.

"Malika, calm down. Solomon wasn't shot, he was the shooter!" Prince informed her.

"What? We don't own a gun. Where did he get a gun from?"

Malika went on and on to the point where she was almost hysterical. She couldn't imagine her son in jail for murder and even toying with the thought made her nauseous.

"Malika, I don't know a lot because I wasn't out here. From what I'm hearing some words were exchanged and that escalated to a fistfight. Sometime during the fight Solomon came out with a hammer and started banging," Prince explained.

Malika shook her head in disbelief. "No, maybe somebody else's kid, but not Solomon. My son is no killer. He would never even touch a gun."

"Yeah, well, tell that to the police who came and picked him up. Malika, there was at least a dozen people that saw what went on out here and they all tell the same story."

"Dear Lord, I need to sit down." Malika stumbled over to the benches and took a seat. "How could I have allowed Solomon to get caught up in this foolishness?"

Prince tried to console her. "Malika, you didn't get Solomon into anything. Sometimes the call of the streets gets too strong and we answer it."

"This is that muthafucka Scar's fault. I know he roped my boy into this shit and I'm gonna kill him." Malika hopped up off the bench, but Prince stopped her.

"Malika, you can't blame somebody else for what Solomon decided to do. I made it clear to everyone in the hood that he wasn't to be recruited but if somebody does something voluntarily it falls on them. Solomon tried to make his movie and took his first knock upside the head. The D-boys swooped down on him about three hours ago, so he may still be in the twenty-fourth."

"I've gotta go see about my son." Malika started off in the direction of the precinct.

"Hold on, I'll come with you," Prince offered.

"Thank you, but you and your crew have done enough for me and my son. I'd appreciate it if you stayed away from us. If I catch you or any of your boys talking to my son again I'm calling the police," Malika said coldly.

"Malika, you know I'd never do anything to hurt Sol." Prince's voice was thick with emotion.

"Which is just why you're going to let him be," she said and disappeared down the hill.

Chapter 34

ANIMAL PEEKED THROUGH THE CURTAIN OF THE MAY-bach like a starstruck kid watching the throngs of people lining the sidewalks that had come out to see them. He had come a long way and he knew that his crew was smiling down on him, but the moment felt empty as none of them were there to share in the moment. His thoughts went to Gucci and what she might have been doing.

"What up? You good?" Soda snapped Animal out of his daze. He was running a lighter back and forth under the blunt to seal it.

"Yeah, I'm straight," Animal said.

"Dude, you've been in a zone all night, maybe you need a lil pick me up." Soda extended the foam cup to Animal.

Animal reached for the cup and caught himself. "Nah, I'm gonna chill with the sip tonight."

"What're you on the water wagon or something?" Soda looked at him quizzically.

"Never that, I just ain't gonna fuck wit that lean tonight," Animal told him.

Chip draped his arm around Animal. "I can dig that, but I got something that will make you feel groovier than any of that liquid death. Peanut butter and jelly." He held up a blunt and a pill respectively. "I'm offering a trip on a magic carpet like no other, my friend," Chip promised and pressed the pill into Animal's palm.

"Why don't you put that shit away, Pookie?" Don B. told Chip. "It's okay for y'all niggaz to get faded, but don't be wasted to the point where you're slurring and shit if someone sticks a microphone or recorder in your face. This is a big night for all of us fellas so let's enjoy it."

As expected the Code Red's grand opening was off the meter. The front of the spot was lit up like Grammy night with spotlights sweeping the air in front of the spot. The police had to close off the area for one block in every direction to control the heavy traffic of luxury cars and bikes pulling up to Code Red. Television reporters and journalists from just about every periodical worth mentioning showed up to try and get the exclusive on the star-studded event. Rappers mingled with actors, businessmen mingled with dope boys, and models with hood rats, and it was all good because of everyone's mutual love for Big Dawg.

It had been entertaining, but when Don B. pulled up with his entourage they stole the show. In synchronized movements the drivers got out of the three black on black Maybachs and came around to open the doors for the occupants. The first car on the line held security. Devil stepped onto the red carpet flanked by seasoned killers and apprentices, who he ordered to fan out and secure the perimeter. Once his people had been given their orders Devil went to stand beside the second Maybach in the line, which held the rappers. The third Maybach in the line contained the window dressing, this being the wayward chicks they decided to roll in with and a select few dudes from the hood who Don B. had selected to come along. They wouldn't have the VIP access of the inner circle but they helped to make Don B.'s crowd look thick.

When the entourage had been allowed their fifteen minutes of fame the real show began. Chip got out of the Maybach first, dressed in a long-sleeved Polo shirt with jeans and Louis sneakers. Soda was clearly feeling himself when he slid from the ride rocking a Brooks Brothers blazer over a black T-shirt. Hanging from his neck was a chain that looked to weigh almost as much as he did with its thick link and eighteen-inch medallion. It was a block of gold crafted into the outline of his home state, with a diamond star in the top right corner.

Animal flinched as the flash of cameras seemed to come from everywhere at the same time. Even behind his super-dark shades the light stung his eyes. Don B. had a mean outfit selected for his newest superstar but Animal took one look at the rhinestone-decorated shirt and knew he would be dressing himself. What he came up with was black jeans, red and gray Pradas, and a red and black plaid flannel that he only buttoned at the neck. On his head rested a Chicago Bulls fitted cap, with his hair spilling wildly from beneath the hat. Don B. had tried to convince Animal to get it braided up before the party but he preferred to let it stay wild. It was a reflection of the mood he was in. The diamond Big Dawg chain he wore was nice and drew quite a few stares but it was the looming Muppet chain that sparked conversation.

Of course Don B. had to make his entrance grander than anyone else's. The first thing you noticed was his jewels. Don B. slid out of the Maybach looking like he had definitely come to play that night. His neck and wrists looked like the Christmas tree at Rockefeller Center, caked in multicolored stones and chains of all makes and sizes. It had taken him an extra twenty minutes just to get everything on. His outfit was just as eye-catching in dark jeans, a red leather aviator jacket with white fur around the collar, and a white scarf flipped around his neck. On his head sat the matching aviator hat with a pair of tinted goggles pulled snugly over his eyes. He looked more like a World War II pilot than a record exec, but he had a style all his own. On each of the Don's arms he sported two ladies dressed in short red Fendi dresses with matching red heeled sandals. Around both their necks they sported diamond dog collars. As Don B. walked the red carpet, holding the leashes of the two beautiful ladies with him, he drew the attention of every camera in the area, which is what he set out to do.

The Big Dawg crew took a group photo on the red carpet, then did a series of individual shots. The photographers and the ladies all paid special attention to Animal. What Don B. had neglected to tell him was that he had arranged for him to take some solo pictures with the winners of a contest they had run on the radio to promote the party. Animal spent the next twenty minutes mustering fake smiles and policing the inquisitive hands of horny groupies. Between the flashes he thought he saw Don B.'s old bodyguard Remo stalking around the velvet rope, but when he looked again he was gone. When he was done with the contest winners Animal was ushered by one of Devil's boys toward the front door to join the entourage. As he passed the line he spotted a familiar face trying to get his attention.

Mimi waved her hands frantically. "I know you ain't gonna walk by me twice in one night. What up, blood?"

"Oh, what's good, ma?" Animal smiled, showing every piece of gold in his mouth. "Yo, let her through," he instructed the bouncer who quickly parted the ropes for the girl.

Mimi was looking like something special in her tight silver boy shorts and high stilettos with the clear heels. Her plum hair was covered by a platinum wig and the fishbowl rhinestone shades she wore obscured most of her face. When she leaned in and hugged Animal it was like everyone stopped and took notice, including the photographers who swooped in with their cameras to get shots of the stunning young couple.

"Damn, Mimi, this is my event and all eyes are on you." Animal motioned toward the camera.

"The people know what looks good when they see it." Mimi posed for the camera, blowing kisses with her pouty lips. All of the girls on the line looked sick enough to throw up as Mimi took multiple pictures with Animal, but there were two eyes in particular that burned more than any of them.

"Animal, we gotta go," Tone called from the door.

"I ain't trying to cramp ya style, my nigga. I just wanted to say hello and good looking out on making sure I got that bread on time," Mimi said, playing with his chain.

"You earned that, ma. But check it out, why don't you roll in with me?" Animal suggested.

"Boy you're crazy. Y'all got enough groupies on the train as it is."

"You ain't no groupie, you're my guest." Animal extended his arm. As soon as she accepted his arm the flashbulbs went off again.

"I hope your girl don't see this and catch no feelings," Mimi said, looking around at the crowd of angry females who hadn't been chosen. She made it a point to stick her tongue out at two especially sour faces on the line.

"My girl ain't nowhere out here, so knock it off. Besides, I've known you since you were like ten and just the thought of having sex with you makes me feel like I need to talk to a priest." Animal laughed and led Mimi into Code Red.

"IT'S A FUCKING MADHOUSE OUT here!" Boots said as they rounded the corner of the block Code Red was on. There were so many people on the sidewalk that you could barely move without someone stepping on your feet, which was bad for her since she was wearing open-toed shoes. It was a little cold for her feet to be out but they were among the only few pairs in her closet that weren't twisted.

"This is just my speed," Jada said, twirling the cherry lollipop between her lips and batting her eyes at an attractive gentleman in a black suit. She had gone for the dominatrix look rocking a leather corset and skintight leather pants. The heel on her high boots was so tall that they had a running bet as to how many times she would fall before the night was over. "Don B. always did know how to bring 'em out."

"Yes, because the freaks sure do come out at night," Gucci gave a Spanish girl wearing a short Dereon dress. The girl and her friend were being ushered through the line by two bouncers. Gucci wondered who they had fucked to get VIP status.

"Oh, ain't that Soda?" Boots tiptoed to see over the crowd where the crew from Big Dawg was taking their photos. "Damn, that nigga is fine, but he's short as hell."

"Gucci, ain't that your man right there in the Bulls hat?" Jada asked, pointing in Animal's direction.

Gucci watched as he took pictures with different women, smiling like he just knew he was the man. "Yeah, that's that nigga." Gucci's voice was cold. "Come on, let's make our way around to the other side of the crowd and see what the line is looking like."

"Why don't we just walk up to the front and tell them who you are?" Boots suggested.

"Because I don't want any of his big-mouthed ass henchmen telling him I'm here yet, now let's go."

Gucci led them around to the other side where there were three lines; one for VIP, one for bottle service, and one for the regular folk. All of the lines were long but the bottle service line seemed to be moving a little quicker so they hopped on that one. As they neared the front of the line she could see Animal being escorted to the entrance and stop short to talk to someone on the regular line. She couldn't see the girl's face but from the way she was dressed Gucci already knew she was a skank.

"Who the fuck is that Animal is talking to?" Jada moved next to Gucci to watch the show too.

"I don't know, but I'm gonna find out," Gucci vowed, pushing her way closer to the front. She watched in disgust as Animal not only took pictures with the girl but walked into the club arm in arm like she was the queen of the manor. The girl must've felt Gucci and her girls mugging her because she looked at them and stuck her tongue out.

"Oh, no this bitch didn't." Boots tried to climb over the rope, but Gucci and Jada held her back. "Gucci, you need to let me mop this bitch, real talk!"

"Boots, hold ya head. I ain't trying to get tossed outta here on no chicken head shit. We're real bitches and real bitches don't get tossed on no bullshit. If they're gonna throw me out tonight it's gonna be for shutting this muthafucking party down. Now let's go compose ourselves and get our strategy right." Gucci led them back to the line. She was ready to explode over what she saw but she had to stay in diva mode until everything was in order. Animal was going to wish he had never met Gucci when it was all said and done.

Jada tapped Gucci and drew her attention to a gentleman on the VIP line who was staring at her. "Damn, Gucci, you must be working the shit outta that Pucci dress because dude been clocking you since we rolled up."

Gucci looked over at the man and took in his measure. He was clean-cut, wearing a nice tweed blazer with a pair of jeans and some Steve Maddens. A gold cross hung from his neck stopping just above his belt. As Gucci and the guy studied each other a lightbulb went off in both their heads at the same time.

"Gucci?" he broke first. "It's me, Stone!" He spread his arms. Andrew Jackson a.k.a. Stone was a blast from Gucci's past that stirred mixed emotions in her. She had had a mean crush on Stone back in the days, but Stone never took their relationship seriously. He was getting money and living the fast life and Gucci wasn't having sex yet so he found another girl who was. Gucci always played it like it was nothing but Stone had been the first guy to really hurt her feelings.

"What up?" she said dryly.

"Gucci, I ain't seen you in years and that's all I get is a *what up*?"

Stone came around from his line and over to hers. "Can a nigga get a hug or something?"

Gucci started to brush him off, but she couldn't resist the opportunity to let him see the woman that little girl had grown up to be. She leaned in and gave him the buddy hug including the pat on the back. "How you been, Stone?"

"You know me, I'm out here living." He popped the chain around his neck so she could see it. It was nice link, but the gaudy cross dangling from the end of it took away from the quality. "So what up, ma? I don't see you uptown no more, you moved outta the city too?"

"Nah, I'm back and forth. Got a lil spot in Texas where I rest my head from time to time," she said coolly.

Stone smirked and nodded in approval. "Blow up or throw up, huh?"

"You know that's been my motto since I was fifteen."

"Yeah, even back then you were about your business, ma. That's something I always dug about you. So what up y'all rolling up in the spot?"

"We're here ain't we?" Jada rolled her eyes. She remembered how twisted Stone had had her cousin and she'd always disliked him for it.

"Still the same Jada, huh?"

"You know it."

"Anyway." Stone turned back to Gucci. "If y'all want y'all can roll in with me and my boys through the VIP."

"Nah, we good," Gucci said, wishing the damn line would get moving. She hadn't put on any stockings with that short ass Pucci dress and she was getting cold.

"You sure, that bottle service line looks like it might be a while." Stone smirked and his boys laughed.

"Gucci, is that you?" A skinny white girl with mouse-brown hair and holding a clipboard walked up to her. Gucci couldn't remember her name but she knew the girl worked for Big Dawg in the publicity department. "What fucking idiots." The girl tapped the clipboard against her head in frustration. "Excuse me," she called to the closest bouncer, "why is she waiting on the line?"

The bouncer looked at them both dumbly and shrugged. "Hell if I know, I'd assume she was waiting to get in like everybody else."

"Are you guys all high off kush? This is Animal's fucking girlfriend. She isn't supposed to be doing the line, are you crazy? Come on, girls." She waved Gucci and her crew over to the bouncer. "You see to it that these girls make it in with no hassle and comp them with a bottle, you can bill it to Big Dawg."

"Right away," the bouncer said and parted the crowd for them.

"Gucci, please don't tell Animal and the guys about this. I'm already skating on thin ice and I kinda need my job," the girl with the clipboard pleaded.

"Don't worry, we're good." Gucci smiled and followed the bouncer.

"Damn, I need to be rolling with you!" Stone called after her.

"Nah, you're VIP, remember?" Gucci said over her shoulder and disappeared into the club.

Chapter 35

ABOUT AN HOUR AFTER FINALLY MAKING IT TO THE VIP and getting situated Animal wasn't feeling any pain. He stood off to the side of the elevated stage where the VIP was situated; looking at the strobe lights as if they were the most beautiful things he had ever seen. Between the pills, the weed, and the liquor he was flying to another galaxy and Chip was his copilot. Mimi stood off to his right dancing by herself sipping a funny-colored drink. Dudes were trying to get at her left and right but Mimi was shooting them down.

"That's a bad bitch right there." Soda nodded over at Mimi. "What up, big homey? Why don't you share that wit ya boy?"

Animal turned his sleepy eyes to Soda. "First off, lil nigga, she ain't my property. Second, she ain't trying to fuck wit yo greasy ass, so you can forget it."

Soda took a gulp of his drink "Come on, dawg, why you cuffing the lil breezy? We can take that back to the telly and get our tag team on. Yo, keep it one hundred; she got some good pussy don't she?"

To everyone's surprise Animal grabbed Soda up by the collar. "Ain't you got no regards for what the fuck comes outta your mouth? I don't give a shit how you do with the rest of these little groupie bitches, but if you come at Mimi sideways we gonna have a problem, feel me?"

"Yeah, man, why you tripping?" Soda's eyes were wide and fearful. Animal never answered, he just shoved him and stalked out of the VIP.

"Animal, what's good?" Mimi called after him, but he kept walking. She gave Soda and Chip dirty looks before leaving the VIP.

"Damn, niggaz getting all sensitive over jump-offs up here in New York?" Soda asked Chip.

Chip laughed. "That ain't no jump-off, that's his niece. They don't share blood, but his brother had a baby by Mimi's mother so they've been like family ever since."

Soda felt like shit for the things he had said to Animal. "Damn, I gotta apologize to my nigga. I didn't mean no disrespect." Soda started after Animal, but Chip stopped him.

"He'll be okay, but it's too soon to invade his space. Let him be for a few and everything will be cool," Chip told him.

"Chip, I spend damn near every day with Animal when we're in Texas so how do you know so much shit about him that I don't?"

"Because Animal just makes music with you. He actually talks to me," Chip told him and went back to enjoying his drink.

Animal hunkered over the bar nursing a Grey Goose with pomegranate juice, sulking. A few groupies pressed him but Animal shooed them away like flies, preferring his own company when he was upset about something. He hadn't meant to react so harshly to Soda's statement but the drugs had him in his feelings.

"Is this seat taken?" a feminine voice called from behind him.

"Beat it, shorty," Animal said without looking up from his glass. To his irritation she took the seat anyway.

"What are you hard of hearing?" Animal spun around and found Kelly's pretty face staring back at him.

• • •

"PARTY OVER HERE, PARTY OVER here," Jada sang as she danced through the crowd. The room was swollen with people and everyone seemed to be having a good time except for Gucci. She twirled over to her cousin and tried to engage her in a bump contest but she was nonreceptive. "Girl, what's up with you, you still tripping off Animal and shorty? If you want we can find that bitch right now and pound her out."

"Now that's probably the first thing we could ever agree on since knowing each other." Boots gave her a high-five.

"Cool it, Cagney and Lacey. I told y'all that I don't wanna make a scene until I'm ready to be the star. Besides, my beef ain't with ol' girl, it's with Animal," Gucci said.

"Well, my beef is about to be with one of these clumsy bitches if they don't learn how to walk. These muthafuckas are killing my toes," Boots said, stepping out of the way of a passing group of girls.

"Well since we ain't kicking nobody's ass let's go to the bar and collect our comp bottle, I'm ready to get my swerve on," Jada said and led the pack toward the bar.

Gucci walked with her click to the crowded bar, careful not to be spotted by one of Animal's people before she was able to get the drop on him. Over in the corner she spotted the girl with the platinum wig freak dancing with some dude. She was still tight at the girl for trying to stunt on them, but she wasn't as tight because at least she wasn't dancing with Animal. Gucci had swept the club twice and there was still no sign of him.

The bar was just as much a zoo as the rest of the club, if not more so because everyone was trying to get a drink. Jada managed to push a hole open near the bar wide enough for all three of the girls to squeeze into. Gucci claimed her bottle of champagne and tricked off on a bottle of Hennessy for her girls. She placed her back against the bar while she sipped her drink and continued to scan the crowd for her man.

"What's up, baby? You wanna dance?" A dude sporting a dry curl and a fake-looking gold chain approached Jada.

Jada looked him up and down. "Does it look like I'm trying to be out there dancing in these heels." She held her leg up. "Kick rocks, son."

"Tramp-ass bitch," the dude mumbled as he stalked away.

"Ya mama's a tramp," Boots called after him.

Gucci shook her head. "Some of these niggaz are just like vultures."

"And some of the niggaz ain't no better," Jada directed Gucci's attention to the end of the bar where Animal was chatting it up with the Spanish girl she had seen outside in the Dereon dress. "Gucci, I know you said you didn't want to cause a scene, but I've had about enough of this shit." Jada took her earrings off and began working on the straps to her boots.

"Fuck it, let's make a movie," Gucci said, holding back the tears. She stormed toward Animal getting angrier by the step as she watched the Spanish girl paw him like she wanted to fuck him right there. They had made it to within a few feet of them when she heard Boots's loud voice behind her.

"Bitch, why don't you watch where you're walking!" Boots was screaming in the face of a girl who was a few inches taller than her.

"Goddammit, Boots!" Gucci started, making her way back to Boots who seemed to get more hyped the closer she got. Gucci knew how it was going to play out and unfortunately she got there too late to stop it.

By the time security made it over, Boots and the girl had their hands locked around each other's throats and both their shirts were ripped. Titties and weave hair flew in every direction as a crowd of spectators cheered them on. In no time security had Boots and the other girl off their feet and on their way to the exit. When Gucci tried to explain who she was and that Boots was with her they threw her out too. The last thing she saw before she was tossed on the street like common trash was the girl kissing Animal on the cheek.

ANIMAL WAS ALMOST SPEECHLESS LOOKING at Kelly in her very short Dereon dress that left so little to the imagination.

"I've never been good at taking directions unless it's in the heat of the moment," Kelly joked. "So why are you over here all by yourself looking like you just lost your best friend?"

"Just taking a break from the camera," Animal said.

"I don't know why. The camera loves you! I saw you out there flicking it up with them chicks."

"So what, you're watching me now?"

Kelly placed the straw of her drink seductively between her lips and took a sip. "A good huntress always stalks her prey before she moves in for the kill."

"You're gonna get both of us killed if you keep dangling temptation in front of me, Kelly. My girl is real possessive over what belongs to her."

Kelly rolled her eyes. "Damn, it ain't like I wanna keep you. I'm just trying to borrow you for a second."

"You don't quit, do you?"

"Nope, not when my mind is set on something I want," Kelly declared. "Animal, don't make it more serious than what it is. All I wanna do is fuck you then you can go back home to ya shorty, what's good?"

Animal thought on it for a very long moment. Kelly was by far one of the baddest chicks he had ever had offered to him, but in the back of his mind he couldn't help but to think how Gucci would feel if she ever found out. At the end of the day he knew he had to do the right thing, even if he didn't want to. "I appreciate the offer, but ain't nothing popping, sis."

Kelly gave him a look somewhere between shock and disappointment. "Damn, that must be one special lady for you to pass on all this." She took Animal's hand and ran it from her breasts to her thighs.

"She is," he said, letting his hand linger on her thigh a little longer than it needed to. A commotion coming from the other side of the club drew both of their attention. From the fake hair flying around Animal already knew what was going on. "Girl fight," he said with a smirk.

"I better get over there and make sure it ain't none of my bitches getting it in," Kelly slid off the bar. "Not for nothing, Animal, you're a real sweetheart." She kissed him on the cheek. "When you get home you make sure you tell that lady of yours how lucky she is."

"I will," he said, watching her walk away.

Animal could've kicked himself for not at least getting some head from Kelly, but he knew it was the devil enforcing the thought in his head. Kelly was a bad chick but she would only be around for a moment, whereas Gucci would be there for a lifetime.

Animal pulled out his cell to text her when the hairs on the back of his neck suddenly stood up, alerting him of danger. He instinctively reached for his gun and remembered that he had left it in his car and they had all rode in with Don B. in the Maybachs, which might prove to be a costly error if things got ugly. His eyes swept through the club in search of the threat and when he saw Rico barreling down on him with some of his boys a huge lump formed in his throat.

Chapter 36

"WELL, WELL, IF IT AIN'T THE LITTLE BOY WHO CALLS himself playing grown man's games," Rico said with a smug grin. Mud and Dirt flanked him wearing expressions that said they wished Animal would try something. "I've been looking for you for a long time."

"Well, you've found me so what's popping?" Animal stood up. He knew he was outnumbered and outgunned, but he was a G with it and wouldn't be intimidated by any odds.

"You talk a lot of shit for a nigga who could get his wig pushed back within a matter of seconds if Rico gives the word." Mud stepped up. The way he kept his hand lingering near his belt Animal knew he was strapped.

"I don't see no gag over ya man's mouth, make it do what it do," Animal said bravely. Mud went to draw his gun but Rico stayed his hand.

"You know," Rico began, "it was genius on your part to beat Lee within an inch of his life and put the idea in his head that I did it, but you had to know that I'm too caked up for them bum-ass charges to have stuck so I'm gonna assume it was a ploy to separate me and Changa, right?" Animal shrugged. "And since I haven't heard from

Ras in a few days I'm gonna assume he's dead, right?" Again Animal shrugged. Rico laughed. "You know when my men first started getting knocked off I thought I was dealing with a whole crew, but had I known it was cockroach ass I'd have stepped on you a long time ago. You were stupid to think you could win a war against me."

Animal sized his opponents up. "Rico, this ain't about no war. This is about me mounting your head on a wall for you having Tech killed. You got all the guns and all the soldiers but I got all the heart, so if you and these goons came in here to try and intimidate me then it was a wasted trip. Niggaz like me wake up expecting to die, so if you wanna rock then let's get it." Animal broke a beer bottle on the bar and squared off to do battle with Rico and his crew.

"What the fuck is going on here?" Don B. pushed through the crowd followed by Devil with about five or six more of the homeys on their heels.

"Well if it ain't the famous Don B.," Rico greeted him with a smile. "I don't see you much since you stopped buying coke from me."

Don B. didn't miss the sarcasm in his voice. "I push a different kind of product now, Rico. But what I wanna know is why you and ya mans got my lil homey hemmed up like this?"

"Ain't nothing but a little unfinished street business between old friends." Rico was speaking to Don B. but looking at Animal.

"Well, street business needs to stay on the street. If y'all wanna have a good time then it's bottles on me all night, but if y'all came in here to act up I'm gonna have to ask you to leave. I don't want no problems in my club, fam," Don B. told Rico and his boys.

Rico measured his words. He may have had more power than Don B. on the streets but in the club with the police and security presence he knew he had no wins. "You got it, big man." Rico backed up. "Animal, I'm gonna see you on the streets."

"I'll see you before you see me," Animal shot back.

"Animal, what the fuck was that all about?" Don B. asked once Rico and his boys had left.

Animal tried to downplay it. "Nothing, it was a small thing."

"Don't give me that. If you've managed to get into a beef with Rico I'd hardly call it a small thing. In case you didn't get the memo Rico is one of Shai's capos."

"Fuck him and Shai. Every man bleeds the same," Animal spat.

"See, now you're just talking stupid. Dawg, I thought we agreed that once we got this music thing popping you were off the streets?" Don B. reminded him.

"I am off the streets, Don."

"Then what was that thing with you and Rico?"

Animal hesitated. "It's complicated."

"Animal, that's not a good enough answer. If you don't tell me what's going on then I can't help you."

"I don't recall asking for your help with this, Don," Animal snapped.

"Don't come at me all sideways like I'm the enemy, lil homey." Don B. raised his hands in surrender. "Look, we ain't even gotta talk about this right now. It's a party and we should all be having fun, smell me? After we leave here me, Chip, and some of the other guys are going to the studio to lay some tracks. Try to stay out of trouble until then." Then Don B. walked in one direction while Animal went in the other.

"Dude, where are you going?" Chip caught up with him.

"To arm myself. If Rico and his hos come back I'm gonna be prepared this time," Animal told him, working his way through the crowd. Chip finally managed to get him to stop completely when they reached the exit.

"Animal, don't put yourself in harm's way. If something is gonna go down then let security handle it, that's what we pay them for."

Animal gave his friend a serious look. "Chip, you ain't from what I'm from so I don't expect you to understand. In the battlefield you can't trust anybody with your life, you can trust yourself."

Animal left it at that and hit the exit.

• • •

ANIMAL TOOK A MINUTE TO look around and make sure the coast was clear before stepping from the safety of the club's security. Rico wising up to him being the one murdering his people happened a little sooner than he expected but he knew it was bound to happen. All this meant was that the gloves were off and it was kill on sight.

He made hurried steps up the block toward Amsterdam Avenue where he planned on hopping in a livery cab and going to retrieve his gun and his car. As he neared the top of the dark block he heard footsteps behind him. Animal waited until the footsteps were close and spun around with his fists balled up. They wouldn't do him much good against a gun, but they were all he had to defend himself.

"Be easy, Rocky Balboa." Mimi threw her hands up.

"Mimi, you know better than to run up on me like that. What are you doing out here, you should be inside," Animal scolded her.

"You know I had to make sure everything was okay. I saw you having a real heated discussion with those dudes in there and I wanted to make sure you didn't need me to watch your back." She flashed the handle of the little pistol she had in her purse.

"I'm good, killer." He smiled. "But seriously though, you should get back inside the club where it's safe. Something might go down out here tonight." Animal looked around nervously. It was the first time Mimi had ever seen him rattled about anything.

"Animal, you know if somebody is at you that means they're at us. We're family," Mimi said.

"I know, baby girl, but not with this. I'm just going across the street to get a cab so I can go get my hammer. I'll be back in a minute, I promise."

"Pinky-swear?" Mimi held up her pinky.

"Pinky-swear." He lopped his pinky around hers to seal the deal. Animal hugged Mimi close to him.

"A'ight, so I'll be waiting for you to—"

Without warning Mimi broke the embrace and pushed Animal to the floor.

"It's a hit!" she cried and drew her gun.

Mud and Dirt took cover behind a parked car just as Mimi's bullets ripped through the ground where they had been standing. Dirt tried to pop up to get a lock on Animal, but a bullet bounced off the car hood hitting him in the eye with shrapnel. Animal called to Mimi to take cover but she was already moving in on her targets hidden on the other side of the car.

"Don't hide, pussies. Come get some of these hot ones." Mimi closed in on her targets. No sooner than Mimi rounded the car, Mud caught her with a bullet to the chest. Mimi's small body flew over the car and landed on the ground a few feet away from Animal.

"Mimi!" Abandoning his own safety he crawled to Mimi, who was lying on the ground with blood running from her mouth.

"Damn this shit burns," Mimi rasped. Tears streamed down her face and mingled with the blood.

"Don't try to talk, baby. I'm gonna get you outta here." Animal cradled her.

"I'm already out of here, big homey. Just tell me that I got them niggaz too," she wheezed, sending more blood spilling from her mouth.

"Yeah, baby. You got them niggaz," Animal lied.

"Good," Mimi said with her last breath and went limp in his arms. In her stillness Mimi looked more like the little girl he had known than the killer he had raised her to be and it broke his heart. Mimi had had a hard life of empty dreams and broken promises, but now no one could touch her. She was at peace.

"Muthafuckas!" Animal took up Mimi's gun and went after Mud and Dirt. Mud had just poked his head over the car when he saw Animal sliding across the hood like an action movie. Animal landed a kick to Dirt's jaw, stunning him, before he put Mimi's gun to his head and pulled the trigger. Without his partner Mud lost his heart and tried to run but he wasn't faster than a bullet. Animal dropped him with one to the head, then gave him two more to his back to make sure he was done.

With a heavy heart Animal walked back around the car to where Mimi's body lay. He felt bad for having to leave her on the streets like that, but he could hear the police sirens closing and there was no way he could avenge her death if he was locked up. Animal reached down and closed the girl's eyes before crossing himself. He whispered a promise to Mimi that he would settle up for her and disappeared into the night.

Chapter 37

WHEN MALIKA GOT TO THE TWENTY-FOURTH PRECINCT she was notified that due to overcrowding Solomon had been moved. She ended up visiting two precincts in the Bronx before finally tracking him down at the Thirtieth in Harlem. After filling out the necessary paperwork the woman behind the desk wearing the sergeant's stripes allowed her a five-minute visit with Solomon. He looked so pitiful sitting in the dirty cell that Malika broke down and cried.

"Baby, are you okay?" Malika held his hands through the bars.

"Yeah, Ma, I'm good," he said, trying to play tough but she could tell he was scared. He was also sporting some fresh cuts and bruises meaning that he had been roughed up at some point.

"What happened? They said you were shooting at somebody but I know there has to be some kind of mistake," Malika said.

"No, it wasn't a mistake, Ma. Some guys had come over to our side of the projects beefing and a big fight broke out. I was scared so I got the gun out of the grass and started shooting, but you gotta believe me, I wasn't trying to hurt anybody." Solomon's eyes began to water.

"Don't you worry. I'm gonna get you outta here tonight," Malika assured him.

"I wouldn't bet on that," a cop who had been ear hustling interjected. "We've got him at the scene of the crime with the gun laying at his feet. Furthermore your boy is a part of that little drug ring they've got going on in the projects."

"That's impossible, my son doesn't sell drugs," Malika said indignantly.

The officer looked at her like she was crazy. "Hey, Bart, come here for a minute, will ya?" He stopped a plainclothed officer that was walking by.

"What's up?" the plainclothed officer asked.

"This lady here says her son doesn't sell drugs."

The plainclothed officer looked inside the cell and laughed. "Are you kidding me? I've been watching this little dude push shit for Scar for the last week. He's so good at it we nicknamed him Charlie Hustle." The two officers laughed and left Malika standing there dumbfounded.

"Solomon, is what they're saying true?" she asked but he remained silent. "Boy, you better tell me something before I reach in that cell and choke the shit outta you."

He sucked his teeth. "Yeah, it's true."

Malika wanted to faint. "Solomon, for as many talks as we've had about the streets what would make you jump out the window and do something so stupid?"

"You!" he snapped. "Ma, day in and day out I watch you scrape and borrow to get through to the next day and it was killing me. Every guy you get with leaves you suffering and you gotta pick the pieces up and start all over again all by yourself. I just wanted to prove to you that I was a man and that I could do more for you than them suckas you keep falling for."

Solomon's words hit her like bricks. With all that was going on Malika had only thought about herself and how hard things were on her. She never once stopped to think of what it was doing to Solomon and hearing it from the horse's mouth cut her deeply.

"Time is up, Ms." a uniformed officer notified Malika.

"I'm gonna get you out of this I promise," Malika told Solomon as she was escorted away. Malika was blinded by tears as she rushed through the precinct lobby toward the exit. Some of the officers who had overheard what was going on looked at her and shook their heads, but the desk sergeant felt sorry for her.

"I'm going on a break," the sergeant said and came from behind the desk. When she got outside Malika was sitting on the precinct stairs sobbing. "Here you go." The sergeant handed her a tissue.

"Thank you," Malika said, dabbing her eyes. "I don't know how this happened. I've done everything I could to be a good mother and it just seems like I'm not doing enough."

"No matter how much we do it never does," the sergeant told her. "We work our fingers to the bone to make sure our kids have the things we need and they still can't get over not having the things they want. Some can fly straight on their own and others need a little coaxing."

"Do you have kids too?"

"Yup, three boys, one girl, and a husband who is in his second childhood." The sergeant laughed. "There are times when I wanna beat myself up for the things everybody else does, but I have to remind myself that it's not me doing dumb shit it's them. You can't get nobody right until you get yourself right, and the first step is learning to love and appreciate you even when no one else does."

"Those are some wise words," Malika said.

"I've been around long enough to learn from trial and error, Malika."

Malika's head snapped up in surprise. "How did you know my name?"

"I know your name from when you showed me your ID, but I know your voice from my husband's voice mail. I'm Dorian, Teddy's wife."

"Oh, my God." Malika covered her mouth in embarrassment. "Dorian, let me explain. I never knew that Teddy was married. We—"

"No need to explain, Malika, because I am so past getting upset with Teddy and his wandering dick. While he's out doing him you can believe that I'm out doing me. When you came in here and I made the connection I started to lose your son's paperwork, but as I listened to what y'all were going through I felt bad."

"Even though I had sex with your husband?"

Dorian nodded. "Malika, it'd be easy for me to be out here trying to put the beats on you for what you've done, but at the end of the day I didn't take those vows with you, I took them with Teddy. You're just a casualty of the sick little games he's been playing for years. If you're smart, you'll leave him alone for good, but if you're dumb you'll keep getting roped into his apologies like I've been doing for the last few years."

"If you know what kind of dude he is then why are you still with him?"

"Out of convenience, of course. Teddy is a low-down dog, but he's got a healthy bank account and owns a few properties. One day I'll wake up and leave him but for now I'm content to let him wonder while I slowly bleed his bank account dry. When he's broke and on his last legs then I'll kick his ass to the curb with the rest of the trash." This got Malika to laugh. "Listen, clean yourself up and go get something to eat. By the time you come back I'll have pulled some strings to have your son released to you with a date for y'all to go to family court. I probably can't do anything about the charges he's facing, but at least he can fight the case from the streets. Be strong because y'all are gonna need each other," Dorian told her and started back up the stairs into the precinct.

"Why are you doing this for me?" Malika called after her.

Dorian thought long and hard on the answer. "Because I feel sorry for you, Malika. You think you're a woman and you're just another baby with a baby trying to make it in the world. Come back in a little while to pick up your son and don't let me see either one of you again, because you've used up your last free pass."

AS PROMISED SOLOMON WAS PROCESSED and ready to go by the time Malika made it back to the precinct. She was so happy to see him that all she could do was hug him and cry. She looked for Dorian to thank her, but she had gone for the night. The new desk sergeant said something about a family emergency that she had to deal with. Malika and Solomon had a long talk about life and his upcoming court case. They had a hard road ahead of them and they had to be on the same page to face it. Solomon seemed like his stay in a cell had possibly scared some sense into him but only time would tell.

When they got to their building there was a crowd of people gathered in front of it. The police had the whole area taped off and wouldn't let anybody inside. On the ground there was a body covered in a bloody white sheet. Malika couldn't see the face, but the corpse was wearing a familiar-looking sneaker. Near the front of the crowd she spotted Jada's uncle Mookie and his partner Fish, whispering among each other.

"What happened?" Malika asked Mookie.

"The chickens have finally come home to roost." Mookie nodded at the lobby. The police were bringing Scar and Lloyd out in handcuffs. Scar was still smirking like it was a game while Lloyd looked ready to cry. "Them boys they was shooting at earlier came back with some guns of their own and their aim was just a little bit better."

"Where's Jay?" Solomon asked frantically.

Mookie removed his do-rag and placed it over his heart. "I tried to tell him to find another game"—he looked down sadly at the bloody sheet—"but the young ones never listen."

"NO!" Solomon collapsed into his mother's arms and screamed over and over into her chest.

Malika tried to console him as best she could, but there was nothing she could do to soothe his grief. She was both saddened and relieved by the sight of Jay lying under that sheet. She was sad because he was a young man with so much potential who just happened to get caught up in Scar's little game, but relieved because she knew that if the wind had blown the other way it would've been her kid under that sheet.

Chapter 38

ANIMAL WAS NUMB WHEN HE FINALLY MADE IT BACK TO his apartment. Chip had been blowing up his phone, but he didn't feel like talking. All he wanted to do was crawl into Gucci's waiting arms and grieve. When he opened the apartment door and saw all of his clothes shredded on the floor and Gucci's bags by the door he knew his grieving would have to wait.

"What the fuck?" He looked around in shock. "Gucci, get your ass out here!"

"Fuck you, adulterer!" she screamed through the bathroom door.

"What the hell are you talking about? Open this damn door!" He banged on the bathroom door.

"I ain't opening shit because I don't wanna see your cheating ass face. My shit is packed and I'm going to stay with my mother." From the rawness of her voice he knew she had been crying.

"Gucci, I don't know what you're talking about so why don't you come out here so we can talk? I've had a bad night and I really ain't up to arguing with you."

"Looked like you were having a good night to me the way you had them chicken heads all up on you at Code Red. Which one did you fuck, the big booty Spanish chick or the young-looking one that was dressed like a stripper? I seen it all!"

"You went to Code Red after I asked you not to?" He was surprised. Now her anger was starting to make sense. "Gucci, that shit ain't what it looked like. I can explain it."

"Explain it to your little bitch on 106th since that's where you've been spending most of your time."

Animal was confused. "Gucci, I don't know any bitches on 106th."

"You're a liar because your car has been parked over there every day this week and don't try to deny it because I had Jada watching ya dumb ass. Animal, I told you not to play with my heart and now you're gonna see what it gets you."

Animal felt his frustration mounting. He had gone through too much that night to have to come home and deal with some domestic shit. "Gucci, I'm tired of talking to you through the door."

"Then stop talking and get the fuck away from me, nigga!"

"Gucci, baby . . ."

"Don't baby me, Animal, because we're past that shit. If you wanna go play with these tramp bitches then do that because I'm damn sure gonna find me a tramp nigga and let him play all in my mouth."

Gucci's threat pushed Animal over the edge and he started kicking the door. "Gucci, if you get out there and try to play me I'll kill ya monkey ass!"

"You keep kicking the door and I bet I'll call the police on you. Ain't no telling what they'll find if they run up in here. Go get all the pussy you want, Animal, because it's a wrap for us."

Animal was too hurt and too angry to keep arguing. "If that's how you wanna play it then fuck you too, bitch!" He gave the door a kick for good measure.

He had been foolish to blindly trust Gucci when she couldn't do the same. He had just lost someone as close to him as his brother

Justice and she was too busy throwing accusations at him to be sympathetic. Animal took a minute to change his bloody shirt and headed for the door. On his way out his phone rang and it was Chip on the line. Animal hit the ignore button and tossed his phone on the bed before slamming the door viciously behind him.

GUCCI LISTENED FOR A WHILE to make sure Animal had gone before coming out of the bathroom. Her makeup was a mess and her eyes were swollen for crying for so many hours. Jada had tried to get her to come home with her, but Gucci declined. She was going to deal with the issue between she and Animal while it was still fresh. It took everything she had not to come flying out of that bathroom and cutting Animal but she knew that she would get weak and end up taking him back after she looked into those passionate eyes. She knew she had been a fool for letting him into her heart the way she did and now she was suffering the consequences of her actions.

She noticed his cell phone on the bed and couldn't help but to play the devil and go through it to see if he had gotten any new numbers at the club. To her surprise it rang as she was doing so. "What?"

"Oh, I'm sorry I was trying to reach Tayshawn," the woman said on the other end.

"This is Animal's phone. Who is this calling at booty call hours?" Gucci snapped.

"I'm sorry to be calling you at this hour and Lord knows I wish I didn't have to. This is Maggie. I'm one of the nurses at the home where Ms. Hanna was staying."

"Hanna?" Gucci asked, trying to match the name with one of the jump-offs in Animal's phone.

"Yes, Hanna is one of our residents at the seniors home on 106th Street."

"That wouldn't be 106th and Columbus would it?" Gucci asked, feeling the knot forming in her stomach.

"Technically between Columbus and Amsterdam, but yes that's the place. I'm sorry, who am I speaking to?" Ms. Brown asked.

"Gucci," she said, starting to put the pieces of the puzzle together in her mind.

"Yes, he's been telling us about you all week. You know we owe you an apology for cutting into your quality time while Animal is here visiting," Ms. Brown joked, but Gucci didn't laugh. She was too sick to see the humor. "Anyhow, the reason I called was to tell him that Hanna had passed this evening. I figured he should know since they were so close. Animal did more for Hanna than her blood kin."

"I'm sorry to hear about Hanna and I'll pass the message along to Tayshawn," Gucci said numbly.

"Thank you, Gucci, and I look forward to meeting you real soon. Take care now." Ms. Brown hung up.

Gucci let the phone slide to the bed as all she could do was sit there with a stupid expression on her face. She had no idea that Animal had been taking care of someone in a nursing home. It was yet another secret in his life he hadn't seen fit to share with her yet. His visits to Hanna explained what he had been doing on 106th, but it still didn't dispel what she had seen in the club.

The ringing phone brought Gucci out of her contemplation. She grabbed Animal's phone thinking it was him, but it was actually hers. She didn't recognize the number, but she picked up anyway in case it was Animal calling from someone else's phone. They had to have a long talk before she made any rash decisions. "Hello?"

"Gucci, this is Chip. I'm sorry to wake you, but I've been calling Animal for over an hour and he ain't picking up," Chip told her in a panicked voice.

"He was here a few minutes ago, but we had a fight and he left his cell phone here. Is everything alright?"

"Nah, shit is fucked up. They found Mimi dead around the

corner from the club. People saw them outside the club together, but Animal was nowhere to be found when the body was discovered."

"Who was Mimi? One of his bitches?" Gucci asked.

"No, she was his niece."

"What?" Gucci's mouth dropped open. Chip went on to give her the short version of Animal and Mimi's relationship and in the process Gucci was able to figure out that Mimi was the girl with the platinum hair she had seen him with.

"Gucci, you still there?" Chip's voice came through.

"Yeah, I'm here."

"Being that Animal pulled a disappearing act the police are starting to ask some real uncomfortable questions. We got some of the guys out combing the streets so hopefully we find him before they do. He knows we had a studio session tonight so me and Don B. are down here now hoping that he shows up."

"Oh, my God. Oh, my God," Gucci chanted, trying to gather something to put on. "Chip, I'll be down there in about twenty minutes, please keep me posted if you hear anything."

"You got it." He ended the call.

Gucci felt like less than shit for the way she treated Animal. He was trying to come to her for help and she couldn't see past her own jealousy to be there for him. Her sympathy suddenly turned to fear as she realized the seriousness of what had been set in motion. Animal was wandering the streets, drunk, emotional, and armed. Things had gone from bad to worse.

DON B. LOOKED LIKE HE had seen a ghost when Animal came skulking out of the shadows. He looked weary, more so than Don B. had ever seen him. "Yo, kid, we've been looking all over for you, are you alright?" Don B. inspected him.

"I'm good, man. Just tired, real tired," Animal said.

"Yo, I got some bad news for you, B., Mimi . . ."

"I already know," Animal cut him off. "Rico's boys laid her down right before I laid them down."

"Rico did this? Yo, that's my word I'm putting some paper on that nigga's skull. It's going down and that's on Blood!" Don B. declared.

"Where the fuck you been?" Chip came flying out of the lobby of the building that housed the studio they were working in. He hugged his friend for a long time. "Man, we were all worried shitless about you."

"Thanks, but ain't no cause for it. You know the Animal is always gonna be alright." Animal raised his shirt and showed them the butt of his gun.

"What the fuck are you doing with that when you're in enough trouble as it is?" Don B. scolded him. "Give that hammer to Devil or one of them to hold for you."

"The last time I trusted another nigga to guard my life I lost Mimi. Giving up my strap is a mistake that I won't make twice," Animal said coldly. As the three of them stood outside debating about the gun two cars pulled up. One was a black sedan and the other was Gucci's truck.

"Animal, we need to talk!" she yelled out the window before the truck had come to a complete stop.

"Fuck does this broad want? She better not come over here on some bullshit cuz I might run up in her mouth the way I'm feeling," Animal said with an attitude.

"Animal, don't start no Ike Turner shit out here," Don B. warned.

"Nephew, what it is?" Remo called from the passenger window of the dark sedan.

"This nigga here," Don B. huffed. "What you want, man? We're in the middle of a crisis." Don B. threw his hands up in frustration and walked toward the car.

"I ain't beat for this shit," Animal said when Gucci stepped onto the curb.

"Animal, please don't walk away. I just wanna talk." Gucci approached. At the angles they were walking at she and Don B. reached the sedan's line of vision at about the same time.

Gucci did a double take as she noticed suspect movement in the back of the car. It only took a split second for her eyes and her brain to connect to send the message to her mouth. "GUN!" she screamed.

THE WORD SEEMED TO DRIP from Gucci's mouth, but by the time she finished it Animal was already barreling down on her. Don B. stood frozen with fear as the guy in the backseat started shooting. Animal ran past and knocked Gucci to the ground before turning his rage and gun on the sedan in a hail of bullets. He could hear people screaming and the sounds of bullets hitting metal but he kept firing. He didn't care who they were or where they had come from, but he knew that he would not let them have Gucci.

By the time his gun was empty the car was a smoking mess of holes and blood. Remo hung out the passenger window with half of his face blown off and dripping down the side of the car. The chick behind the wheel had a gaping hole in her head. The man who had been shooting at Don B. lay halfway out the back of the car with his chest opened. He was a brown-skinned kid who Animal had never seen a day in his life and would never see again.

"Drop that hammer, muthafucka!" Animal heard someone shout. When he looked up a half-dozen police cars had appeared seemingly out of nowhere. "Lay that pistol on the floor real slow," Detective Alvarez said, keeping his gun pointed at Animal's head.

Animal thought about holding court, but the pleading look in Gucci's eyes stayed his hand. As slowly as he could he lay on the ground and allowed himself to be captured.

"You know, my partner bet me that if we laid on you long enough you'd do something stupid," Detective Brown said, squeezing the handcuffs and yanking Animal roughly to his feet.

"Save the speech and take me in, pussy," Animal capped.

"Wait, this has got to be some mistake," Gucci pleaded with the detective with tears in her eyes.

"No mistake, baby. We caught your man at the scene and still holding the murder weapon. It don't get no sweeter than this!" Detective Brown said proudly.

"Partner, you better come take a look at this," Detective Alvarez called from where he stood examining the bodies. When Brown walked over to see what his partner was looking at his eyes got wide. "Do you remember this dude?"

"Hell yeah, for as much time as we've spent chasing him. That's Shannon Jones, the brother of that little girl Dena who Don B. was said to have raped. Shit, had we known that we could've picked Animal up on a bogus charge earlier so that he couldn't have been here to save Don B.'s maggot ass."

Detective Alvarez looked over at Don B. "You are one lucky muthafucka."

Don B. shrugged as if it was nothing, knowing that a few seconds prior he had been ready to shit his pants.

"Too bad we can't say the same thing about your buddy." Detective Brown yanked Animal by the arm. "And you"—he looked at Don B.—"we'll catch you on the come around."

"Do you want us to take him downtown?" one of the uniformed officers offered to transport Animal.

"Hell no. We're delivering this one ourselves," Detective Brown beamed.

"Oh, Animal, I'm so sorry, I was wrong about you cheating on me and I'm so sorry for ever doubting you." Gucci sobbed as the detectives carted him away.

Animal smiled. "It's all good, baby cakes. Sometimes this is just how it plays out for a nigga. I might be a minute so do you think you could find it in your heart to wait for me?"

"Forever and a day, baby. Forever and a day!"

"And let nothing short of God change that." He winked.

"Get your ass in the car." Detective Brown shoved Animal roughly in the backseat.

As they drove away from the scene Animal weighed his trip back to New York. One thing he could say was that it had been a colorful one. He had got to be a celebrity in his hometown, even if it was only for a week. Though he had crippled Rico's organization, Rico was still out there somewhere. When he woke up the next morning he would probably read the paper and have a good laugh at what had become of his enemy. It didn't matter though. Animal was going to prison for a long time but they couldn't keep him forever. He would carry his grudge with Rico until one of them was in the ground.

He looked out the window at Gucci's weeping face and felt a warm sensation in his chest. Even with the best lawyers he was going to have to do quite a bit of time for the shooting, but knowing Gucci would be in his corner would make it possible for him to stand strong no matter how much time they hit him with. They say that love conquers all and from what he had learned during his time with Gucci, Animal believed that very strongly.

Epilogue

IT WAS BACK TO BASICS FOR JADA AFTER THE DRAMA AT the club with Gucci. It had been fun hanging out with her cousin, but Gucci kept a little too much drama for Jada's taste. She was looking forward to getting back to her grandmother's apartment and getting a good night's sleep. The next day it was back to business.

She was surprised when she got home to find the living-room light still on and her grandmother talking to someone, especially when she was normally asleep at that hour. She figured that it was one of the neighbors with some more of the drama that they loved to bring to the Butler house, but when she rounded the corner and saw who was sitting on the couch her jaw dropped.

"Mommy, Mommy, guess who came to visit us?" Jalen pulled her by the arm.

"Girl, I've been trying to call you all night to tell you to come home, you know it's rude to have people waiting for you like that." Ms. Pat was going on and on, but Jada was just standing there dumbfounded. "Well, ain't you gonna say something?"

Jada tried to find the words but she just couldn't.

"Yeah, ain't you gonna show ya baby daddy some love?" Cutty asked, bouncing little Miles on his knee.

"Oh, hell nah," Jada finally managed to blurt out before she fainted.

AFTER THE TROUBLE WITH SOLOMON Malika decided she had had enough of Douglass Projects. Taking just a few personal items she packed her and her son up and went to have a long overdue talk with her parents. She had expected to have to whine and beg, but surprisingly her parents had missed her as much as she had missed them, especially her father. It was high time that he got to know his grandson and the woman his little girl had grown into.

THAT MONDAY MORNING THEY LAID Mimi to rest with a quiet ceremony that included just a few friends and loved ones from the block. She had no family, but an anonymous donor had made sure she had a beautiful homecoming. A carriage pulled by two white horses rode her through her projects one last time before she was taken to the cemetery in Linden, NJ. Mimi might not have been loved by many, but the few who loved her did so beyond measure.

RICO'S NIECE HAD A BEAUTIFUL wedding ceremony at St. Michael's Cathedral. Rico had to pull quite a bit of strings to make it happen, but nothing was too good for his niece. Carmen had insisted that the wedding was off-limits so the only people there who he had street ties with were Shai and Swan. He tried to thank Shai for the little tip he gave him about Animal, but Shai barely said two words to him. It was as if he was upset that Animal had failed to kill Rico. No matter, Shai was on borrowed time anyway. When Rico was able to restructure his inner crew he was coming for Shai's throne.

Rico came down the stairs flanked by all the wedding guests, throwing rice at his niece and her new husband. When he got down to the bottom of the steps he saw a little black boy wearing thick glasses peddling flowers. "Shoo, shoo, don't you see we're having a wedding here?"

"I'm sorry, sir, I'm just trying to hustle off some of these flowers," the boy said timidly.

"We've got enough flowers so take a hike." Rico shoved him.

"But not like these, they smell really nice." The little boy held one of the bouquets up for Rico to inspect. Rico noticed that there was something wedged between the flowers and when he looked closer to inspect them Ashanti pulled the trigger.

The bullet went in Rico's throat and out the back of his neck, spattering the bridesmaids with blood. When Rico dropped to his knees Ashanti shot him again in the gut. Brasco came next, firing a shot into Rico's back as the wedding guests watched in horror. Even Nef had finally gotten his hands dirty and gave Rico two shots. Shai's men moved to intervene, but Shai stopped them as he knew that this was not their battle.

As the young gunmen were leaving Ashanti stopped and pointed his fingers at Swan in the shape of a gun and made a popping sound with his mouth. "See you around, playboy."

AS ANIMAL HAD EXPECTED THE judge remanded him and ruled that he be held without bail until his next court date. The attorney Gucci had hired for him tried to dispute it but the judge wouldn't hear it. The witnesses and the police painted a picture of Animal as a remorseless killer who wasn't fit to walk the streets and the judged believed them. This was a battle that Animal would have to fight behind the wall. Detectives Brown and Alvarez were floating so high on their horse that they volunteered to take Animal to Rikers Island.

"Looks like we finally got your black ass, huh? Big bad Animal about to spend the rest of his life in a cage, how fucking ironic is that?" Detective Brown taunted Animal, but he wouldn't feed into it.

"You know for as pretty as you are, kid, I'd hate to be you when your ass touches that rock." Alvarez laughed.

"Man, both of y'all can suck my dick. Just either take me to jail or shoot me and put me out of my misery, but please stop talking," Animal said and busied himself looking out the window. Ahead of them there were some men directing traffic around some construction that was going on near the on ramp to the BQE.

"What the fuck is this?" Detective Alvarez grimaced at the construction.

"Fuck it, J. Throw the lights on and go through it," Brown suggested.

While the two detectives were arguing about their best course of action, Animal saw what they didn't which was one of the construction workers pulling a gun.

Animal hit the floor of the car just as the shooting started. Glass shattered all around him and he could feel Detective Alvarez lose control of the car. The sedan jumped the curb, striking two cars and a fire hydrant before coming to rest on its side. Animal used his legs and slid over broken glass out the back window of the car. He felt like his arm was broken and it was hard for him to breathe, but he kept crawling. Through his blurred vision he could see a brindle pit bull stalking toward him. The dog leaned in and snarled in Animal's face. He was so hurt that if the pit decided to maul him all he would be able to do was lie there.

"Isis come." He heard a voice through his fog of pain.

Animal focused his eyes as best he could and followed the dog to the voice. He looked up and saw a pair of green eyes staring down at him from a coal-black face. "Damn, I know I'm in hell if you're here," Animal mumbled.

"Nah, you ain't dead. There's someone who's been waiting a long time to see you and we have need of your unique skills. Get him in the van," the green-eyed man ordered someone Animal couldn't see.

"Where are you taking me?" Animal asked, trying to stay conscious long enough to hear the answer.

"You let me worry about that. Just think of it as a family reunion," the green-eyed man told him. The last thing Animal heard was the green-eyed man's all too familiar laugh before the darkness took him.

K'WAN KEEPS THE STREET FICTION GAME ON LOCKDOWN

Visit the-blackbox.com and sign up to receive GANGSTA WALK, a never-before-released free short story from K'wan